The Perplexing Problem
of the Porcelain Bandits

A Novel by Dan Johnson

THE PERPLEXING PROBLEM OF THE PORCELAIN BANDITS

Copyright © 2010 by Dan Johnson

Wonderful Terrific Publishing
San Francisco, California

Cover Design by Aaron Best

ISBN 978-0-578-05773-6

Printed in the United States of America

To everyone who encouraged me along the way

How It Started

The doorbell interrupted Jenn mid-sentence.

"Must be UPS for you, Thomas," I said.

"I don't think so," he said. "My next order shouldn't come in until tomorrow; I tracked it this morning."

"Well, somebody's gotta get it," I said.

Jenn and Thomas immediately put their fingers to the side of their noses.

"All you," said Jenn, grinning.

A cop was at the door. He was an Asian guy, shorter than me, a bit overweight, carrying a battered notebook and a weary, lined face.

"Hi," he said. "Do you live here?"

"Yeah," I said. "Is there anything wrong?"

"I'm afraid there is," he said. "Does Brent Scalia live here, also?"

"Sure," I said. "What did he do?"

"I'm afraid I'm going to ask you to come with me," he said.

"What did *I* do?" I asked.

"Nothing," he said. "I need you to come to the medical examiner's office."

"The hospital?"

"No," he said. "The morgue. Brent Scalia is dead."

The morgue is a place that you never want to visit while you're still not dead; the building is in a severely industrial area of SOMA on Bryant Street near the freeway overpasses, a few blocks from the county jail. The cop let me sit in the front seat on our ride down.

"Tough day?" I said.

"Yeah," he said. "Shuttling you there is the last thing I have to do before I clock off. Spent most of the day in the Tenderloin answering pick-up calls."

"What's a pick-up call?"

"Someone's passed out on the sidewalk, and a well-meaning tourist calls the cops to come pick him up. The guy on the sidewalk just wants to sleep; nobody else really cares, but we have to call in the paramedics and a social worker. A big mess each time, for someone who just wants to lie there in a haze and not bother anyone. But if you call, we respond. "

"Oh," I said. I had been going to empathize and talk about how my day at work was kind of a pain, too. I kept my mouth shut.

At the morgue, the two-man security team made me walk through a metal detector and patted me down -- in case I was there to stab corpses, I guess. I signed a bunch of forms declaring that I was there with no ill intent and wasn't allergic to dead people, and then an old guy with wispy hair and a white lab coat took me to an elevator. He said nothing as we descended three levels to a little room with a metal door that opened with a wheel lock.

The wheel made no noise as it turned, and the old man pushed the door open with a couple of fingers. It must have had great bearings; that door was at least six inches thick. Inside, it looked *exactly* like the morgues on bad medical TV shows, right down to the brushed aluminum walls and the one shelf that someone had left open.

"Whoop, we can't have that," said the old man. "Something might decay." He cackled, walked over to the shelf and pushed the gurney back inside, then closed the door.

"Let's see, now where's your friend…" he said.

"Housemate," I said.

"Housemate," he said. "Right." He took a palmtop computer out of his pocket and started to peck at it with the stylus.

"They gave us these a few months ago," he said. "Something about being able to more efficiently track our guests. I kind of miss my paper, but…ah, here he is. Number sixty-three. Hit by a car in SOMA just today."

He walked over to a handle that looked like every other handle in the room and pulled out a gurney, then gestured me over.

"Is that Brent Scalia?" he asked.

I looked down. There, lying on a bright steel table, looking nothing more than asleep, was the guy who'd lived downstairs for four months. On the TV shows, the dead people look like they're asleep. He could have been asleep, except that his shoulder was cranked far forward, and one side of his head looked flat and was matted with blood. It was definitely Brent, though. He slept on his side; we all knew this because he had a tendency to conk out on the couch during Monday Night Wrestling. He liked to drink orange juice in the mornings while eating Total and watching ESPN. He was about five foot five and had a little bald spot in his black hair. When he'd interviewed to be in our house, he'd said his pet peeve was when people took water glasses from the kitchen and kept them in their rooms. He hadn't become a friend yet.

And now he was lying on his back on a steel table. He'd probably been hit when he was on his way back home from work. His off-white button shirt had come untucked. Brent always wore off-white shirts to work; I'd made fun of him for it after I noticed, and he'd pointed out that wearing the same thing every day made it easier to get out of the house. His skin was paler than usual, and his left arm was twisted low across his body, his elbow at a hard right angle, but the hand backwards from where it should have been. I could see his fingernails; they were ragged and bitten. The edge of his bald spot was just visible under his curly hair.

"That's him," I said.

"OK," said the old man. "You have to come upstairs now and take care of some paperwork."

"What happened to him?" I asked.

The old man looked at his forms. "Didn't the cops tell you?"

"I mean, I know he was hit by a car," I said. "But I don't know anything else."

"Says he got hit by a car," he said. "That's about it on the coroner's notes. There's a copy of the police report here. Want to read it?"

"Not right now," I said.

"Make sure they give you one when you go upstairs," he said. "Sometimes they forget about that kind of thing."

Upstairs, I filled out some forms. The forms had lots of words, most of which I didn't really understand. I mean, I read them – it's impossible to *not* read if you know how – but they didn't register. It was like reading a school assignment that you knew the teacher would forget to ask questions about; I read it, but not really.

Except for the last form, which read, "next of kin statement."

"I can't sign this," I said to the nervous-looking woman behind the counter.

"What do you mean?" she said, twirling her hair around her finger. She had been twirling and untwirling her hair ever since the old man had dropped me off at this counter, which I guess was where everyone in the city came to sign away dead bodies. She had a pretty terrible job.

"I mean I'm not the next of kin," I said. "I just live in the same apartment."

"Lived," she said.

"Huh?"

"Well, since he doesn't live at your house any more, you should use the past tense," she said.

"What?" I said.

"Respect for the dead should include proper grammar," she said. "You won't believe what some of the people who come through here say to me."

"I believe it," I said. "His room is... *was* downstairs from me, off the kitchen. The cop brought me here to identify the body."

"Well, since your signature is on these other forms, the body is now your responsibility," she said. "It would be very helpful to us if you could notify the next of kin so we can get this last form signed and release the body to them. Once the body is identified, we like to get them out of here as soon as we can."

"OK," I said. "Wait...what if I hadn't identified the body?"

"Then we'd keep it as a John Doe for three weeks, then we'd cremate it," she said, snapping her gum. "But it's much better now that it's been identified – you have a little more time to find the next of kin and get him out of here."

"Does this happen often?" I asked.

"People with no families?" she asked. "All the time. Half the homeless people they haul in just go right to the burner – they have no ID, and we have no way to track 'em down."

"Right," I said. "OK. Can I have a copy of the police report?"

"The police should have given you that," she said.

"They didn't," I said. "And the cop is gone."

"Well, you *should* go over to North Station and get a copy from them," she said. "But I've got a few of them here, and nobody ever notices if there's one less piece of paper in the final packet for a stiff."

She handed me the report. I left. The day had turned dark, and I was standing on the sidewalk with no one to give me a ride home. A homeless guy had made camp in the little hollow between the stairs and the building, sheltered from the wind. He had stretched a tarp from his cart to the top of the stairs, weighing it down with water-stained books. I peeked in; he was watching a Giants game on a battery-powered television, and he pumped his fist as the batter swung and missed.

Naturally, there was no bus stop anywhere near where I was, so I started walking north. After two long blocks, I noticed a faded yellow stripe on a stoplight pole, with a faintly stenciled "19" that had been partially obscured by a tag that read "Goat Fornication." A bus stop.

The 19 bus makes a loop through South of Market, running under several freeway-overpass homeless camps, the courthouse, and the police station. It continues north of Market Street through the Tenderloin, a good neighborhood for scoring your daily supply of pre-processed street pharmaceuticals. The bus that showed up had everyone - the gap-toothed methamphetamine freaks, heroin addicts with brown sores oozing through threadbare sleeves, over-the-hill hookers commuting back from a night in jail, a worn-out security guard coming off shift, and two well-dressed young Chinese boys, holding hands and staring openly at everyone else. I couldn't find a seat, so I stood to the side of a zombie-thin man with well-picked scabs on his nose and lips. He mumbled and sniffed at me when I reached over him to pull the cord that signaled the driver to stop.

I waited on the bus platform for about ten minutes, along with several other forlorn-looking people.

"How long you been waiting?" I asked the group.

"Ten minutes," said a voice. "Maybe twelve."

"Not so bad," I said.

"Wait and see," said the voice. "MUNI will screw up."

They sure did. My group waited for another twenty minutes before any bus showed up. While I sat on the bus, I read the report. Most of it was boring – the time of the incident, the name of the reporting officer, the names of the paramedics who'd responded, the total time between incident and the road clearing. I skimmed over that and read over the report of the actual accident.

Witnesses McDonnel and James observed the victim walking along the sidewalk at approximately five-thirty p.m. on Wednesday, July 18. Victim slowed to look at his cellular phone, removed the phone from his pocket and started a conversation. Victim was then struck from behind by a dark red, dark green, or dark blue sport-utility vehicle, which had come up on the sidewalk and then accelerated. Witnesses put the speed of the vehicle at approximately 40 miles per hour. Reporting officer notes that this speed would be possible, and since the victim was struck near a corner at the end of a long block, this story checks out. No witnesses were able to confirm the license plate of the vehicle, although Witness 1 is fairly sure that it contained a 2 and a V. This incident is being judged as a hit-and-run accident pending further investigation.

That was it. The report itself took up all of four pages. By the time the number 6 dropped me off two blocks down the hill from my house, the journey had taken me over an hour and a half. I could have walked in less time.

The front door was locked, and I remembered that I had neither key nor phone, so I held down the door buzzer until I heard some footsteps come thumping down to the door. Thomas.

"Alex," he said. "Where have you been? We tried calling you."

"I left my phone in my room," I said. "Sorry – I kind of left quickly."

What's going on?" he said. "Where were you?"

"At the morgue," I said. "Brent is dead."

Chapter 1

It was Tuesday night, the last normal night at the house before it all started. When I got home from a long after-work ramble around the city, Jenn was on the couch under a blanket, reading a magazine with the television on low. Her brown hair was pulled back into a tight ponytail, but she didn't have quite enough hair to pull it off, leaving a couple of strands on either side that fell in front of her eyes. One hand turned the pages of the magazine, the other brushed errant hairs behind her ears. She looked up briefly when I reached the top of the stairs, and then looked back at her magazine.

"You're back late," she said.

"Anyone else here?" I asked.

"Not yet," she said, and looked back down at her magazine.

I trudged upstairs to my room. We were two of five housemates; our place is large for San Francisco. It takes up the top two floors of a three-story Victorian house. The ground floor is a one-bedroom apartment; a quiet couple whom we don't see much lives there. The living room and dining room are downstairs, which is the second floor of the building, along with a normal front porch and enclosed back porch. One of the bedrooms is next to the kitchen, and the downstairs bathroom opens on the hallway near the stairs. Four bedrooms and one bathroom upstairs, a hall lined with fading gray carpet, threadbare enough to see the outlines of the sub flooring beneath. I live in the middle on the right, Jenn in the middle on the left, Shawna wedged into the smallest room on the far end, with Thomas in the largest room at the near end of the hallway, next to the top of the stairs. The hallway is decorated with four black-and-white photos of cats that the previous tenants left behind.

We live in San Francisco, right on the border between Cole Valley and the Upper Haight. Cole Valley is quiet, slightly gentrified, the kind of place where you live when you're done living in six-person houses and are ready to have that little one-bedroom flat that you can fill with things. It is a safe and relatively clean neighborhood, with crepe restaurants on the corners where young mothers in designer tracksuits gather for late-morning coffee and group baby-watching.

The Upper Haight was once known as Haight-Ashbury, and it still exudes a gentle seediness. The main feature of the neighborhood is the legions of homeless kids who wander up and down Haight Street, panhandling tourists for beer money, shooting heroin in the side alleys, and generally making pests of themselves. I'm pretty sure that most of them come from Marin and have trust funds for their periodic trips to rehab.

If you ask me where I live, my answer depends on who you are. For job interviews and talks with people who are older, wealthier, or respectable in some way, I'd say Cole Valley. For younger people, hipsters, women I'd like to go out with, and people from out of the city, I'd say "the Haight." Never "Upper Haight," because saying "Haight" implies the "Upper" rather than the "Lower." It's complicated.

The words "San Francisco" are so loaded – once most people hear them they think of steep hills and cable cars full of drag queens eating Rice-a-Roni. That's not really how the city is – although I'm sure that that particular cable-car/drag queen/instant-dinner thing has happened at one point or another – it's kind of like any other place, but with a more enhanced weirdness. From my window, I could just see over the roof of the place next door, and on clear days I could just make out the ocean to the far west, a place I went to even less often than I could see it through the fogs and mists of the Sunset. I took off my shoes, dumped off my shoulder bag on top of the small pile of worn-but-not-dirty clothes that took up one corner of my loveseat, and went downstairs to join Jenn.

She moved over slightly when I entered the living room, and I sat down on the other side of the sofa, pulling some of her blanket over to cover my feet.

"Watching anything in particular?" I said. "There's a band I like playing Leno at eleven."

"Not really," she said. "Change away."

I flipped through the channels until I found a *Simpsons* rerun.

"Haven't you already seen this one?" she asked.

"Yeah, but it's funny. This is the one where Homer really has to go to the bathroom, and they end up at the casino, and…"

"Right. You know what happens. Why watch it?"

"Because it's better than anything else on. You'd rather watch

Desperate Housewives?"

"No. Is it on?"

"I have no idea. If I knew, I wouldn't be a twenty-six-year-old guy from San Francisco named Alex Baker. I'd be a forty-two year-old homemaker from Duluth named Myrna with a banker husband and three kids with three different soccer practice locations. I make it a point of professional pride *not* to know when *Desperate Housewives* is on."

"Professional pride? You're in marketing. Nobody knows what exactly you do. You have no profession."

"Professional guy pride."

She grinned. "Professional guy? Have you looked at yourself? You're the polar opposite of a successful personal ad: *'Twenty-six-year-old white guy stuck in a permanent state of arrested development. Five foot ten, blue eyes, generic brown hair, skinny…"*

"Hey, I'm not skinny. Hipsters are skinny. I'm slender."

"Right. *Dresses like a skate rat kid from the early 1990s. If you like the short-sleeve-over-long sleeved t-shirts and the look of pants that are slightly too big, you'll think I'm pretty hot. Extra points if you can tolerate the Clash, get worked up over inanities, and don't mind eating burritos for dinner three times per week."*

I opened my mouth to say something witty in return but was interrupted when the door downstairs opened and slammed, and footsteps started to clomp their way up.

"Lock the door!" shouted Jenn and I in unison.

The footsteps paused, then clippety-clopped down the stairs, paused for the muffled shooting of the bolt on the downstairs door, and began their heavy trudge back up to where we sat.

Thomas was six foot three and two hundred pounds, slim, but he walked like a fat guy, making the house shake when he walked up the stairs. He claimed it was because he had heavy bones; I thought he was just constitutionally incapable of being quiet.

"Right, I'll talk to you later," he said, snapping his cell phone closed. He turned to us. "What's up?"

"Leno comes on in twenty minutes," said Jenn. "We're going to watch because Alex likes the band."

"Who are they?" asked Thomas.

"Dropkicks," I said. "A punk crew from Boston."

"If they're on Leno, they're not a punk band," said Thomas. "Being on NBC destroys any punk cred."

"Who are you to argue?" I shot back. "You're an investment banker. How would your knowledge of Eurotrash trance music and radio-hip-hop qualify you to say what's punk?"

"Oh, you're making me livid," said Thomas. "I know what I know."

"Which isn't much," said Jenn.

"I'm livid," said Thomas. "*Livid.*" He stomped upstairs. Jenn and I laughed, and the spoon next to my water glass rattled with each of his steps.

On the television, a puffy-looking Catherine Zeta-Jones was pimping T-Mobile cell phones. It still weirded me out that she made her splash in *Zorro* as a Latino woman, but she's actually Welsh; her accent on the commercials threw me every time.

"God, I hate Michael Douglas," I said.

"What?" said Jenn, looking up at me from her issue of *Make*.

"He ruined the fantasies of every guy my age by marrying her. Sure, now we're aware that if we were to be nearly sixty and a terrible actor we'd be able to pull a girl like Catherine, but it also reminds us of college, when all of the hot girls freshman year were dating seniors, so you had no shot. Now, we're in our twenties, and all of the hot girls are with fossils like Douglas. It's ridiculous."

"That's the stupidest thing you've said tonight," said Jenn.

"What about when I said that Ron Popeil's inventions were the epitome of American culture?" I said. "What about when I declared that all South Floridians were foot fetishists? What about when I said that it was obvious that Ricky Martin *wasn't* gay? All of those were far stupider than the Zeta-Jones rant."

Jenn sighed. "Alex, it's been forever since you've been on a date; why would you possibly care about who Catherine Zeta-Jones is sleeping with?"

"Because she's setting a bad example for the people I *could* be dating," I said.

"Only ten minutes until Leno, and then I can go to bed," Jenn said.

"Don't you want to watch it with me?" I said.

"No," she grinned. "I wanted to keep you company while you watched TV, because you're always complaining that we watch too much TV, and you don't watch with us much. But, when you do, it's fun because you say so many stupid things. But if you watch something you actually like, it's no fun. So I'll go to bed when the show you actually want to watch comes on."

The door downstairs opened and a pair of feet started to bounce their way up the stairs.

"Lock the door!" we shouted.

The steps receded, the deadbolt thudded, and the steps resumed. Shawna came into the room, looking like that Chinese girl who used to get all of the calculus homework right, came to San Francisco after college, and then turned herself completely around at Burning Man. Now she did lots of yoga, straddling the line between hippie and hipster with a manic grace.

"Oh my God, you guys," said Shawna. "You're here again, watching television like slugs. I just got back from my contact improv class...I learned how to be a table. A table! Isn't that awesome? Do you guys want to go into the kitchen and be tables with me for a few minutes?"

"Can't," I said. "Leno's on."

"Oh, you'd rather watch him than do something that's going to make you feel better and make you touch another human?" she said. "That's fine. I met this guy tonight, and he was cute, so I got his phone number. Should I call tonight? No, I shouldn't. I should call tomorrow and make him have dinner with me or something. Maybe coffee? Or tea? OK, I need to do some yoga before bedtime. 'Night!" She ran up to the third floor.

Jenn and I looked at each other, waiting. Five seconds later, Shawna came running down the stairs.

"Oh my God, did I tell you? I'm going to shave my legs tomorrow! I've got a job at a school and they want me to wear a skirt, and I'm tired of wearing tights, so I'm going to do it."

"Interesting," I said. Shawna didn't have all that much leg hair, as far as I could see.

"It's more than that," she said. "It's epic. I gotta go give myself a trim. 'Night!"

"Wow," said Jenn. "She's going to give herself a haircut in the downstairs bathroom and leave hair in the shower drain again. Brent's going to be pissed."

"Who wants to tell him?"

"Not me," said Jenn. "He'll find out in the morning, when he showers in a bathroom with hair clogging the drain."

I whistled. "Is he home yet?"

Jenn shrugged. "I don't know. I haven't seen him in a couple of days. His door's closed, but he could have beaten everybody in and is just hanging out in there like he usually does."

"What about Leno?" she asked.

"I don't think I can take it," I said. "Waiting for everyone else to come home is still more funny than giant chin boy is ever going to be."

She left. I stayed up with the TV off and re-read a Daniel Pinkwater book. Such was a night at our house, the day before it all happened.

It all started with toilets. I was seeing a movie at the AMC on Van Ness the day after our Zeta-Jones discussion. I had been feeling a little bit low, so I bailed out of work a couple of hours early and headed up to the theater on the 38 bus for the last matinee showing of a new Michael Bay summer blockbuster. After all of the explosions and plot twists were done, I headed to the bathroom.

Movie theater bathrooms have improved lately; the can was the kind of place you'd expect to see on the executive floor of an investment bank. All of the urinals were occupied, so I walked to the far end to the open disabled-use stall. I stood there, peeing, and I noticed two things:

1) The toilet was an automatic flusher, although it lacked the cool motorized seat-cover thing that they have at airports.
2) Both the toilet and the auto-flusher were made by a company called "Toto."

The latter wouldn't have been a big deal, as I'm not a stoner and would not stand there peeing and have delusions about Dorothy's little dog barking orders to a crew of commode-manufacturing Munchkins. But *every* toilet I'd ever seen was manufactured by American Standard. Those guys made the urinals in my elementary school, the fancy low-volume porcelain wonder that graced the powder room in my rich high-school pal Darren's house in the hills, and even the pee-troughs at the baseball park.

So what was this Toto company? Were they taking over the monopoly that was once held by American Standard? Was this another example of a foreign company with sweatshop manufacturing putting one over on good old American organized labor?

I finished, left, and walked down Van Ness to Haight Street to the 71 bus home. It was late rush-hour; the bus was packed to the gills with the last wave of work crowds, among the usual assortment of sociopaths, homeless teenagers, street zombies, and exhausted shift-workers.

Thomas was home when I got there. He was eating chips with salsa and watching the local news.

"Dude," I said. "Do you know anything about toilets?"

He gave me a look of *oh-my-God-here-we-go-again*. "No, Alex, I don't think about toilets. I do things with them that you shouldn't discuss in polite conversation. Why are you asking me about toilets?"

"Because I was pissing in a urinal that wasn't American Standard when I was at the movie theater just now."

"Aren't *all* toilets American Standard?" he asked.

"I thought so. Are ours?"

Thomas shrugged and ran a hand through his spiky brown hair. "I have no idea. I've never really thought about what make our toilets are when I'm using them."

"Let's check." Thomas, who apparently didn't have anything better to do, followed me as I walked across the living room to the downstairs bathroom and checked the toilet. There, on the back side of the bowl, flanked by a couple of hairs of dubious origin, was the American Standard logo. Upstairs was the same, except that the whole room was much dirtier, and the logo was *sans* hair. We were an all-American Standard household.

"Huh," said Thomas after we'd ensconced ourselves in the living room again.

"Yeah," I said. "Weird."

"Come on, let's do some research," he said. This was his normal mode of operation. Flaky, distractible, but curious about absolutely everything.

His room was cluttered but clean. Thomas's bed was in one corner, and the wall near the windows was dominated by a huge desk, smothered with a flat screen monitor, printer/FAX/scanner, lamp, USB hub, and innumerable papers. The chair was an Aeron that Thomas had liberated from a failed dot-com. He swept some papers to the floor, exposing a keyboard. The computer came to life; Thomas clicked a few keys.

"Experience the pinnacle of personal hygiene with the TOTO washlet," said Thomas.

"What?"

"The TOTO website," he said. "They capitalize every letter in 'TOTO,' although I can't figure out what kind of acronym it would be."

"Tough On…" I said. I couldn't think of what the second two letters could possibly mean for a toilet company.

"What's a washlet?" I said.

"It kind of looks like a midget toilet," said Thomas.

He did some more clicking around, and I watched. The TOTO website made me want to go and wash myself; the design was so yuppified I was afraid that we were going to break something just by mousing around. Everything was brushed aluminum and FLASH cartoons and the sleek minimalism that you always see in downtown loft condominiums.

"Stupid brushed-aluminum décor," said Thomas. "On toilets. That makes me livid."

"Check American Standard," I said.

Thomas opened up a new window and browsed over to the site. It was kind of broken; the front page graphics didn't show up. Thomas found a navigation bar and clicked on "toilets." The main graphic showed up this time, showing a simple white porcelain toilet that looked exactly like the one that I grew up with. Not a washlet in site.

No Plunge, it said. *Engineered to virtually never clog.*

"That's the working man's toilet," I said.

"You got that right," he said. "I get the feeling that an encounter with the aftereffects of Taqueria Cancun would make that washlet cry for mercy. But that No Plunge can probably take anything we could dish out."

"What are you guys doing?" It was Jenn, looking even more disheveled than usual. She worked for an education policy agency with a staff of forty-three women and two men. Jenn spent most of her time trying to avoid office politics, which sounded more exhausting than actually doing any work.

"You know about American Standard, right?"

"Sure," she said. "They're the toilet guys…"

Jenn was interrupted mid-sentence by a buzzing. The doorbell. Nobody ever rang the doorbell.

Chapter 2

On the day after my visit to the morgue, we had a house meeting. Such meetings usually only happened at times of planning ("We're having a party. Who's doing what?"), times of anger ("The hair in the drain clogged the tub, and now it's overflowing") and times of confusion ("How did pieces of banana get into the toaster?") This was the first time we'd met in a time of tragedy. It sounds kind of awful that we waited that long to have the meeting, I know, but Thomas had been called back to the office when I'd gotten home, and Shawna had disappeared at some guy's house. I'd left for work after everyone else, and it didn't feel right to tell the other two by e-mail. So I started the meeting by telling Shawna and Jenn what had happened. They both cried for a little while. Thomas put his arm around Shawna after a few seconds. I stared at the floor; I hadn't cried at all, and I felt bad because I hadn't. The air felt thick with shame.

"So," said Thomas. "What are we going to do?"

"Well, we gotta find a new roommate," said Jenn.

"Before we do that, what should we do with his stuff?" asked Shawna.

"Um....you guys forgot something," I said.

Everyone looked over at me.

"Shouldn't we get in touch with his parents?"

"Does anyone *know* Brent's parents?" asked Thomas. "I've never talked to them."

We all shook our heads. Brent had come into the house through Craigslist, like all of us (although Shawna had known Jenn beforehand), and we didn't keep tabs on each other. We hung out, sure, but exchanging emergency contacts was a bit beyond the pale.

"OK, how do we find them?" Thomas said. He was slipping into organizer mode now, asking questions, leading the room. I really wished that he had been the one to answer the door when the cop came. He dealt with million-dollar transactions at his job; he probably would have known what to say at the morgue. We would probably know more and would not have been sitting there in uncomfortable silence as he asked the question.

"Well, have we looked around?" he asked, looking at me.

"I went through his room," I said. "His cell phone wasn't there, which should mean that his wallet and his bag are probably still at the morgue."

"Why didn't you take it?" asked Jenn.

"It's his stuff," I said. "And I think they'll only release it to the next of kin."

"Well," said Jenn. "You can explain to them that without the stuff, we can't find the next of kin, right?"

"Sure," I said.

"Great," she said. "Can you go down there tomorrow? I bet he's got numbers in his phone."

Huh? I was the go-to guy for morgue issues now? I really didn't want the responsibility, but to not go would seem like sour grapes. Tomorrow was a Friday, and if I told my boss that I needed to take off early to go to the city morgue to check up on some things about my newly-dead housemate, he'd surely let me go. I'd spend an hour at the morgue, then hit the bars early.

"Sure," I said. "I'll get out of work a little early and head down."

My boss was as predictable as I'd thought he'd be, so I ended up at the morgue just after lunch. The morgue on a Friday afternoon was as much of a morgue as any business is on Friday. Well, perhaps more morgue-ish. At my office on Fridays, the only thing that gets done after lunch is FreeCell tournaments. The older folks play FreeCell, that is. Anyone under thirty-five has bribed the IT guy to bypass the "not-work-related" filters on their computers and spends their time managing fantasy sports teams, reading stupid news stories, updating their online dating profiles, Google-stalking old high school flames, selling stocks, instant-messaging friends, forwarding scads of no-longer-funny e-mails to lists of long-forgotten acquaintances, writing Rants and Raves for Craigslist, playing online poker for real or imaginary cash, furtively Photoshopping pictures for online Photoshop contests, or blogging. The morgue felt like that, but quieter. When I walked into the front door, the same nervous-looking woman was at the front desk, filing her nails with a red emery board and making absolutely no noise while doing so. Deathly quiet. The door clicked shut behind me, echoing in the room.

She gestured to the two plastic chairs to the right of my door.

"Someone will be with you shortly," she said.

The chair was uncomfortable in an elementary-school-auditorium kind of way. My legs were too long, so I had to bend my knees as I sat, forcing my tailbone directly into the hard plastic of the chair without the agreeable padding of my butt in to cushion it. I'm not tall – about five foot ten if I'm wearing big shoes. After a couple of minutes of discomfort, I stood up.

"I *said* that someone would be with you shortly," said the receptionist. She was still filing the same nail.

"The chair isn't too comfortable," I said.

"But you're supposed to sit while you wait for someone to be with you," she said.

"I'd love to," I said. "But the chair isn't very comfortable."

"I can't do anything about that," she said. "But before someone will be with you you'll have to sit down."

I sat down. She filed her nails for another minute, then looked up at me.

"How can I help you?" she asked.

"I…" I said.

"No, before I can help you, you have to come up to the desk," she said. "I don't want to strain my ears listening for you all the way across there."

I walked over.

"What can I help you with?" she asked.

"I'm here to see if I can pick up the personal effects of one of the people here."

"One of the dead people?" she asked.

"Yes," I said.

"Sure," she said. "I assume that you're the next of kin?"

"No," I said. "I'm a housemate. I need to look at his stuff in order to find the next of kin."

"Oh," she said. "That's kind of odd. Can I have the name of the deceased?"

"Brent Scalia," I said.

"S…k…."

"No, c," I said. I ended up spelling Brent's last name for her letter by letter.

"Ah, yes," she said. "And who are you?"

"Alex," I said. "Alex Baker."

"Alex," she said. "Well, you *are* on the list here as the one who identified the body, so let me send down a request for Mr. Scalia's things."

"That's it?" I asked. "Aren't you going to ask me for ID?"

"Honey, there are lots of strange people in this city," she said, taking out her emery board again. "But I have yet to meet someone low enough to come into the city morgue and use a fake name to steal a dead man's last possessions. Now just take a seat over there and someone will be up with what you're looking for in a little bit."

I sat back down in the plastic seats. My tailbone immediately started to ache. Usually, I carried a bag around containing a book or two, a pen, and the ubiquitous San Francisco layers in case of fog. I'd finished my last book, I'd forgotten to go to the library, and the morgue was light on reading materials. I sat.

And sat.

Stood.

Sat.

Stood.

Sat.

For about a half an hour.

The door to the basement opened, and the same white-haired old guy from the previous week showed up, carrying a brown cardboard shoebox. He nodded to the receptionist, who ignored him. Then he looked at me.

"Are you Alex?" he asked.

"Yes," I said.

"Here you go," he said, and handed me the shoebox.

Inside was a smashed cell phone, wallet, hoodie, small shoulder bag, and a white envelope with a corporate logo for the return address – JWP&C. The envelope had been opened already; it contained a pay stub from the same company, made out to David Jones. A David Jones who lived at our address.

"Huh," said Shawna. The two of us were sitting in the kitchen having chips and salsa for breakfast; Jenn and Thomas weren't up yet. They weren't *good* chips and salsa, because Shawna had bought them. I always buy the good ones, thick chips made from real tortillas, dark brown, without those even brown spots that the people who make Tostitos manage to put on every single chip. I buy the salsa that comes in little plastic tubs in the refrigerated section of the grocery store, hot as I can find. Everyone in the house always bludged off of mine, so I tended to run out, hence Shawna's chips. She was always broke, so she'd bought on-sale Pace and an on-sale pound bag of plain Doritos. The chips tasted like recycled paper, and the salsa was as bland as a Nebraska shopping spree. In this case they were welcome; after the bombshell at the morgue, I'd gone to a bike messenger bar called Zeitgeist and pounded down enough beer to buzzify a stadium full of English soccer fans. Eating anything with zest would have caused an internal Verdun.

"So let me get this straight," she said. "Brent wasn't Brent."

My head hurt. Shawna's voice was on the higher-pitched side of things, without any of the mellowness that the Chinese seductresses always have in kung fu films.

"I don't know," I said. "He worked as David Jones, but the drivers' license in his wallet was under Brent Scalia."

"So who *was* he?"

"I'm not sure," I said. Shawna and I had spread out the entire contents of Brent's life, stuff from what the morgue had given me and what we could find in his room, in front of us on the table. A drivers' license in the name of Brent Scalia. A second drivers' license and a Social Security card in the name of David Jones. A collection of life memorabilia as nonspecific as they come – Red Sox pennants, books about baseball, iPod, laptop computer, khaki clothes for the office and jeans for the weekend. No address books, birthday cards with return addresses, day planners, or the like. His iPod playlist was full of bands that everybody had heard of. The laptop was opening to a user named "Brent," but it was protected by a password and had automatically shut down after I tried to log in three times, noting that any future failed login attempts would render the machine permanently inoperable. I didn't know that was even possible; score zero for my hacking ability.

"Wait," she said. "When I was temping, they made me fill out an emergency contact in the little form I filled out before I could start working. I bet his company did that, too. Could we call his office?" she said. "Where did he work?"

Brent hadn't talked much about work. I remember one time he came home seeming stressed out; when I asked him about it, he had mumbled about "giving a presentation to the CEO of the company" and disappeared into his room. I knew that he worked downtown, and he left in the mornings much earlier than I did and got home erratically, between four-thirty and midnight. Brent dressed for work like everyone else downtown – a collared shirt and khakis, black or brown shoes. He wore a baseball hat when it rained, because he didn't like to have the rain in his eyes as he walked up the hill to the N line. He wouldn't have been that special – just another short guy on the light rail, absorbed in the daily free paper, iPod buds coming out of his ears.

I turned his pay stub over. He'd grossed nearly forty thousand dollars so far this year, from Jackson West Phillips and Cairney.

"731 Sansome," I said.

"Where is that?" asked Shawna.

I wasn't sure, so I walked out to the living room and picked up my laptop from the sofa, where I'd left it the night before as I'd surfed around looking at stupid video clips in a vain attempt to stay awake long enough to drink a quantity of water that would stave off my hangover. I popped it open and opened up Yahoo Maps.

"Corner of Sansome and Pacific, looks like," I said. "Interesting neighborhood."

"What's interesting about it?"

"Well, it's not really the financial district, not really North Beach, not really Chinatown, not really anything," I said.

There was more than that. I knew the area well. Brent's office was smack-dab in the middle of the old Barbary Coast, an area on the edge of downtown that was all landfill that had gone in around abandoned tall ships in the 1800s. Back then, the Barbary Coast was nothing but alleys and filth, prostitutes, gambling, saloons so vile that dive-bar-loving hipsters would run away screaming after one look at the entrance. The city had looked the other way, as cities do when half of the government is down in the depths of the sex district every night. Over time, the ships rotted away and the buildings were built, and the disease and dirt of the Barbary Coast changed into the cellblock skyscrapers and white-collar crime zone known as the Financial District. Remnants of the Coast turn up every now and then; some time ago they were excavating the foundation of a new forty-story high-rise right off of Embarcadero Center and turned up the skeleton of one of the old Panama Clippers.

"We should call them," said Shawna. "They might be wondering what happened."

"Well, they won't be wondering until Monday," I said. "And they won't be open on the weekend, so we can wait until then. It's pretty close to my office...I can go."

And that was that. We finished the salsa, and I took Brent's pay stubs up to my room and put them on my corner couch and spent a few minutes picking up laundry from the floor. By the time I finished up Shawna had gone off to yoga class, Thomas was sprawled out on the couch in his usual Saturday spot, watching the Giants pre-pre-game show, and Jenn was attempting another batch of low-fat cookies. I joined Thomas on the couch for a little while, and after the Giants started losing in the second inning, my phone rang. My friend Gerald was hosting an afternoon cribbage tournament in an hour at Café Abir, and I was invited. He was also a good brain to pick, and I had some questions about the Brent conundrum.

"Wanna come?" I asked Thomas. His six foot three inches completely covered the couch; one of his knees was sticking through the hole in his Saturday morning sweat pants.

"No," he said, shaking his head. "There's a guy spinning records late tonight at the DNA Lounge and I want to be on top of my game for that. Going to one of Gerald's oddball events isn't a good way to relax."

"Why do you have to rest to go out?"

"Because unlike you, I have to get to the office every morning at the crack of dawn because I have to track the New York markets. And I had to wear a suit every day this week because the regional managers were in town."

"You *like* dressing nicely."

"I like it when I choose to dress nicely. I don't like it when other people make me. You would understand if you actually owned any decent clothes. Your wardrobe makes me irate, you know. I have to take you shopping."

"Shopping is not something I do," I said.

"You make me irate," he said, yawning. "Totally irate."

"Seeya," I said, and headed out the door.

Getting to Café Abir was a pretty easy task, in theory. Down the hill to Haight, down Haight to Divisadero, then north. Haight Street is no longer the counterculture domain that everyone says it was back in the Sixties, which I never really believed. The instant people start saying that an area is full of counterculture types, all of the wannabes move in to start taking advantage of the cachet of living in a counterculture place. It's doubtful that the Haight was counterculture for much longer than a few weeks back in 1966. Now we have the Gap and a Ben and Jerry's and a bunch of boutiques that sell shoes that nobody I know can afford. Those places are mobbed every weekend with suburban teenagers. The counter-culture vibe is supplied by a tattoo studio and a couple of head shops that make their living peddling exquisitely expensive blown glass bongs to the aforementioned suburban teenagers, as well as a few homeless people who've adopted the hippie look to work the street along with the gutter punks and their ironic "Give us money for weed and beer" signs.

All of them and more were out in force when I reached Haight Street. It was more crowded than usual – a solid wall of people was milling on the sidewalk, the streets were packed with cars, and navigating through the crowd was difficult. I made my way to the intersection of Haight and Ashbury, where an electric Muni bus had come off of the overhead power lines while attempting to pass a double-parked Hummer. The entire road was blocked, and the throngs of shopping-bag-toting tourists who were waiting to get photos of themselves at the Haight/Ashbury sign were restlessly shivering in the foggy damp. It didn't get any better a block down, where another bus had also come off of the power lines while attempting to take a left up the Masonic hill. Traffic and people were snarled all the way down to Buena Vista Park. Just another Saturday.

As I walked, I called the San Francisco Police Department's North Station, which is where the reporting officer for Brent's accident was based. The woman on the other end of the line was very polite, very friendly, and told me absolutely nothing. No, they had no more information on the case. No, it was not SFPD policy to keep any objects of a deceased person after they've been catalogued, even in an investigation.

"Hang on," she said. "At the moment, there doesn't seem to be an investigating officer assigned."

"Why not?" I asked. "Isn't hitting someone with your car on a sidewalk a crime?"

"Yes," she said. "But our unit that investigates pedestrians killed by cars is stretched pretty thin. There's usually a three-month lag between the incident and when the officers have the free time to do any follow-up."

"How can they possibly do any follow-up after three months?" I asked.

I could almost hear the shrug coming from the other end of the line. "We have a personnel crisis," she said. "If you want to do something about it, come on in and take the police entrance exam. Unless it's a homicide, there's not much we can do."

"How could it not be a homicide?" I asked. "Someone drove a car into him and he's dead, and they took off. That's murder, right?"

"According to the officer and the witnesses, nobody was positive that the vehicle in question was actually trying to target your friend. Without motive, it's vehicular manslaughter, and that investigations unit is, as I said, overwhelmed."

Great. I hung up. I was nearly to Abir, anyway.

Café Abir is a coffee joint with ten beer taps, the kind of place where students sit and play with their laptops all day. It's dark and comfortable, with wood tables on the floor and a few couches and low coffee tables on a mezzanine. The coffee is decent, and they sell vegan cookies. It's the kind of cafe that my friend Gerald's parents worried that he'd hang out in when he moved to San Francisco.

Gerald is from Indiana, and his parents are convinced that he lives in the modern-day Gomorrah; they mail him every San-Francisco-related clipping from *News of the Weird* along with handwritten notes asking him if whatever perversion mentioned in the article happened anywhere near his house. It's unlikely – Gerald lives in lower Pacific Heights. He's an organizer, a doer, a world-class stoner, and he dresses like all three. He looks like a management consultant who does efficiency studies for Burning Man. From his space on one of the couches, he gestured me over.

"Hey," he said. "They're cool with us doing this here, but buy something every couple of hours."

"Right," I said. "Too many people hanging out?"

He nodded. "Apparently one of the neighbors has an open network, so they've been besieged over the past week or so by laptop gypsies. They're going to ask the guy to password-protect it, but he's been out of the country for a month."

I grinned. "That's life."

"That's life *now*," he said. "Ten years ago, this wasn't a problem." He reached into his pocket and pulled out some dark brown crumbs."

"Brownies are an exception to the rule?" I asked.

"No," he said. "I bought a brownie here, then crumbled it up with one of mine in a Ziploc bag. I'm eating both, so it's cool."

"Why didn't you just eat a couple before you got here?"

"I did."

Oh. He was high as a kite; as usual, you couldn't tell. I went to get some coffee. The guy behind the counter was everyone's stereotype of the independent coffee bar barista; star tattoos on the backs of his hands, small earrings, a Keith Richards haircut and a too-tight Replacements T-shirt. He was maybe twenty years old; his attempt at an ironic mustache was wispy.

"Small coffee," I said.

He smiled. "Sure thing. Room for cream?"

Coffee – hot, brown, bitter. The perfect drink for a cold summer day. I walked back up to the couches and grabbed an empty seat in front of one of the cribbage boards. My partner was Judy, a slender brunette with a wardrobe straight outta Hammet. She even had forearm gloves and a cigarette holder with an unlit cigarette at the end.

"Hi," she said. "I'm twenty-six and I have a boyfriend."

"Kind of a weird way to introduce yourself," I said.

She shrugged. "I like to get sexual tension out of the way. For what it's worth, you're pretty cute."

We sat down and started to play. After a few hands, the conversation mellowed enough for me to ask what was on my mind.

"Anyone ever have a roommate who died?"

The other three people looked at me, then looked at their cards and resumed playing. The glasses-and-sweater guy to my left spoke first.

"I heard about a group house where the new roommate moved in and then died of an overdose, leaving behind a suitcase full of cash. They didn't tell anyone and tried to keep the money."

"James," said his partner, a plump girl with a ring through her lip. "That was the plot of *Shallow Grave*. We saw it the other night."

"Was it a good movie?" asked Judy. "I've got fifteen for two, fifteen for four, and a run for seven."

"Not bad," said the plump girl. "It's by the *Trainspotting* guys. A little immature, but still worth seeing.

"But has anyone had it happen for real?" I said.

"Not anyone I know," said the plump girl.

We continued the conversation while Judy and I continued to get killed. We went one and three in the pool-play round, shunting us to the conciliation brackets, where we would have had to win every game *and* have a good point differential to make it to the championship game. Judy and I switched from coffee to beer. Nobody had anything useful to say about dead roommates with dual identities.

"I was talking about the life/death thing with a friend of mine the other day," said Gerald, who was sitting next to me and Judy. "She was excited because she deflowered a virgin this past weekend."

"How old is she?" I was on my third Anchor Steam and feeling nice and mellow.

"She's thirty, he was twenty-four," he said. "She was doing the born-again-virgin thing ironically during her second year of nursing school. Anyway, they were talking about sex and whatnot, and one of the guys in their program was like 'Wow, you guys are virgins? I'm a virgin, too!'"

"And from there the hunt was on?" I said.

Gerald grinned. "Exactly. My friend and him ended up dating for a bit, then they got together." He paused. "Now she gets to live forever."

"How's that again?" asked Judy.

Gerald paused and put his beer down.

"There's an old story," he said. "You only really die when everyone who knows you or knew you has died. As long as the memory of you is still around, you're still alive, until the last person who knew you is gone. With my friend, it went like this. You never forget the first person you sleep with. Whether you're a fundamentalist who marries his high school sweetheart or a total player who makes Wilt Chamberlain look like a priest. Nobody ever forgets. So, this guy, he sleeps with my friend, he's never slept with anyone before – this guy will never forget that girl. She's immortal."

"Wow," said Judy."

"Not only that," said Gerald. "There's the generational aspect to it, as well. If this Texas guy goes ahead and tells his children all about his first time, with a good description, do they qualify as remembering her? If so, she's going to live freakin' *forever*."

"Your logic is impeccable," I said.

"Ain't it?" asked Gerald. "Interesting story, though, don't you think?"

I nodded. I think he was saying that if I really wanted to find out something about my roommate, I'd have to find the first person Brent had slept with. I thought about it for a second, then chucked it. If I didn't know his real name, how was I going to find an ex? Post a Missed Connections ad? Even if I could do that, where would I post it? I had no idea where Brent was from, no real clue where he had lived before living with us, and nowhere to start looking.

"Hey," said Gerald. "Don't look so down, Alex. It's been a great day."

"You're not stuck with an ex-roommate in the morgue and a nagging sense of guilt because you haven't the first idea what to do about it," I said.

"Where'd he work?" asked Gerald.

"Downtown," I said. "I've got a pay stub somewhere. I'm talking to them first thing next week."

"Good call," he said. "But..."

"What?" I said.

"This smells weird," he said. "If I were still in college and scoring weed from guys I don't know, I'd walk away from this deal, metaphorically."

"Fifteen for two, one-twenty nine!" shouted the guy at the championship table. "Game over!"

"Whoop," said Gerald. "Gotta take care of my responsibilities."

"Thanks for the idea," I said.

"Just remember," he said. "Keep your eyes open."

He clambered over the back of the couch and hopped up onto the championship table. His too-long jeans made a slight scriffling sound as he landed. Gerald waved his arms, and the cheers and claps of the crowd faded out.

"Ladies and gentlemen," he shouted, "thank you all for coming to the first annual Café Abir Dominoes and Cribbage contest. First off, I'd like to apologize to everyone who came here to play dominoes, as all we did was play cribbage. We'll find some dominoes next time. Secondly, I'd like to acknowledge the skill and fortitude of our champions – Lila Monaghan and Charles Wikowski, please stand and take a bow!"

The two winners stood and staged elaborate, ballet-worthy bows. Charles then knelt down and kissed Lila's hand. She blushed, grabbed him by the arms, pulled him to his feet, and stuck her tongue down his throat. Charles stiffened in shock, then grabbed her and kissed her back. Even the non-players in the coffeehouse roared in appreciation.

"Looks like we have a double win," said Gerald. "I have it on good authority that these two just met today! Congratulations, guys, you win a cribbage board, two free beers here at Café Abir, and free admission to the next Cribbage/Dominoes night here. Please see me to claim your prizes. Everyone else...beer's a dollar off for the next thirty minutes, and I'll be behind the bar, so drink up! Exact change will be appreciated."

He hopped down from the table, then did a Spider-Man move

over the bar and started to pull pints into glasses. If it were possible for human beings to actually glow, Gerald could have lit up a darkened stadium. He lives for this kind of thing – being the center of attention, the guy that makes things happen and then soaks in the adoration of his friends. In the past, he'd done scavenger hunts, water-balloon fights in the park, games of Squirtgun Assassin that had taken in what seemed like half the city, Nerf golf tournaments, dim sum restaurant crawls, you name it. He worked from home and was stoned most of the time; I think that's where most of his ideas came from.

I ordered a Kronenberg and settled in a couch to sip, relax, and watch the crowd. Charles and Lila were sharing an easy chair, alternately making out and slamming down beers brought to them by people in the crowd. Judy was sidling ever-closer to a thin boy with a starving-student look. Everyone was laughing and talking to each other, and I had just decided to get up and mingle when I felt my phone vibrating in my pocket.

Bzzzzzz. Bzzzz. Bzz

It was a text message from Jenn.

If you're interested, I baked some cookies. Want me to save some before Thomas kills them?

I texted right back.

Yes, please. You're the best.

She replied.

Can the sweet talk – yours are in foil in your room. Ever think about making the bed?

I clicked the phone shut and headed home. If I was lucky, those cookies would still be warm when I got there.

Saturday night, at home, hanging with Shawna and Jenn, watching *Clerks* for the three hundredth time on the Independent Film Channel. I don't think that the IFC has any real business showing *Clerks*; Kevin Smith isn't exactly indie any more. Once you can cast Jennifer Lopez at will, you're pretty much The Man. Of course, there were things we *could* have been doing. San Francisco is a buffet of options for the young person in search of entertainment. By ten o'clock, dinner was winding down, the bar crowds were starting to heat up, the clubs had opened their doors to the poor students who showed up early to knock $10 off of their cover charges, the ravers had come out of their daytime hidey-holes. It was paradise.

But we weren't out in it. Sometimes you have to mellow out with homemade cookies and a four-dollar bottle of wine. And, by going to bed early Jenn and I would be able to beat the next-morning brunch rush.

Sunday breakfast is a great idea that has spiraled completely out of control. I'm not opposed to the concept – wake up at eleven in the morning with a terrible hangover, wander down to the diner on the corner (obligingly serving breakfast food until noon), and eat a ton of decent breakfast food for five bucks.

Those days are gone, though. Somewhere along the line, brunch stopped being just a hung over late-breakfast and became *brunch*. Things got weird. Nice restaurants started making the Sunday meal a staple for their ultra-bourgeois customers, wealthy investment bankers began to hire babysitters for four hours on Sunday mornings, and it became easier to find pumpkin pancakes with caramelized bananas and a huckleberry demiglaze than waffles with pure maple syrup and a side of bacon. Some places in the city are so full of cougars and open-collared suit guys that you start looking around for the *Sex and the City* cameras.

My generation isn't any better – if you go down to Boogaloos in the Mission or the Pork Store Cafe in my neighborhood, the crowds of people in tight clothes and impractical sunglasses overwhelm the sidewalks, and the see/be seen factor overwhelms the point of the whole thing, which is to eat. The only way to avoid it all is to wake up and go as early as you can and power down your first meal of the day unscarred by people with elaborate morning makeup and small jeans.

I had to pound on Jenn's door for two minutes at eight thirty in the morning before she answered. She was in her comfortable pajama pants and a beige tank top, and she didn't look particularly happy.

"What?"

"It's breakfast time," I said. "Remember last night? We were going to go get breakfast?"

She blinked her eyes and rubbed them.

"I can't believe you actually woke me up this early," she said.

"I had to. I can't go alone, and if we're not out of here in half an hour, Kate's will be mobbed, we'll be starving, you'll be grumpy, and we'll hate each other."

"Which would be different from how I feel about you right now in what way?"

"You'll get over hating me now if we eat quickly. If we don't eat quickly, you'll still hate me for getting you up and you'll hate me for being around when you're hungry. Besides, it's my turn to pay."

"You're right," she said. "I'll be ready in a few minutes. Don't walk close to me, though. I might forget and accidentally throttle you."

Jenn was the only person in the house whom I woke; she was my usual weekend breakfast buddy. Thomas slept in hard on weekends to make up for work, and Shawna always took an hour to get ready. Jenn moved quickly after waking and didn't have a boyfriend. After a quick debate, we decided to walk down the mile to Kate's Kitchen in the Lower Haight. We got there at five till nine, and a bleary waitress sat us down.

"I can't believe people get up this early," she said.

"We're losers," said Jenn.

"I wish *I* was," she moaned. "My boyfriend was up until three-thirty in the morning blowing rails with his gay friends. I had to give him four of my muscle relaxants to get him to stop twitching in bed. You guys look like you've slept – I wish I had your relationship."

Jenn snorted. "He's my housemate, not my boyfriend."

"Amen to that," I said.

"Oh, sorry," said the waitress. "It's an honest mistake – coming in together early on Sunday screams 'couple', you know? You guys need menus?"

"I don't think so," said Jenn. "I'll have the fruit orgy and he'll have the Farny Garney and hush puppies."

"Done," she said. "Coffee?"

"Two," said Jenn.

We sat at a table in the middle of Kate's, next to the wall. It's a happily San Francisco place – a huge map of the country covers one wall, sketches by local artists are hung at eye level, and a blend of downtempo and reggae blasts from the kitchen. It's famous for pancakes, the Farney Garney sandwich, and sports-metaphor omelettes that change ingredients with the seasons. It would be quiet until 10:15, when all of the tables would suddenly fill, names would go on a list outside, and our unperky waitress would probably lose her mind. But early it was a good place to eat.

Jenn had managed to pull together a good look in two minutes. She is one of those effortlessly attractive people – medium brown hair, a small nose, dressed frugally well by keeping tabs on the local vintage shops and H&M sales.

We didn't say much. I checked out the pictures on the wall, which looked like they were painted by an African Hieronymous Bosch on Xanax. Jenn had bought the Sunday *Chronicle* on our way down the hill, and she passed me sections as she finished with them. There wasn't much in the way of news, although I got a bit of a kick out of one of the ads.

"Check it out," I said. "There's a toilet sale at the Home Depot over in Oakland."

Jenn lowered the Datebook section. "And I would care why?"

"It's funny," I said. "I'd forgotten– Thomas and I were checking out toilets online before the cop picked me up to take me to the morgue. It's like everything's coming up toilet in my life."

"You are so weird," she said.

Our food came then and we dug in. A middle-aged lesbian couple wandered in with an obscenely cute baby. An old man sat down with the front section of the Sunday *Chronicle* and started to read. He'd be gone before ten, so nobody gave him static about reading and taking up space. The music started up – early Police, before their extreme-pop stage, when Sting wasn't a twelve-hours-of-sex Tantric weirdo but just another punk from England with spiky hair and torn clothing. God, it would have been great to have been around back then.

"What are we going to do with Brent's stuff?" she asked.

"I hadn't thought about it," I said. Brent hadn't been big on decoration – he had no photos or knickknacks – but he did have a bed, a dresser, a bunch of clothes, and a laptop computer. When I'd ransacked his room, I hadn't even moved the gym shirt he'd left on top of his closet door to dry. The laptop was useless; logging in to his account was still impossible. "Do we keep it?"

She shuddered. "That's morbid."

"Do we donate it?"

"I don't know."

"Well, what happens to stuff that people own when they die? I mean, say you're an old guy and you die – do your kids just take your old-man clothes? It's be a shame to waste them, but…"

"You wouldn't fit in Brent's clothes, Alex. You'd need to lose three inches and gain twenty pounds."

"I know that. And I don't want his clothes."

"You're criticizing someone else's fashion sense? Do you own anything but t-shirts from British punk bands and jeans?"

"I wear buttoned shirts."

"To *work*. I've never seen you put one on voluntarily. Maybe that's why you're single."

"Because my shirts don't have buttons?"

She took another bite of melon. "It's not the buttons, it's what they signify. Girls like to look at guys when the guy looks like he cares what he looks like. You look like you're actively trying to get people to look away."

"We won't donate his clothes," I said. "If we can find his parents, they might want them."

"How can you find his parents?" she asked. "You're still not sure of his real name."

"I can at least try," I said. "We owe him that. We can't just chuck his things until we really know who he was. Until we know that, his stuff is all we have to go on."

She nodded, chewing slowly, not looking away from me. I got a little embarrassed – talking like a movie hero isn't my usual style – and I looked away first.

Monday. My day to check in at Brent's old workplace and see what I could turn up. They'd have missed him on Friday, and at least I'd let them know that his absence from work wasn't an instance of slacking. He didn't deserve to die and *then* get fired for lack of attendance. The company name looked like that of a law or accounting firm, so I'd have to get over there before the official close of the workday at five.

In order to do that, I'd have to get out of my job early. As I said before, this isn't much of a problem. By three o'clock on Monday, most of the marketing department was catatonic. My cube neighbor Raymond had already changed into a bright-orange shirt and gym shorts in preparation for an ultimate frisbee game, and Valerie from across the hall was furiously writing a detailed blog entry about her weekend of debauchery. She was closing in on forty and three years post-divorce. I was too scared to go out drinking with her – the word "cougar" didn't do her justice.

"What's a synonym for 'hammered'?" she asked.

"Smashed?" I said.

She shook her head. "That's not quite what I'm looking for. I'm trying to illustrate more of a classy drunkenness."

"So like slightly-swaying-old-man-drunk, rather than fratboy-vomit-in-a-garbage-can drunk," I said.

"Bingo. That's exactly it. We were at Top of the Mark on Saturday night and this guy who was like sixty-five kept hitting on us by telling us all about how he'd owned his place in Pacific Heights for like thirty years or whatever, and how he'd just installed a hot tub. Totally insinuating that we should come back and hang out in his hot tub."

"Why didn't you?"

She grinned. "Not because we would have minded hot-tubbing. But we probably would have had to look at him naked. Old. Gross."

"Snockered," I said.

"Huh?"

"Snockered. It's an…"

"Right," she said. "Perfect. An old-guy-drunk word."

Our boss Phil showed up right then, doing his thing where he walked through the cubicle farm and asked what was going on. He wasn't a Lumbergh - he dressed nicely but never wore those ridiculous colored-but-with-white-collar-and-sleeve-shirts – but he was still the guy who had to go through the painful half-year ritual where he told us that our performance had been average or just barely above, and that was why we were only getting two or three percent raises. Aside from that, he was a decent enough guy. He even put our drinks on the corporate credit card sometimes when we went out for

Thursday evening happy hours. Still, when he came by, we all tried to look busy.

"What's shaking?" he asked.

"The usual," I said. "Just trying to get a few things out the door before I have to take off."

"What? It's only three."

"Yeah," I said, "But I have an appointment– remember, I e-mailed you about it a few weeks ago?"

"Oh," he said. "Right."

This was total bullshit. There was no e-mail. It didn't matter because even if he looked for the e-mail (unlikely) and came back to me the next day with the point that he couldn't find the early-leave-request-e-mail, I could always blame the e-mail system – a multiple-hacked version of Lotus Notes that seemed to think that the server was a Doberman and our messages were Snausages. He'd never go that far, though – if he came back to me and admitted that he hadn't read the e-mail, that would be too close to admitting that he never read *any* of my e-mails, a fact that we both knew was absolutely true. But he knew that I knew that his calendar always showed that he was stuck in meetings from ten in the morning until the end of the workday on Fridays during ski season. It was kind of like the office version of Mutually Assured Destruction.

"So I'll be gone in about twenty minutes," I said.

"OK," said Phil. "Anything serious?"

"Can't really talk about it," I said. That's what I always said. If someone had been keeping track, they'd have noticed that I had more doctor's appointments than a chronically incontinent hemophiliac. Nobody was keeping track.

"Well, break a leg," he said. "See you tomorrow."

See you tomorrow meant that Phil was going to go back to his office and not emerge until five fifteen, when he'd barrel straight from his door to the exit door in the hopes of not encountering *his* boss, Howard Maloney, who would sometimes demand progress reports or flow documents, which would mean that the rest of us would get panicked overnight e-mails from Phil demanding that we produce appropriately long PowerPoint presentations with enough jargon to satisfy Maloney. Marketing is weird. All we did was produce

PowerPoints, and somehow that was all that we needed to do.

I headed north on Montgomery to Jackson, then crossed over to Sansome. 731 was a nondescript white building with glass doors and a copy shop on the first floor. The directory on the outside listed Jackson West Phillips and Cairney on the second floor. I dialed the code on the little phone pad.

"Jackson West Phillips Cairney," said a female voice.

"Hi," I said. "Um, I'm here to talk to someone about Brent...I mean, David Jones."

"Oh, we were wondering about him," she said. "Why don't you come up?"

The door made a buzzing sound, and I pushed it open and walked to the elevator. It was a slow elevator, the kind that makes mysterious groaning sounds. When the doors opened, I walked into an office that looked almost exactly like mine, a gray-walled cubicle farm with a receptionist who looked vaguely like Phoebe Cates from *Fast Times at Ridgemont High*, sitting behind a frontless desk that showed where her lithe legs *would* have been if she hadn't been wearing knee-high, heeled leather boots.

She looked up at me as I entered, and her gaze stopped me in my tracks. I stood there, stunned, for a few seconds, until the elevator tried to close on my shoulder bag. She smiled; obviously this had happened before.

"Hi," she said. "Did you just buzz in?"

A tongue stud flashed when she talked.

"Yep," I said. "I'm here about David Jones."

"Right," she said. "Let me get you Gabriel Beck. He's David's boss."

"Was," I said.

She cocked an eyebrow.

"Oh," I said. "Um...yeah."

"Huh," she said, then bent her head to the phone. I couldn't overhear what she was saying.

"Have a seat," she said. "Gabriel will be right out."

Gabriel kept me waiting for ten minutes, then appeared from a side door that was so flush with the wall I hadn't noticed it before.

"Ah, you're the one with news on our missing fellow," he said.

"Come into my office."

I didn't like Gabriel. He was like Pigpen from *Peanuts,* except instead of being surrounded by dirt, he was enveloped in a cloud of smarm. Gabriel wore a light blue Lumbergh shirt, no belt, and suspenders. His desk was littered with four to-go Starbucks cups, and he had a coffee-stained StressBustR squeeze ball next to his computer mouse. I sat down on the hard plastic chair across from him, and he folded his hands and smiled at me. One of his front teeth was fake; the gumline around it had turned dark from coffee and cigarettes. He closed the smile and started to talk.

"So," he said. "What's going on with David? Why isn't he here explaining why he bailed out on a project that was on deadline for Monday, leaving me to cover for his lazy ass all weekend? Is he off in one of those rehab centers? He didn't strike me as someone with a coke problem, but you just never know with you kids." He ran a finger slowly down his gray-stubbled cheek. "And it really doesn't speak well for him that he sent someone else to talk for him instead of just picking up the phone…when you see him, you can let him know that we're seriously considering our other options as far as his employment status is concerned."

"David's dead," I said. "He was hit by a car the other day after work."

"Oh," said Gabriel. He didn't say anything, and I waited for a bit, then filled the silence.

"I'm one of his housemates," I said. "But…"

"Well, I guess I won't be firing him, then." said Gabriel. He looked at me.

"Yes," I said. "But…well, I need to get in touch with his parents. We don't have their number, and, um…we didn't know him as David Jones."

"What was his name?" asked Gabriel.

"Brent," I said. "Scalia. Brent Scalia."

"Oh my God," said Gabriel. "Do you know what this means?"

"That he was a strange guy?" I said.

"No," he shook his head. "It means that we could get *sued.* If it comes out that we hired someone with fake documentation, we could be in huge trouble. We're a financial institution. Have you told the newspapers about this yet? If you haven't, don't. One second."

He punched a button on the phone. "Morgan? Can you pull David's HR file and bring it over here, please? The whole thing. I *know* there are some things I'm not supposed to see; bring them anyway."

Gabriel hit the button again and turned to me. "Do you understand what a revelation like this can do to a business like ours? I don't think you do. Christ, I've got a case of the Mondays!" He started to twitch, and little half-moons of sweat had appeared under his arms. He started frantically typing, muttering as if I wasn't there.

"He's dead, so he won't complain, and all we really have to do is get rid of some of his e-mails or assign some to my name, and we can say that we fired him before he kicked the bucket. All of mine asking where he was were to his work e-mail, and all we have to do is figure out when his last sent mail was and then manufacture a termination letter for that evening." He looked at me, and his voice changed. "I'm sorry to say this, but David was fired right before his unfortunate passing. Perhaps it was a suicide."

"Are you joking?" I said. "I've just heard you change his status right in front of me. You can't do that."

"Of course I can," said Gabriel. "If you'd waited another week we would have recorded his hours for last week in payroll and it would have gone to the payroll company, but…that went out on Friday. There's no record of this conversation. If it's not on paper or in the database, it doesn't exist. Of course, you'll want to notify his parents. I'm having Morgan bring in his personnel records. Let's just go out and get them."

Gabriel grabbed me by the arm and took me over to the door. He bustled me across the office, never letting go of my elbow as he did so. The secretary from the front was kneeling in front of a file cabinet, a pile of manila folders stacked to her left.

"Did you find it?" asked Gabriel.

"Yep, here it is," she said, handing over a folder. "Just got it now. Both copies that we had in the files."

"Great!" he said. "You do good work, Morgan."

Gabriel took the papers out of the folder and dropped them into the industrial-sized shredder. It hummed, whirred, and spit out a stream of paper spaghetti into a can filled with similar-lengths of paper spaghetti.

"There," he said, smiling. For the first time, the smile reached his eyes.

"Did you just shred his employment records?"

"Shred what?" he said. "He demanded his records after we fired him. We gave him the originals, and these copies have been unfortunately lost. Morgan, can you please escort him out? All the way out."

Morgan walked over and took my arm, leading me to the elevator. At some point she had undone two of the buttons of her white dress blouse, revealing a very smooth swath of pale upper-chest skin. It wasn't cleavage or anything, but if that kind of thing is staring you in the face it's kind of hard not to look. The door opened, we entered, and Morgan didn't let go of my arm.

We walked out onto the street. Morgan reached inside her blouse and brought out a thin metallic case. She clicked it open and took out a thin cigarette and tiny lighter.

"I take smoke breaks every hour," she said. "Although I don't smoke, in case you were wondering." Click. Flame. Inhale.

"I wasn't," I said. "Wondering, I mean. I don't smoke either. But I don't have problems with people who do. I mean, I don't like smoke much, but I think people should be able to..."

My babbling was interrupted by the roaring of a diesel MUNI bus. She grinned at me again. I could feel the scorching waves coming off of my cheeks, and I could be pretty confident that I was now roughly the color of a Roma tomato. A real one, not the crap they sell in the grocery store in the winter.

"So..." she said.

"Nice to meet you," I said.

"I didn't," she said. "Do you have a name?"

"Alex," I said.

"I'm Morgan," she said, extending a hand.

"I got that," I said. I'd left Roma tomato behind at this point and was now approaching ketchup.

"Um..." I said.

She raised her eyebrows in the way that mothers do to a three-year old who's having trouble finding the right words.

"You need some help," she said. "I might be able to help you."

"How? He shredded everything."

She snorted. "So?"

"What do you know?"

She snorted again. "Not here."

We paused.

"So, do you…uh…maybe want to get a drink sometime?" I said.

Her eyebrows fell, and she smiled. "That's more like it.."

"Great," I said, reaching into the pocket of my shoulder bag and coming up with a battered black PaperMate. "I don't think I have any paper."

"You don't need one," she said. She drew a small card from her cigarette case and took a pen out from behind her ear.

"Here's my number and my e-mail," she said. "Call me any time."

"OK," I said. She smiled again when she handed me back the folder. "Nice to meet you, Alex."

"Same," I said. She turned around and walked back into the building, her heels click-clacking as she went.

Chapter 3

Drama-free house needs new roomie - $650

Housemate wanted for mellow Cole Valley apartment. The place is more like a house than a classic flat — we have the top two floors, and the bottom is taken up by a big garage and storage area. We're two girls and two guys, looking for someone of either gender. We're straight but not narrow, don't have any pets and aren't looking for any, 420 friendly as long as you use our (awesome) front porch, and we don't care what you eat, because we eat everything. One of us is a vegetarian, and that's never been a problem. We all work, and it would be nice if you worked enough to be able to pay the rent. The storage area has laundry so you won't need to deal with the maniacs at the laundromat down the street.

"Think that works?" asked Thomas.

"Fair enough," I said. "Post it."

Thomas reached down to his mouse and clicked the "Accept Terms of Service" button, and our ad was out to the world of Craigslist. We started to get replies right away. Thomas read them aloud as they came in.

Hi, I'm a student at San Francisco Institute for Holistic...

"Next."

Your house sounds like just what I'm looking for for me and my Pekingese...

"Next"

After I finish touring the world as part of a mixed martial arts Ultimate Fighting collective, I'm looking for a place to settle down...

"Next."

Wow! Your place sounds great! I run my own candle-dipping business, so I'll need to use most of the kitchen for four hours per day...

"Next."

And so on. Thomas and I went through e-mail for two hours, e-mailed three people back and set up appointments for the following evening. Forty-five minutes each, back-to-back-to-back.

"Only a week until the first of the month," he said. "I hope we find somebody."

"E-mail the girls," I said. "If they can make it for the interviews, that would be good, too."

Thomas turned back to his laptop and wrote a quick note. "Done," he said.

"It won't be that bad," I said. "And if none of them work out, we can probably handle an extra hundred and twenty-five apiece if we have to deal for another month without a newbie."

Our living room had two couches. The one facing the television was yellow, ugly, and more comfortable than a Brookstone massage chair. The other was an oversized love seat, sitting at a ninety degree angle to the large sofa. I sat on the big one with Jenn. Thomas and Shawna were on the love seat. We had brought one of the chairs from the kitchen table and put it in front of the television – the potential roommate would sit there and be faced by us on two sides. The evening had already started badly; two of our potentials had e-mailed during the day to flake out on us. I was bummed, as I'd planned on my usual housemate-interview technique of two beers per person. So I had started early and was three in by the time the doorbell rang.

I put my finger to the side of my nose and looked around. Everyone but Shawna had our fingers up. She was looking out the window, twirling a strand of dark brown hair on her finger.

"Oh, what are you guys doing?" she asked, after noticing that we were all staring at her.

"Nose game rules. Answer the door," said Thomas.

"Oh, OK," she said. She bounced up and thudded down the stairs.

"Do you think she even knows the nose thing?" I asked.

"Doubtful," said Thomas. "But that's why we love her."

"Looking to get a little down-the-hall action?" I asked.

Thomas reached down, balled up a stray receipt, and threw it at my head. "That'll be the day."

Shawna came back up the stairs with a midget in tow. The guy was *small*, two inches shorter than Shawna at least. And she was barefoot – he was wearing black dress shoes with thick heels, along with khakis and a tucked-in red polo shirt.

"Everyone, this is Darren," said Shawna. We all said our respective names.

Darren sat on the chair across from all of us. His feet didn't touch the ground, so he swung his legs back and forth as he sat. I took a sip of beer.

"So," said Thomas. He leaned back slightly on the couch in a confident-banker pose; he'd used it on me when I'd interviewed to move in the year before. "Why don't you tell us about yourself. Are you from around here?"

"I'm Darren," he said "I come from Antioch."

"Where's that?"

"It's in the East Bay. Kind of over the hills."

"Oh."

Thomas leaned forward, then leaned back. I sipped my beer. Shawna started to roll up her pants, revealing sparse, stubby leg hairs. Why hadn't somebody put some music on?

"Do you work in the city?" asked Jenn.

"No, I work over in Oakland," said Darren. "I've never lived in the city before."

"Where did you move from?"

"Antioch."

"Oh, so you've…"

"I grew up in Antioch, then went to Antioch junior college, then I finished my degree at Berkeley," said Darren. "I managed to save a lot of money by living at home for the first two years of college, and for the past two years I've saved money by living in Antioch. My parents didn't charge me rent, as long as I did the dishes after dinner and mowed the lawn once per week. I saved a lot of money that way." Darren's feet were swinging back and forth furiously, and he was leaning far forward, on the edge of his chair. I'd have been worried about him tipping over and smacking into the coffee table if he hadn't been such a shrimp.

"So…why are you moving to the city?" I asked as I reached down to grab another beer.

"My dad took me aside the other day and told me that it was going to be time for me to leave soon." He was smiling when he said this, and his eyes were glistening, reminding me of that one scene in *the Shining* when Nicholson sticks his head through a wall. There was no way he was going to see Brent's old room; the knife rack was right near the entrance and I wasn't going to let him near anything sharp.

"I have a few questions for you guys," he said, taking a neatly folded piece of paper and a pen out of his pants pocket.

"Shoot," said Thomas.

"Well, do you have any pets?"

"No," I said. "That's why we said we didn't have any on the ad."

"Well, you can't be too careful, I always say," he said, and laughed. His laughter sounded like someone was torturing Bart Simpson, a strangled, gargling high-pitched cough. He made a note on his piece of paper.

"And do you have high-speed Internet?"

"Yep," said Thomas.

"Anyone here allergic to down? Is there a laundry in the building? How often do you expect people to clean the lint filter?"

And on and on. I don't know that any of us had ever cleaned the lint filter. I'd have been hard-pressed to point out where it was on a topographical map of our laundry room. We didn't answer that question, and Darren didn't seem to care. He kept firing off queries and making quick marks on his little piece of paper. After twenty minutes of interrogation he flourished the paper, thanked us, and told us he only had one more question:

"Are you guys OK with having my parents come over every now and then to check on the place?"

Pause.

"Um…we can talk about that, definitely," said Thomas.

"OK, good," he said. "I think that's the last on the list that my mom made."

"Your mom?" I asked.

"Yeah, she gave me this list of questions to ask you, and I'm going to take the answers back to my parents to make sure that this place checks out with them."

"Oh," I said. "Are they the kind of parents who would freak out if they see that I left my bong in the bathroom?"

"What's a bong?"

"Broom," I said.

"Oh, I don't think mom would care about that. But I'll make sure to ask," he said. "Is that all?"

I nodded.

"Nice to meet you," he said, and walked down the stairs to the street.

Thomas took a look at us one by one. Then he slowly drew one finger across his throat. "Looks like we're in for the long haul," he said. "But where did the bong come from? You don't have a bong."

"It was a test," I said. "He failed."

I went to work the next day. Wednesdays were referred to as "Hump Day" by George, who works in accounting and sits next to the side door, which I use to enter the office because it goes nowhere near Phil Hampton's desk on my way in. It's not like Phil cares, but if *his* boss were to see him not caring about me coming in twenty minutes late every day, Phil might get in trouble. I'm the kind of wage slave who looks out for his immediate superiors.

"Happy Hump Day, Alex!' said George as I skulked in.

"Yep," I said.

I don't encourage George's cliché-ridden office patois. I never respond happily, I never mention how glad I am that the week is almost over, I never imply that I'm going to knock back a few cocktails after the day, or that I can't wait for the weekend because I have big plans. I say "yep" or "yeah," and walk right by. And George continues to say things like "Happy Hump Day". I think his need to be cheerful is directly attributable to his job. As a fact-checking accountant, the guy is supposed to look over the spreadsheets and balance statements that the other accountants produce and point out any errors that have been made. It's not just boring, it's meta-boring. His life must be terrible. But I didn't feel bad enough for him to hang out with him outside the office; there are some lines that you just can't cross, and hanging out with accountants-of-accountants is one of them.

When I reached my desk, there was a Post-it note on my computer screen.

Alex,
Come see me when you have a minute,
Phil.

Weird. You only left a Post-It on a screen when you really wanted your message to get across. Usually we just sent e-mail or instant messages. Voicemail for bigger issues. Post-Its are the one thing that you can't ignore – everybody looks at their screens all day, and the physical object negates the "it must have been lost in the system" excuse.

I booted up my computer, quickly checked my e-mail and the smoldering wreckage of my fantasy baseball team, and wandered over to Phil's mega-cube. As a mid-level boss of low-level guys like me, he didn't rate a real office, but his cube had three walls of desk as opposed to my two, and he rated a real Aeron chair instead of my Staples leatherette special. Phil was looking at his stock account when I walked up behind him and knocked on the metal top lining of his cube.

"Hey Phil, you wanted to see me?"

"Yeah, Alex," he said. "One second."

Phil clicked a button, closed a window, then turned around.

"Have a seat," he said.

I cleared a space on one of his desk surfaces and sat down. It was a weird perspective – Phil's taller than me, and from where I was sitting I could see the beginnings of a bald spot. His scalp was red and mottled where the thinning hair had let the sun through.

"What's up?" I said.

"Well, lots of things," said Phil. "I don't know how to tell you this, and it's a very difficult thing for me to say, but…they're letting you go."

My heart jumped into my throat, then plummeted down to my large intestine.

"What?" I said.

"There's a massive restructuring going on," he said. "I just found out about it on Monday. The whole department is going to be let go."

"Wow," I said. "What's going to happen to everybody?"

"Well, if you want to reapply for another job here, you're welcome to do so, but…off the record, that's probably not going to happen. Later on this afternoon someone from Human Resources will come by to take you through the logistics of it all."

"What's going to happen to you?"

Phil shrugged. "They're switching me over to manage the

accounting department. I don't know why."

"Why are you sticking around?"

He gave me a rueful grin. "I have two kids and a mortgage on a house down on the Peninsula. I figure I could live for about one week without my normal source of income. I have to stay. Be happy you're leaving. It's not going to be pretty around here."

"How many other people know?"

"You're the last to come by," he said. "I left notes on everyone's computers."

"Well, I had an emergency e-mail that came in…"

Phil shook his head. "Alex, I don't care. I think you were earlier today than you've been in five months. It doesn't matter any more."

"So what do I do now?"

"Well, you have to hang around here until Human Resources comes to get you, so you can probably go back to your cube and do what you always do."

"OK," I said.

"And Alex," he said. "It's been pretty obvious to me that you've been skating here for a while. You're really quick when you're doing something you give a shit about, and you notice things that nobody else does. That's a talent. Find something you give a shit about; it might be good for you."

"Thanks," I said after a moment. We shook hands and I walked away. It occurred to me as I walked off that that might be the last conversation I ever had with Phil. He lived down south, I lived in the city. He was in his forties and went to the gym every morning before work to fight an unending and vocal battle against the encroachment of a spare tire. I routinely battled weekday hangovers and subsisted on burritos and banh mi. After today, there was little chance that we'd ever run into each other again. And he'd given me a variation on the "wasting my talents" lecture that I'd been getting ever since high school.

When I got back to my cube, my computer didn't work. It was on and everything, but when I used my login name and password, it wouldn't let in. I picked up the phone to call over to IT, but the phone gave me nothing but a fast-busy signal. Oh. Right. I'd been laid off. Big companies did this sort of thing to prevent disgruntled employees from raising any kinds of hell. I didn't want to raise hell; I wanted to check the Giants and A's schedules for the next month to see how many weekday day games I could attend before the season ended. Stupid company. What was I supposed to do now?

I could have cleaned out my desk, but I didn't have any personal items other than a Word of the Day day-by-day calendar that I had stopped maintaining. The Word of the Day had been "pecuniary" since January 14. I could have gone for coffee, but there was a chance that the IT folks would have deactivated my ID, and I wanted to find out what kind of severance I was getting.

So I started to flip through the day-by-day calendar. Disinformation, ratiocination, mechamorphosis, galactophage, groak...I flipped through nearly 200 words and got to that day's word: finale.

"A little bit obvious," I said.

"Alex?"

I looked up. A woman stood in the doorway of my cube, clutching a banded packed of manila folders. She gave off the same wankerish stench as George from accounting, but the resemblance ended there. Where he was frail and zit-ridden, she had flawless skin and a pleasantly physical plumpness. Her glasses were big and round, and she had one of those multiple-metal-bead chain things hanging from the ends, just below her bobbed hair. I hated her on sight.

'Yep, that's me," I said.

"So, Philip has already talked to you," she said. She spoke quickly, kind of like a DVD player on 1.2x speed. Her voice needed some WD-40. "I'm Clarissa from HR, and I'm here so you know about what's going on and to tell you how sorry the company is to have to let talented resources like you go. However, the company is going to do the best job it can to speed your transition and make it as productive as possible for you."

"What happens now?"

She sighed, as if I had interrupted her soundtrack. "So, the company is going to give you a severance package equivalent to six paychecks, payable semi-monthly. After that, if you have not yet found a new employer, you will be eligible for unemployment insurance, which will be in the equivalent of, for you, approximately nine hundred dollars, semi-monthly, unless you choose to take out taxes. I have all of this information here. And you'll be able to get medical insurance through California COBRA, which we highly recommend. I have information on COBRA here in your folder, as well. Do you have any questions?"

"Um…no, I don't think so."

"So, if you do come up with any questions, the Human Resources Department has been authorized to answer those questions for you for the remainder of the week. Please feel free to call us during business hours anytime up until this Friday. Here is your packet. Please leave the building within the next thirty minutes."

She slapped a manila envelope onto the desk and walked off to deliver her news to whoever else was still around. When I did my first interview with the company, the representative from Human Resources was a slim woman with a last name that ended in "anov," facial features carved from ice, and a Bond-girl body. Is Human Resources divided that way? Hot girls for intake interviews on the left, plain ones with screechy voices for layoffs? And why was it that the only people who ever worked in HR were women and gay men? And had the company just given me *three months* of severance pay?

Two hours later, Gerald and I were sitting on opposite sides of a picnic table at Zeitgeist, San Francisco's only real outdoor bar. It sits in an odd corner of the city, where the fog is split on its way from the ocean by the two fingers of Twin Peaks. If the fog belt were a hand, Zeitgeist would be sitting right in front of the webbing between forefinger and thumb. The back patio is almost the size of a baseball infield; the ground is gravel and dirt, the picnic tables are mismatched, and outhouses line the rear wall. A large man takes care of a half-barrel barbecue, and the PA plays nothing but punk, country, and rockabilly. Gerald had brought a cribbage board and was happily smoking both me and a joint while we shared a pitcher of Velveteen Rabbit India Pale Ale.

"So what do you do now?" he asked.

I shrugged. "I dunno. I could try to find a new job, but…not for a little while. I figure I can just mellow out for a month or so. It's not that often that you can get a chance to just hang around."

Gerald nodded. "You got that right. I'm usually so busy, I don't get any downtime." His cell phone rang with the opening chords to "Master of Puppets." Jarring, but effective.

"Hey," he said. "Tomorrow and Friday? Um…yeah, I can probably do that. Eighty per hour OK? Cool?" He hung up.

I'd never known Gerald to have a straight job; he seemed to just pick up whatever work came around. He'd done web design, kitchen remodeling, sold weed to friends, ran focus groups…all sorts of things.

"How do you get to do what you do?" I asked. "Fifteen for two, run for five."

He shrugged. "I know a few people. Stuff just kind of works out. Fifteen for two, fifteen for four, double run for twelve. I'm ten away from skunking you."

"Luck, all luck."

"You make your own luck," he said, taking the tweezers out of his Swiss Army knife and using them as a makeshift roach clip. "Any news on your housemate?"

I paused for a second. Did Gerald really want to know about all of that? We were friends, yes, but usually just doing-stuff friends. Not important-stuff friends. Still, he was looking at me expectantly, so I told him the whole story, starting with Brent's other name and ending with Morgan. He whistled through the gap in his front teeth.

"She hot?"

"Yeah," I said. "In the 'I might be wearing a vinyl corset under this suit' kind of way."

"Huh," he said. "You found a new roommate yet?"

"Interviewing people," I said. "Not that fun."

"Hm," he said. "Is the secretary worth seeing?"

"She's cute," I said. "Worth meeting for a drink, anyway."

"You don't have anything else to do," he said. "You should call her."

"Now?"

"Sure," he said. "All that wait-five-days stuff is idiotic. If you want to call, call. If you don't, don't. The rules are written by the people who run *Cosmo*. If they knew anything, they'd be married and happy with real jobs instead of running the same differently-worded articles every month. So call."

"Now?"

"Why wait? At the very least, it'll start your pain a little quicker, and you'll recover faster. I'm going to go refill our pitcher, and your out-call list better have her number at the top. Double run for eight. You're skunked."

He picked up our empty pitcher and walked inside to the bar. The guys at the table across from me pulled out a small pipe, packed it, and started taking hits. Hank Williams started to sing "My Son Calls Another Man Daddy." I pulled out my cell phone and dialed Morgan's number. It rang twice, then she picked up.

"Hello?"

I paused – I'd been expecting voicemail, which is what you always expect to get when you're dialing someone who doesn't have your number. If it's a new number, it's voicemail; that's the way you do it. Weird.

"Hello?" she said again.

"Hi, Morgan, it's Alex," I said. "I met you just, um, the other day."

"Oh, right, David's roommate." she said. "Yesterday. What's up?"

"I was wondering if, um…" Reason! I needed a reason to ask her for a drink. I had to say something that implied that there was something I wanted to do with her aside from just have a few drinks and some fun without our clothes on. I had to say *something*.

"I kind of wanted to talk to you about Brent…David," I said. "I was wondering if maybe we could get together to talk about him."

"Oh, sure," she said. Was that a touch of disappointment? "I'm free tonight, actually. Will you meet me?"

"Sure," I said. "Tonight I'm free." Of course I was free tonight. I was free every night. Days, too.

"Great," she said. "Meet me at the Dover. You know where it is?"

"I can find it," I said.

"The r and the e are backwards," she said. "D-o-v-r-e. Eight o'clock."

"Cool," I said. "See you there."

"Bye."

Gerald came back with a full pitcher. "Let me see that phone," he said. I flipped it open and handed it over. He clicked a couple of buttons, then grinned. "Well, you either did it or called a random number for two minutes just to fuck with me," he said. "Good job. When are you meeting?"

"Tonight at the Dovre. You know where it is?"

He whistled. "Wow, she's a tough girl. It's a divey place down near where Mission meets Valencia. What time?"

"Eight."

"Two hours to kill, huh? That's a lot of cribbage for you to lose."

"Who's going to lose?"

He smiled with his mouth closed. "Your deal."

I walked from Zeitgeist to the Dovre. It's a distance of about a mile and a half through the Inner Mission, ground zero for the kind of nightlife that straddles the hipster/yuppie junction. The rocketing real estate prices haven't driven out all of the poor folk yet. Mission Street at Sixteenth is still a little slice of the third world, a place where wheelchair-bound pimps yell at you as you pass by, the hookers have track marks between their toes and next to their eyes, and the dealers use the front tables of taquerias as open-door offices. At night, rats flit past in the darkness of the alleys, over and around the piles of clothing that cover sleeping people.

One block away, Valencia Street teems with Armani suits and Ugg boots, as well-heeled twenty-somethings with financial district jobs and no fear of a Thursday hangover flock to martini bars and jungle-beat-infused sushi, pounding back fifteen-dollar Ketel One cocktails. I walked down Mission; drug dealers make me less uncomfortable than yuppies.

Things calmed down as I went further south. Sallow hipsters smoked cigarettes in the soft red light that spilled out of the front doors of dark bars, metal grates were pulled down over the entrances to the carnicerias and fruit stands. One guy on the corner was packing up his churro cart, and he looked at me with a hopeful eye. I shook my head no, and he flipped the top over on his cart and locked it with a *chunk*.

A small red neon *Dovre* sign sticking out of the bottom floor of a corner row-house was the only indication that the place existed. There wasn't the usual knot of nicotine fiends outside; and as I walked in and inhaled the stale stench of old tobacco smoke, I understood why. The Dovre was one of the few bars left in the city that still let people smoke despite the ban. Five or six guys were gathered around the jukebox at the far end of the room. Morgan was sitting by herself. She wore a black knee-length skirt and was tapping a thin cigarette against her chair. The ashes were falling onto a carpet stained from years of people doing exactly what she was doing.

She smiled as I sat down next to her.

"Hi," I said.

"Hi," she said, touching my arm.

"What's happening?" I said.

She shrugged. "Not much. The usual. Work, gym, meeting guys in smoky bars."

"You meet lots of guys in smoky bars?"

"No," she dropped her cigarette and crushed it into the carpet. "I come here because the guys who hang out in smokers' bars are usually too old to want to bug me."

"What if they do anyway?"

She shrugged. "I take care of them."

I signaled the bartender with a finger and ordered a glass of Wild Turkey on the rocks.

"A Manhattan," Morgan added.

The bartender nodded. "Sure thing."

"So…" she said.

"Um…" I said.

This felt date-ish. Dates aren't really my thing, and first dates, the one-on-one getting-to-know-you part, give me the verbal dexterity of a mime with foot-in-the-mouth syndrome. I sat for a couple of seconds, trying desperately to think of something to say. My mind was blank. Then it started to fill with G.I. Joe characters. That wouldn't work. M.A.S.K.? Thundarr the Barbarian? Voltron? Thankfully, the bartender came back with our drinks, and I took a strong slug. The bourbon burned my throat on the way down, my eyes watered, and I could feel my pulse speeding up. Why was I sitting in this stinkhole of a pub with this woman? Because I wanted to sleep with her, obviously, but there was something else, something… there was this guy, wasn't there? He had a name… I took another drink. The '80s cartoons disappeared, and I remembered.

"Brent," I said. "David."

Her face went from smile to somewhere else. "What do you want to know about David?" she asked.

"Brent," I said. "I know him as Brent."

"Do you want me to call him BrentDavid? That's awkward."

"No," I said. "David is fine."

She drew out a pack of Benson and Hedges menthols, put it to her lips, flicked a lighter to the end, and puffed twice without inhaling, turning the end bright red. I stared at the ember.

"I know a few things," she said. "He started working for us about six months ago as an analyst..."

"What do you guys do?"

"Nothing too exciting. We do financial services with a legal bent. Or legal services with a financial bent. Somewhere in the middle, I guess. What do you do?"

"I used to work, until today."

"What happened?"

I shrugged. "Got laid off."

She touched my shoulder. "That's terrible. I'm sorry. What are you going to do?"

"I don't know. Find a job after my severance runs out."

"Good plan," she said. "So specific, too."

She was smiling. Sarcasm. This was going *wonderfully*.

"So David wasn't weird or anything?" I asked.

She shook her head, looking oddly disappointed. "No, not really. Gabriel said that his resume was good enough to get in the door, and he gave good interview."

"Where'd he work before?"

"I don't know – I don't have a copy of his resume, and I can't get into Gabriel's computer. I knew him day-to-day. He showed up on time, did his work, ate a lot of clam chowder from the San Francisco Soup Company, and always left at five o'clock on the dot."

"Wait," I said. "Always?" Brent/David had never come home earlier than six-thirty in the four months that he'd lived with us. Sometimes he came home at nine or ten, and he had always said something about a deadline, or a tough day at the office, or something like that.

"Yeah," she said. "It was bordering on strange – it wasn't like he'd stop what he was working on in the middle of whatever it was and go home. He'd be done by about ten of five, then clean up his desk, and be out the door. His desk was always super-clean, and sometimes people would come to see him at five past, and if they hadn't seen him earlier in the day, they'd ask if he'd even been in that day. He even cleaned his coffee cup out."

"Who does *that?*"

She shook her head. "David, apparently."

"Where would he go?"

She shook her head again. "I have no idea, but it'd be good to know. Want another drink?"

I tried to count back from the double-shot of Wild Turkey through the three (or was it four?) pitchers that Gerald and I had put down in the course of his vicious cribbage beatdown, but the only number I could come up with was somewhere between six and ten. I had enjoyed a brief bout of sobriety before the whiskey, but that was long-gone. Maybe this could go somewhere.

"Yeah," I said. "Same thing."

She ordered for the both of us. Manhattan, Wild Turkey on the rocks.

"So," she said. "What do you think? I was working only a few desks away from a guy with two names. I think that's interesting." She took a long pause, dragging off her cigarette. Her voice was almost husky. "Someone with two names. Someone who wasn't what he seemed. I wish I knew why he was doing that, what he was doing down in SOMA on a weekday afternoon. It's fascinating." She leaned closer to me, putting her cigarette awfully close to my face.

"You're right," I said. "Maybe I'll try to find out where he was going."

She leaned closer to me. "Good idea." I could smell the smoke on her breath, and I didn't care. "I think you should call me soon, and let me know what you've learned."

I swallowed. Her mouth was inches from mine, and I could see the tiny lines on the sides of her eyes. The lines wavered when I blinked my eyes. I wanted to shake my head and clear my thoughts but she was too close. "OK," I said.

She drew back, turned to the bar, drained what was left of her drink, and leaned over, close to my ear.

"Call me," she whispered, and brushed her lips against my cheek as she moved her head away. The kiss left a cold spot where her lips had been.

Then she was gone.

Chapter 4

I'd like to say that I woke up on my first full day of unemployment with a spring in my step and a song in my heart. I didn't. When I woke up the fog was in with a vengeance, coming through my tiny open window and covering everything in my room with a layer of moisture, just enough to make me shiver right when I got out from under my covers to go to the bathroom. I had a hangover, one bad enough to make me want to both stay in bed for the day and get some breakfast to try to kill it. After a few minutes' debate, breakfast won, and I went downstairs.

Nobody was home. Thomas and Jenn had normal day jobs, and Shawna had started another temp job at the Sound Healing Institute. I went downstairs to the kitchen, where a tray of cinnamon rolls sat on the table with a clean spatula and a note.

Alex,

Congratulations on the layoff! I made these for you last night, but I bet you didn't see them and went right to bed. Eat away!

Jenn

PS: Did you find out who Brent's next of kin are? We were talking about it last night and it'd be a good idea to nail that down. E-mail me, ok? I need some entertainment.

I dug one of the cinnamon rolls out of the pan and stuck it in the microwave for ten seconds. Delicious. Jenn was neurotic, anal-compulsive, and had a flair for the dramatic. But she could bake like a champ, especially in times of stress. Pastries as a cure-all; it was kind of nice.

The microwave beeped and I dug in. The thing was ridiculous – at least a full stick of butter, pure sugar glaze, and enough cinnamon to make my eyes water. Another success from my baking-crazed roomie. As I ate, I started thinking about what I had to do, and I grabbed a pencil and made a list:

-     *Clean my room.* This was *always* on the list. I think it has deep childhood roots; whenever I'd go to my mom and say "I'm bored," she would tell me to clean my room. I never would. This pattern continues today, except that I tell myself I'm bored, and then I think that I should clean my room. I never do.

- *Figure out who Brent's next of kin were.* This was more of an immediate problem than the bacterial colonies that were probably developing in my rug. To find his next of kin, I'd probably have to learn more about him. In order to do this, it would help to:

- *Find a picture of Brent.* I didn't have one on my computer, but I could probably scan one from his driver's license with Thomas's help. Thomas was a scanning-and-photoing maniac; he photo-documented everything he did. One time, I caught him taking his camera out of the bathroom after he'd been in there for quite a long time. I wasn't going to make any accusations, but I did see a picture the next day on ratemypoo.com in which the toilet looked *really* familiar. Once I had a picture of Brent, I needed to walk around and show it to people. I wasn't entirely sure where this would take me, but that's what the P.I's on television do, and it usually works. Why wouldn't it work for me?

- *Figure out something by the next evening.* Because if I had something, Morgan might sleep with me. Maybe.

Two cinnamon rolls, twenty minutes, and three segments of the just-before-noon news later, I took a shower, which wouldn't have been notable, except that I didn't notice the hair ball that clogged the drain while I let the water warm up, turning the experience into less fun, more gross.

After showering, I fired up my laptop and brought it into Thomas's room. When scanned and blown up, Brent's driver's license shot wasn't the most flattering pic; his thinning brown hair was sticking up, his eyes were swollen and puffy, and the shadows made his already thick eyebrows look like they connected on the left side of his nose. But it was still he. I cropped out his head and shoulders from the rest of the photo, and printed a couple of color copies. The result was a bit blurred, but it was Brent.

It took me four tries to leave the house – I forgot my phone, caught and broke my shoelace on a protruding brick, then made it two blocks away before having a paranoid thought that I'd left the door unlocked. I went back and checked; it was locked. I was hungry, so I got off the bus a little bit early and stopped off for a burrito. The burrito was good, and while I was happily chomping away at my table, a guy came in and started ranting about a teenage girl who'd pulled a knife on him on the bus. The cops showed up, they emptied out the number 6 bus that he'd come from, and then the cops searched the handbags of everyone who had been on the bus. Naturally, they found no knives. The crazy dude then thanked the cops and walked up Market Street – the opposite direction from the bus. By the time I made it back to the sidewalk outside of Brent's office building, it was half past two.

I started hitting up pedestrians when I got to within a couple of blocks of the building where Brent had worked. When I took out the piece of paper with his picture on it and started trying to catch people's eye, everybody started talking on their cell phones, reading the newspaper, or intently looking across the street. It was strange; I guess that the legions of political recruiters and smiley-faced Greenpeace kids had inured the downtown masses against any kind of random social interaction. After about ten minutes of hanging out outside the building, I gave up.

The ground floor of Brent's building was a copy/print shop; I wandered in. The front room was long and thin, with one desk near the door and a hallway that led to a door at the rear. Nobody was sitting at the desk. I leaned over, looking for a bell or an intercom, or some way to signal that a customer was waiting. Nothing. I waited for about five minutes, taking laps around the desk, clicking the keys on the computer behind the desk (it was locked, so I couldn't sit down and play Solitaire). I went outside and back in to see if it triggered a bell, then shrugged my shoulders and walked down the hall to the door.

The rear room looked like the heavenly playground of a typesetter's dreams. Three huge monitors were set up on the side wall, hooked up to a copy machine that was easily thirty feet long. The rest of the room was taken up by four copiers and a giant black box with a long feeder that could only have been a giant automatic scanner. Three guys were sitting in the middle, playing cards. They were all dressed identically in white polo shirts and khakis.

"Hi," I said.

All three guys looked up at me.

"Break," said one, and stood up. He was short and chubby, with olive-dark skin. His hair stuck up in the back; the top of the tuft might have come up to my nose.

"What can I do for you, Mr....?" he said. He sounded like a high-pitched Connery-era Bond villain.

"I'm Alex," I said. "I'm hoping you can help me."

"That's what I asked you," he said.

"Right. Do you know this guy? He used to work at Jackson West upstairs." I took out the picture and showed it to the guy.

"Hm..." he said, tapping a finger on one of his chins. "Let me think...can I see it, Mr. Alex?"

I handed him the photo. He held it close to his face, rotated it a full 360 degrees, then walked over to his two compatriots, who had busied themselves by throwing cards at each other.

"Guys, do you remember this man?" he asked.

The two other men leaned forward to look at the picture; neither got up from the floor. The Bond villain knelt down, and they held a soft conversation in a language I had never heard. Then one of them started nodding, the second guy on the floor nodded, and the Bond villain got up and walked back over to me.

"We know him," he said. "Mr. Jones. He used to come in here, but only with orders for copies from upstairs. One time he spilled his coffee on the work order, but that was the only time anything happened."

"Oh," I said.

"Yes," he said. "That was strange, it was only the other week. He had a much bigger coffee than he usually did. Usually he got a...the middle one?"

"I think they call it a grande," I said.

"Yes, graandey. This time, he had a ventey."

"One of the big ones?"

"Yes, and I remembered making a joke. Mr. Jones, you are drinking too much coffee today. Then he shook his head, reached for the work order, and knocked his coffee on it. It was very stained, but he didn't seem to mind much. He seemed quite tired."

"Thanks," I said. "Can I have my picture back?"

"Oh, yes," he said. "What do you ask for?"

"He was my housemate," I said. "He's gone now."

"Ah," he said. "People disappearing. Just like the old country."

My next stop would have to be Starbucks, which represented something of a problem. There were three within sight of 731 Sansome Street. Brent could have been a regular at any one of them. I thought for a moment and decided that the first one to check would be the easiest to get to – slightly downhill, instead of up, and only one street crossing.

The Starbucks was like any other. The staff was cheerful, multi-ethnic, and under twenty. I waited in line behind two well-dressed women with layered haircuts who were chattering about the problems they were having with their gardeners.

"You'd think that for nine dollars an hour they'd learn English," said the brunette.

"Well, you could pay them less until they do," said the blonde.

"Boy, that's a *wonderful* idea," I said. "Why don't you make them wear little stars, too, so people can pick them out on the street?"

"Who asked you?" asked the blonde.

"Nobody," I said. "But if you're going to have an inane conversation in a public place, don't be surprised if someone chimes in."

She wrinkled her lips, as if smelling something for the first time. "Come on, Larissa," she said. "No reason to be harassed here when we can get frappucinos down the street."

Her friend gave me a dirty look as they left.

"That was cool," said the girl behind the counter. "They come in bitching and moaning every day and never leave a tip. What can I get you?" Her ebony skin was perfect, her hair was pulled back into tightly-wrapped braids, and her braces flashed with reflections from the fluorescent lights. Her nametag read:

Try a Pumpkin Latte
Amy

"A small coffee, please," I said. "And a question."

"I don't date customers," said Amy. "Even ones who drive out people I hate. I gotta follow my own rules."

"No, not that kind of question," I said. "Do you recognize this guy?"

I pulled out the picture from my pocket, unfolded it, and showed it to her.

"What are you, some kind of Magnum?" she asked.

"An extra-large condom?"

She giggled. "No, the TV show. My dad was really into it and has all the DVDs, with the guy with the mustache. Tom something."

"Selleck," I said. "Tom Selleck."

"Right," she said. "He's a hottie."

"The picture," I said. "You know him?"

"Sure," she said. "I recognize most of the afternoon regulars."

"What do you know about him?"

She smiled. "He was a good tipper. He even tipped when he paid with his Starbucks card. He wasn't one of those guys who come in, order, and pretend that you don't exist, either. He'd talk to you."

"About anything in particular?"

"Sure," she said. "What was weird was that he *never* bitched about his job. Everyone else in here is always complaining about how their boss is making them put together fifty-five PowerPoint slides by four p.m., or that the secretary is screwing up their dinner reservations, or making jokes about three o'clock being the Infinite Hour."

"Whoa," I said. "Other people do that?" I'd thought that the three-o'clock-goes-on-forever joke was only one that we had used in my office.

"Everyone knows that," she said. "It was on Craigslist. Your guy, though, he always said things were going well and asked how we were doing. Except one time. It was the other week; he ordered a venti latte instead of a grande, and that was weird. I had to re-key the order. He looked tired, and instead of using his Starbucks card, he paid cash. And he didn't buy a new card, which he would have usually done. He had me keep the change from a five, which was weird, because that's only thirty cents, and he usually tipped a buck. And he didn't ask how we were; he just took off. I guess he was having a bad day."

"Has he come in since then?"

"Nope. What's this all about, anyway? I don't even know that I'm allowed to answer questions about the customers..."

"Nothing," I said. "He's my housemate, and...uh...we're trying to figure out what to get him for his birthday."

She cocked her head at me and gave me a look. "Right. And this job is my first step up the corporate ladder. I'm young, not stupid. If you're going to bullshit me, at least try to do it plausibly."

"He's missing," I said. "And I'm trying to find out more about him."

"You lived with the guy?"

"Yeah," I said.

"You white guys are so weird," she said. "Live so close to each other, but you never even talk."

"It has nothing to do with being a white guy," I said.

"Yeah?" she said. "Anyone else you know would live like that? Your coffee's a buck."

I gave her a dollar, and dropped another one into the tip jar.

"Thanks for the help," I said.

"Sure," she said. "I hope you find out more."

I walked over to the condiment bar and added cream, sugar, and a plastic top to my coffee.

"Hey, mister," said Amy.

I turned around.

"Your friend. That last day here, he paid in cash, and along with it, he accidentally gave me a receipt from a place called the Lucky Dragon Duck. I don't have it, but I remember it because it was such a weird name, there were Chinese characters on it, and it was for something like six hundred dollars."

"Thanks, Amy," I said.

"You're welcome," she said. "Come back any time. One hundred percent tips are gonna get me through college."

Chapter 5

Housemate wanted for mellow Cole Valley apartment. The place is really more of a house — we have the top two floors, and the bottom is a single-room place occupied by a young couple. We're two girls and two guys, looking for someone of either gender. We're straight but not narrow, don't have any pets and aren't looking for any, 420 friendly as long as you use our (awesome) back porch, and we don't care what you eat, because we eat everything. One of us is a vegetarian, and that's never been a problem. We all work, and it would be nice if you worked enough to be able to pay the rent. Oh yeah, the house has laundry, so you won't need to deal with the maniacs at the laundromat down the street.

Please be at least somewhat socially competent — we don't care if you're directly out of college (we all were there at one point or another), but if you have just come out of your parent's basement, you're probably not the guy for us. In other words, we don't care if you're young, as long as you can act like you're at least 22.

"So what do you do?" Thomas was playing point man again, sitting in the middle of the couch, still in his work outfit of a black button-down and khakis. He'd taken off his shoes and socks, and was tapping his flip-flops on the floor.

"I'm a healer," said the prospective housemate, a slimly built guy named Nadav with a deep tan and three knit bracelets around each wrist. He spoke with a slight, harsh accent.

"You're a doctor?" asked Jenn.

"Oh, no," he said. "Not Western medicine."

"Acupuncture?" I said.

He shook his head again. "Much more than that. I'm a fourth-level Reiki practitioner, and I also practice massage and yoga therapy, as well as other kinds of bodywork."

"Oh, neat," said Shawna. "Where did you learn?"

"Up in the redwoods, near Garberville," he said. "There is this wonderful community of people, they all live in the forest, and the dormitory where you stay while you learn is an old school bus."

"How long were you up there?" she asked.

"Two years," he said.

"Wow…" said Shawna. "That's a long time."

"It was the most beautiful experience of my life," he said. "I can't wait to settle here in San Francisco and bring my skills to the people who need them."

"Where are you living now?" I asked.

"Here and there," he said. "Sometimes with friends, sometimes in my van."

"How do you find clients?" I asked.

He smiled again. "I can't imagine that I'll have a problem with that. This is San Francisco, the city of love!" The accent got thicker. He sounded like Billy Crystal in *The Princess Bride*.

"So you don't have any clients yet?"

He shook his head.

"And where were you hoping to do your work?"

"I can spread out people on the dining room table?" he asked. "A hard surface is necessary. Oh yes, I am also a vegan. Everyone in Garberville said that if you come to San Francisco and live near Haight Ashbury, people are vegans. You must have a wonderful vegan kitchen!"

"Well, not really," I said. "Listen, we've got someone else coming in, so we'll give you a call."

"Oh, I don't have a phone," said Nadav. "I use e-mail at the drop-in center down on Haight Street. Just send me e-mail with when you want me to move in."

He padded downstairs, his sandals making very little noise.

"Well," said Jenn. "He would be the only guy in this house who knows how to go up and down the stairs without shaking the whole place."

"Right," I said. "Have you ever seen the aftermath of a vegan in the bathroom?"

"It's a full-bean-and-lentil toilet assault," said Thomas. "Along with all the roughage they eat...disaster. I don't want to incur the toilet paper expense. If we had a washlet, maybe."

"What's a washlet?" asked Shawna.

"A high-pressure butt hose that comes out of the toilet," said Thomas. "We saw it on the toilet company website."

"Oooh...like colon cleansing?" asked Shawna. "I always wanted to have that done."

"Not really our thing," said Thomas. "I'm sure the landlord would be happy if we replaced the toilets, but it's not what I feel like doing with my time."

"Amen to that," I said. "Ours function just fine, when we can use them."

"What's that mean?" asked Thomas.

"Asparagus," I said. "You made some last night, didn't you?"

He smiled. "Yep. Sixteen spears."

"Is there any kind of neutralizer you can buy?" I said. "Like Bean-O for Asparagus? Is there an Asparagus-O?"

"Not that I know of," said Thomas. "Studies show that only about 22 percent of people even *have* asparagus pee. I'm one of the lucky ones who's got it."

"*Why* do you know that?" I asked.

"I looked it up once," said Thomas.

"Yeah, but why?"

Thomas shrugged. Sometimes he just looked stuff up.

"There's a more pertinent question," I asked, looking at him. "How'd that guy get past our initial filter? I thought we agreed we were looking for someone with a job that enables him to actually pay the rent, and definitely not someone who wants to spread out strangers on our dining room table and do energy healing."

Thomas shrugged. "I don't know. I never e-mailed him. I just got the note that we were having someone come by tonight."

He looked over at Shawna. I looked over at Shawna. Jenn looked over at Shawna. She had cocked her head to one side and was using both of her hands to put a little braid in her straight black hair

"What?" she said. "Just because I'm the house's resident kind-of-hippie means that I'm going to invite someone I met on the street passing out healing flyers over to see if he can live with us just because he was cute and foreign? Wouldn't it be nice if I weren't the only Asian person in the house?"

"He was Israeli," I sad.

"That's practically Asia," she said. "And he *was* cute, wasn't he? I didn't know he was vegan, though. If someone isn't respectful of my need to eat cheese, I don't want him to live with us."

With that, she stood up and went into the kitchen. The rest of us traded looks for a few seconds. Jenn grimaced, then reached over and picked up a book. Thomas and I ended up looking at each other.

"Repost the ad?" he asked.

I nodded. "Post away. It's only Monday – maybe we'll find someone before the week ends."

Friday dawned sunny and new-roommateless. The fog had lifted early, and only the merest wisps remained when I rose at the crack of ten and made some bacon. When I was working I never had the chance to have bacon at home. My new status as a man of leisure gave me the time, and I had prepared for the morning by purchasing a pound of uncured center-cut no-antibiotics no-additives free-range bacon for ten dollars from the natural food store down the street. The girl behind the counter had looked at me harshly; she was probably a vegan activist.

As my bacon sizzled, my eggs quivered, and my cereal crackled and popped, I went online to finally see if I could find out anything about the Lucky Dragon Duck. I would have looked earlier, but I'd held off looking until after two fruitless days of showing Brent's photo around town. Then I'd taken Thursday off. So now I looked. Google was useless, and the Yellow Pages came up empty, as did Citysearch, the *San Francisco Chronicle* online, sfist.com, sfstation.com, metroblogging San Francisco, Restaurants.com, *Lucky – the magazine about shopping* online, sfcityguides.org, the Chamber of Commerce, *Hello, San Francisco!*, KPIX's "what's happening" list, *Time Out San Francisco*, Craigslist San Francisco, *San Francisco* magazine, *The San Francisco Examiner*, Gayguide.com, Mistersf.com, Genderqueersf.com, and several Cantonese newspapers that I had no hope of reading but occasionally printed an English character. Nothing. Zilch.

I closed my computer and took my four slices of bacon and covered them with scrambled egg. What to do? If something wasn't on the Internet, it either didn't exist or didn't want to be found. Or, I couldn't find it. I fired up instant messenger and pinged Thomas while I chomped away.

Thomasrox: Whassup?
Alxbkr: Need some searching help. You busy?
Thomasrox: Yeah, really important stuff.

Thomasrox: My boss asked me to "un-TLA the SAP, CBA, and NAB files."

Thomasrox: I have no idea what that means.

Alxbkr: Hahaha. Sucker.

Alxbkr: Can you do one of those business database lookups for the Lucky Dragon Duck here in San Francisco?

Alxbkr: It's a business, but I can't find it.

Thomasrox: Hang on.

I finished my bacon and eggs and took them to the sink to wash off the dishes. As I was scrubbing, my laptop beeped.

Thomasrox: Nothing in Hoovers, Dun/Bradstreet, or USABusiness.

Thomasrox: Why you want to know?

Alxbkr: Brent used to go there, I think.

Thomasrox: Oh. Weird.

Alxbkr: What?

Thomasrox: Dunno. Just thinking. I never really talked to the guy.

Alxbkr: Yeah?

Thomasrox: Different schedules, different whatever.

Thomasrox: I feel kinda bad.

Alxbkr: Nothing you could do.

Thomasrox: I know. Bad karma.

Alxbkr: Yep. I hope I can find out what he was all about.

Thomasrox: You think this place will tell you?

Alxbkr: All I got.

Thomasrox: Hope you find something.

Alxbkr: Thx.

Thomasrox: L(9-1)r

Nothing to do but go down to Chinatown and scope around the old-fashioned way. I assumed that that was the old-fashioned way, as I'd never really scoped around before without knowing an address. I wasn't looking forward to it – Chinatown is no picnic on nice days when it's close to the weekend. But I didn't have anything else to do, and I really wanted to be able to tell Morgan something other than, "Well, I know he got his coffee at Starbucks." I hadn't called her –

whenever I opened my phone, I imagined telling her that I hadn't found out anything, and I thought of her being disappointed with me, and I'd close my phone.

I took the bus downtown; the middle-of-the-day crowd is much mellower and more well-behaved than the rush-hour folks. Maybe investment bankers and dangerous psychotics are vinegar and baking soda to each other. Or maybe I just got lucky. I got to the intersection of Powell and Market in only twenty minutes. Throngs of tourists were lined up at the cable-car turnaround, and two old men were standing on boxes, taking turns haranguing them about Jesus, backed by a large sign that said "Jesus Savs." When I got closer, I could see that someone had penciled in a caret and an "e" where it should have been in the first place.

Chinatown lies on the other side of Union Square, our version of Fifth Avenue. It's the kind of place where people take shopping breaks at the Armani Café. The crowds were thronging strong as I walked up the hill – Japanese families with four kinds of cameras, neon-spackled Germans, shorts-socks-sandals couples from Altoona and Rock Island. I'd never bought clothes here, and I remembered why as I elbowed people out of my way.

The gate to Chinatown is on Grant, one block from the Square. An arch spans the street, an odd blocky thing that looks like a pagoda father with two lil' pagodas. Underneath it on the right is a shop that sells ornately carved jade and certified thousand-dollar antiques. On the left is a store that flogs "Property of Alcatraz" shirts, little foot-massage balls, anime lunch boxes, and machines that will turn your penny into a cable car for fifty cents. The shop on the left was doing a brisk business.

I wasn't entirely sure what I was looking for – all I knew was that a place with kanji on the receipt and a weird name was probably a Chinese business, and most of the most-odd Chinese businesses were still in Chinatown. The main streets were alive with guttural Cantonese and lilting Mandarin, open-air markets hawked dirt-streaked purple vegetables, and older people milled around in the streets clutching pink plastic shopping bags filled with the night's dinner. Newly-arrived immigrant women stood on the corners, passing out fliers hawking cheap dim sum, and old men sat in alley doorways, playing mah jongg and smoking hand-rolled cigarettes.

I started with the alleys, where the tourist sheen gives way to urban oddities. The shops on Grant deal in paper umbrellas and sweet-and-sour chicken, but you can still buy live pigs for the slaughter on Waverly Place. Some of the old buildings used to be brothels, gambling houses, or opium dens, and they still have the odd doors and peep holes to prove it. There's a wall where the bricks are uneven; some of them stick out, some are horizontal or only half-bricks. It looks kind of like a Dali painting come to life. Those odd bricks had been melted in the great fire of 1906; the wall was a memorial for the people who had died that day.

After a few blocks of wandering I ended up back on Grant Avenue in front of the Golden Dragon, a generic-looking three-story palace of a restaurant, the kind of place that has one menu (pot-stickers and General Tso's chicken) for tourists and another (braised pig's feet and fermented tofu) for locals. The lunch rush hadn't started yet, and most of the tables were empty when I walked in.

"Hi," I said to the host, a younger guy with longish, John-Woo-movie hair, starched vest, and bowtie. "I'm hoping you can help me out."

"One second, please," he said. He turned to the guy behind him. I couldn't see who he was talking to – the podium blocked my view. "You pay now!" he said.

"I told you, I'm short," said a voice with an accent I couldn't place. "I'll just hop out to the ATM and get twenty bucks, and then I'll make up what I owe you."

"No credit," said the host. "You're going to work."

"I can't work here," said the voice.

"No excuses," said the host.

"Wait," I said. "How much does he owe?"

"Four dollars thirty cents," said the host.

"I'll pay for it," I said. I leaned forward and gave the host a five. He nodded, reached into a drawer, and gave me seventy cents back. The guy behind the podium skipped out – I didn't get a good look at him because the host was staring me right in the eye and I didn't want to look away. He was small, with black hair, and he flitted by in less than an eyeblink.

"Lunch for one?" said the host. His accent was thicker, more Chinese than when he'd been talking to the not-payer.

"No, I'm just looking for a place," I said. "Have you heard of the Lucky Dragon Duck?"

He hesitated just a touch, then said "Lucky Dragon Duck? It's a restaurant? Our food is better. Look at our menu. Best sweet and sour chicken in town." He whipped a thick, laminated menu out from under the host stand and thrust it into my hands.

"I'm not a tourist," I said. "The Lucky Dragon Duck? A place? The Lucky Dragon Duck?" I was raising my voice as I talked to him, doing that thing that Americans do when they think that English isn't getting them as far as they like. He just looked at me with a steady gaze. I was close to yelling when someone yanked on my arm and pulled me out the door.

The guy pulling me was short. Very short, five feet tall, maybe, with his shoes on. Those shoes were odd; black wingtips peeking out below wide-leg jeans so flat they must have been ironed. He pulled me up Washington Street, nearly bowling over an ancient woman who had set up a kiosk to sell stress-buster balls and video CDs. She yelled at us as we rumbled past. He yanked me left, into an alley so small that an open door would block it.

"Are you crazy?" he asked. "Are you completely, totally, absolutely insane?" His English was perfect, with that odd accent. It was the same voice I'd heard earlier, the guy who couldn't pay his bill.

"Wh.."

"Shut up," he said. "Don't talk. Don't gesture, and for God's sake don't turn around or move at all; I don't want anyone walking by to see your face."

"You have to be making some mistake," I said.

"Why do all of you Americans talk like you're in a Hitchcock film?" he said. "That's *exactly* what Cary Grant said in *North by Northwest,* except that *he* actually had a point, whereas you walked right into the Golden Dragon and asked about…that."

"What?" I said.

"What you asked about," he said. "I'm not stupid enough to talk about it out loud with a white fellow. Why are you asking about it in *there?*"

Dan Johnson

"What's so special about the restaurant?" I asked.

He gave me the same look that my mother used to give me when I had tried to make up an illness and stay home from school.

"It's only the place where the Tongs went crazy and slaughtered five people back in 1977," he said. "It's only the site of one of the most famous gang massacres ever to take place in the city. Not to mention all the stuff that the media never got their hands on. Tell me, now, *why* were you in there, asking that question?"

I hesitated, then told him the Brent story, abridged, ending with the receipt.

"Got a picture?" asked the little man.

"Sure," I said, taking the oft-folded paper out of my pocket. "You recognize him?"

He looked at the picture, blinked several times, then re-folded it and put it in his pocket.

"No," he said.

"Can I have the picture back?" I asked. "I want to show it to some more people and see if anyone recognizes him."

The little guy laughed. "You must be joking. Are you this stupid? You really don't want to be tossing that name around.. Don't do it."

"I have to," I said.

"Why?" he said. "If he's mixed up with that place…"

"What do you know?" I asked.

"Enough to know not to ask," he said. "Look, I'll do you a favor. You got me out of a tight spot back there. Give me the photo, give me your phone number. I'll ask around."

"Why would you do that for me?"

He looked away, then back at me. "I was in a tight spot. It would have been very bad for me to spend more time in there."

"Why were you there in the first place?"

He shrugged. "Sometimes you have to go places."

"What's your name?"

"Nothing I want to tell you," he said. "This is a one-time favor, OK?"

"What's the Lucky Dragon Duck?" I asked. "Where is it? At least tell me that."

He looked over his shoulder again, then turned to me. "It's a place where people gather," he said with his voice low. "The kind of people who wouldn't take kindly to someone asking about the place where they gather. Get my drift?"

Not really. With that description, the Lucky Dragon Duck could have been anything from the mayor's office to a crack den.

"How will I know when you've found anything?" I asked.

"I'll call you," he said.

"How?" I said. "You don't even know my name."

"Oh, right," he said. "Write down your number here." He held out a small piece of paper and a stub of a pencil. I put the paper on the back of my hand and scrawled my cell phone number on it.

"Can you read that?" I asked.

He held the paper up in front of him and squinted.

"Yep," he said, then folded the paper up and put it in his pocket. "I'll be in touch," he said. He walked out of the alley. I waited a few seconds, then followed. He had disappeared into the crowd.

"Let me get this straight," said Gerald. "You paid for this guy's lunch?"

"Part of it," I said.

"And he wasn't cruising you? You didn't end up with your clothes off in some slavery massage parlor?"

"No," I said. "I called you up and now we're here."

Here in this case was Red's Java House, a waterfront greasepit and bar, just under the Bay Bridge and off a dock where the big cruise ships tie up. We were sitting in plastic chairs on the back deck, splitting a pitcher of Budweiser and some cheese fries. The sun beat down on the back of my neck.

"And this is all because you're trying to track down your now-dead housemate, who may or may not have been the guy that you thought he was?"

"Yes."

"And it may have something to do with the Golden Dragon? That place is *terrible*. I think the sweet and sour chicken I had there was coated with rancid molasses."

"Yeah," I said.

Gerald shook his head and took a big swig of beer.

"Why are you getting all mixed up in this?"

"I'm not sure."

He grinned at me, a grin that said *I know why*, and my phone chirped before I could come up with a response. The LCD screen said "Neighbor," because Jenn's room was across the hall from mine.

"Hey," I said.

"I'm off work early," she said. "Where are you?"

"Red's on the water," I said. "Having a beer with Gerald."

"Mind if I join you guys? I'm half a minute away."

"Sure," I said. "Swing by. We'll be here for a bit."

"Who was that?"

"Jenn."

"Ah yes, your attractive roommate who you've lived across the hall from for over a year and claim to have never seen unclothed."

"Stop," I said. "Jenn's like my sister."

"Christ," he said. "Hanging out with you is like being in seventh grade, without the embarrassing public erections and feelings of inadequacy when confronted with a training bra."

"What?"

He shook his head. "Forget it."

"Uh...huh. Well, here she is now."

I turned around, and there was Jenn, looking slightly out-of-place in her work clothes – long black skirt, leather boots, dark tank-top under a sheer blouse, brown hair pulled back into a very tight bun, carrying an overstuffed shoulder bag.

"Hi," she said. "Hi, Gerald. Long time no see."

"Jenn," he said. "Good to see you."

She smiled. "Yeah."

"Want a beer?" asked Gerald.

"Dear God, yes." she said. "Alex?"

"Right," I said. I went to the bar and bought a hefeweizen, Jenn's favorite. She and Gerald were grinning at each other when I got back.

"Skipping the gym today?" I asked.

"Yeah," she said. "I got out of work early because my boss, the woman who reads the Oprah day-by-day calendar and leaves the sheets on my computer when she wants me to learn some kind of lesson, had an ultrasound. When she has an ultrasound at eleven, she goes home. *Her* boss also had an ultrasound, at one. So I got to leave early."

"Two pregnant bosses?" asked Gerald.

Jenn and I both laughed.

"That's the tip of the iceberg," she said. "Right after I started there two years ago, all of the women started getting knocked up. The whole place is one giant reproductive cycle. It's gotten to the point where I don't look twice when someone's pumping breast milk in the bathroom, and I've seen water break three times. I'm only twenty-six. I'm too young for this shit. I work in a made-for-the-Lifetime network movie, without the inspiring recoveries from terminal cancer."

Gerald exploded with laughter, spraying beer all over me.

"You win," he said. "That's it, I surrender, it's Appomattox Court House, Waterloo, Stalingrad, Dunkirk, and Yorktown all in one. That's the funniest goddamned thing I'm going to hear today, and it's only mid-afternoon. I might as well go home and stare at the wall for the rest of the day..."

"Is he always like this when he's high?" asked Jenn. "I mean, I know he's stoned all the time, so is he always like this?"

"Perhaps it's better to ask if he's always like this when confronted with a woman of your excruciating hotness," I said.

Jenn rolled her eyes. She has this weird way of rolling them; somehow she's able to start rolling with her left eye, and then, a few blinks later, start the right eye, so it looks like one eye is pulling the other as they roll around her face. The first time I saw her do it I was really weirded out, but I was used to it by now. It was a new one for Gerald, and when he saw it he snorted, blowing beer all over me yet again.

"Holy shit," he said. "Did you see what you just did?"

"I rolled my eyes," she said. "If you keep spitting beer all over Alex I'll probably do it again."

"Are you helping him with his mystery solving?" asked Gerald.

Jenn looked at me. "The search for the Origins of Brent?"

I nodded. "Things are weird with that," I said.

"You two are so screwy," said Gerald. "Has it occurred to you how unbelievably strange it is that you're poking around trying to find out what your housemate was doing after he's already dead? Why didn't you find this stuff out *before* he moved in?"

"You don't ask that that kind of thing," I said. "When someone interviews, it's not like your question is 'So, do you have a fake name?' All you really care about is whether or not the guy is going to pay the rent on time, won't make a mess of the living room, and does his dishes. Everything else is kind of a moot point."

"What if he's an axe-murderer?" asked Gerald.

"Cliché," I said. "There really aren't any axe-murderers. When was the last time you read about someone actually being cleaved to death with an axe? It just doesn't happen any more. Modern serial killers are more subtle."

"You get my point," he said.

"Right," said Jenn. "I mean, we just didn't know him that well yet. I know that he liked to watch baseball down at the bars on the weekends. I went with him once, and he was yelling at the TV because the Red Sox were losing. He didn't like it when you brought glasses into your room from the kitchen; he'd said that during his interview. And there was one time he came home early, and I was home, and nobody else was there. We made tea and talked about things. Or…well, I talked about things. He kept asking me questions about what it was like to grow up in Oklahoma, whether or not we had dust storms like they always show on the Weather Channel, and if my parents were still together."

"You didn't ask him anything?" I asked.

She shook her head, staring down into her glass. "No. I wish I had. I mean, we lived for four months with the guy and I have no idea if he has any brothers or sisters, or if his parents are still alive, or anything like that. He might as well have just been an ATM, like a place where we just went to get the rent from. It's sad."

The sun had migrated west, and as we sat not talking it slipped behind one of the big hotels that lined the waterfront on the city side, plunging a little area around our table into shadow and dropping the temperature. We sipped our beers, and I shivered. Nobody said anything for a few minutes, until a stray thought penetrated my solid wall of guilt.

"Wait a second," I said. "Jenn, Brent was a Red Sox fan? Was he from Boston?"

She nodded, dislodging a strand of hair from her bun, then pushing it back. The pencil that was holding it all together clattered to the concrete patio. She leaned over to pick up the pen, and her hair fell out around her shoulders.

"Great," she said. "One thing goes, then everything goes. Story of my life." She straightened up and started to re-wrap her hair. "I'm trying to remember, because I was baking when he was talking to me, and my glaze wasn't coming out quite right. Let's see…I asked him if he was from Boston, and he said he grew up around there, and his dad was a rabid baseball fan, and he kind of couldn't help it. It was like talking to someone who still looks at their old baseball card collection or who used to really be into comic books, but actually still is. They're embarrassed about it, but it's still what they're really into, you know? Anyway, yeah, he was planning on hitting every game when the Sox came to town to play the A's this year, and he was pretty excited because he'd read about a group of Red Sox fans that always sit in the bleachers to argue with the locals. He thought it would be fun to sit with them."

"Wow," I said. "How come you didn't mention that before?"

"It's baseball," she said. "I told you all the important stuff."

I took out my phone to make a call.

"Where do you store the suitcase battery for that thing?" cracked Gerald. It's an old joke. I haven't replaced my phone in a couple of years; it's battered and scratched, and sometimes I have to hit it in order to make a call go through. I don't care. I'm saving it for the day when retro cell phones will be trendy, like fixed-gear bikes, trucker hats, and drinking Pabst Blue Ribbon over beer that has flavor. When that day comes, I'll be the coolest guy in town.

"You'll rue the day you said that," I said.

"Rue the day? Who *talks* like that?" he said.

"Guys who don't need to mine *Real Genius* for a snappy comeback," I said.

I punched two buttons, and Thomas picked up, answering with his full name because it was a work extension.

"What's up?" he said.

"Are you online?"

"Of course," he said.

"Aren't the Red Sox coming to play the A's this weekend?"

I could hear keyboard clacking and mouse clicking on the other end of the line.

"Yeah. Four game series, starting tonight."

"Want to go to a game?"

His smile was so wide and so instant it came through on the phone. "Sure," he said. "I haven't been in a while. When?"

"Tomorrow?"

More clicking and clacking. "Trying to find tickets...it's sold out."

"Can you find some bleacher seats somewhere?"

"Craigslist, here I come," he said. "I'll make it happen. The game's at one. We're leaving by ten so we can make it to batting practice."

"You got it," I said. "Seeya at home."

"Bye."

"What was that all about?" asked Jenn.

"Under the Euro exterior, Thomas is a baseball fiend," I said. "This is the second time the Red Sox have come to the area this year – they played the Giants a month ago. We go to the game, find the group of Red Sox fans in the bleachers, and see if any of them know Brent. What could possibly go wrong?"

I met Morgan that night at Lucky 13, a rock and roll bar on Market Street on the border of the Castro. The jukebox blasts punk and metal, the bartenders are a giant, tattooed couple who once went on Jenny Jones because the show's producers were desperate to have a heavily inked woman for a show titled "I love large breasts." Lori was on duty that night, wearing a leather bustier that showed off the multi-hued Chinese-style dragon that dove down into her cleavage. The bar was crowded with grease-haired rocker types and scared-looking young professional woman out slumming for bad boys to take home. I sat at the far end of the bar, munching on stale popcorn, nervous. I didn't have much in the way of information to give her, but I didn't want her to forget about me.

Morgan settled in next to me without a sound, brushing her leg against mine as she hung a tiny brown purse on the hook below the bar. She mouthed a word, but I couldn't hear it over the music and the crunching of my popcorn.

"What?" I said.

She smiled and placed her hand on my leg. "I said, 'hello,'" she said. "What do you say to that?"

"Hello," I said. "What would you like to drink?"

"I got one when I walked in," she said. "If I'm already holding a drink, none of these boneheads will offer to buy me one."

"What's wrong with a free drink?"

She shook her head. "Nothing, technically. But if I accept one, then I have to speak for at least two minutes to whoever bought it for me, plus he's got a license to come up and talk to me for the rest of the time I'm at this bar. By buying my own and coming and sitting down next to you, nobody will bug me."

"Because they'll think you're with me?"

Morgan smiled without showing her teeth. Her lipstick was dark, almost black, nicely complementing the deep burgundy of her small t-shirt. With that and her jeans and dark leather boots, she looked like an evil version of Winona Ryder.

"Well," she said. "I *am* with you, aren't I?"

"Um…I guess," I said, having no idea if that was what she wanted me to say.

"For now you are," she said. "So, Alex. What do you have for me?"

"Not much," I said. "I found out that Brent used to get coffee at Starbucks, was most likely from Boston, and has something to do with a place called the Lucky Dragon Duck."

Morgan put her drink down sharply.

"What was that last one?"

"The Lucky Dragon Duck," I said. "Weird name, huh?"

She picked up her drink and took a sip. "Yes…yes, it is."

"Do you know it?"

She shook her head quickly. "No, I don't. I just think it's a ridiculous name. I mean, why name your shadowy conspiracy organization something that sounds like a greasy take-out place in an Iowa mall?" She laughed. "That doesn't make sense. It's a red herring, Alex."

"Right," I said. "I'm going to the ball game tomorrow to try to track down anyone there who knows him. Maybe I'll find out something."

She turned towards me and grabbed my wrist, pulling me close.

"You'll tell me when you find something out, won't you?" She breathed that last into my ear; I could feel her exhalation tickling the tiny hairs on my lobe, and I shivered.

"Yeah, of course," I said. "Why wouldn't I?"

"Some people can't be trusted," she said. "I have to go." She leaned forward and brushed the corner of my mouth with a kiss, then grabbed her purse. "Can't forget this," she said. "Bags don't grow on trees, you know." She hopped off her stool and walked through the crowd to the door.

"Dude, is she with you?" asked Lori, the heavily-inked bartender. "You should keep that one close."

"I don't know," I said. "I mean, I know, but I don't..."

Lori gave me a knowing smile. "Yeah, I know."

Chapter 6

Saturday dawned cold and foggy. Thomas and I both were wearing shorts with our fuzzy slippers when we met up in the kitchen at nine-thirty. I had my backpack ready – sunscreen, baseball hat, extra t-shirt, fleece pullover, full water bottle, a printed copy of my scanned picture of Brent, and a notebook.

Thomas was decked out in Giants gear – hat, wristbands, and old-school Will Clark jersey. Ordinarily you wouldn't wear that going to Oakland. I mean, it's not like the loyalties of the Bay Area are as fractured as they were in New York in the '50s, when Yankees fans didn't dare venture over the Manhattan bridge to Brooklyn, but you can still get a good ribbing by wearing green and gold to the San Francisco side and vice versa. It's worse in Oakland – the place has had an inferiority complex ever since Gertrude Stein said, "The trouble with Oakland is that when you get there, there isn't any there there." That statement isn't really true, but the sentiment still rankles. Even before they won the World Series, the Giants got all the attention of the local media, their games sold out, and they've got a beautiful stadium right downtown. The A's have won four World Series, only sell out when the Sox or Yankees come to town, and have had four different radio stations in the past ten years. Oakland fans can be a little bitter.

"Aren't you asking for it, dressed like that?" I said.

"Ordinarily, I would be," he said. "But the place is going to be swarmed with obnoxious Boston fans. I'm the lesser of two evils."

"Why not just wear an A's hat?" I asked. "I've got an extra somewhere."

He looked at me as if I'd suggested that cooked sushi was better than the raw stuff. "I'm no sports bigamist," he said. "My devotion runs deep."

"You're sick," I said.

"Yep," he said. "But I'm also a genius." He walked over to the fridge, opened it, and pulled out two one-liter bottles of Pepsi and a half-full bottle of Jim Beam. Thomas poured out a third of each Pepsi and filled the rest with bourbon.

"I really don't feel like paying seven dollars for beers," he said.

"Not bad," I said.

"Let's go."

"Go" meant taking the accordion-style bus down to Market and switching over to an under-the-bay BART train. Ordinarily, ten o'clock on Saturday would be a pretty quiet ride, but the train was mostly full, and we walked through three cars before we could find seats. Most of the people were from Red Sox nation – stockinged pennants, red jerseys, and re-discovered dropped-*r* accents littered the train.

The Coliseum has been around since the seventies and looks it. Whoever was in charge of making buildings back then would have been a wonderful designer of gulag dormitories; the stadium itself is a ten-story-high football-centric monstrosity. We walked around to the bleacher side and wound our way down to the sixth row in right field. The first five were already packed with the drummers – rabid, maniacal A's fans who brought congas and snares to every game, giving the place a touch of the atmosphere of a Brazilian soccer match.

We sat for batting practice. Or, rather, I sat, and Thomas made his way down to the railing next to the field with his baseball glove and tried to shag home-run balls. He came close only once; the bleachers are about forty feet above the level of the field, and you really have to nail one to get it up there. I sat and he shagged for nearly an hour, as the seats around us filled up with green-and-gold hometown loyalists and white-and-red-clad Bostonians. Cheers and jeers started going back and forth, the teams took the field, and I got to work.

"Excuse me," I said to a goateed man in a many-stained Mike Greenwell jersey.

"If you're here to talk about the '88 LCS, get out of my face before I punch it," he said.

"No, it's nothing like that," I said. "Have you ever seen this guy?" I pulled out my picture of Brent and unfolded it. "I think he hung out in this section the last time the Sox were in town."

The guy squinted, then shook his head.

"I don't think so," he said. "He a local?"

"He lived here," I said. "But he was a Red Sox fan. I think he was in the bleachers for the San Francisco series last month."

"Oh," he said. "Lemme see that again."

He took the picture in both of his hands, squinted hard, took off his 2004 World Series Champions hat and used it to shade the paper, turned it all the way around, put his hat back on, and squinted again.

"Maybe," he said. "He might look kind of familiar. You know where he comes from?"

"Not really," I said.

"Why do you want to find him?"

I took a deep breath. "He died last week," I said. "I'm trying to find his parents."

"How do you know him?"

"He was my housemate," I said.

The guy took off his hat again, looked at the picture, then looked at me. "This guy lived in your house and you don't know who his parents were?"

"Uh, no."

"Why?"

I started to talk, then stopped. Why didn't I know? On the other hand, why would I know? We didn't have a house phone; when we ordered pizza the guys on the other end would have to ask us for the address, as their automatic address-finder things wouldn't work on a wireless. Nobody got mail except for birthday cards and bills, and Brent hadn't had a birthday while he'd lived with us, I don't think. He'd never really had any visitors, and his parents didn't live in town, so they never came by to say hi or check out the house.

"I don't know," I said. "We just didn't."

"Weird, man," he said. "That's weird."

It wasn't, really. What would have been weirder would have been if we *had* known his parents; we'd negged a potential roommate mostly because it looked like we'd have to get to know his parents. How would I have ever come into contact with them?

"Right," I said. "Any idea about him, though?"

"How tall is he?"

"Short," I said. "Five-five, five-six, maybe."

"Hmmm…" he said. "Can't really say. But I was only here for one game last series; you probably want to talk to someone who was here for the whole thing."

I was about to ask him if he knew anyone who had been there for the whole thing, but then the first batter of the inning came up, and the guy exploded out of his seat, screaming incoherently. There was no way I could get anything out of him while the Red Sox were batting, so I headed back down to our seats, where Thomas was happily sipping his illicit drink and bobbing his head in time to the drummers.

"Great stuff, isn't it?" he asked.

I nodded, took a drink, and watched. The drums only let up when nothing was happening, which meant that I was only able to walk around and show Brent's picture to people in the gaps between innings. Practically, this mean that I was only able to talk to one person per inning break, as I had to have conversations that were exactly like the one I'd had with the bearded guy, which took a while, and I wasn't even able to ask around every inning break, because the caffeine-and-alcohol doubleshot was forcing me to the bathroom every twenty minutes.

By the sixth, the A's had gone up four to two on an Eric Chavez double that skidded barely fair over the first-base bag, I'd talked to four people, and I was sick of telling the same story over and over to drunk maniacs who kept dropping their *r* sounds.

"One more," I said. "I'm only going to talk to one more person, and that's it."

Thomas had finished his bottle and was happily yelling at the Red Sox left fielder, who couldn't possibly hear him over the racket of the drums.

"OK," he said.

"Seriously," I said. "This was probably a stupid idea."

"Not really," he said. "This is an awesome game."

"I think I'll ask that guy, and be done with it," I said.

I pointed to a man who was standing three rows back - a gaunt, overly tan fellow wearing a tattered red windbreaker and sweating in the warm weather. He was at least in his seventies, and his glasses were held to his face with a black elastic band.

"Why him?" asked Thomas. "His brain is probably so mushy he thinks it's Reggie Jackson vs. Carlton Fisk out there. Hell, he's probably wondering why Jimmy Foxx isn't playing first base."

"Who was Jimmy Foxx?"

"The guy who used to hold the home run record for both clubs. Played for the Sox and the A's back in the '30s."

"Why do you know that?"

Thomas shrugged. "It's better than filling my head with the stupid crap I'm supposed to know for work. They put all of these arithmetic models together to predict market behavior, and then they trash all of them every time there's a chance to jump on a bandwagon. At least baseball stats are consistent."

"Barry Bonds and steroids," I said.

"Point taken," he said. "But it's still more honest than your average stock trade."

On the field, the Red Sox had loaded the bases with two out, but Justin Duscherer struck out Kevin Youklis with a nasty slider, and people stood up for the seventh-inning stretch.

"Back in a tick," I said.

"A tick," said Thomas. "Stop trying to be English."

The old guy was sitting on an aisle, so I was able to stand right next to him when the fake organ started playing "Take Me Out To the Ball Game." He didn't sing, and when he noticed that I was looking at him instead of singing, he started to talk.

"Stupid tradition," he said. "This isn't even a tradition; the only place where they used to sing this idiotic song was at Wrigley Field, and Harry Caray would lead it. Then the Cubs kept stinking but they had that national television thing, so everybody started doing it. Stupid. So stupid."

"Um…" I said.

"Are you about to tell me that it's a *good* thing? Thousands of people singing inane words while staying completely off-key? Do you think this is good? It heralds the end of civilization!"

Those last words were almost at a yell. I took a step back, then removed the picture of Brent from my pocket.

"I'm looking for this guy," I said. "I'm hoping you can tell me something about him."

"He owe you money or something?" asked the old man. "You don't look like a sharpie to me." His *sharpie* came out *shaaa-pie*.

"No," I said. "Well, kind of. He used to be my housemate, and

I'm trying to track down his parents."

"Aaah," he said. He snatched the picture out of my hand and peered at it from about six different angles. "Yes, Brent."

"You remember his name?" I blurted.

He gave me a look that oozed scorn. "I can tell you the name of the guy who pinch-hit for Bobby Doerr at an away game versus the Chicago White Sox in 1953," he said. "I don't forget names."

This grumpy old guy was the first person I'd met outside of the house who knew Brent as Brent. I could practically see the mystery unraveling before my eyes. I was getting close, I was...

"Brent is a good name," said the old man. "Not as good as Bobby, though. Doerr was a *player*, you know?"

"Right," I said, "But about..."

"He'd come up there with his white pants stained dark with dirt, resin, and 'bacca, and he'd chew out the pitcher, chew out the fans, then smoke the ball anywhere he wanted it to go. Not like these guys who chew pieces of blasted *gum*. If you're over twelve, you got no business chewing gum. It's 'bacca or nothing."

As he said this, he shifted something from his left cheek, which had been invisible to me, to his right cheek, a chaw big enough to make him look akin to the squirrels in Golden Gate Park at the onset of winter. He bit down on violently on the tumoric mass, then spat a five-inch stream down at his feet. Some of it splashed on my toes, and I cursed myself for wearing sandals.

"But about Brent..." I said.

"Good kid," said the old guy. "From Slummerville, he said."

"Slummerville?"

"Somerville," said the guy. "Suburb of Boston. Good Irish place – some of Whitey's gang used to hang out there."

I wasn't sure why the old guy was throwing in a *Leave it to Beaver* reference, but I ploughed on.

"Do remember anything else about him?"

"Sure," said the old guy. "He sat next to me last time I was here." *Chew.* "He was one of those young fellas who wanted to talk baseball and nothing but baseball, so we had a fine old time, even though the boys lost."

He sat down, and there was about six inches of bench to the right of him. "Sit down, boy," he said, patting the small empty area of bench. I sat in the aisle next to him, hoping that my pants wouldn't end up with 'bacca stains. The A's were coming to bat, and the old guy started to chew with more intensity.

"Yeah, we talked a lot about Yaz and the Sox in the '60s," he said. "The kid hadn't been born, but he had a lot of knowledge about those teams. It was like he'd read a lot of books about 'em, I thought. But no, he was just a baseball card nut...YES!" The leadoff batter swung and popped the fifth pitch sky-high, over the bullpen mound to the side of the left-field foul line. An easy catch for the third baseman, and the Red Sox loyalists roared their approval.

"Turns out he was kind of famous with those kids who collect bubble-gum cards," said the old guy.

"What?" I said. Famous? Bubble-gum cards? No, wait. He probably meant baseball-card-nuts. Brent had been into baseball cards? I'd had no idea.

"He had a rare Yaz card from 1968," he said. "Not the Triple Crown year, but the one where he was the only .300 hitter in the league. Turns out that about ten cards were printed backwards – they had Yaz hitting right-handed instead of his natural left." *Chew. Spit. Splatter.* "BRADLEY, YOU'RE A BUM. A BUM!"

I'd never heard anyone actually called a bum at a game before. Most of the people I knew preferred the more vile cuss words. I liked the old guy's better.

"Apparently it caused a fuss," said the old guy. "I don't care about cards myself, but your friend was really excited about it. He'd just sold his card for something ridiculous. Apparently it made a magazine or something like that."

A magazine. Brent had been in a magazine. I wrote that down on the back of my paper.

"You don't know what magazine, do you?"

He snorted, chewed, spat, and splattered. "Why would I waste my energy paying attention to that kind of stuff? Cards that aren't worth anything. Ugh. No point. Now, if you're talking about great '60s players, people whose cards should be worth something, you're talking guys like Rocky Colavito, who would have been as good as Williams if he hadn't been hurt. Or DiMaggio, who should be in the

Hall of Fame…"

"Joe DiMaggio's not in the Hall?" I asked.

He gave me the same look of scorn. "*Dom* DiMaggio," he said. "The best damn center fielder there ever was. His brother was overrated, if you ask me. So was Mantle. Boozehound who couldn't keep his ankle on straight with a plaster cast…"

And on and on. I couldn't get up while the inning was still on, and the A's were taking pitches, drawing walks, generally doing everything to prolong the inning except score. Then there was a long conference at the mound, after which there wasn't a pitching change, which I could have used to get out of there and give my butt muscles a break. All the while the old guy prattled on.

"…and *he* should still never show his face in Boston again. Everyone says Buckner, but I'd buy that guy a beer. Hurst, what a bum. What kinda pitcher gives up five runs to a damned National League New York team and puts us in a position to lose on a bad-hop grounder? Skinned alive, that shoulda been him…"

"Can I ask you a question?" I asked.

"I don't like being interrupted much," he said. He didn't continue, so I spoke.

"How come you're here, not back at home in Boston?"

"My kid moved here," he said. "And I wanted to be closer to him, so I moved. Stupid San Francisco mixed-up seasons and no winters. I fly back to Boston every February just to get some cold weather and be around people who keep to their own business."

I took that as my cue to leave, and walked down to our seats. Thomas was sipping on the remains of my drink.

"Any luck?" asked Thomas.

"I think so," I said. "Maybe. Why are you…"

"Oh, well, the game's almost over," he said. "I thought you wouldn't mind."

"No, not really," I said. "But you owe me a beer."

"OK," said Thomas. "You know, you've missed all of the good parts of the game."

"Don't remind me," I said. "Or I'll make you buy me another beer for being an I-told-you-so housemate."

"I never told you anything," he said.

"The principle is the same," I said. "You're still a back-seat driver, even if you're riding shotgun."

The rest of the game was wild. In the top of the ninth, with the A's still up two runs, their middle reliever went wild, hit two batters, and walked a third to load the bases with one out. The pitcher went out, the closer came in, and immediately picked off the runner at first, who had strayed too far from the bag and fell down after twitching the wrong way on a pickoff move. That was followed by a dink single over the third-base bag, with the runner on second base staying put after a near-perfect throw home just missed the scoring runner there. Four to three.

The drummers had gone crazy, conjuring up a beat that reminded me of the island sacrifice scene in the original *King Kong*. People were stomping on the seats, screaming obscenities so awful they could have come from the other dimensions of a Lovecraft novel. Odd geometries, horrific lines, the works. Thomas was up and yelling; I was standing and smacking my hand on the empty Pepsi bottle, making a satisfying *thunking* sound.

Low and outside, ball one. Batter steps out of the box, adjusts his wristbands.

Curve, snapping from high to low, across the plate, taken for strike one.

Change-up, swung at and missed, strike two. Batter backs out of the box, blows a large pink bubble, stares hard at the pitcher, steps back in.

Ball two, fastball up and outside. Ninety-nine on the radar gun.

Ball three, fastball in the dirt.

The noise of the crowd was palpable, seething, organic. I felt like I was part of something alive, connected. There's nothing like the last inning of a game with the winning run only ninety feet away.

Pitch – fastball, in on the hands, fisted out towards left field. Left fielder running in, running, running, stumbling just a touch, diving forward with the glove out, the ball popped out of the glove but the fielder turned over while sliding on the ground and kicked the ball with his foot. The still-alive ball went straight up, then came down into the left fielder's bare hand. Catch. Out. Ballgame.

Pandemonium. I hugged Thomas, the guy behind me who just

before had used a word so bad I don't think they even know it in England, a heavily tattooed gangster-type who squeezed nearly all of the air out of me, and an ancient woman who was trying to leave with her just-as-ancient husband. I think I might have broken her; something definitely popped as I gave her my bear hug. I hope it was just her back cracking and not an important bone.

"How was the game, boys?" asked Jenn when we got home. She wrinkled her nose. "Yuck. Why do you smell like bacon?"

"It wasn't our fault," I said.

"What, someone else put swine-smelling cologne all over you?" she said.

"No, we were just hanging with some fans who were grilling some post-game bacon." *Some,* in this case, meant three pounds. I don't know why those guys had three pounds of bacon, and I don't know why they insisted on grilling it all, but I do know why they made us eat three pieces for every beer we drank; they were evil. Pure evil. I felt like someone had forced an iron-sheathed cactus into my digestive tract.

"Well, you two should shower," she said. "And change clothes. A potential is coming by to interview in fifteen minutes."

My hair was still dripping as I leaned over Thomas's computer to check the e-mail.

Hi. I'm twenty-four and moved to the city six months ago. I am moving out of my apartment, because it was a six month sublet, and it is coming due fairly soon. I work at a non-profit in the Presidio, and your place sounds like it's close to the 43 bus, so I could get there quickly.

The 43 on time? Might as well say that James Dobson will be inaugurating the next Mr. Gay.com.

I am hoping to be in a house where it is clean, the people are friendly, and you hang out some, but not too much. See you soon, Patrick

"See?" said Thomas. "Sounds sane."

"Too sane," I said. "The really crazy ones always are."

"One sec," I said. "Mind if I check out something real quick?"
"No problem," he said.

I clicked over to Wikipedia and did a quick read-through of their article on baseball cards. I was hoping that Brent's sale would have been notorious enough to make in into the entry, but no such luck. A few clicks put me on the web forum for *Beckett's Baseball Card Monthly*, where I left a simple message asking if anyone knew anything about a guy named Brent who'd sold a rare Yazstremski in the past year or so. Right when I finished typing, the doorbell rang. We looked at each other, shrugged, and walked downstairs.

He was tall. Very tall. So tall that he had to stoop over as he crested the stair to avoid bonking his head on the sloping ceiling. He was slim but not skinny, and he stood with that little slouch tall people do when they're forced to interact with short folks. His blonde hair was floppy, kind of bowl-cutty, and it fell down into his eyes as he strode into the living room, taking two steps to cover a distance that always took me four.

"Hi," he said, folding himself into our usual chair. His knees stuck up to mid-chest level, although his feet were on the floor.

"Six-ten," he said.

"Excuse me?" said Thomas.

"I'm six foot ten," said the guy. "It's what people always ask me." His voice was low, a sub-bass rumble.

"Patrick, right?" said Thomas. "Do you go by Pat?"

"Not since the *Saturday Night Live* skit," said Patrick.

"Fair enough," said Thomas. "Patrick it is."

"So, Patrick," I said. "What are you all about?"

He smiled. It was an easy smile, the kind of grin that comes from someone who spends quite a bit of time with a smile on his face. It wasn't that he was amazingly good-looking, although his face was classically square and handsome, kind of like a very large Dick Tracy. He just exuded niceness. "I work at Save the Blue Bay, a nonprofit. We're interested in water pollution issues in the San Francisco Bay, and spend most of our time working with industry to try to find ways that they can dispose of their waste without causing harm to the local ecosystem."

Shawna sat up straight and looked him in the eye.

"That's amazing," she said. "It's great that you're doing that kind of thing,"

"Yeah," he said. "We do really good work."

"What do you do for them?" I asked.

He smiled again. Jenn sat up a little straighter.

"Mostly office things," he said. "I gopher around, take care of the printer and toner orders, maintain the fax machine, stock the fridges, that kind of stuff."

"Ah," I said. "Overeducated and under-used, huh?"

He smiled again. It was weird – this was the first time he'd smiled directly at me, and I felt myself sitting up a little straighter.

"I guess so," he said. "I mean, I didn't go to college for four years to learn how to do that."

"What did you do in college?" asked Thomas.

"Computer science," he said. "And photography."

"No basketball?" I said.

"They kept trying to get me to play," he said. "But Caltech doesn't have a real team, and I wasn't there to try to be drafted."

"Makes sense," said Jenn.

I finished my beer and walked the empty over to the kitchen to recycle it. As I was digging around in the bottom of the fridge for another bottle, Jenn came in and leaned down, close to me. I could feel her breath on my ear.

"What do you think?" she whispered.

"Not bad," I said. "Probably the most sane guy we've met."

"He's so *tall*," she said.

"Hot?" I said.

She turned pink. "Yeah. Something about a really tall guy…"

I sighed. I'm not tall, I'll never be tall, and hearing about how hot tall guys are kind of chuffs me. It's not like being tall has all of the advantages. Sure, you can reach things down from the top shelves in the kitchen without needing a footstool, but I bet that all of the respect and higher salaries aren't worth the airplane pain and constant weather jokes. Right. Yep.

"Something about him, though…" I said. "I've seen him somewhere before."

"He's kind of tough to miss," said Jenn.

"Yeah, but it's not like I hang out down in the Presidio," I said. "He seems kind of bland, too."

"Bland can be good," said Jenn. "Living with two drama-queen boys is enough."

"Drama queen?" I said. "I'm no drama queen."

"No, you're right," she said. "Things just happen to you. Like that time that Shawna accidentally spilled coffee on your Strummer biography and you moped around the house for three days after. Right. No drama there at all." She turned around and walked back to the kitchen, her grubby-around-the-house pants swishing. I cracked my beer with the opener I kept on my keychain and followed her.

"...and I don't really have that much stuff," Patrick was saying. "Just a bed, some personal things, and a few books. Is it OK if I use some of the empty bookshelves in the next room?"

"Sure," said Thomas. He was radiating warmth, friendliness, all of the things that said *we're totally going to let you live in this house*. Totally out of character. "Any more questions?"

"Just one," I said. "I mean, it doesn't sound like your job is much more than an internship, and it's kind of expensive here in the city; I'm just curious..."

He smiled again. "I do have a couple of side businesses. Most people in San Francisco do, you know?"

"Internet stuff?" asked Thomas.

"That's part of it," said Patrick. "I'll tell you about it sometime; sounds like you've got some business experience that's a bit more intense than I do."

"Sure," said Thomas. "No problem."

"Oh," said Patrick. "And I sometimes make a bit of noise in my room with the door closed...but never after ten o'clock."

"*That's* no big deal," said Jenn. "Alex blasts his music until midnight, and we don't care."

"Blasts?" I said. "I don't blast."

She snorted. "Right. I can hear it from my room with both doors closed. That's blasting."

"Whatever," I said. "You just have sensitive ears."

"That's it, then?" asked Patrick.

"Yep," I said.

"Great to meet you all," said Patrick as he unfolded himself from the chair. He leaned over and shook all of our hands in turn, then straightened. "You have my e-mail address?" he asked.

Thomas nodded. "You bet," he said. "We'll be in touch, we just have to…"

"Talk about it. I know," said Patrick. "Take your time." He turned around and walked down the stairs, his monstrous feet barely making a sound as he walked down the stairs. We all waited, straining to hear him leave; the door closed with a soft *click*.

"Wow," said Jenn. "He didn't slam the door. I thought it was a male imperative to do that."

"No," said Shawna. "We just live with selfish, insensitive boys."

"Obviously," said Jenn. "So, um, we like this guy, right?"

Thomas nodded. All three of my roommates looked at me, and I didn't nod. I squinted, frowned, and did all of the facial things that you do when you're trying to convince people that you're thinking hard about the problem at hand. Actually, I wasn't – I had started thinking about Jenn's pants on the way back from the kitchen, and how she looked pretty good in grubby pants, and then I started thinking about Morgan in grubby pants. Did she even own grubby pants? Was she a sweats type of girl? Old jeans? Or soft silk pajamas? You can tell a lot about a woman by her comfortable pants.

"Alex?" Jenn said. "You OK?"

"Yeah," I said. "He seemed like a good guy, but…"

"But what?" said Shawna. "Too much of a hippie for you because he works at a place that isn't evil?"

"No…it's just…well…can we sleep on it?"

"Of course," said Thomas. "But I'll say right now that I'm definitely, at this point, OK with him."

The meeting broke up then. Thomas went up to his room to play online poker – he had it in his head that he was going to play his way into the World Series and use his winnings to pay off his student loans. Jenn stayed in the living room to read a book and watch *Project Runway,* and Shawna started the nightly process of burning the bejesus out of some dinner vegetables. I had no food in the house and no desire to be anywhere near the kitchen while Shawna set fire to her produce, so I threw on a sweatshirt and walked down the street to find some food.

I ended up three blocks away on Haight Street, walking west towards the park. The night hadn't fully fallen, and the window-shoppers and preppie kids were slowly giving way to the weekday nightlife crowd, a crew that's not gay, not straight, not hippie nor hipster, but an odd mix of all of those mixed in with the crusty street kids. The crusties look like Mad Max meets Woodstock, a bizarre amalgamation of punk hair and homemade clothes. Guys in stenciled leather jackets right out of a heavy-metal parking lot sat on the sidewalk, strumming acoustic guitars while singing Paul Simon, stopping mid-song to ask me if I could spare a dime, change, or money for beer, sir? Half of them had dogs, and half of that number didn't bother to cover up the track marks on their sallow forearms and pockmarked faces.

As I walked, I passed places and mentally checked off what I didn't want to eat. Vietnamese noodle soup was out, as was crummy pizza, sandwiches, breakfast-crepes-for-dinner, Thai, vegan burgers, grilled meats on a skewer, falafel, high-end pasta, pan-Asian noodles, pub food, and all raw salad wraps. Sometimes I think it would be nice to live in a neighborhood that only had one restaurant, with only one food item available each day. At least that way I'd just go and eat and not spend so much time wandering around by myself trying to figure out where to go.

As usual, I settled on a burrito. Boston has seafood, New York has their pizza, Chicago has hot dogs, Santa Fe has green chile, and Des Moines has whatever the hell they eat in Iowa. Here, although the guidebooks will tout the glories of local crab and sourdough bread, the locals subsist on food logs, over a pound in weight, nearly a foot long, wrapped in foil, and well under ten bucks. Taqueria El Balazo was humming as I walked in; it's a split-level place where the counter for ordering faces you when you walk in. I ordered a super carnitas (fried pork) burrito, stocked up on pico di gallo and cilantro, grabbed an issue of the free *San Francisco Bay Guardian*, and prepared to chow down.

The stories in the *Guardian* were the standard free-weekly-lefty-investigative muck of the city: an exposure of the downtown business's fleecing of the city coffers without any specific examples, the semi-monthly "Transitions" column (a first-person perspective column from a girl who was in the process of switching gender), previews of upcoming indie-rock shows with captioned photos showing four slender glasses-wearing lads, and the sex column, which this week featured a question from a youngish straight man who wanted to know if any organization existed that could train him in the art of being a nude sushi model.

I finished most of the articles and was paging through the back section escort ads as I mopped up the remains of my salsa with the last dregs of my free chips…and then I remembered where I had seen Patrick before. The ad wasn't big, but it was full-color, and featured a photo of Patrick, *au naturel,* with a black star over his crotch.

M4M tall fetish outcall/incall. 6'10", I'll make you feel smaller than anyone else can. Built, slight BH, no bears, 7.5", uncut. Your place or mine – I have everything we need in my personal mini-dungeon, right at home. In by eight, out by ten. No overnights. Leather boys welcome!

I ripped the ad out and recycled the rest of the paper. When I got home everyone had retired early to their rooms; rather than bother anyone, I just taped the ad to the door of the upstairs bathroom with a scrawled post-it saying *let's keep looking.* As I finished, Thomas padded down the hall, clad in his night-time normal of boxers and a t-shirt.

He took a look at the ad, looked down at me, and shook his head.

"Bummer," he said. "I was kind of looking forward to being the second-tallest guy in the house."

"What's the problem?" It was Shawna. She crowded in next to Thomas, edging me out of the way. "I don't think it's our place to judge what he does in his spare time."

"You're absolutely right," I said. "It's not. And if he had some other space I'd be perfectly happy to have him as a roommate. However, I'm not really up for having the room next to the kitchen being a part-time BDSM lair."

"Yeah," said Thomas. "And this doesn't speak too much for his intelligence. There are places down South of Market where you can rent dungeon space for client meetings and deduct the cost; I don't want to live with anyone who isn't smart enough to make use of that kind of financial incentive."

"Are you serious?" I said.

He shrugged. "Not really. If I had problems with living with financially dumb people, I'd never have let you move in."

"You think I'm dumb?"

"No," he said. "Financially dumb. Why don't you have a job yet?"

"Because I have severance," I said. *And I hate working*, I didn't say.

"OK," said Shawna. "Thomas, do you mind taking a look at something for me?"

"Sure," he said.

They walked down to Shawna's room at the end of the hall, and Thomas slammed the door. I smoothed out the newspaper with the palm of my hand, then walked back to my room to go to bed. I hadn't bothered to take my phone with me as I'd gone to dinner. The face's light was on, and a little envelope with a pen was in the upper-left-hand corner. A text message, probably Gerald wanting to meet me for a nightcap or some such.

Look at Spotend Alley

Then come Wednesday 9 pm to Dashiell Hammett Way.

The message was from a number I didn't recognize. I popped open my laptop and checked to see if Gerald was online – he wasn't, so I sent him an e-mail with the message in it, asking him to meet me for coffee tomorrow – Sunday morning.

Chapter 7

My mind was moving around pretty quickly as I walked up Divisadero Street the next morning. I had spent a few minutes last night Googling around and had found out where Dashiell Hammett Way was but had come up with a complete blank on Spotend Alley; it didn't show up on any of the major search engines or mapping sites, and I'd given up and ended up scrolling through old music videos. I remember falling asleep with my fingers still on the keyboard, dreaming that love was a battlefield. As I walked, I kinked my neck back and forth to work out some of the stiffness.

"Spare any change, man?" Another homeless man; he looked in his sixties, which probably put him at about forty-two.

"Sorry, got nothing," I said.

"Thas' all right, have yourself a wonderful day," he said. His words slurred through his broken teeth.

"You too," I said.

"I'll try," he said as I walked away. "Don't stick yo' head where it don't belong."

Gerald had already staked out a seat in one of the armchairs when I reached Café Abir. He was drinking a pint glass of what looked like coffee with cream and was reading the local section of the *Chronicle*. A driving hat was perched on top of his head, and he was wearing a corduroy sport jacket; he looked like a hipster English professor.

"Alex," he said. "Get yourself something wiry, my boy."

"Boy?" I said. "I'm older than you."

"Only in years, not where it really counts."

Gerald *always* got the last word. I went to the counter and ordered a café au lait from the nose-ringed, black-dreadlocked, Edward Scissorhands-pale guy behind the counter.

"Au Lait, sure," he said, in a tone of voice that made a funeral director sound like a cheerleader.

The coffee was dark, nutty, and strong; I could feel it in my bones as I set down next to Gerald, who was scratching away at a crossword puzzle. I didn't say anything. Interrupting him during a brain game was a no-no.

"Catechism...python...Tolstoy...Twiggy...Milne...marathon...fo rkball," he said. "Done."

"How long?"

"Twenty-two minutes," he said. "Not too bad. It was a tough one today."

I didn't say anything, and waited as he looked over the puzzle again. Even as stoned as he normally is, the guy is a crossword fiend and a Scrabble ninja. Eventually, he folded the paper, put it down, took a sip of his drink, and looked over at me.

"OK," he said. "What do you want to talk about? Please don't tell me this has something to do with finding you a job. You know how I feel about friends of mine working in cubicles."

"Not at all," I said. "It's more about finding a place here, an alley I've never seen."

"GFE," he said.

"What does that mean?"

"It means 'Google Fucking Exists,'" he said. "Don't you read Dan Savage?"

"Yes," I said. "But I must have missed that column somewhere in between the pegging one and the one where he named something disgusting after a Senator. But Google doesn't help on this one."

"What makes you think I would know?" he asked. "You know as much about this place as anyone."

"Because you know things I don't know sometimes," I said. "Do you know Spotend Alley?"

Gerald put his cup down, then picked it up, then took a drink, stirred it, and took another drink. It wasn't as if a giant dark cloud had covered him over and he'd become a beast or anything like that; it was as if I could see his mood, and the mood itself had gone from a sunny day to scattered clouds with a chance of rain. He leaned forward to talk to me, and the smile that usually played around the corners of his lips had gone.

"I've been there," he said. "Why in God's name do you want to know about that place?

"Something to do with my old roommate," I said.

"Why are you going so crazy with this?" he asked.

I shrugged.

"No, I'm serious," he said. "Dude, I've known you for two years now, and the only time that I've seen you devote this much energy to something was…shit, it came close when you were watching wrestling all the time."

Right after I'd moved in, I had become completely addicted to the Monday night wrestling shows. Right at nine, I would boot everyone else off of the television and start yelling at the Rock and the Undertaker and the other super stars of the sports entertainment world. I finally stopped when I realized I'd spent the better part of a workday reading retro-focused wrestling websites because I wanted to get a better sense of the history of the sport.

"But this is something else," said Gerald. "Seriously, why do you care?"

"I don't know…" I said.

"Not good enough," said Gerald.

"I mean, part of it was just that I kind of wanted to find out what had happened," I said. "And then there's Morgan, who *really* seems to want to know who Brent was, and…"

"And you're trying to ID your dead roommate so you can jump his former co-worker?" asked Gerald. "Classy. Were you saying something else?"

There was something else. If I were to kick the bucket, would anyone I hung out with know whom to tell? Like Brent, I did all of my calling with my cell phone, and if that got munched, nobody would know who I talked to. My work emergency contacts had probably been deleted when I was let go. My parents had briefly glimpsed Jenn and Thomas when they'd come around to visit earlier in the year, but they hadn't swapped phone numbers or anything. I didn't know Brent that well, but I wouldn't want *my* parents to find out that I'd been cremated two years after the fact. It didn't seem right to leave Brent that way, either.

"Well…" I said. "I kind of think it's the right thing to do. If I don't do this, who will? I mean, what if his parents back in Boston are worried about him?"

"Boston, huh?" he said.

"Yep," I said. "He was from Boston."

"Spotend Alley," said Gerald. "That's near Grant."

"It's in Chinatown?"

"Yep. I remember it because it was one of the few alleys that *wasn't* on the 'Alleys of Chinatown' tour I took a few years back. We walked by it, but the guide just mentioned it in passing and walked us right over to Waverly to check out the old dude who plays the violin and will give you a bad haircut for five bucks. It stuck with me, and I remember looking it up…"

He paused and dug into his backpack, coming up with a battered notebook. "I brought an old notebook before that tour because I wanted to mine it for a scavenger hunt that I planned …I think this is the one."

Gerald flipped through the pages, muttering to himself and nibbling on a brownie.

"Here we go," he said. "I have written down 'Spotend Alley – headquarters of Chinese Fraternal organization. Organized to take down PRC.'"

"PRC?"

"The People's Republic of China," he said.

"So what does this mean about Brent?"

Gerald shrugged. "How should I know? Was he mixed up in some kind of weird bring-China-back-to-democracy movement?"

"Not that I know of," I said. "We never talked politics."

The only person in my house who ever talked politics was Thomas. He wasn't quite a Republican, but lots of people in his job were, and after a long day at the office, he usually needed some deprogramming. One time he was reading *1000 Books To Read Before You Die* while we were watching a news report about another right-wing-politician-with-young-boy scandal, and I cracked that I should write a book called *100 Closeted Republicans to Have Gay Sex With Before You Die*, and Thomas didn't get the joke. But Brent…no. The only time I heard him say anything remotely political was after he'd been delayed for an hour on a late-night MUNI train and had raged on and on about how whoever ran public transportation in San Francisco should be recalled, skinned, and shot.

But everybody said stuff like that.

"He wasn't a really political guy," I said.

"What was he into?"

"I really don't know," I said. "Baseball. His job. eBay, apparently."

Gerald folded up his notebook and put it back in his backpack, then took his last sip of coffee.

"Kind of weak, man," he said. "You live with a guy for four months and you can't even say one thing about him other than that he may not have really been into politics? I think that says something about you."

"Me? What about everyone else?"

"Who?"

"Um…my roommates?" I said. "None of them are here asking about something that might be able to track down who this guy was."

"Do you have anything else to do?" asked Gerald.

Good point.

"What matters is that I'm here now, and I'm trying to do the right thing," I said.

Gerald laughed and took off his hat, running his fingers through curly black hair. "You sound like one of those 'don't commit suicide' videos they made us watch in third grade," he said. "'Trying to do the right thing' is something mayoral candidates say after they've been caught with a glass pipe, three rocks, and a transvestite hooker. You may be doing something approaching the right thing, but you're not *trying* to do it. You're kind of stumbling around, like a Plinko chip that happens to hit the big money. If you find out anything about this guy, the finding-out part certainly won't be your fault."

"I appreciate your confidence," I said. "Really."

He shrugged. "I tell it like it is sometimes. You really ought to bring Jenn along when you do this."

"Why…so you can hit on her?"

Gerald laughed hard. "No," he said. "She doesn't seem to be into stoners. I think that she tempers you a bit."

"Hm," I said.

"Be careful around Spotend," he said. "It gave me an odd vibe."

"Where is it?" I asked.

He ruffled through his notebook. "Weird," he said. "I don't have that written down. I think it's one of those alleys that doesn't have a sign and isn't on a map. Maybe it's off Kearny? I'm not sure. You might have to ask someone, but…"

"But what?"

"It's that weird vibe thing," he said. "It's not that democracy thing, it's that our guide rushed on by. Tour guides don't just do that. I'd just be careful who you ask."

I walked back home, feeling that caffeine tingling in my spine and head. Thomas was working at home when I got there, sitting shirtless in his boxers, madly clicking his mouse and typing a few keys, then doing it again.

"Alex," he said as I walked past his room. "Check this out."

"What's up?"

He pointed at his computer screen; he was fooling around on eBay, and he'd come up on a page that said *Gallstones.*

"Gallstones?"

"Gallstones," he said. "Some guy passed his gallstones, and now he's eBaying them. I'm bidding."

"Why?"

He shrugged, then up-clicked his bid. "Why not? I don't know anyone else with a set of gallstones in his room."

I looked around his room. His bed was the slept-in equivalent of the post-battle Somme. Somehow, his sheets had gone sideways, and his mid-weight blanket was completely on the floor. Both pillows were smushed together, as if they had been copulating during the night. All of the posters on his wall were free trade-show booth decorations from large corporations, except for one real art piece – a Klimt print that he'd found on Craigslist and purchased at a steep discount from a guy who was leaving the country for undisclosed reasons, fast.

"Where would you put them?"

"In a fish tank. What do you think?"

"I think it's a terrible idea." That comment was from Shawna, standing in the doorway wearing men's boxers and a T-shirt. Something didn't compute here. I was the guy without a job, and two of my employed housemates were lounging around in the house, wearing underwear.

"Aw, come on," said Thomas. "They're neat. Look, they're kind of hot pink. Or fuchsia."

"Fuchsia?" Shawna walked over to the desk, nudged me out of the way, and leaned over. She smelled sweaty, as if she'd just done one of her harder yoga routines. "That's kind of gay."

Thomas grinned at her. "I can use a word like 'fuchsia' without fearing for my heterosexuality."

She arched her eyebrows at him. "Why would you fear for that? Feeling like a little less of a man these days?"

"I don't know," he said. "Should I?"

She rested her hand on his shoulder. "I think all of you males in this house are big giant amazing men, you know? Much more manly than all of the guys in my contact improv class; I think some of them take the class just so they can run their hands all over the girls. They'd be too scared to make a real-life move."

"Run their hands?" asked Thomas.

"Yeah, it's kind of like being back in junior high when you'd be making out with someone and they'd put their hands under your shirt but over your bra and you'd be thinking 'come *on*, man just go ahead and slip them under there,' but they'd never do that. It was awful."

"And the guys would end up with blue balls," I said. "It goes both ways."

"Whatever," she said. "I'll trade your seventh-grade blue balls for pregnancy, hormone swings, and societal pressure to lose ten pounds."

"Don't," said Thomas. "Lose ten pounds, I mean."

"What business is it of yours?" I said.

"Shut up, Alex, he's being sweet," said Shawna. She punched Thomas on the arm, then flounced out of the room. I watched her go; you could see the little lines of her calf muscles flexing as she walked down the hall.

"What was *that* all about?" I said.

Thomas shrugged. "Hey, I just won the gallstones!"

"Don't they have a whole 'not-selling-body-parts' thing going on?"

"I guess they don't care if they're your own parts. If I got into the business of selling other people's gallstones, it might cause some problems."

"Right," I said. "I'll now continue on to my room, where I was going before this conversation started, and I'm going to attempt to forget that it ever happened, because the idea of having someone else's gallstones in the house is a little weird."

My room was kind of a mess. Copies of free weeklies and *the Onion* had taken over most of the sitting space on the love seat I kept in the far right corner, and the floor was littered with bus transfers, ATM receipts, and paystubs. My hamper was surrounded by clothes, because I never bothered to walk over to the corner to actually put them in. I shot them, basketball style, and my jumper sucks. My *London Calling* poster had a drooping top-right corner, and some of the boxes that I kept under my bed were sitting on my nightstand.

So I straightened and, in doing so, ended up going through the boxes. I don't know why I kept them around – it's not like I'm really emotionally invested in Christmas cards from 1997, postcards friends have sent to me from all over the world, and high school yearbooks. I swept some of the papers off of the loveseat into a plastic bag for recycling and paged through the yearbooks. Geez. Nine years since high school. One of the photos was of me and a couple of friends milling around in the quad, looking like we're having a serious conversation. I remember the day pretty well; we had been standing around munching on crackers and kind of joshing each other, and the photographer had come up and asked us for a yearbooky pose. So we'd started emoting; in the photo, Nick is pointing at me, I'm holding both hands over my chest in a *what, me?* gesture, and Kevin and Dustin are standing across from each other, arms locked on shoulders in a perfect imitation of a slow dance or the conversation you have when you tell your best friend that your girlfriend might be pregnant.

One of my junior high history teachers had been list-obsessed; instead of writing essays or doing multiple-choice exams, he'd force us to write endless lists. Ten Reasons Why The South Seceded. The Six Most Important Battles of the Revolutionary War. Five Landmark Events in Reconstruction. Eight Diseases Imported to America by Europeans. Stuff like that. I didn't remember much from the class, except that it stuck in my head that lists were a good way to get things done. I took a record store flier that had come in the previous week's *Guardian* and started to scratch out a list on the back:

Things I know about Brent.

1) *Not tall. Five foot six.*
2) *Black hair. Curly, thinning a bit*
3) *In good shape. Went running sometimes, went to the gym (he said)*
4) *From Somerville, near Boston*
5) *Said he was twenty-six.*
6) *Worked at some kind of firm, doing not exactly sure what (records shredded. Great)*
7) *Ate spaghetti, even more than anybody else I know. Usually with marinara sauce (note to self — there's still half a bottle of his Newman's Own in the fridge. Do something about it)*
8) *Something to do with the Lucky Dragon Duck, which is probably some sort of Chinese thing.*
9) *Morgan knows something about him. Or wants to know something.*
10) *Somebody else wants to see me at a possibly-sketchy Chinatown alley to maybe talk about him.*

That was the sum-total of what I had been able to accomplish in several days of not much work. Lots of "maybes" and missing information. Sam Spade I was not. I wasn't even Inspector Gadget. I went to sleep, unhappy.

"Hi." It was Jenn, home from work early. She was dressed in a summer work outfit – a slim black tank-top/light jacket combo with a skirt and knee-high black boots. With heels. She probably stood almost as tall as me with those heels.

"It's a party here today," I said. "What brings you home?"

She stalked into my room and sat down on the bed, pausing to smooth out some of the covers. "When I rode the bus in to work today I knew it was going to suck. The driver was super-surly, and he made me take my pass out of my purse and show it to him because he said the laminated pocket was too reflective, and people had been getting away with fake passes that way. Then I was sitting next to a homeless guy who proceeded to pee in his own pants while he was sitting there, then stumbled off the bus, leaving me to make my way past his seat without getting any of his pee on my clothes. Then I got to work and my computer was all messed up, which meant that I had to deal with our sadistic IT staff, which is one guy, and he thinks I'm hot, so he takes forever to fix my computer, all while staring at my chest. It's really hard to take something apart while staring at *these,* so he nearly electrocuted himself. By the time he was done, I had to go to a meeting with my boss where I learned that she'd just read *Who Moved My Cheese?* and was getting ready to implement those management principles at EDC. I was sitting in the lunch room eating the fruit salad I made yesterday, almost ready to start on the real part of my lunch – the leftover pad thai from last night, and *it* happened."

"More pregnancy stuff?"

She shuddered, and buried her face in her hands. "They were sitting in the lunch room, chowing down on giant pastrami sandwiches, the really big ones that are smothered in mustard and coleslaw and God knows what else, talking about whether or not they were going to save their placentas or *eat them.* And then they started to discuss placenta flavoring, as if there was some sort of thing they could add to it to make it taste better. Someone actually uttered the phrase 'lemon-thyme placenta.'"

"It could have been worse," I said. "They could have said 'tarragon-curry tempeh with stir-fried umbilical cord.'"

"Good point," she said. "I need to get a new job." She walked back across the hall.

I followed her the five feet into her room. She was sitting on the futon that she used as a bed, pulling on her right boot, which was partially unzipped down the back. Her face was turning red with the effort, and I could see the muscles on the back of her arms quivering.

"Want some help?"

She shook her head and pulled some more, turning her face the color of a ripe tomato. After a few seconds, her hands slipped off, and she slumped backwards.

"Fine," she said. "I give up. Can you take them off for me? Apparently even that little bit of physical coordination is too much for Jenn Saunders today." She spread her hands out to the sides, untucking her top from her skirt.

"Hang on," I said. I knelt down, held the top of her boot with my right hand, and pulled the zipper down an extra two inches. One hard yank, and the boot came off. Ten seconds later, Jenn was wiggling her toes and breathing happily.

"Thanks," she said.

"You're welcome."

"No, seriously," she sat up and shook her hair out of the severe ponytail she wore it in while working. "I'm sorry I exploded all over you just now...I just needed to vent."

"Not a problem," I said. "I still owe you."

She leaned forward with a saucy grin. "Yeah, you do," she said.

Yep, I owed Jenn big time. About two months after I'd moved into the house, an old friend of mine from college had come down to visit, and we'd gone out drinking on a Friday night. Gerald had joined us, and in five hours, we hit about seven bars telling fantastic stories, pounding down more shots, and generally making asses of ourselves. By the time we got home, I was having a hard time recognizing my feet as my own, and we tried my keys in four different doors before we got to my place.

I had passed out, and I had a very fuzzy recollection of waking up in the morning, nearly tripping over my friend, and going to the bathroom. I awoke to blazing sunshine. In Jenn's futon. She was sleeping with her head to my feet. I panicked and sprinted downstairs to the couch in the living room. My entire existence flashed before my eyes – what had happened? How had I ended up in Jenn's bed? Was the house going to kick me out instantly? I huddled in a miserable, head-pounding hungover state for an hour, until the stairs thudded and Jenn came down, dressed in sweats and running shoes, which were quite becoming.

"Alex," she said. "I'm going to class. But we'll talk."

I had spent the whole day in agony, not eating or drinking enough water, battling fear and a hangover that would have felled a quartet of Russian generals. When Jenn showed up at five in the afternoon, I was sitting on the stoop waiting for her, ripping the leaves off of the branches of any plant I could reach, thinking about how much it would cost me to rent a hotel room for a couple of weeks while I looked for a new place.

"So," she said, sitting down next to me. "I don't really want to talk about how it is that you came into my room last night reeking of booze, tripped, fell into my bed, and went right to sleep with your feet in my face. I also don't want to talk about how you were breathing so heavily I thought you were going to throw up on me, and so I had trouble sleeping. Nor do I want to talk about the practice GRE I just tanked because I didn't sleep more than two hours last night."

"I'm…" I said.

"Stop," she said. "Here's the deal. One: for the next twelve months, every time that the two of us are at a bar, and I want a drink, you buy it. Two: If you do not fail at point one, I will not tell Thomas or Shawna about this little mishap. OK?"

I breathed out. "OK."

"The subject is closed. By the way, have you showered today? You smell a little funky."

And that was why I owed Jenn.

Chapter 8

My Tuesday day-planner, if I'd had one, would have been a big mass of white space. No job interviews, appointments, meetings, last-minute consultations, operations, road trips, coffee klatches, brunch soirées, lunch fetes, dinner parties, get-togethers, charity balls, fund-raisers, concerts, gatherings, shindigs, time-consuming chores, errands to run, lawn socials, park picnics, barbecues, or clambakes. In other words, it was a perfect day to go down to Chinatown and check out Spotend Alley for myself.

After rising, cooking myself a bowl of Frosted Flakes with buttered-and-honeyed English muffins, I got dressed and played Find The Cell Phone. As usual, I had forgotten to hook it up to the charger that I kept plugged into the wall next to my bed, with the cord on the nightstand. By far the most logical place to put a phone, but in my half-drunk state the previous night, I had probably put it somewhere creative.

On the bookcase, next to my keys? Nope.

Hiding away behind my laptop, which I had left open all night? Uh-uh.

Tangled up in my comforter, which I'd tossed on the floor after getting out of bed? No dice. Eventually, after picking up papers, completely stripping and making my bed, recycling most of the mail I'd had piled on top of the stereo, and digging all of the clothes out of my hamper, I found it lying in the drawer of my nightstand. I plugged it in while listening to the two voicemails that had appeared during the evening.

Voicemail One was from Gerald, wondering if I'd be around for a drink or two at a downtown bar at about five that day.

Voicemail two was from Morgan, asking me to please meet her for a drink at seven that evening at the Hemlock in the Tenderloin.

I clicked the phone closed and thought for a second or two, then sent them both a text message:

Can't make it. Sorry. Busy.

Morgan would wonder about that one, I was pretty sure.

Chinatown was colorless, washed-out. Today the fog had stayed in, turning the downtown skyscrapers into fading ghosts, their upper floors almost translucent as they blended in with the mist. I was wearing a fleece and a rain jacket, and I cinched up the hood as I walked under the arch on Stockton Street. The old man at the front of the kitsch shop was swathed in a giant down trenchcoat, and he barely waved at the people who walked by.

I walked as quickly as I could, weaving through the crowds of tiny Chinese women in bulky overcoats and nearly running over a shivering tourist couple as they pawed through low-priced sweatshirts and ski caps. They both wore sandals; his pale toes had turned a light blue under the nails.

"Bloody California," he said as I walked by. "Couldn't go to bloody Blackpool in the summer like normal, we had to come to bloody San Francisco and freeze our bums off for five hundred quid extra...."

Everyone knows Mark Twain wrote that "the coldest winter I ever spent was the summer I lived in San Francisco." It's a great phrase, but he didn't write it. Nobody knows who coined that particular saying, but it's pretty accurate. I'm always amazed at the number of people who come into town in July and August clad only in American flag T-shirts and too-short shorts. The guidebooks warn about the fog; half of the pubs in town have "fog" in their names, and people still come here convinced that San Francisco is the California they see in *Baywatch,* awash in beach volleyball, barbecues, and the occasional cardio-pulmonary resuscitation session.

It doesn't work that way here. When the fog is in hard, there is a hush over the city, people speak in soft tones, and the whole place feels like the set for a Bogart movie. As I walked up Stockton Street, I kept expecting to see a shady, trenchcoat-clad character shuffle his way out of an alley, make a hard-to-see transaction with a mysterious black-jacketed man, and disappear into the gloom down towards the bay.

I walked around for half an hour, just wandering. I did not see my short, Hitchcock-loving friend and didn't find Spotend Alley, so I walked down Waverly for a third time, intending to give up and go home. The street was slightly different when I walked down it for the third time of the day. Before, right across the street from a brick-and-door façade that advertised *live poultry fresh killed* in faded raised red letters, the door next to the barber pole had been closed. The door was now open, and a portly Chinese gentleman was sitting on the stoop, scratching out unholy melodies on a battered violin. A sign in the window said *Haircuts $5. Cash only.*

A haircut wasn't what I'd come to Chinatown for, but I sort of needed one, and I couldn't go home without *something*. So I walked up to the old man and looked at him while he played. After a minute or two of really repulsive music (I don't know much about classical, but I know bad), he glanced up at me and broke into a three-toothed grin.

"Haircut?" he said.

"Yes, please," I said.

He gestured with one hand towards the interior of his shop, and I walked in ahead of him. The place was small. Just one barber chair, two waiting chairs, a clouded, cracked mirror, and one set of plugs for the clippers. The cracked mirror was lined with Chinese-written stickers, and several broken combs were scattered on the floor.

"What kind cut?" he asked.

"Um…just a haircut," I said.

"Shave?" he asked.

"Sure," I said. "How much?"

"Shave two dollars," he said. "Seven for both,"

"Deal," I said.

"Haircut first," he said, and got to work.

He started to bustle around the shop, dipping combs and scissors into a phial of blue liquid on his counter, and rummaging into his drawers until he came up with a satisfactory pair of clippers. They started buzzing as he plugged them in, and he snapped a blending comb into place and went to work.

I like haircuts. I like it when they use the little mister to dampen my hair, then snip it away, bit by bit. I like the tickling sensation as the razor goes past my ear. I like the cool feeling when the barber gets rid of the little fuzzy tufts that grow on my neckline. I even like it when they trim my sideburns, even though I'll just shave the suckers off when I get home. I'd get my hair cut every four weeks if I could afford it, or if I wasn't so lazy.

Not this time. The barber plugged in his clippers and gave a Nicholson-in-*The Shining* cackle. I wanted to get up from my seat right then, but he clamped a hand down on my shoulder and started in on the right side of my head. I don't know where the guy had managed to purchase a pair of *blunt* clippers. It felt like he was trying to yank out my hair with a fork.

"Ow," I said.

"Not hurt," he said. "Clippers can't cut you."

I kept my mouth shut; if he could cause this kind of discomfort with a pair of safety clippers, God knows what he could have done with a pair of scissors. He clipped away for a couple of minutes, running the buzzing machine over my head in a random pattern. The mirror was facing right at me, but it was clouded to the point of uselessness right where my head was; I looked like one of those guys on reality TV who hasn't signed one of the release waivers.

The buzzing stopped.

"You want layer?"

"Um...I don't think so." The last time I'd had a layer-type cut, I'd been a sixteen-year old kid with one of those two-tone long-on-the-top bowl cuts that had been popular at the time.

"How much from top?"

"An inch, maybe?"

"One inch, OK." He drew a pair of scissors from the cylinder filled with blue liquid, snipped them experimentally a couple of times, then grabbed a fistful of hair at the top of my head and yanked up. I clenched my teeth and made a dying-frog sound. He snipped and snapped away; I could see two and three-inch clumps of brown hair landing on my shoulders. Great. The guy was turning me into a Marine.

"All done," he said, a minute later. "Look." He turned the swivel chair slightly, letting me look into the blur in the mirror where my head should have been. "Good, OK?"

"I can't quite see..." I said, leaning forward to get up.

"No, not get up yet," he said. "Keep towel, time for shave."

"I don't know if I need a..."

"Sit, sit, no talk," he said. "Talk I might cut you."

My mouth snapped shut.

The old man walked over to a decrepit exposed-copper sink on the far side of the wall and cranked the handled to the left of the faucet. After a few seconds, the sink started to emit a banshee's moan, and steam began to rise from the basin. He took a yellow towel, soaked it in the water, wrung it out, then came over and lay the towel over my face. The towel smelled like a retirement home full of dogs that have just come in out of the rain. I breathed through my mouth.

The towel came off, and the barber started to lather me up with what felt like a steel-wool brush. I jerked my head to the side, and he grabbed the top of my head again and held me still while he finished sanding my face. He kept his hand on the top of my head as he reached over and pulled out a safety razor. I breathed easier; if he'd had a full-bladed throatcutter job I probably would have bolted, shaving-cream face and all.

He scraped, I winced, and about two and a half minutes later he was wiping off the remains of the shaving cream from my face with the same damp towel.

"There," he said. "Shave. Cut. Seven dollar."

I dug into my walled and came up with a five and three ones. "Here," I said.

"Ah, tip," he said, grinning. "Thank you."

"You're welcome," I said. "There's one thing…"

He raised his eyebrows; the lines on his forehead were labyrinthine.

"Do you know Spotend Alley?"

His eyebrows darted downwards, his frown hid his eyes. He shook his head.

"No." He turned around and picked up his violin and the bow. "Nobody smart asks where Spotend Alley is." His accent was mellower, less Chinese. "And if they did know things, they would not tell you."

"What, are the Tongs going to swoop down and take me away from right off of Grant Street?"

"Kearny," he said. "Just north of Jackson."

He looked hard into my eyes, then shrugged and shouldered his violin.

"Go away," he said. "Send friends for haircuts and music. Something happen to you, then I still get the business. Thanks for big tip." He started to saw away at his violin, producing what might have been Bach's Second Brandenburg Concerto, if Bach had been deaf, armless, and insane.

Kearny is down the hill at the Easternmost border of Chinatown, a buffer zone between the ethnic burg and the financial district. I walked down, hugging myself against the wind, heading north on Kearny, passing by the Lucky Sandwich Shop, Naan N Curry, Electronics Cheapest!, and the Happy Bar ("Where Good Friends and Girls Meet.") Were they implying that girls couldn't be good friends? Or that you had to be a good friend to meet a girl? An alley branched off of the street just north of the intersection with Pacific. It was unsigned and was definitely more of a space than an alley. The entrance was partially blocked with several wooden pallet-crates. I wedged myself in around them, accidentally rubbing my right hand against one of the crates, driving a splinter right into the top of my second knuckle.

The alley cleared up after I made my way around the crates. It was about five feet wide, and the buildings on either side were tall enough to block out the sun. Someone had strung laundry along most of the metal of one of the fire escapes. The underwear flapped softly in the breeze.

About thirty feet along, the alley ended at a small door with flaking brown paint, a shade under six feet high. Had it been open, I could have walked through it and just missed scraping the top of my head. I tried the knob; no dice. A black mailbox hung on the wall next to the door; it was the kind of mailbox you'd expect to see on a townhouse in an old neighborhood of an East Coast city; square, with a metal hinged top and a fleur-de-lis on the front.

I opened the box and looked at the mail inside. Nothing particularly interesting; an offer for an American Express Gold business card, a flier from Sparhawk of the Green Party on why he should be both Supervisor and member of the School Board at the same time, and a business letter from something called the Friends of the Republic of China, West Coast Brotherhood Empowerment Division, addressed to David Jones care of the Lucky Dragon Duck. I put back the flier and the offer and looked at the envelope– the outside reminded me of the "thanks for applying" letters you get from colleges that don't want you. I was about to open it, when I heard footsteps on the other side of the little door. I put the letter in my bag and I walked back out of the alley as quickly as I could, not sure if this latest waste of time was more or less of a waste of time than everything else I was doing.

An e-mail was waiting for me when I got home.

From: GaryScheff@beckettscards.com
To: Alex Baker
Alex,

Sure, I remember that sale. It wasn't as big of a deal as I think you think it is. Your pal managed to find two dozen Yaz rookie cards that were slightly flawed. Not cosmetic flaws from use or from sitting in a drawer, but the kind of flaw that a stamp collector looks for. I wrote the story about the cards - the deal was that the card had Yaz batting right-handed. He was a lefty. I think he sold them for around a thousand bucks apiece. Quite a haul for a lucky find. He sold them to a shop in Providence. We wrote a couple paragraphs about it in our "notable sales" column. I did the interview with him, but it was a really short deal. I just confirmed that the sale had gone down, and he gave me the link to the archived item. It's http://ebay.com…

The address continued. I made a mental note to follow up on it at some point the next day; it was time to head out for the evening's mental game. Pub trivia on Tuesday nights at the Bitter End was a house tradition in the sense that we made it when we could. What with Brent dying and trying to find a new housemate, we hadn't gone in a couple of weeks, so Jenn had sent out an e-mail to everyone requiring our attendance that night.

Getting to the bar from where we were was kind of a pain; back when I was working downtown I'd just work – well, stay in the office - late and grab the Geary Street bus. From our place, I had to take a streetcar out to Ninth Avenue and then a bus across the park. It wouldn't have been a big deal, except for the guy who parked his car on the streetcar tracks while he ran inside the Yellow Submarine Sub Shop to get a sandwich. When I got off the train, I got a great view of the #44 bus going the other way, and the next bus was a thirty minute wait. When it dropped me off at 6th and Clement Street, my whole journey had taken over an hour. For three miles. I should have walked it.

The Bitter End is an Irish bar in an Asian sea, a neighborhood that used to be Russian, Ukrainian and Gaelic but had become mostly Chinese over the years. The streets were packed to the gills with late shoppers as I walked down Clement, looking to kill a little bit of time before seven o'clock.

"Look out!" shouted an old man. I jumped to the side as he hopped out of a truck and trundled past me, a skinned pig draped over his shoulders. The truck was labeled in Chinese characters and the English words *Meat Co.* He carried the pig into a butcher shop, and I followed. It was a madhouse of people, and the guys behind the counter were chopping, grinding, and gutting with a ruthless efficiency, their white coats and aprons spattered with blood and fish guts. I stayed at the butcher shop for about fifteen minutes, finally leaving when an ancient woman twisted the neck off of a chick before she left, leaving the head on the floor for everyone to step on.

Two bookstores and one iced coffee later, I wandered into the Bitter End. The place was generic *faux*-Irish, complete with black-and-white pictures of James Joyce on the walls and a never-ending cast of thick-accented bartenders who managed to flout the immigration laws much more easily than people who were unlucky enough to be born south of the border instead of across the ocean. It wasn't crowded, and I found Thomas quickly enough. He looked every inch the off-duty banker – neatly pressed shirt with the top two collar buttons undone, untucked from his slacks. He was poring through a copy of *Street and Smith's* when I sat down.

"What's with the magazine?" I said.

"It's for fantasy," he said. "And I've got this idea about card values relating to the trade value, so I wanted to bone up before we hit the trade deadline. What's with your hair?"

"Don't ask. Who's coming?" I asked.

"Everyone," he said. "Even Shawna."

"Cool," I said. She was always a wildcard for trivia. She was as dependable as she was for anything else. In other words, not much.

"Beer?" he asked.

"Newcastle," I said.

"OK," he said.

As he got up, a hand pushed on his shoulder, sitting him back down. She was dressed in jeans and a white blouse, with brown hair tied up tightly underneath a scally cap.

"Drinks, lads?" she said. Her brogue was strong.

"Newcastle, and a Sapphire and tonic."

"Guinness."

"You got it."

Jenn showed up about ten minutes later, settling into the seat I'd saved for her next to me and dumping her oversized gym bag under the chair. Her hair was wet, and the circles under her `eyes were darker than usual, making her usually calm face look overly thin and raccoonish. The waitress showed up with our drinks and ice waters on the side. ,

"Thanks for thinking of me," Jenn said, knocking back a quarter of her gin and tonic, then slamming down an entire water. "Long day."

"Looks like it," said Thomas.

"You have no idea," she said. "What's with your hair? It looks like you went to a Marine barber with advanced Parkinson's."

"You don't want to know," I said.

We all ordered fish and chips. Shawna showed up right after the waitress left the table, and Thomas sprinted after her to add another fish/chips and a salad. She smiled up at him as he talked with her, and she put her hand on his shoulder before he walked back to the table.

"What was that all about?" asked Shawna.

"Not much," he said. "I put in our orders, and she asked where I was from."

"You did it again, didn't you?" I said.

Thomas had a habit of putting on a fake English accent whenever he was talking with someone from Europe. It drove the rest of us nuts – he was from southwest Chicago – but he didn't see anything weird about it.

"What?" he said.

"The accent thing," I said.

"I don't do an accent," he said.

We all stared at him.

"Livid," he said. "You guys make me livid."

"Alex, what happened to you?" asked Shawna.

I was about to answer, but the microphone crackled, and the host came out. He was a big guy with a thin beard and thinner hair on top, extraordinarily large around the middle, always dressed in an XXL black T-shirt, black jeans, and very white running shoes.

"All riiiight," he said. "Welcome to the Bitter End's world famous Trivia Night. If you haven't done this before, it's simple. You all have answer sheets and pencils, and there are six rounds, ten questions per round. I'll read the questions, you write down the answers. Don't cheat – that means no Blackberries, Palms, or cell phone calls to your friends. Oh, and name your team – the best team name wins a special prize."

The mike crackled again, and the Pogues started to blare over the PA. We huddled up and started scratching out team names, throwing out the cheesy, the too-vulgar, and the obvious, before coming up with Belle's Balls and Sebastian's Discs.

"That won't win us anything," said Thomas.

"Yes it will," I said.

"Nobody knows Belle & Sebastian," he said.

"People do who own music that has lyrics," I said. "The world doesn't revolve around Paul Oakenfold, you know; maybe it's time to evolve your musical taste a bit."

"What's good is good," he said.

I snorted. "Right. Someday you have to explain the logic that gives you a collection that's mostly on tape and doesn't include any songs that don't have an organ solo."

"I like the organ solos," he said.

"Then you should go to church," I said. "Lots of organs there."

"Enough of that, children," said Jenn. "We're about to start. Who's the scribe?"

"You do the writing," said Thomas. "Nobody will be able to read our scribbles."

The questions at the Bitter End were a paean to the late-Generation X set – rounds always included a history segment, a television segment, and a music round where they blasted thirty seconds of a song and you had to identify it. The second-to-last round was always a sheet with smudged photocopied photos of celebrities that you had to identify, and the last round was a difficult grab bag.

What song did Pink Floyd name after their drug-addled original frontman, Syd Barrett?

"Another Brick in the Wall."

"No, idiot. That one came *well* after Barrett quit the band."

"Ask Thomas. Floyd's a stoner band."

"I was into jam bands in college, not stoner bands."

"What's the difference?"

"Jam bands are all about the atmosphere and the concert. Stoner bands are for college students to listen to while they smoke pot order pizza while they're forgetting about their final exams."

"I think it was a Syd song."

"Jenn? You know this?"

"I *do* know a few things about music. More than you, probably."

"What do you mean by that?"

"I mean, if it wasn't an English band who flamed out in the early '80s, they might as well not exist to you."

"That was cruel."

"It's 'Shine on You Crazy Diamond'," said Jenn.

"How do you know that?"

"My dad had the album," she said.

What is the world's fastest mammal? That is, with no mechanical assistance?

"Deer. I nearly hit one of those with my mom's car when I was growing up."

"I say rabbits. When I was in New Zealand…"

"Gee, Thomas, did you get to go to New Zealand last year? I've never heard that before."

"Shut up. In New Zealand they want you to run over rabbits because they're invasive, not native. I tried to run one over, and that little sucker was *fast*. I must have been going thirty miles an hour."

"You guys are all screwed. It's a cheetah. They had it on the Discovery Channel."

"I think we yield to the guy with no job. Cheetah it is."

Approximately one hundred years ago, San Francisco was nearly leveled by an earthquake and fire. What was the month and day of that event?

"Shit, that's hard."

"How can it be that hard? Everyone here knows that."

"*I* don't know it."

"Does anyone here know it?"

"April 18th," I said. "Early in the morning."

"Why do you know that?" asked Jenn.

"I like to read history books," I said.

This auteur became famous for making his first film for a pittance, and setting it on top of a Quick Mart and video store that shared the same building. Who is he?

"God, that's easy. Kevin Smith."

"Kevin Smith is *not* an auteur."

"Who cares? We know the answer to the question."

"Yeah, but it's the principle of the thing."

"Alex, you don't have any principles."

"That's not true."

"Right, I forgot one. One of your principles is that when I'm thirsty, you should flag down the waitress and get me another beer."

"I have to pay for your beers. Why do I have to flag down the waitress?"

"Why do you have to pay for her beers?"

"I can't really tell you."

"Is it some kind of CIA thing?"

"No. It's an Alex-and-Jenn thing."

"Is that like a Thomas-and-Shawna thing? I'm feeling left out."

"What does *that* mean?"

"Nothing, really."

Songs appearing on the music round: "I've got You Babe," by Sonny and Cher, "Little Bit O' Soul," by the Music Explosion, "Don't Believe the Hype" by Public Enemy, "The Little Drummer Boy" by David Bowie and Bing Crosby (quite possibly the worst song ever recorded). The trivia meister was cackling with glee as he played that last one, and the bar resounded with shouts of "Turn it off!" and "Please, turn it the fuck off!" He didn't, and we were treated to nearly three minutes of "pa-rum-pum-pum-pum" squealed to the most screeching organ line ever devised in the early '80s. He ended by going with "Opposites Attract" by Paula Abdul, and "Private Eyes" by Hall and Oates. That last one had the entire bar singing along, out of key, with percussion provided by the pounding of beer glasses. We got every one of those right.

Celebrity round, beer pitcher number five.

"Who the *fuck* is that?"

"Don't worry about that one."

"Seriously, that looks like the guy who played Doogie Howser halfway through a botched sex change operation."

"OK, we can totally get some of these. That's Reese Witherspoon, that's Cate Blanchett…"

"No it's not, it's Gwyneth Paltrow."

"Are you sure?"

"They're the same fucking person."

"Dude, it's Gwyneth."

"No, it's Cate. Cate was in *Lord of the Rings*. This chick was not in *Lord of the Rings*."

"We get *Us Weekly* in my office. I know."

"In the office? Who subscribes?"

"Our receptionist. She's from Jersey."

"Hey, *I'm* from Jersey."

"It's OK, Jenn. You've shed most of the Jerseyness."

"Remember when I said that you were aggravating?"

"I think you said 'exasperating.'"

"Whatever, you're both."

"So is it Cate or Gwyneth?"

"Put it to a vote."

"Cate."

"Cate."

"Gwyneth."

"Cate."

"Majority rules."

At one point or another during all of this, Thomas brought up the roommate situation and money, as in what were we going to do about the rent. Shawna had the smallest room, so she paid the least. Thomas had the biggest, so he paid the most. Jenn and I paid the same. Brent had paid a touch more. Shawna, as always, was worried about money. I didn't really care, and none of us wanted her to move out because she couldn't afford to. So, Thomas took out a napkin and worked out a formula whereby she would chip in an extra hundred bucks, the rest of us would absorb the extra at about $175 per person, and she'd do some extra cleaning.

"But Shawna doesn't know how to clean," said Jenn.

"I do!" she said. Her skin was an off-rose color and her eyes were glassy.

"I bet I have to remind you," Jenn said.

"I can't bet," Shawna said. "I don't have the money to do it."

"If I *don't* have remind you within three weeks," Jenn said, "I'll do your cleaning. If I do, you do my laundry while I'm at work on one of your days off."

"Done." They shook hands, filled beers, and clinked glasses.

We came in fourth place, behind a group of eleven University of San Francisco graduate students, a group of Genentech scientists, and two old guys with massive beards who looked like rejects from a ZZ Top cover band. Fourth is out of the money, but the old guys didn't want their small team award and gifted us their free two pitchers of beer.

The bar slowly emptied out. I was pleasantly soused; not so drunk that I'd have trouble walking out the door, but buzzed enough to make standing up an interesting experience. Thomas and Shawna were pretty wrecked - show-us-your-tits, New Orleans drunk.

"Paula fucking Abdul," said Thomas. "I remember waking up to that song when I was like six. 'Straight up now tell me do you want to love...'"

"Me forever!" yelled Shawna. "When I'm caught in a hit and run!"

Then together: "Da-da-dada-da!"

The giggled, collapsing into each other.

The waitress came by. Her black shirt had come untucked, and she had the weary look of someone who's got four more hours to go on her shift.

"You guys want any more, or..."

"We'll take the check," I said.

"Here you go," she said, taking a printed receipt out of the pocket on her mini-apron and dropping it on the table. "I'll get that whenever you'd like."

"Wait a second," I said. "Can I declare credit-card roulette?"

"What's that?" asked Jenn.

"It's easy," I said. "Who's in?"

"I am," Jenn said.

"I am," said Thomas.

"Out," said Shawna. "This sounds like macho guy bullshit."

"OK, cool," I said "You pay what you owe." I eyed the receipt. "Should be about thirty apiece."

"Not too bad," said Shawna, throwing in a twenty and a ten.

"We put the money in the middle," I said, "and we call over the waitress. Hey, can you come over here?"

The waitress walked back over to our table from the bar. "Can we use your hat?" I asked. She nodded. "Just put it on the table," I said. "So, each of you give me a credit card."

I produced a jet-black MasterCard that I had had since I was a freshman in college. Jenn handed over a United Airlines Miles Visa. Thomas dropped in an Amex.

"We ask our waitress…what's your name?"

"Vanessa." Her voice had the same Irish lilt, but she now sounded weary.

"We ask Vanessa here to draw each card out of the hat. The first several cards – in this case it's only one – are free and clear, out of the game. The second-to last gets the sixty bucks in the middle of the table. The last one pays the bill."

"What's this game called?" asked Vanessa.

"Credit card roulette," I said. "Best bar game ever."

The two tables next to us had started to show an interest in our game; the three guys were leaning over, listening.

Vanessa reached her hand into the cap, mixed it around, and pulled a card.

"Jennifer McLaren," she said.

She reached in again.

"Thomas Rockland."

"Yes!" shouted Thomas. He reached over and pulled over the sixty dollars that were lying in the center of the table.

"That leaves – Alex," she said.

"Fair enough," I said. "Run it."

I pounded the rest of my beer and poured another from our half-full pitcher.

"Shit," I said. "That's a hundred bucks."

"I wouldn't worry about it," said Thomas. "What goes around…" he paused and let out a tremendous Viking belch… "comes around."

"Easy for you to say," said Shawna. "Alex doesn't have a job. That's a lot of money."

Thomas snorted. "Three months of severance? I think he'll be OK."

"I'll probably not starve," I said.

I tuned them out, got up, and wandered to the back of the bar to try to find a bathroom. The bar wasn't quite as crowded as it had been at the height of the trivia contest, but I still had to throw a few elbows as I made my way through the clumps of people that surrounded the tables. I even caught a dirty look from a white-baseball-cap clone, but I just winked at him. Frat boys tend to get scared if you act gay, and this one was no exception; he whipped his head back around to his crew so fast his hat nearly came off of his head. What is it with people who love wearing the South Carolina hats that say "Cocks" anyway? And why would you wear it in San Francisco, unless you were advertising an upcoming trip out of the closet?

By the time these questions had finished running through my head - well, they weren't *running* so much as *reeling* - I was standing in the bathroom, waiting for one of the two urinals to free up. The Bitter End had recently stopped posting the sports pages above the urinals and had replaced them with ads framed in bulletproof plastic frames; originally, the ads had just been posters, but they got peed on by people who would rather read the box scores than be assaulted with ill-spelled pitches for male enhancement pills.

One guy finished up, shook, and walked right out the door. I took his place, shaking my head.

"That's annoying, isn't it?" asked the guy next to me, an utterly average-height/weight guy with goofy puffy blonde hair.

I'm not much on toilet conversation, not because I'm afraid that the guy next to me is going to try to check me out or that somehow by partaking in such conversation I'll lose my membership in the Guy Club, but because peeing, like other bodily functions, is something that's best kept to yourself.

On the other hand, I wasn't a rude person, so…

"Yeah," I said. "I hate it when people don't wash their hands. It's gross."

"Oh," said the guy. "No, dude. The advertising. It's bumming me out."

"Why?"

"Because it's lame. I'm sitting here with my junk in my hand, and the last thing I want to read about is that this guy here with the porno 'stache is going to save me money on my auto insurance."

"Oh, right," I said. "I guess that would be a bit…"

"You know what *would* be cool?"

Trapped. "What?"

"If they had, like, computer screens here, flat ones. And they were hooked up to eBay, and you could say what you were interested in buying, like, you could say 'baseball card' and it would pop up with some of the baseball cards that were on eBay, like, right then. Then you could see what was going on that you could buy on eBay."

Baseball cards. eBay. eBay. Baseball cards. Something was going on here, and the guy at the urinal next door was getting excited.

"…and then you could just put your thumb on the screen, and it would read your thumbprint and it would be connected to your credit card! And you'd buy something, like a ridiculous camera or a Barry Bonds card or even a *car*. You could start, like a business. You could fund your own business while taking a piss. Wouldn't that be the piss?"

"Sure," I said. Financing a business, though…it made me remember something.

It had been a terrible day at work, one of those days where a scheduled raise meeting had been preempted because one of the online games I'd been playing had somehow put a trojan horse onto my hard drive that had sent out e-mail to everyone in my department containing an audio file that said, in a Speak and Spell voice "Alex watches zebra porn on his computer now! Alex watches zebra porn on his computer now!" I'd been forced to go to IT with my hat in my hand and get a thirty minute lecture about accessing unapproved websites from a guy who clearly had his machine dialed into World of Warcraft and was using the old game-with-pause-screen-that-looks-like-spreadsheet dodge. What do IT guys need with spreadsheets?

When I got home, grumpy and hoping to blow off some tension, Brent had been sitting on the easy chair in the living room, sipping on a bottle of my Anchor Steam and clicking his laptop mouse button every few seconds. He had started talking right when I walked in.

"Hey," he had said when I walked in. "I'm drinking one of yours; I'll replace it, don't worry."

"Not a problem," I said. "Whatcha doing?"

He grinned. "eBay," he said. "Cards and business, my friend. Cards and business."

We sat, drank beer, and watched wrestling. Brent never moved the computer off of his lap. He must have been auctioning off baseball cards the whole time. After learning the Yaz connection, I'd thought the baseball cards were the business But what if they weren't? *Start a business,* the toilet guy said. Maybe Brent was funding more than the six-pack he'd bought for me the next day.

The toilet guy was still going on "…and then she was like 'it's Montreal, my friend, you can touch what you want,' and I was like 'whoa, they totally don't let you do that at home,' and then I put my hands on her tits, and they were fake, and I could feel the bags crinkling, you know? It was crazy; I'm never dealing with fake ones again. That shit's just not natural."

"Wow," I said. "That's something."

"Damn right," he said. "I speak Bibles full of truth."

He zipped himself up and walked over to the sink, muttering to himself. "Bibles full of truth. *Bibles.* Man, I gotta remember that line."

"The Gas n' Sip kid in *Say Anything* already beat you to it," I said softly. He didn't hear me, and left the bathroom still muttering. I realized that I had been standing at the urinal without urinating for several minutes, so I zipped myself up and went to the sink to wash my hands. The soap was that weird bubbly stuff that they have nowadays; I kind of miss the powdery scouring soap that we had in elementary school. It felt terrible on your hands, but at least you knew they were clean.

The bar had emptied out even more when I left the restroom; the tables were still full, but I no longer had to maze my way through the crowds. When I reached our table, the scene was similar to when I'd left.

"It's that fucking accent," said Jenn. "I hate it when you do that."

"I haven't done that in weeks," said Thomas.

"No, that's not true," she said. "You did it an hour ago. It's weird and it freaks me the fuck out," said Jenn. "You're from Illinois, not England. The only thing the two places have in common is that they both start with a vowel."

"Hey guys," I said.

"Can we change the subject?" asked Thomas.

"Let's just bail," I said. "Thomas will spring for a cab."

"Why me?" said Thomas.

"Because you won roulette," I said. "It's only fair."

Chapter 9

The tinny opening chords of "Should I Stay Or Should I Go" roused me from my dream. It had been a good one – I'd been building a racing scooter with Leslie Nielsen, Shelley the Waitress from *Twin Peaks,* and Brent. Brent and Shelley had been getting along fine, and he'd had his hand on the small of her back when the guitars started up. I hate being woken up by my phone, and it was worse now that I hadn't used an alarm clock in several days. My heart jumped up into my skull and rebounded back again, and I spasmed an arm out to grab the phone, knocking my half-full glass of water all over my nightstand in the process. Cursing, I picked the phone out of the growing puddle. It was 9:32 and my head hurt. I didn't recognize the number but I flipped my phone open anyway.

"Hello?" My throat was dry, and my voice sounded like rocks dropped on a slate floor.

"Is this Alex?" the voice was dry and quiet.

"Yes," I said.

"Oh, good. This is Donald Sherwood from the San Francisco City Medical Examiner's office. Is this a good time?"

Is there *ever* a good time to hear from the morgue? "Sure, no worse than any other."

"Well, we're calling because we're interested in knowing if you've had any luck in finding out who might be the next of kin for the body of the man here for whom you're listed as the informational contact."

I took a few seconds to sort through all of the words and figure out what he was asking me. Oh, right. Next of kin. Not something I knew.

"Um…not yet. I'm still trying to track them down."

"See, that's kind of a problem, because we are running a bit short on space here, especially with all of the people who catch hypothermia out in the park because of the fog and end up here. And it is not out of the question that in the next few days if the fog stays in, we might run into a situation where someone new coming in might need your man's space in our facilities. So it would be great if you could come on in and tell us who that next of kin is as soon as you possibly can so we can clear up space."

"What happens if I can't?"

Donald sighed loud enough to hurt my ear with the buzzing. "Well, then, we would take your friend's remains and catalog them, then we would do a near-complete heat elimination."

"What's a heat elimination?"

He sighed again. "We put the body in the incinerator."

"Oh. Wow. Um…can you call me before you do that?"

"We usually call the next of kin before we do that."

"Right, but I'm trying to *find* the next of kin."

"Yes, OK, all right, we can give you a call before we do that. I'll make a note in the file. I urge you to hurry, though, especially if the fog stays in the city like it is supposed to. You wouldn't believe what we've seen in here. Just yesterday a man came in who had been living down at the far end of the park near the windmill for nearly two years, living off of the scraps in one of the garbage cans from the soccer field. Apparently, people leave oranges and whole loaves of bread in there."

"Jesus, man," I said. "It's only been a couple of weeks."

He shrugged. I could hear it over the phone. "I'm just the messenger," he said. "We don't have the resources to keep people in cold storage for a long time, and we try to keep our space as open and flexible as we can, in case there's a cold snap or a bad variety of heroin that goes around. Oh, and by the way, you *are* incurring storage charges while the body is here."

"Thanks," I said. "I'll give you a call."

I closed my phone. Great. I really needed to find Brent's parents. Whoever they were, they deserved to get a look at their son the way he looked now, before the City of San Francisco decided to turn him into ashes. And I had no idea what the storage charges were, but they'd probably eat up most of my severance.

"I can't believe you invited a girl to come by," said Jenn.

"Why not?" asked Thomas. "It's not like any of the other people we've talked to have been remotely normal. They've all been guys. Maybe there's a connection."

"Of course there's a connection," I said. "All men are crazy."

Jenn hit me. "Can't you get anything right? You got it backwards."

"Backwards?"

"Yes," she said. "All *women* are crazy. All men are just assholes."

We were sitting in the kitchen, waiting for another potential housemate to come by. It was eight o'clock, and Jenn had already changed into her comfortable outfit for the evening – a pair of ratty sweat pants, faded yellow t-shirt with short-cut sleeves, thick wool socks, and fleece-lined slippers. She was wearing her glasses and was picking at a plate of leftover stir-fry. Thomas was still in button-down/slacks work clothes and was working his way through a massive lamb schawarma sandwich from the Mediterranean Flavors of the Sea, which did not serve seafood of any kind.

My phone vibrated. I opened it – a text message.

Dashiell Hammett Lane at eight. Be on time.

Right. My meeting that night. I closed my phone.

"She seems sane," I said. "And we changed the ad. Check it out."

Wonderful Cole Valley house is looking for a fifth – guy or girl - to fill an empty bedroom. The place is big, with kitchen, living room, dining room, front and back porches, lots of shelf space, etc. Room is off the kitchen, big enough for a queen bed (at least), with floor space. There's a bed and furniture already in the room, or you can bring your own.

Please be normal. By "normal" we mean that you should be able to pay the rent on time, understand that cleaning is not *a hypothetical concept, understand that while you may be a vegan, we're not, and we won't bug you about your diet if you don't go nuts on us. Also, we all work outside of the house. We don't care if you work from home sometimes, but you can't run an entire side business from here.*

We are three guys and two girls, doing different things, but we all get along well. Drop us a line if you're interested. $700/month plus utilities ($30 in the warm months, about $50 when it's cold).

Mandy looked like she had come straight from milking the cows on a Minnesota dairy farm. Blinding blonde hair, blue jeans, running shoes, a red-and-white checked shirt, set off by a dark brown wool scarf. Her hair was damp from the fog and hung limp and lifeless over her right shoulder. She was smiling when she sat down across from us; her eyes stopped for a second at me, flicked down to my hands, then moved along. I took another sip of my beer and waited for

Thomas to start things up. I couldn't shake the feeling that I'd seen her before.

"So," Thomas said. "What's happening?"

"The usual," she said.

"What brings you here?" He asked. "I mean…from your e-mail it sounded like you're in a pretty sweet situation."

"Yeah," she said. "Well, kind of. I'm a live-in caretaker for an older woman with MS, out in Noe Valley. It's me and three other women, and we basically live in her huge mansion house, and each of us is on shift at any given time, and one of us has to be there all the time. We live rent-free, and we all have a food budget."

"Why leave? What's to hate about that?" asked Jenn.

She shrugged. "Nothing. I've been doing it for a year, and it's time to move on and do something else. And I'm a little tired of changing adult diapers and being on call."

"What else do you do?"

"I'm an administrative assistant," she said, flipping her hair from one shoulder to the other.

"For what?"

"A non-profit," she said. "Downtown."

"Cool," said Thomas. "Jenn and I work downtown. Shawna does a few different things."

"Neat," she said. "It's so convenient here; you can just hop on the train a couple of blocks away, right?"

Thomas nodded. "Yep. You can get downtown in about twenty minutes."

"Thirty is more realistic," I said. "Especially when the trains are too crowded and you have to wait for the next one."

"That's fantastic," she said. "Waiting too long for the train can really raise your stress level."

I laughed. "I don't know if I'd call it *fantastic*," I said. "It's kind of annoying."

"Does it stress you out?" she asked.

"Alex doesn't have much stress right now," said Jenn. "On account of the part where he doesn't really do anything any more."

"Except for…" I said.

"That one thing," said Thomas.

"You're not working?" asked Mandy.

"I got laid off a little bit ago," I said. " I was working for…well, I was working for one of those companies that does stuff you've never heard of, for other businesses you've never heard of. I was in marketing, which means that I was trying to make it so that people would hear of us. Since nobody's ever heard of the company, and they got rid of me, I guess I wasn't too good at my job. I'm kind of going through my options right now."

"And if your options are sleeping until eleven and spending way too much time watching videos online, that's a good description of it," said Jenn. I stuck my tongue out at her. She grinned. Mandy laughed, and we all joined in.

"Laughter is a pretty good stress-buster," she said. "But most of your stress is coming from your reactive mind, you know. If you can get rid of that, you can really turn your stress levels around."

"Huh," said Shawna. "That's kind of neat. I'm really into yoga, and that helps me out a lot."

"Yoga is something you can do," said Mandy. "But it's a little more physical. I'm talking about your engrams."

She looked at us with those wide eyes, as if she was waiting for someone to say, "Oh, *engrams*. Of course."

We waited.

She looked around, still smiling that Stepford smile.

"You know," she said. "Engrams are like, bad memories, trauma. They're like complete recordings of bad things that have happened to you. And once you get rid of them, you can be in the Clear. I'm still a preclear, but I'm getting close, and I performed my first audit the other day."

"Close?" I asked. I was beginning to remember where I'd seen her before.

"Yeah," she said. "This is so great. I really think that this is the kind of place where I could prosper. Do you mind if I leave you guys a book? It might help you make your decision."

Thomas choked. I handed him a beer, and he took a swig.

"Sure," I said.

"Great," she smiled again, so wide that I thought her face would crack. She reached into her satchel and pulled out a large trade paperback.

Dianetics, by L. Ron Hubbard.

"Well, that's how they get you," Thomas said after she left. "There's always that little knot of cute girls who are downtown who try to get you to come to a free showing of the Hubbard movie, and you're thinking, 'hey, maybe this is one of those situations that never happens, like getting picked up in a laundromat' and then you look at the little card they give you and it's Scientology. The cute girls are all automatons. I'd have better luck trying to score with Tom Cruise."

"Pig," Shawna said, hitting him on the shoulder. Thomas then hooked his arm around her neck and pulled her into his lap, where they proceeded to wrestle for a few minutes. It was about then that I'd checked the time: seven fifteen. I was supposed to be at Dashiell Hammett Lane at eight, so I left and picked up a bus down on Haight Street.

I had read *The Maltese Falcon* after moving to the city. It's one of those books that you're supposed to read when you move here, along with *On the Road, The Joy Luck Club, Howl, Tales of the City,* and *The Electric Kool-Aid Acid Test. Falcon* had been my favorite of any of them; it captured the city as a place, before it became "San Francisco," when the city was a city, instead of an amalgamation of hope, ideas, and literary excess. Tonight was a night that Hammett would have liked – a dark, quiet evening with heavily-scarved people scurrying along the sidewalks.

The fog was coming in fast when I got off the bus at the Powell Street stop near the cable-car turnaround. A long line of tourists wound from the "board here" sign around the rope fence that separated the sidewalk from the tracks. Most of them were bundled in wool caps and down jackets; the wind was blowing steadily down from the hills, carrying a damp mist that wormed its way through jackets and sweaters and touched your skin with a clammy fingertip. The two beers I had drunk during the interview with the Scientologist were itching to leave, so I started to look around for a place to drain my bladder.

Ordinarily, I would have gone a block over to Stockton street to take advantage of the big bookstore there or up a few blocks to the

Borders, but my eyes stopped and rested on the little oval-shaped metal building on the sidewalk a few yards away. It was about ten feet high, and the walls had the bumpy texture of alligator skin. A sign near the roof said "Cable Car turnaround public toilet."

I had seen the public toilets around town but had never used one. My curiosity got the better of me, and I walked up and pressed the button. A panel slid aside. The whole space was about twice the size of an airplane restroom, but it was entirely metal. Even the toilet was steel, almost chrome in its shininess, with no moving seat to sit on; I wondered how women managed without falling in. The little room smelled like glass cleaner, antiseptic in its sterility. A little sign above the toilet read

Welcome to this San Francisco public toilet. After you enter, the door is locked from the outside, and can only be opened from the inside. After you leave, the entire area will be sterilized with a chemical disinfectant for thirty seconds. This disinfectant is completely harmless to humans. Please remember to take all of your personal belongings with you after you leave.

Above the metal toilet was a red button labeled "flush." Next to the toilet was a cone-topped box toilet paper dispenser, exactly like the ones they had in my elementary school. Some things never change. I did my business, hit the "flush" button, then opened the door to leave. The door shut behind me, and an LED above the door flashed red. I tried to open the door and it was locked; from behind the door I could hear a *shhh*ing sound, kind of like the whistling of a popped bicycle tire.

"Does that thing work?" asked a shambling voice.

A trenchcoat-clad old man with a gray, scraggly beard and a pair of mismatched shoes was speaking to me. He was wearing a faded green army rucksack, his hair was slicked back from his forehead, and he didn't smell bad.

"I guess so," I said. "I mean, the toilet flushed and everything."

"Thank God," he said. "They wouldn't let me in to use the restroom at Borders; they thought I was a homeless fella. Can you believe that? I've got a place to sleep, and I go there every night, but they still won't let me in. "

"Weird," I said. "Good luck."

"Thanks!"

I walked along the tourist line and headed up the hill. It was a seven-block walk up Powell to Dashiell Hammett, which lay near the top of Nob Hill. Powell Street goes up right through the heart of what was, that night, an unusually-quiet Union Square. The trophy wives had gone home and the shops were closing. I trudged up the hill, passing the a retro-'50s diner with a blinking marquee of a roller-skate clad waitress. One of the LEDs in her mouth was out, giving her a gap-toothed smile. I pulled my jacket a little tighter and kept walking.

When I reached Bush Street, the businesses gave way to a series of mid-rise apartment buildings. I took a right and walked half a block to Dashiell Hammett, which was bigger than an alley, but not quite a Way. Parked cars lined the left curb. I headed up; the street was exactly a block long, and the slope between Bush and Pine was steep. I started to breathe hard. Only one of the three streetlights was functioning; I went up to it and stood beneath. After a little while, my legs started to ache a bit, so I sat down diagonally, leaning my back against the lamp and bracing my feet against the tire of the Mini Cooper parked nearest to me.

"Alex," said a voice. It was medium-pitched, with an accent somewhere between New Zealand and South Africa. My short friend from Chinatown. His voice came from behind me, on the other side of the Mini Cooper. I started to turn around.

"Don't turn," said the voice. "I don't want you looking at me."

"Why not?"

"Because you might start to recognize me on the street, and I don't want you to react. If someone's following you and sees you, I could be in big trouble."

React? How could I *not* react? The guy was four feet tall.

"OK," I said. "What am I here for?"

I could practically hear him rolling his eyes. "You wanted to know what your pal was doing at the Lucky Dragon Duck. I know."

"He was trying to line up financing," I said.

"Shite," said the little guy. "How did you know that?"

"I figured it out," I said. No need to tell him that I hadn't been entirely sure, and he'd just confirmed it. I could feel his frustration – it made me feel good. Sam Spade probably felt this way all the time.

"What I don't know is what he was financing."

"I've got some leads on that," said the little guy. "But nothing yet. The important thing is that he *didn't* get his financing through the LDD. They turned him down flat."

"Any idea why?"

"My source there said, 'Because it was the stupidest fucking idea they'd ever heard of.'"

"Hm."

"I have to go now," he said. "But I'll be in touch."

Two footsteps, and he was gone. I turned around to an empty alley. The fog was thick, and I couldn't see to either end. Stupid idea, he'd said. Hm. I took out my phone and texted a *where-you-at?* to Gerald. He pinged back in less than a minute. I took a left and headed down the hill.

We sat in a back booth at the Blu Light, a neo-yuppie Chinatown bar where the bartenders were young, attractive, and gave everyone enough static to make me wonder if they tested for the sassiness gene as a job prerequisite. Our server was a wide-grinning, voluptuous black woman who might possibly have been twenty-one and called us both "hon" with no trace of irony. Our booth was one of those slim only-for-two jobs that made it look like the two of us were on a pre-dinner drinks date. Gerald was having a Blu Martini (which was exactly like a regular martini, but three dollars more), and I was having an Anchor Steam.

"Weird," he said. "What did you see?"

"Nothing," I said. "I never got a good look at him this time. But he's hard to miss. I mean, he's tiny."

"Huh," he said, taking a drink. "I think you should drop this, Alex."

"Drop it?"

"Yes," he said. "I hate to point out the obvious, but this is pretty *weird*. Night meetings in an alley? Text messages from phone numbers you don't recognize? Small guys who talk like Raymond Chandler characters? This is odd. Maybe there are dark forces involved."

"Dark forces?" I asked.

Gerald shook his head. "I don't know, man. It doesn't get a whole lot darker than this."

"It does," I said. "You told me to come to this place. If there's a root of all evil, it's here."

Behind Gerald, two men in expensive suits were jostling for the attention of a half-Asian girl in a black miniskirt and camisole. She was flirting heavily, leaning into one man and then the other, resting a hand on a shoulder there, playing with her hair, acting like a bar girl. The guys were older, middle-aged investment banker types. Nobody was going home with her, but she'd get some free drinks out of it, and the two guys would get to feel attractive again before going back to their estates and children in Hillsborough. It's a dance I've seen a million times, and I hate it as much now as I did when I first saw it.

"Just think about it, all right?" asked Gerald.

"OK, I will," I said. "Gotta go."

"Where are you headed?"

"Meeting Morgan in the Mission at ten-thirty."

"She stays out late," said Gerald. "When do I get to meet her?"

I shrugged. "I don't know what her deal is. And we're not really seeing each other."

"Maybe you should figure that out, too," said Gerald. "Obviously, she wants to hang with you. You should have sex with her."

I spit out my beer. "Jesus," I said. "Could you be any blunter?"

He shrugged. "That's what you want. I just say what's on your mind. You should just text her and ask; it's easier that way."

"You might be right, but I gotta go," I said.

"Be careful," said Gerald.

"Why did you text me?" asked Morgan. She was wearing a mesh top with three-quarter sleeves, a black tank-top underneath, and her hair was pulled into a ponytail. She had been waiting for me at a center table when I walked into The Connecticut Yankee. "I hate texting," she said. "Don't do it."

Great start. "Two in a row," I said. "Fantastic."

She sighed, reached into her purse, pulled out a package of cigarettes, tapped them into her palm twice, then stood.

"Get yourself a drink," she said. "I have to go powder my nose."

She walked toward the back and I went to the bar, where a genial bearded guy was manning the taps. He was talking to a pair of sorority girls down at the other end, under a signed, yellowed photo of Dominic DiMaggio. After a minute or two, he and came over and arched a questioning eyebrow.

"Guinness," I said. "Two, please."

"Ya got it," he said.

I looked around; the place had sports bar décor. Endless photos of guys in uniforms lined the walls, along with Wheaties box covers, baseball gloves in glass cases, signed jerseys, and a couple of hockey sticks. A small stage took up one corner, and a guy with long hair and an Abercrombie sweatshirt was playing around with the public address system. He looked suspiciously like a sound guy for one of those bands consisting of guys who get out of college with an everstoned love of the Grateful Dead and decide to make a go of it touring fratty bars and playing out-of-tune versions of *Terrapin Station*. If they started playing, I'd have to leave. Several groups of people were clustered around tables, eating plates of fried food.

"Two Guinness," said the barman. "Eight dollars."

I gave him a ten and took my beer back to the table. He had poured it well; a smooth head, and the tiny little bubbles were cascading down the side of my glass. Three sips later, Morgan sat down. She smelled slightly of cigarette smoke, and smiled when she saw her fresh drink.

"Guinness," she said. "Good."

She reached across the table and took my hand. "I'm sorry that I snapped at you just now," she said. "It's just that I hate texting. I got dumped by a guy that way once, so I don't text any more."

"Oh," I said. "OK."

"How are things?" she said.

"Not bad," I said. "Kind of weird."

She turned my hand over and pressed my knuckles down into the table, then started to trace the lines of my palm with her finger. "Tell me about it," she said.

I hesitated. She listened through the whole story without a word, leaning forward, continuing to trace the lines in my hand with her fingernail. When I finished, she had tears in her eyes.

"You don't know yet what he was up to?" she asked, squeezing my hand. "You really don't?"

"No," I said. She was squeezing hard, tight enough to grind the bones of my hand against themselves. "What's wrong?"

"My job," she said. "Remember my sleazy boss?"

"Yes," I said. "What happened?"

"They fired me," she said. "I came in in the morning and my computer wouldn't boot up, and the locks on my desk had been changed. When I went in to talk with my boss, he had a paid security guy in a suit there waiting to escort me out. The guy looked like he'd flunked out of the Secret Service for being half-Cro-Magnon, and he smacked my ass as we got out of the elevator. I told him I'd sue, and he laughed and said that there was no way anybody would believe me, that he'd testified in dozens of trials and knew judges. I didn't know what to do, so I kind of lost it. I was really glad to hear from you, even if it was a text. And that's not all." She smiled at me. I felt my heart beating faster.

"I haven't told anybody this," she said. "Not yet. But I think I can trust you."

"Sure," I said. "I'm pretty steady."

"Well," she said. "I'm pregnant."

If I had been walking, I would have stopped in my tracks. My first thought was *well, I'm glad it's not mine.* Followed by *who's the dad?* And then, I'm not proud that my third was *if he's out of the picture, maybe I can play the hero and she'll want to sleep with me.* I batted that last one away.

"Yeah," she said. "And my asshole boss terminated my job right when I had one more day to sign up for another year of benefits, so I'm not eligible for COBRA any more, and good luck getting anything else all on my own, because I'm sure that pregnancy is a pre-existing condition."

"Jesus, Morgan," I said. "What are you going to do?"

"I was hoping you could help with that," she said. "The kid is Brent's."

"What?" I said.

"It's not that hard, is it?" she asked. "The kid is Brent's. I'm going to have his kid."

Well, I'd now found Brent's closest relative. That relative just happened to live inside the uterus of his former girlfriend.

"It's important," she said. "Once the baby can be DNA tested, I can get some kind of child support through Brent's estate. You're helping to deal with that, right?"

Shit. What to say?

"There are some problems," I said.

"Oh," she said. She looked down at her drink, then up at me. Her eyes were ringed with dark circles, circles of no sleep and lots of tears. "Whatever the problems are, I really hope you can solve them," she said. "I need to make sure that this child has a good life."

"Yeah," I said.

She stood up and walked away. Her walk was still a sashay, sashay-ish enough to turn heads as she moved. I watched, thinking vaguely about the best way to see that sashay without anything on top of it. Then I shook my head, feeling my face start to burn. There are levels of low, and lusting after your dead ex-roommate's now-pregnant girlfriend is right down there. I stared at the table until I felt as badly as possible, then left.

Shawna and Thomas were both home when I got there. They were sitting together on the bench at the kitchen table, munching on cinnamon rolls, she leafing through a copy of *The New Yorker*, he playing a one-handed version of *Sonic the Hedgehog* on his IPhone using a Sega Genesis emulator. I sat down on one of the chairs.

"Where have you been?" asked Shawna.

"How do you know I've been anywhere?" I said.

She rolled her eyes. "One: you're wearing your clothes. Two: You came up the stairs. Three: you're not carrying any food. Four: if you'd been here, you'd have noticed the note that Jenn left at the top of the stairs telling us to please eat the cinnamon rolls she baked tonight, and you would have gone directly to the fridge and popped one in the microwave instead of talking with us."

"Good job with the logic," said Thomas. "There's hope for you yet."

She reached over and slapped his wrist, leaving a light mark on his skin. "I can be logical," she said, laughing. "I just choose not to be most of the time."

"Don't hit me," he said. "That hurt."

"Hurt?" she said. "Little me hurting big...strong...you? I doubt it."

"You're getting off-topic," he said. "Alex, where were you?"

"A bar," I said. "With Morgan."

"Who's Morgan?" asked Shawna.

"She's his nemesis," said Thomas. "Someone he's been after for a couple of weeks, trying to figure out if she's into him or not, the way he always does if someone who is of the female persuasion says three words to him."

"Ah," she said. "So he may be doing the transformation from Morose Lonely Single Alex to Happy Alex?"

"Happy Alex?" I said. "I'm happy most of the time."

She patted me on the wrist. "You're avoiding the question. And no, you've been Morose Lonely Single Alex for nearly a year."

"Well, there'll probably be more of that," I said. "She's definitely not into me."

"What, did she say that?"

"Did you foul up when you were unhooking her bra?" asked Thomas. "That's always a deal-breaker."

Shawna gave him a look. "Why, has it broken lots of deals for you?"

Thomas grinned. "Until I was about fourteen. Then I started to get it right."

"No, that wasn't it," I said.

"Oh, so you *did* figure out the bra," said Thomas. "Our little boy is all growed up now!"

"No, not that," I said. "She's, um, pregnant."

That shut them up. I took the silence as an opportunity to go over to the fridge and take out two of Jenn's cinnamon rolls and pop them in the microwave. The beeps as I pressed the buttons were loud and piercing over the soft hum of the fridge.

"Jesus," said Thomas. "You got her pregnant already?"

"What are you going to do?" asked Shawna. "I mean, you'll have to move out; we can't have a baby here with Thomas's Union Square club music blasting at all hours of the day. Babies need to nap."

"It's not Union Square club music," he said. "It's dirty house."

"Appropriate," she said. "Given your room. But you do go to

Union Square clubs sometimes."

"I don't really mean it," he said. "Some of my friends are Euros, and that's where they hang out."

"Yes you do mean it," said Shawna. "You're as Euro as it gets. There was that one time that you woke me up because you hadn't carried your keys because you thought that they wouldn't look good in your jeans when you were at Ruby Skye. Remember that? That was pretty serious Euro clubbing, I'd say. I think."

"Irate," said Thomas. "I'm irate that you remember that."

"Guys," I said. "It's not mine."

I could almost feel the air pressure in the room collapse when I said that. The microwave beeped its finish, and I took out the rolls. My first one was denser than lead, covered in gooey melted sugar, and delicious.

"Oh," said Shawna. "That's good."

"Are you guys going to stay together anyway?" asked Thomas. "I mean, that's the kind of thing that could really put some pressure on a new relationship."

"No kidding," said Shawna. "One time in college I had this friend who got preggo from this dude who wasn't her boyfriend, and he was a total simp and decided to stay with her and help her decide if she wanted to keep it."

"We're not together," I said. "She's helping me with the Brent thing, that's all."

"Don't help her too much," said Thomas.

"Yeah," said Shawna. "Definitely don't stare sensitively into her eyes as you run your hands up the perfect arch in the small of her..."

Her voice faded as I walked up the stairs. One time, after a five minute disjointed monologue that had started with the flavors of Starburst and ended up with Sri Lankan politics vis a vis the Tamil Tigers, Shawna had accused me of being a terrible listener. To my mind, hanging out with her forced you to be a good listener; it wasn't like you had any choice. She didn't take it personally when you left in the middle of one of her sentences, but I still felt a little weird about doing it.

When I got to my room, I tossed my jacket on my little couch, took my cell phone out of my pocket, and plugged it in. The phone had been dead for a couple of hours; I had left it on for the entire night before, and the messaging I'd done during the day had killed the battery. I stripped down to my boxers and walked down the hall to grab a shower.

After I finished showering, the message light on my phone was drinking.

"Alex, Gerald. It's not late yet. Can you meet me at the Castle tomorrow at three? I just had a brain flash."

I hopped online and checked my e-mail. Two offers to increase the size of my penis, four tips on super-hot stocks that were set to explode above fifty cents per share, a letter from a guy who was looking for someone to share the bounty of a Ugandan minister who had died in prison after an embezzlement conviction, someone looking to sell some cut-rate wild boar testicles (*that* was a new one), and a note from Jenn.

Alex,

You ok? I went to bed and before you got home. Eat some of the cinnamon rolls — they'll kill your hangover. Drop me a note and let me know that you made it back OK. All right?

Jenn

Jenn,

Yep, I'm fine. Ended up getting kind of wasted with Gerald. Just got in, will probably head to the Castle tomorrow at around three. Wanna come? Hope your day is going well by the time you get this in the morning.

Alex

Chapter 10

The Edinburgh Castle was on the outskirts of the Tenderloin, a neighborhood that the guidebooks always characterize as "rough," "colorful," or "sleazy." The books are all wrong. The 'loin mixes the thrills of an open-air drug market with the filth of a homemade outdoor latrine, a dirty reminder of everything that can possibly go wrong in an American city all rolled up into ten square blocks. The bar is on the west side, right on the edge, but I had to walk up a few blocks in from where my bus stopped. When I got off the bus, an old mustached man was loudly declaring his candidacy for the House, Senate, Presidency, and position of Insurance Commissioner on behalf of the United States Marijuana Party.

I passed a colony of homeless people huddled against the cyclone fencing next to a vacant lot. Two people were writhing under a pile of sleeping bags, their scabbed feet entwined and clawing at the air. Twenty feet away, a skeletal man was wrapping a rubber tube around the one good arm of his female friend. As I approached, he pulled the tube tight with his teeth, took out a needle, and jabbed it into one of the bulging blue veins of her arm. The look on her face went from scrabbly and scared to relieved to passed-out in less than ten seconds.

"Hey, wake up," he said, slapping her in the face. "You gotta do me now. That's the deal."

"Thas' no," she said. "No can. I can." She roused her head in a jerking motion, like a student fighting to stay awake during a boring lecture. After a few seconds, she nodded off again, slipping down the fencing to the sidewalk, where she sat, her head lolling off of her boneless neck. The man shook his head in disgust, gripped the syringe in his teeth, and began to wrap the rubber tubing around his right arm. I walked a little faster.

The homeless people thinned out as I walked north, giving way to people who were saner, but no less colorful.

"Looking for action?" The man was wearing a blonde wig and a red miniskirt with a plunging neckline that revealed his fine brown chest hair. His arms were flabby; what had once been muscle had turned to ripples of skin and cottage cheese under his arms. His knee-high boots were scuffed to a light tan.

"Sorry," I said. "It's a little early for me."

"Come back later," he said. "We'll ha' a party." He batted his eyes, looking like a bizarro Jessica Rabbit. I kept walking, past more men dressed like movie versions of bordello dreams, tired women in tube tops that hung loosely off of crack-waif bodies, dealers in huge coats standing on the corners, sizing up each person who walked past.

"Rocks and black tar," one said softly as I walked by. "In this mornin', rocks and black tar."

I shook my head, being careful not to meet the man's eyes. An E-Z Payday Loan and Check Cashing place had a line out on the sidewalk; it must have been welfare day. The door to the Y-Not Lounge was open; dark figures lurked at the bar, served by the toughest-looking woman I had ever seen. One of the drunks looked at me as I was looking in, and he smiled, teeth shining yellow in the sepia light. I walked faster.

One block from the Castle, the sidewalk was blocked by another homeless encampment, so I crossed over to the other side and waited to cross at the red light. A bike messenger passed me. He was wearing fog-proof body armor of long underwear, baggy shorts, and windbreaker. He cruised easily up the street, swinging out of the bike lane to avoid two quivering crackheads who were shoving each other into the middle of the street. The messenger looked back and yelled, and one of the crackheads took off his hat and threw it after the bicyclist. My light turned green, and I crossed the street.

I was breathing quickly when I got to the Castle. The place was dim and nearly deserted, with Scottish flags hanging from the high roof rafters. Gerald was sitting on a high stool at the far end of the bar, leaning forward in a close conversation with a cheerily plump blonde bartender. A soundless television was playing a loop of Premier League highlights, and the jukebox was softly spitting out the Pixies. I took off my jacket and hung it on one of the hooks below the bar, then hoisted myself up on a stool.

"…and, get this, he nearly dies," said Gerald.

"You're kiddn'" she said in a thick burr. "No fookin' way you can die of constipation."

"I'm serious. He was completely blocked up, so full of his own shit he looked like he was about to give birth."

"What d'ye *do* when ye've got that?"

Gerald smiled darkly. "Well, first thing we tried was hot green tea. Lots of it, with ginseng and mint. We figured a lot of caffeine would be just the thing to give him the runs. No dice. So, we went nuclear. He had a package of Ex-Lax; he ate half of them in ten minutes, then walked into the outhouse."

He paused and took a sip of his beer, which was darker than the wood paneling of the bar.

"One second, love," she said. "Can I be getting you somethin'?

"What's he got?" I asked.

"Anchor Porter," she said. "We got one of the first kegs of this year's batch."

"That works," I said.

"One second," she said. "Then your friend's goin' to finish his story." After spinning a coaster down the bar to a spot directly in front of me, she put a pint down, leaned on her elbows, and gave a green-eyed stare to Gerald.

"So?" she said.

"So," he said. "That didn't work, and he was *dying.* I mean, his hands were on his stomach, he was paler than an Irish vampire, and his cheeks were all puffy. I figured we had to get him to a doctor, but we were hiking, no car or anything, so I headed out to the road and stuck out my thumb."

"Good luck in this bleeding country," she said.

"You'd think that, but we were in the sticks, so the second car that goes by pulls on over, and it's this woman with a little VW Golf that's completely full of junk she was hauling over to a swap meet in town – the town happened to have a real full-service clinic. She moved some of her potting soil and drove us over there, basically in each others' laps. The clinic was one of those small-town places where you don't even have to have an appointment, just pay fifty bucks and you can go see a doctor. So we go in there, and I wait around in the waiting room reading *Time* magazines from 1982, and then he comes out of the office, this look of fear on his face."

"Fear?"

"Yeah, like he was about to go into a test he hadn't studied for. So I ask him what's up, and he says…"

Gerald chuckled, coughed, sipped at his beer, and continued.

"He says, 'We gotta go find a drugstore and a public bathroom.' I go, 'Why?' He goes, 'Because they gave me a prescription for a suppository and an enema, and I have to get them and then find a place to use them.' At that point I was about to lose my *shit* laughing, but he looked so terrible I stifled it back. We walked into town from the clinic, about half a mile, me carrying his pack and him practically doubled over from the pain. There was a Rite Aid on the outskirts of town, so he went in there to fill the prescriptions, and I started asking people in the parking lot if there was a place where my friend could use the toilet."

"How did people react to that?"

"Crappy. Most people looked at me weird and kind of stood back like they do in movies when a character is confronted with a crazy person. I had no idea people actually edged away in real life. But one dude who was there to recycle cans told me that there was a new outlet mall in town about three blocks away, and they had shiny new bathrooms. After he told me that, my friend comes out with a little pill bottle and a big blue box labeled 'Enema.' Naturally, he puts the box down and sits next to the door of the Rite Aid to wait for me, and everybody who comes out the front door sees him sitting there, pregnant and bloated, five days' worth of beard, with a big 'Enema' box next to him. People friggin' ran away."

Gerald took another drink and leaned forward towards the bartender. She was listening raptly, leaning forward on her elbows, her top baring just the slightest bit of cleavage.

"We walked over to the outlet mall," said Gerald. "I was carrying his backpack again, and he was carrying the big blue Enema box. It wasn't even an outlet mall, really, just a two-story building with white hallways and little Ann Taylor and LL Bean one-room shops with enough space for a few folded sweaters and pairs of shoes. The bathrooms were clean, though. So I left him in there to do his business and went outside to lay in the park. Half an hour later, he comes out."

"And what then? Had he really rammed a pill up his arse?"

"Well, not really. He said that he had tried. 'I was sitting there,' he said. 'And I had that suppository in my hand, and I was reaching back there, and I just got scared, and then I pushed really hard, and everything just came out.' I asked him, 'Well, what was it like?' He goes, 'Well, now I know what it was like to have a kid, and nobody's ever going to use that toilet again.'"

The bartender threw her head back and gave a throaty, bosomy laugh. "You're right," she said. "That's a tale worth a beer. This 'un is on me for the both of yous."

"Many thanks," said Gerald, holding out his hand and raising his eyebrows in a question.

"Brylie," she said. "You are?"

"Gerald," he said. "This is my friend Alex."

"You're good company on a lonely afternoon, Gerald," she said. "Stick around a bit."

"We're not going anywhere any time soon," he said. "Mind giving us a second? There's a small thing I want to discuss with Alex."

"Sure," she said. "Just give a wave if you need a refill." She walked to the other end of the bar, took out a newspaper and pencil, and started to fill out one of the puzzles, looking up every few seconds at the television.

"Was that a true story?" I asked.

"Sure," he said. "As true as true gets."

I took another sip of beer and looked around the bar again. We were the only two customers. Five booths snuggled against the far wall, and a pool table stood at the top of three stairs in the back. The high ceiling was ringed with a slim, porch-like walkway, lined with two-person tables, all empty. Four chandeliers provided a soft yellow light. When it was crowded, it was probably warm and welcoming. Now, it was still.

"What's happening?" he asked.

"SSDD," I said.

He nodded and took a sip of his beer.

"One thing I did find," I said. I took two sheets of paper out of my shoulder bag. Both were was covered in Chinese characters.

"Kanji," he said.

"What?"

"*Kanji* is what they call Chinese writing," he said. "It's what these symbols are called in Japan."

"Oh," I said. "I always just called it Chinese."

"That's because you're a Philistine," he said. "What is it?"

"Beats me," I said. "I don't read Chinese."

"No, idiot. Why are you showing it to me?"

"Oh," I said. "It was in my inbox this morning – the guy who'd interviewed Brent for that record baseball card sale e-mailed it to me this morning. Apparently Brent had screwed up and e-mailed it to *him*, and the baseball card guy thought I might be interested in it."

"Has anyone else seen it?"

"No," I said. "You're the first person besides me who knows I've got it."

"And it's all in Chinese?"

"Yep."

"Did Brent speak Chinese?"

I shrugged. "I have no idea. At this point, he could have been a closet ninja and it wouldn't surprise me."

"Well, I think that it would behoove you to get this translated," he said.

"Who do I know that speaks Chinese?" I said.

We sipped our beers for a few seconds, then I took out my phone, dialed, and asked a question. Shawna nearly took my ear off through the phone's speaker.

"Why are you assuming that I read Chinese?" said Shawna. "Not all Asian people can read kanji, you know."

"I'm not assuming,," I said. "I'm asking because sometimes you speak Mandarin to your parents. Can you read kanji?"

"Of course I can," she said. "But that's not the point…"

"The point is that it would be a big favor to me if you could translate this paper for me," I said.

She sighed, loudly enough to make Gerald wince. "Yep, I can do it. Where are you?"

"The Edinburgh Castle."

"Oh! I'm right around the corner – I just finished doing hot yoga. I'll be there in five minutes."

She showed up in three, in full yoga-mat-over-shoulder glory. Her black hair was tied up in a tight bun, her socks clashed, and her clothes were soaked in sweat to the point where her light green sports bra was completely visible through her white shirt. She took a quick sip of my beer and then grabbed the papers from my hand, leaving sweat imprints where her thumbs touched the paper.

"This is Chinese, all right," she said. "I'm better at speaking than writing – this might take me an hour or so, and I want to talk through a couple of things with the people at the studio. Are you guys going to be here, or should I just get it to you when I see you at home?"

"Home's fine," I said.

"Great!" she said. "See you there!" She whirled out of the bar.

"One more?" said Gerald. I nodded.

One became two, then a third and then a fourth, because Brylie the bartender wanted to thank us for the entertainment. Shawna wasn't home when I finally walked in the door, and the rest of the rooms in the house were dark and silent.

Chapter 11

I think my mood may have been better the next morning if I hadn't

1) Woken up in my clothes from the previous day.
2) Left my shoes right next to my bed so that when I swing my feet down to the floor so I could go to the bathroom, my heel and arch came right down on the part of the shoe that's both thin and well-supported. That hurt.
3) Had a dry throat and the taste of slaughtered cat in my mouth.

When I pried my eyes open, I saw that Shawna had pushed a couple of papers under my door. After brushing the scum out of my mouth and spending some quality toilet time voiding my digestive system of as much of the previous night's excesses as I could, I packed my laptop and Shawna's translation of Brent's Chinese letters and headed down to Coffee to the People for some breakfast. Coffee to the People is the picture of what people think a San Francisco café should look like, full of socialist magazines, bespectacled graduate students, and laptop-wedded wannabe future dot-com millionaires. Ten in the morning on a weekday, and it was hard to find a table; didn't *anybody* work for a living any more?

I ended up sitting at the large table in the center, as all of the smaller tables were taken up by laptop people who were using the place as a virtual office. Of course, to the casual observer, I was exactly the same – laptop, scattered papers, a pen. But it was different – *I* wasn't getting paid, and I basked in a glow of moral superiority. I sipped coffee, nibbled on my bagel, spread out my three newspapers (our two alt-weeklies and *the Onion*) and started to page through them to get myself into the reading-stuff mindset.

Well, I tried to. Sitting at the small table nearest me was a short-haired man with an enormous red-faced watch. He was dressed in jeans and a t-shirt tight enough to show that he spent an just a bit too much time at the gym. His laptop was a PC – heretical in this town – and a little Bluetooth microphone/headset was wedged into his left ear. Right when I sat down, his Blackberry rang with the tone of

Cher's "Do you Believe?" and he clicked his headset on.

"Hello?" he said, loudly. His voice was upper-ranged and hoarse, like Clint Eastwood on the way down from a helium inhalation binge.

"Yeah, I haven't seen that note," he said. "Hang on a sec." He clicked several keys on his laptop. "No, no, it doesn't seem to be up."

Clicks and clacks.

"Oh, really? No way he's doing that. I think that they're trying to make a move, or at least test the market….no, I think that the market will easily…yeah. Oh, definitely. Hang on…."

He stood up, reached over his laptop to the manila folder on the other side of his table, and started shuffling them.

"Oh, wait, I have another call. Hang on." He reached down to his Blackberry and clicked a button.

"Hello? Yes…no, I'm not at home. I'm at a café in the city. No, no, I won't be able to pick those up tomorrow. The day after is fine. Oh, and can you see about picking up those tickets to the *Lion King* on Saturday? Fantastic. Oh, wait, I have someone on hold on the other side, so I'm going to have to let you go. Great."

As he talked, he leaned back and gestured with both hands, biceps twitching and bunching as he conducted a nonexistent orchestra.

"Sure, I guess I can stay here," he said, then laughed. "No, no, no, I haven't. I guess I could fix something up instead of going to the gym. Oh, no. Not that one. I go to Gold's now. No. OK. OK. See you soon."

He clicked his Blackberry again, then started clacking away on his laptop. I stopped obviously not-looking at him, and looked at the papers on my section of my table again. There was yet another story in the leftier of our two weeklies about the continuing scourge of downtown condo conversions.

"Hello?"

I jerked my head up. The overly-muscular business guy was talking again, this time with his right hand on the earpiece, making his bicep flex. It was big, the size of a small grapefruit. His voice was loud, just the right timbre to pierce through the low conversational hum of the café.

"I don't think we have full penetration there," he said. "It's just not our market, and the synergy just isn't there; they're not particularly innovative. Would that really be a *Moneyball* approach? No, I realize that we're not in the baseball business, but the principles are the same – we have to find a place where the spots in the value chain just aren't correctly priced, and move in on them. Yes, *exactly*. Well, or like finding a stripper before she's moved on to the movies and locking in a management fee before she gets big."

He laughed, a giant belly laugh, stretching backwards and putting both hands behind his head. Small sweat stains were blooming underneath the sleeves of his t-shirt, and I could see little bumps on his wrists from where he shaved his arms.

"Right," he said. "Good one, huh?" he laughed again. "No, no, did she really *say* that? No. I'll send her an e-mail to have her give me a call. Does she have a Blackberry? So she'll get it." Clickety-clackety-clickety. He talked as he typed.

"Your..conduct..was..less..than..professional..please..confirm..meeting..to.. discuss..situation. All..best..Darius. OK, I sent it off to her, so she'll get that and be able to understand what the situation is and how it's affecting her productivity and the way that the business is operating. Our efficiency, really, it affects. No, I didn't see that. I haven't...no, I've never been to Whistler. Just Vail and Aspen. Really? That big? Wow. Yeah, Vail is so much like Aspen was back then, so...Canada, though. I hear that they eat French Fries there with gravy. Gravy? Gravy! I can't imagine what that would do to your cholesterol count...no, still no refined sugar, but I can eat honey and sugarcane. They say that it helps you with your weight, but I'm more worried about my BMI. Body-Mass-Index. Oh, it means a lot; exactly what you should be looking at if you want to achieve peak performance. Peak, yes. Just like they say in *Cheese*. You haven't read *Cheese?* Really, Jay, it's the best thing on how to survive change that I've ever read, and it goes by quickly. Yes, on the plane on the way to and from Vail. Yes, it's that easy."

That was it. I ripped a piece of paper out of my notebook, scribbled thirteen words on it, folded it into a paper airplane, and threw it at the guy. It sailed, twisted, and hit him in the ear. He stopped talking and looked at me. I gestured to the airplane, which had fallen to the surface of the table.

"One second," he said.

I gestured towards the airplane again, raising my eyebrows in the universal "look at it" gesture. He picked it up, unfolded it, and his eyes widened in shock, then looked at me. I smiled at him.

A minute later, he had packed up his things. I could *feel* the tension easing as he went out of the room. When he went out the door, I walked my things over to the little table and spread them out. I started to crumple up the paper airplane, then decided to leave it out on the table, so that anyone who passed by could see what I'd written.

I know it's important, but can you please keep it the fuck down?

The skinny counter kid walked over to clean up some crumbs that the guy had left on my table, took a look at the note, and chuckled.

"Nice," he said. "That guy was a tool."

"What else did he do?"

"He came in here about two hours ago, ordered a decaf coffee for a dollar ten, didn't tip, and sat there yapping. Two people who were sitting near him just took off. I went and tried to ask him to take the phone outside, but he just kept talking and gave me a dirty look, and he was big, and they don't pay me enough money to get beat up by guys like that."

"He wouldn't have beaten you up," I said.

The counter kid shrugged. "You never know. This isn't my place, anyway. If I was a manager, maybe I'd take those risks. But thanks."

"Sure," I said. I didn't begrudge him, but why did everyone have to wait for me to do something stupid before telling that yuppie idiot to be quiet? If this kind of thing kept up, we'd be forced to listen to people discussing their hemorrhoid removal methods at four-star restaurants.

My phone started vibrating; I took it out of my pocket to check the phone number. It was Morgan. I flipped the phone open.

"Hey," I whispered. "One sec; I'm in a café, let me go outside." I left my papers and my half-done drink on the table with my jacket on the chair, picked up my laptop, and walked outside to the sidewalk.

"What's up?" I said.

"Can I come over tonight?" she said.

"Um…sure," I said.

"Great. I'll be by at six. We'll have dinner."

I went back into the coffeehouse and tried to look at the papers on the table, but failed. What was Morgan doing? Did I need a haircut again? What was wrong with me? She was pregnant. You don't plan on making it with someone who's pregnant. But what if she *wanted* to? I couldn't turn down the advances of a woman in need, especially one who looked that much like Veronica from *Heathers*.

I shook my head and took out Shawna's translations. They only took up two lines:

Use LuckyOne13
Pass Yazman

Huh? I looked at the two lines for the rest of my cup of coffee, trying to figure out what they could possibly mean. Nothing came to mind by the time my coffee was done, and I found myself thinking about Morgan again. Was her hair black naturally, or just dyed? She'd always worn tights when meeting me…wow. There was no way I was going to face this without some help.

Jenn,

Hey, I've got someone coming over tonight and I don't have anything to drink, really. Can I

a) *Get some advice on some decent red wine to drink, the kind that is kind of classy?*

b) *Barring that, borrow that bottle that's in the cabinet above the fridge that you haven't touched and has been there for two months?*

You coming home normal time tonight?
Alex

Ten minutes later.

Alex,

No, you can't have the wine. It cost me sixty bucks and is for a special occasion, and anything involving you and some girl probably does not count as a special occasion. And I have a bad feeling about this…

But, since you won't listen to me…go down to the store on the corner of Haight and Clayton and ask the guy there if they have any remainders from their last months' shipment, and buy whatever costs about ten dollars. That'll be a fifteen dollar bottle, and if this girl complains about that, she's not worth keeping around.

Home at six. Try not to be drunk when I get home. See you then.

Jenn,
Just because I go through a six-pack every time someone comes over to look at the place doesn't mean I'm drunk. Drunk would be half a bottle of rum. Six beers in two hours is kid stuff. Besides, maybe we'll just have a glass or two.
Alex

Alex,
Congratulations, you're an alcoholic.
Jenn

Jenn,
Don't you feel like that's a bit pejorative?
Alex

A,
Yes. That was the point. You should feel bad about spending all your severance on booze while the rest of us have to be productive. And how's that finding-Brent's-next-of-kin going? Are they going to drop the body on our porch while we're interviewing the next housemate? That would kind of suck.
J

J,
I'm getting very close to figuring out what's going on.
A

Alex,
You're a crappy liar. Even over e-mail.
Jenn

Jenn's last note came in at 5:45, after I had finished sterilizing my room. My big *London Calling* poster had come undone on one of the top corners a few days before, so I had to bring up a chair from the kitchen to be able to climb up to the top of my dresser and re-stick the corner with sticking plaster. Transferring my pile of clean clothes from the love seat to my dresser took more time than I thought, as I had to refold everything. I hadn't folded clothes since my layoff and remembering how to do it took a few minutes. Folding clothes is *annoying,* especially when you have to follow it up by vacuuming, window-washing, dusting, and showering off the grime that accumulates when you clean.

After I'd finished, I walked down to the liquor store at Haight and Clayton. Two guys on BMX bikes were circling around at the corner, standing up on their pedals as they rode, their baggy pants touching the crossbars of their bikes at the crotch. The owner of the corner store was an affable Palestinian man who went by either Yasser or Nasir; I'd be willing to bet that neither was his actual name, but that he got a big kick out of having similar names to famous PLO or Egyptian politicians, so he used both.

"Hello, friend," he said. Never "my friend," always "friend" here, to everyone, as if all who walked in the front door were automatically on the friend side of things. I wondered if he'd say the same thing to someone who walked in with a 12-gauge and a mask. Probably.

"Hey," I said. "Do you have any remainders from last month's wine shipment?"

"Yes," he said. "Red or white?"

"Red."

"One second, friend," he said, and disappeared into the back.

"OK, I've got some," said Yasser/Nasir as he emerged through a curtain of clear plastic from the room in the back. He put a bottle of Syrah and another of Cabernet on the counter. "Ten dollars each for you. Usually the girl from up the street buys them, but she hasn't come in this week, so…"

"That's Jenn," I said. "I live with her."

"Oho!" he said. "You're a lucky man. She's a very pretty girl."

"No, no," I laughed. "It's not like that. We're just roommates. There are five of us. Well, four. Until we find a fifth. I mean, there are four of us in four different rooms, and a fifth room that we need to put somebody in."

"Oh," he said. He wrinkled his thick eyebrows and leaned

forward. "Are you sure? I think such a pretty girl and a good man like you…"

"God, no," I said. "Something with Jenn? She's anal-compulsive and cried one time when she was watching *Father of the Bride Part II* because she thought the relationship between the girl and her father was so moving. She watches the Food Network all the time, and when it got over ninety degrees last summer she was sleeping curled up with a bag of ice. That and she doesn't really like me like that. And I'm not into her, either. Which why we're not a thing. All that stuff."

He shrugged and put the bottles in a brown paper bag. "What you say may be true," he said. "Pretty girl, she."

I handed him a twenty. "Have a good night," I said.

"You too, friend," he said.

When I got back, our house felt tense, like that scene in *Animal House* where Otter and the crew walk into the bar where Otis Day and the Nights are playing. I could feel the air crackling right when I walked in the door. Voices were coming from the kitchen – two girls. I walked quietly up the stairs, trying to catch what they were saying and who they were.

"…so what are you going to do?"

"We'll see. I'll probably start putting my resume together in a couple of days."

Voice one was Jenn. Voice two was Morgan. This could not end well. I sprinted up the rest of the stairs and burst into the kitchen. Jenn was in her usual baking place, leaned up against the counter with her arms crossed in front of her. She was wearing spandex shorts and a tank-top; she must have just come from the Gym. Morgan was seated at the kitchen table, one black-tighted leg crossed over the other, sipping from a glass of water. She put the glass down when I came in. Light red marks stained the rim.

"Alex," she said. "Hi."

"Alex," said Jenn. "You have company."

I'd never heard words actually drip before. One greeting dripped honey, the other acid.

"Jane was just telling me all about how you all became roommates," said Morgan. "It was fascinating."

"And Morgan was telling me about how she lost her job," said

Jenn. "That sounds just awful."

They both looked at me as if I was supposed to talk. I think I was supposed to go over and give Morgan a hug. Were we at the hugging stage? If we had been dating, I mean, been on dates with dinner and awkward conversation, we would definitely be at the hugging stage. But it didn't feel quite like a huggable moment, there in the kitchen.

"Um. Hi guys," I said. "Everything OK?"

"Sure," said Morgan. "Although…"

"She was just saying," said Jenn. "I guess she and Brent were very close."

"Well, as close as you can get to someone you've only known for four months," said Morgan.

"That all depends on the kind of person you are," said Jenn. "Some people get as close as they can pretty quickly."

"Are you like that?" asked Morgan.

Jenn shook her head, then walked over to the refrigerator and leaned on it, tapping her right foot. "No, not really," she said. "I'm a tough girl to get to know."

"I'm a little more open," said Morgan.

"I can tell," said Jenn.

"Um," I said. "Weren't we going to talk about Brent?"

"Oh, we already did," said Jenn. "I told her how you told me that there wasn't anything new."

"That's right," said Morgan. She looked at me and arched her black eyebrows, asking *is that true?* without actually saying it.

"Well…" I said, then stopped. Even I wasn't so dense to miss that Jenn was throwing daggers at Morgan. Barbed daggers. With poison. Morgan was staring at me with a look that either said *take me upstairs and undress me now* or…well, or something else that I couldn't figure out. I was torn. A third of me was reacting to that unspoken first phrase, on the off chance that it was what she was actually saying. The second third was disgusted at my thoughts and was sincerely thinking about running upstairs and jumping out the window in order to shut down my out-of-control libido. The last third was listening to Jenn, who was telling me to clam up. I went with Jenn – at least she probably *thought* she had my best interests in mind. Nobody else in the room did.

"Yeah," I said. "Nothing new."

"We're not even sure if he had a real bank account," said Jenn.

Morgan brightened at that. "Oh, I know he did," she said. "If you can get into that, I'd bet you'd learn a lot. It could be helpful."

"To who?" asked Jenn.

Whom, I thought, then stashed it.

"To his relatives," said Morgan, looking directly at me. "But that's it. I've got to be somewhere, so no dinner. Alex….call me?" She near-whispered those last two words, in a way that shouldn't have been hot but was.

"Jane…nice to meet you."

"Jenn."

"Right," said Morgan. "Jenn."

She brushed her hand up my sleeve again, as if she was painting a fence. "Remember," she said, and she swept out of the kitchen in a whirl of black. I watched her go, then stood for a few seconds, willing my heartbeat to slow down.

"Wow," I said.

"You're an idiot," said Jenn. She brushed past me and headed up the stairs. She smelled like fruit soap under dried sweat.

"What?" I said.

Nobody answered; I was alone in the kitchen. I looked at my bottles of wine, then put them in a side cabinet. What was wrong with me? I could have made something up, and maybe had the rest of my evening with Morgan set up. She clearly wanted…well, *something* from me, and that was clearly a big problem because she was *pregnant.* Ugh. I shook my head again. I should have told Jenn about the pregnancy – maybe then she would have been more friendly. That was it. That was why Morgan left. I decided to ask Jenn if she could maybe be a little more welcoming, so I went upstairs. Her door was closed. I almost knocked. on the door, then stopped. Jenn was already mad. I'd talk to her in the morning.

Chapter 12

The following Monday, Shawna had the day off from her job working the desk at her yoga studio, and she insisted that I go with her to Good Vibrations, a woman-owned positive-vibe sex shop down in the Mission. I really had no need to go there, but it had been a crummy weekend – Jenn had gone off to Napa, and Thomas and Shawna had both worked, leaving me to putter around the house and mope about the city feeling bad about my pregnancy-lusting self. By Monday, I was feeling pretty low.

"I don't need to go," I said. "I'm currently single, and I really don't feel the need to electronically stimulate my *own* prostate."

"You have nothing better to do," she said.

"Yes I do."

"You're watching *Blind Date*."

Game, set, match.

It was sunny in our neighborhood; the intense fogs of July were beginning to give way to the more wispy evening-only mists of August. I wore sandals with my cargo pants. Shawna was wearing overalls with the legs rolled to just below the knees, Birkenstocks, and an old T-shirt with a crossed-out-penis logo.

"Nice shirt," I said. "Now everyone's going to think that I'm the straight lesbian-friend guy."

"Isn't it great? I got it when I was running the Queer Alliance at Wesleyan."

"You're straight," I said.

She laughed hard, clutching her belly, her black hair falling in her eyes as she bent forward.

"When I was there the Alliance was so disorganized that they let me and my friend go ahead and plan all the events. We put on the best Queer Prom that the university had ever seen, and paid ourselves out of the budget. I ate out on that dance for months. It was a minor scandal when we came out as unqueer, but eventually nobody cared because we threw a good party."

If Shawna had seemed organized, they must have been in some serious trouble. The previous year, she had freaked out looking for a certain pair of flip-flops, and in trying to find them had taken all of the clothes out of her drawers and closet and stacked them all in the hallway. Eventually, she'd found them stuffed between her mattress and box spring. They had been there so she could feel them while she slept and thus wouldn't forget them in the morning.

"Didn't you have a moral problem with that?" I asked.

"No," she said. "If we hadn't spent that money it would have gone back to the school's general fund, and it might have ended up somewhere distasteful."

"Like the College Republicans?"

She looked at me as if I'd grown an extra ear. "Don't you know anything? There *are* no Republicans at Wesleyan."

We walked in a zigzag pattern, crossing streets when there were no cars or the light was green, up and over a hill and down to the Castro. The sun had brought out the boys; the sidewalk was crowded with tank tops, ripped shoulders, freshly shaved heads, and tight biker shorts. Shawna walked slowly, whiplashing after every gelled fauxhawk or set of waxed calves.

After hanging a left on 18th Street, we headed downhill, past Moby Dick's, the Man Hole, and the corner coffeehouse that brewed one cup at a time and marked the gay/straight boundary to the Mission. Tight-shirted muscle boys gave way to tighter-shirted chestless hipsters.

The front of Good Vibrations was opaque. They didn't go for the black-curtains-and-furtive-exit vibe; instead, they had a light-colored treatment with bright letters and maniacal calligraphy. We entered through the glass door and walked down a curtained hall. I'd never been inside before; it was lit up as well as your average bank, and there were none of the creepy trenchcoat guys around who usually hang out at sex shops. A giggling couple were standing next to the dildo rack; they couldn't have been more than twenty-two.

"Double?" he said. "*Double?* Why would you need that?"

"Silly," she said, punching him in the arm. "Think about it."

"Right," he said. "But you've got *me*. Why would you need more than one extra?"

She rolled her eyes so hard her head moved in a circle. "You do go on business trips sometimes, sweetie…"

"That's so wonderful," said Shawna.

"What, double penetration?" I said.

"No, people *communicating*," she said. "They're having a conversation honestly, and they're working out their issues. Isn't it beautiful?"

I shrugged. Shawna is my only housemate that I've ever actually fought with, and our one big argument was about our communication styles, and how I don't communicate what I'm actually trying to say. That's what she said it was about. I always thought that we were fighting about how she kept taking stuff out of the sink and only half-washing it, resulting in dishes in the cabinets that were caked with crusty pasta sauce and parmesan cheese crumbs. We ended up resolving it by agreeing to listen better to what the other person was saying. After promising to do that, she started practically sterilizing the dishes. Whatever works.

"What are we here for?" I asked.

"Well, I was thinking that you broke up with whatshername a long time ago, and I need to spice up my life..."

"Has it been long?."

She shook her head. "A good girl never tells. But if I were to hit a dry spell, it's good to be prepared."

Shawna wasn't a use 'em and lose 'em type of girl; she had the misfortune to fall in love with every single boy she brought home and had her heart broken when they didn't measure up to whatever her standards happened to be at the time. Those standards changed on a near-daily basis, which resulted in some awfully weird conversations between her and her beaux.

Shawna: You can't possibly be wearing that.

Long-haired guy: What?

Shawna: That t-shirt was made in Myanmar! Don't you know what happens there?

Long-haired guy: Um....no.

Shawna: *How can you not know that?*

Long-haired guy: (blank face)

Shawna. Get out! Get out! I never want to see you again!

And so on. That conversation had been in the upstairs hall while three of us were downstairs with hangovers, watching infomercials on one of the channels with three digits. The long-haired guy had come downstairs, looked in on us with a face blanker than Paris Hilton's at an astrophysics convention, and left. This was in no way an isolated incident. That hadn't happened in a while, though. I guess that was why we were at the store.

"So really, this is just an excuse to come here," I said.

"Yep," she said. "And you needed to get out of the house. For a guy with money and nothing to bring him down, you sure mope a lot."

She walked up to the woman behind the counter and started in on an in-depth explanation about how this one man in her life hadn't paid enough proper attention to her, how his tongue really hadn't been strong enough, and that the barbell on a tongue piercing was really better used as strength training, and did they have anything in stock that simulated the feel of a barbell on a pierced tongue?

"Preferably one of the slightly-curved ones," she said. "They're the nicest."

The woman behind the counter would have been perfectly cast as the matron in a gonzo BBC adaptation of a Dickens novel. She was plump and smiling, with one dimple, crooked teeth, graying hair, and a small stud in her nose. Her outfit was a large and billowing variation on business casual, with sleeves that brushed the counter when she gestured.

"I think we can help you and your partner here out," she said.

"Oh, we're not partners," I said.

"Fine," she smiled. "Fuck-buddy?"

"Housemate," I said.

"That's right," said Shawna. "But his issues are much worse than mine."

"Uncooperative partner?" said the matron. "We get a lot of guys like that. We can usually solve it with some kind of Fleshlight-ish device."

"Fleshlight?"

"It's relatively new," she said. "It looks like a flashlight, but you take the top off and it is a very-good reproduction of the female mouth or genitals. I hear it's really great."

"Really?" said the guy over at the dildo rack.

"Hey, I…" I said. My face was getting hot.

"Yep," said the matron. "Our friend here is in the market for one."

"But…"

"Neat," said the dildo guy. "Can I get a look at one?"

"And why would you need *that?*" asked his girlfriend.

"Well, you go places, too," he said.

"And that's why you have a hand," she said.

"Oh, so you're saying that it's OK for you but not for me?" he said.

"Guys…um…" I tried to think of a way to stop what was coming.

The two of them had come over to the counter and were squaring off. He was about six feet tall and she would be lucky to scrape the bottom of five with shoes on, but it was clear who held the power. He was leaning back, blinking, wiping drops of sweat from his forehead, and would have been backpedaling if the counter hadn't been in the way.

"I'm just saying that it's kind of unfair," he said.

"Unfair?" said Shawna. "No, unfair is seventy-five percent of the pay you make. Unfair is forty-two hours of labor followed by two weeks of maternity leave and then unpaid time off. Unfair is you guys looking at my boobs like they're a television show or a hot car. Unfair is voting rights that still aren't in the Constitution. *That's* not fair."

The smaller woman looked up at Shawna, her eyes huge. She looked like a kid playing pickup basketball who's just had Michael Jordan added to his team.

"Wow," she said. "That was amazing." Her boyfriend's mouth was hanging open, making him look like an over-tall *Scream* painting, but real. "Come on," he said, taking her hand. "We should go."

"No," said the girl. "You can go. Whatever direction I'm not going."

"What?" he said.

"That's it," she said. "It's over. Go."

The guy looked at her, then looked at me with a pleading look, then exited. The girl waited a few seconds before leaving.

The matron at the counter crossed her arms and watched them go, then shared a meaningful look with Shawna.

"Come on, Alex," she said. "We should go, too."

"But you didn't buy anything," I said.

"Oh, I'm broke," she said. "At this place, I'm kind of like those people who go to Barnes and Noble just to sit on the couches and read without buying."

So we left, and I was no closer to understanding my housemate than I had been when we'd walked out of the house two hours before.

That night, Thomas and I were at the Rickshaw Stop, the bar at the San Francisco Hipster Center of the Universe. The place is hard to find; it's near the intersection of Fell and Van Ness, where thousands of cars do a back-and-forth wiggle to get south of Market Street and onto the freeway. To find it, you have to look for an unsigned door with the soft red light, as if it were a massage parlor, a bordello, or one of the places that toe the line in between.

We were there because of a DJ that Thomas knew and a band I thought I would like. Ringing London were a group of guys from Oakland who dressed like they were from the East End of London in 1978 and played "blazing cool smashing punk anthems right out of the Mick Jones/Joe Strummer songbook" according to the *SF Weekly*. The DJ called himself Caravan, and he spun punk/jungle mixes. The show was a doors 8/show 9 deal; when the bus dropped us off at 9:15, there was a fixed-gear bike locked to every parking meter on the block. Inside, an unnamed opener had already started. They were all right; a guy and a girl behind two racks of keyboards, equalizers, mixers and an IMac, blasting out screamcore with a trancey, thumpey beat.

We sidled up to the bar and ordered cans of Pabst Blue Ribbon – overpriced at three bucks, but an easy buy for a crowd that thought nothing of dropping a Benjamin on a vintage Judas Priest concert shirt. Thomas and I were the squarest-looking dudes there. Every other guy sported a waxed mustache, the women were young, flat-chested and slim, and star tattoos were a dime a dozen.

"Cool crowd!" yelled Thomas over the din.

"Yeah," I shouted. "Let's go upstairs."

Upstairs we went. The balcony stretched half the length of the club, overlooking the stage but hiding the bar. All of the seats were converted from rickshaws that the owners had purchased at a Bangkok fire sale. Thomas and I settled into one large enough to put us close enough to talk but not enough to force contact, and we started to shoot the shit.

We ran through our normal spate of arguments – punk vs. techno, jeans vs. work pants, San Francisco vs. New York (We both agreed that New York wins on nightlife because of the open-until-four bar thing, but I always refused to give in to his contention that the Big Apple has better cheap food. No way. Burritos beat bagels any day.), and the idiosyncrasies of our housemates and the people we'd been having in to replace them. The opening band finished and packed up, and we were able to talk at a normal non-shouting level.

"I don't know," I said. "I mean, we've already paid an extra month's rent to cover the empty room; maybe we should lower our standards."

"No way," said Thomas. "No stoners or BDSM guys, remember?"

"Just somebody normal, like Brent."

Thomas snorted. "Normal in the mixed-up-in-some-weird-Chinese mafia thing way? That's not normal. Hey, did you get anything out of that translation Shawna got you?"

I shrugged. "Not really. It was a few nonsense words. Use LuckyOne13, Pass Yazman."

Thomas swallowed his beer hard.

"You can't possibly be that stupid," he said.

"Thanks," I said. "What do you mean?"

"Use is a username. Pass is a password," he said. "That's obvious. How could you not know that?"

"Shit," I said. "You're right. God, I'm a crappy detective. Maybe I should just stop doing this."

He scoffed. "Right. Because you're going to put so much effort into it before your severance runs out. You can spend every day at the bar, or play detective. It's probably better for you to detect."

"I gotta go to the bathroom," I said. "Want another beer?"

"Sure."

I thought about what Thomas had said as I walked down the stairs. Sure, we did have an obligation to Brent's memory – if I died, I'd certainly want someone to make sure that my parents knew and that some kind of piece of my memory remained. And impressing Morgan was a pretty good idea, but she was pregnant, which made impressing her not the best idea. And why was all of this *my* responsibility? Thomas was right that everyone else in the house worked; it would be nice to have some more help. I hit the door of the bathroom pretty hard when I walked in.

The bathroom at the Rickshaw was your typical indie-rock-dive hole. The urinals (American Standard; I checked) were yellowed with age, and the water was blackened with the remnants of a cigarette butts. It was disturbing that the smokers stubbed their cigarettes out on the sidewalk, then made the effort to bring them inside in order to throw them away in the toilet, but who understands hipster smokers? The walls were a hodgepodge of band stickers and post-ironic Sharpie graffiti. I read some of it as I stood there at the urinal.

For great head, exercise brain.

What do you call someone else's cheddar? Nacho Cheese.

And below that – *if you're going to make a pun, make sure it's a gouda.*

Beware of the lucky one.

Huh. Why would Brent's user name show up here? And now that I was thinking about it, what was it a user name to? Without that, it was pretty much useless. But again, why would it show up on the wall of a bar? And what were they the user name and password *to*? I could try the laptop again, but the default login username had been "Brent," not "LuckyOne13". It had to be the key to something else, some kind of online account. eBay, maybe?

"Dude, um, are you going to finish up there? Whoever's in the stall is doing some serious damage, and you're kind of standing there…"

"Oh, sorry," I said. I zipped myself up and vacated the space, going over to the sink to wash my hands. The soap was the powdered stuff that they had in the bathrooms in my elementary school.

I picked up two more glasses of PBR at the bar and walked upstairs. Thomas wasn't there; our rickshaw had been bogarted by two guys in all-over camouflage gear, fake bullet bandoliers, and tied-backwards headbands. I stared at them until one of them sneered back at me. Downstairs, Ringing London were setting up. The singer, resplendent in jeans, a studded jacket, and an *Exile on Main Street*

Jagger hairdo, tapped the mike twice.

"Hey," he said. "So we were supposed to go on after DJ Caravan, but he sliced off the end of one of his fingers backstage while he was chopping up some buds to roll a joint with, so we're going to play a longer set. Sorry if you wanted to see him; apparently you can't do a whole lot of record spinning without all of the fingers on your left hand. Anyway, we're Ringing London, and we're going to play some songs. This one's called 'I'm Cool.' One, two, three four..."

The band launched into a three-chord fuzzed guitar power-pop song. Eight measures in, the guy started singing:

I've got my horn-rimmed glasses
And my fixed-gear bike
And I love my girl
'Cuz she used to be a dyke

My hair's long in the back
I got a mustache, too
My belt buckle's huge
I'm a hipster through and through

I'm Cool!
I'm cool!
I'm...so...fucking....cool!

"What do you think?" Thomas appeared out of nowhere and leaned down to scream in my ear.

"I think I'm in love with them," I said.

He grinned. "You would be."

The band ran through a long set – the song names that I caught were "Pabst is the Best," "I Drink Fernet," "My Mother Was A Hippie," "You Have Brakes On Your Bike, You Pansy," "Double That Soy Latte," "I Fit Into Women's Jeans," and a full-fledged remake of the Clash's "Should I Stay or Should I Go?" called (I think) "Should I Shave or Should I Grow?"

Classic.

Their set lasted for over an hour and drove the skinny, spectacled crowd over the edge. The singer slung insults left and right ("Hey, how much did you pay someone else to give that jean jacket that worn look?" "Wow, it must have been great to see Iron Maiden's 1982 tour when you were still in the womb," "You'd be really threatening in that black hoodie if you weighed more than Nicole Richie," and so on), and the audience responded with ironic booing and nonstop dancing. Since everyone was white and arrhythmic, the result looked like the beginning montage of a '70s cop show cast entirely with seizing epileptics.

Thomas and I left after the band was done. I'd bought a CD and a few stickers and had no desire to soil the night by checking out the burlesque dance troupe that had been called in at the last minute to fill in for DJ Caravan. Trying to catch one of the Haight Street busses was a roll of the dice at this time of night, so we hoofed it. We walked past a video store, and six burly men piled out behind us, arguing. They were all bearded and muscular, with tight shirts of various colors, washed-out blue jeans, and haircuts so close they could have been refugees from a boot camp.

"Why were we there again?" said one. "That was a waste of time."

"Well, it's not *me* who wanted to go scope for young butt," said another.

"At a video store?"

"We need to go to a bar."

They peeled off after a block and went left towards Market Street, probably heading to one of the leather/bear joints on the south side. Ahead of us, a homeless guy was standing in front of the open door of an abandoned fridge, his legs spread out wide. As we approached, he exhaled, zipped up, gave us a smile, and shuffled off.

"I don't think I've ever seen a fridge used that way," I said.

"Well, the inside *kind* of looks like a toilet," said Thomas. They're both white and all."

"Except for the part where they're not the same," I said. "That was disgusting."

"Price you pay for living in the city," he said.

We walked home in thirty minutes, never seeing the bus. It's a two-hill walk, and we were both breathing hard by the time we ascended our stairs and walked into the living room. Jenn and Shawna were there, each taking up one couch, wrapped in blankets.

"Good show?" asked Jenn. Those were the first words she'd said to me since Friday.

"Great," said Thomas. "Even without Caravan."

"The DJ," I said. "He didn't show."

Jenn shot me an annoyed look. "Believe it or not, I remember the guy's name from the e-mail when Thomas invited all of us. Amazing that my brain works, doesn't it?"

"Testy," I said, wincing. Was she still mad at me?

"She's just bitter," said Shawna. "Another one of her friends showed up pregnant at work today."

"What's the total now?"

Jenn grimaced. "Out of thirty-nine women at my job, seventeen of them are now pregnant. If you're wondering, that's forty-three percent. It's now completely impossible for me to have a conversation that doesn't involve due dates, labor times, or cervical dilation. I'm going crazy."

"You should have come with us," I said. "It was like the Clash done by people who think like me."

"Great," she said. "A second version of the stuff I've been forced to hear every day for the past year. Why don't you expand your horizons?"

"Because they're the only band that mattered," I said.

"Anything else happen?" asked Shawna.

"Well, we saw a guy peeing in a fridge, and a group of older gay men out looking for some action. Typical night."

Jenn grinned. "You should have stayed home," she said. "We had fun."

"Watching the Food Network?" I said. "Just kill me."

"Philistine," she said.

That was when I knew we were OK.

The next afternoon, I was sitting with Gerald in the back of Ruby's, an impossibly dark bar in the dead zone on the west side of Potrero Hill, nursing an Anchor Liberty Ale and listening to him talk about the midpoint between Generation X and Y cultures and how it wasn't that we weren't well-adapted to being office workers, but that office worker culture hadn't adapted to us. One of his friends had been canned after hacking together a twelve person Mario Kart game on his office network using Nintendo 64 simulators, and Gerald was, by proxy, on the warpath. He had been drinking and smoking since eleven in the morning. His words had started to run together; he wasn't slurring them, exactly, but putting two co-workers that close would result in a sexual harassment suit.

"I mean, it's not like he was actually playing an Xbox so that everyone can see; he was just taking a break and blowing off a little steam. It's the same as going to the water cooler and talking about the latest football scores or any other kind of corporate jackassery."

I nodded, not really listening. It wasn't that I disagreed with him; God knows that I'd screwed around at work enough, when I had been working, to warrant several dozen firings. Despite that, staging a retro-console video game deathmatch tournament using LINUX simulators mounted on company PCs seemed the guy was going a bit far. But I didn't say anything – Gerald was rolling like Bluto Blutarski.

"Turns out his boss is one of those guys who has Google as his home page, then types the Web address into Google, then clicks on the first link that comes up. That's how he thinks things work."

I knew guys like that. William Wallace, who was one or two levels above my old boss, would do that. He had never gotten any of our jokes, either, even when I called him "Mel" on a dare during a meeting.

"No, it's not Mel. It's William," he had said, right before typing http://www.yahoo.com into Google on the conference room projector machine. He had punched the enter key, then clicked on the link, entered his username and password into Yahoo, had run a search for "disambiguated applied plastic materials," then lectured all of us about how our efforts weren't resulting in a positive-trending search-engine optimization.

"Hey, I'll be right back," I said to Gerald, swinging my leg back over the bar stool. "Drank too much water this afternoon."

"Squirrel-bladder Alex," he said. "Don't worry, our friend behind the bar will probably listen to me. Another Anchor, please." The bartender nodded and started to fill a pint glass; I walked toward the back wall, trying to clear my head. I'd slept, woken up, eaten, and met Gerald at Ruby's before lunchtime. Unemployment was rough.

Ruby's was a study in cinderblock. The owners were avowed communists and had apparently fallen in love with the Moscow-housing-project look. Old propaganda posters dotted the walls. Gas masks, bomb casings, and stern-looking bronze faces hung from the ceiling. To get to the bathrooms I had to walk through an unmarked steel door and down a hallway so cramped that you'd have to turn sideways if anyone came the other way.

The bathroom itself was mottled gray plaster, and an "Out of Order" sign hung on a string over the hole where the urinal should have been. I walked into the stall and tried to close the door behind me; it swung open and hit me in the butt. If you were sitting, you'd have to prop it closed with one leg. Ruby's had apparently tired of scrubbing the graffiti off of the walls; a small chalkboard hung on the side of the stall.

The Lucky Ones was scrawled on it, vertically, upside down, on the right side. The handwriting was different than what I'd seen at the Rickshaw Stop – it was blocky and deliberate, the lettering of a kid who has just been called to the front of the class. I zipped up and got out of there.

"You forgot to flush the toilet," said the bartender when I got back to my stool.

"How do you know?"

He grinned, his teeth barely visible under his thick, gray-shot beard. "Because I've been running the water to wash the dishes since you left, and I didn't lose any pressure to a flush."

"Oh….sorry, do you want me to…"

"Don't worry about it," he said. "The evening crowd usually gets to the point where they miss the bowl, so flushing is kind of a moot point. The whole thing will smell like piss by nine anyway."

"I saw it again," I said to Gerald. "The Lucky Ones thing. On the wall."

"In the bathroom?" he said. His beer was nearly empty, and his voice was on the verge of bleary.

"Yeah," I said. "It was his username for something."

"Um…OK," he said. "What for?"

"What do you mean?"

"Jesus, Alex. I'm completely hammered. Don't make this harder. What...is...it...username...for?"

"Oh," I said. "I don't know yet."

The bartender leaned forward. "Are you guys talking about weird stuff in bathroom graffiti?"

"Yes," I said.

His eyes opened wide, then flicked to either side, as if he was making sure that nobody else was listening. There couldn't have been; we were the only people in the bar.

"I've been wanting to talk to some people about this," he said. "But..."

"But what?" I asked, my voice down to a whisper.

"Have you guys ever considered that maybe the World Trade Center wasn't brought down by planes?"

"The demolition thing," said Gerald. "People were talking about that years ago..."

"No, not that," said the bartender. "That's just a cover-up. The towers didn't really collapse; they did fall, but they didn't collapse. See...they're *underground* now. The government is scavenging what they can and selling them on eBay to fund secret spy programs against us."

"eBay?" I said.

"Yeah," he said. "That way they don't have to report it in the budget."

"eBay," I said.

eBay. Duh. Usernames. Password. I needed to get on that. After my next drink.

The weather improved as early August faded into mid-August. Instead of fog-socked days and damp, dreary nights we were treated to wispy mornings, and sunny afternoons. I had stopped wearing wool socks at night, and my sandals started up their permanent residence in the corner of my room. I even rescued my pair of shorts from the bottom of a drawer and decided to wear them on my hangover walk. The house smelled odd; whoever had gone out last had left the windows open. The street didn't waft in a *good* smell.

More of a combination of damp air, a whiff of garbage, a little weed, and the unmistakable reek of unwashed person.

I had my breakfast (cereal, milk, sugar, a banana) and walked down the stairs to go outside. The door stopped short after about a foot when I opened it and a voice said "Ow!"

"Oh, sorry," I said, not sure what I was apologizing for. Opening my door when I lived here? That wasn't really a sorry-able offense.

"No problem, man," said the voice. "I just didn't know you were coming out."

I opened the door again and got a look at who I'd hit. It was a street kid, clad in a black hoodie with patches advertising the Casualties and the Misfits. His fine blonde hair was matted, as if he were trying to grow dreadlocks, but his hair was too straight and thin to pull it off - it looked like someone had tried to make a crown of thorns out of spaghetti. His eyes were clear, though, and he had no ink on his face. He was probably new and hadn't soaked up the Haight long enough yet to really spiral down.

"You got any spare change, man?"

I shook my head. "Sorry, not today."

"OK," he said, and smiled. "I really don't need the money, but I think you're supposed to ask if you hang out here. I'm just traveling around, you know?"

"Sure," I said. "No offense taken."

"Seriously, man," he said. "I don't need anything. Check it out." He knelt down and opened up a lumpy rucksack. "I got a computer and everything."

Sure enough, he did; a sticker covered iBook. I wasn't sure what he wanted me to say, so I just said "cool."

"Yeah, you can keep up with everything that's going on," he said. "I was actually working on one of the networks around here this morning. Don't worry if it was yours; I wasn't downloading porn or anything. I work part-time for a little design company in Austin. They don't care where I am, as long as I get my coding done. I had to do a big build today, so I was just uploading that. It's cool."

"No problem," I said. "Keep yourself safe out there."

"I'll have to be a lucky one to do that," he said.

I had taken two steps away from the front door after my last sentence, but that stopped me in my tracks. "What did you say?"

"I'd have to be lucky," he said.

"No," I said. "You said you'd have to be a lucky one. What did you mean by that?"

He blinked and ran a hand through his hair. "I don't know, man. I mean, what does it mean to be lucky?"

"No, a lucky one," I said. "Did you get that from somewhere?"

"Dude, why do you care?"

"Because I do," I said. "Why didn't you just say 'I'm lucky.'?"

He looked at me. I looked back at him. He blinked, obviously thinking.

"I think I picked it up somewhere," he said. "It doesn't really sound like something I would say. Maybe online, maybe just around. But I haven't been here but two weeks, so I don't really know anybody. Maybe it was an online thing."

"Online," I said. "You picked up the phrase online."

"That would make the most sense, man," he said. "I mean, I don't really talk like that normally."

Online. Of course. I turned around and opened the door again.

"Hey, if you're not going anywhere, do you mind if I hang out here?" he asked. "I have a little more work I could do, and if the cops hassle me I can say that you know I'm out here."

"Sure," I said.

I'm not a big geek. I mean, I have a computer and I know how to look things up and book airline tickets, and whenever I go home my parents have some computer problem and I'm usually able to fix it by reinstalling a program or rebooting some things or checking on the wires. But I'm not a virtual-life person or Thomas-class efficient type with an IPhone synched to his laptop that can be auto-dialed from two floors away. I'd forgotten to check my e-mail that morning; that might sum it up.

I started to dig through the previous nights' clothes that covered my little corner couch. My two-year-old laptop was lying under my favorite old flannel shirt, and when I flipped it open, it beeped angrily at me and powered down. Low battery. Where had I put the power adapter? Naturally, I had thrown most of the clothes on top of my two surge protectors. After chucking all of the floor clothes into to my closet, I found the power adapter, plugged in next to my stereo cords and the long extension that went to the reading lamp next to my bed. After plugging the laptop in, it worked fine, so I settled down on my couch and started looking with my fingers.

I Googled "the lucky ones" and came up with a low cost spaying and neutering clinic, an independent film featuring a C-list relative of Drew Barrymore, a site with a bunch of movies featuring normal-looking people doing normal-looking things, an article about survivors of an East Asian tsunami who had converted to evangelical Christianity in order to benefit from contributions made by a megachurch in Kansas, a breakdown of the lyrics of the song by Loverboy, the story of a boy from rural Maine who was in the middle of a boot-camp-style rehab program, and zombieanarchy.com. Nothing even remotely close to what I was looking for. That's the problem with the Internet these days; there's so much crap, it's absolutely impossible to find out what you're looking for with a wide search.

So I started poking around in a few other places – I checked Myspace and Facebook for combinations of those words, then scoped around on the San Francisco city website, ending up on Craigslist in the rants and raves section, scrolling through endless screeds both for and against various types of racism, Republicans, and bears. The bear rant was pretty weird – I couldn't tell whether the guy had something against large carnivorous mammals or hairy gay men.

Two hours had gone by, and I hadn't found anything of use, other than a guy out near the beach who was selling a CD of some live Clash rarities that were pretty much impossible to find. I e-mailed him asking about pricing, then went back to the message boards and ran a desperation full-text search for "lucky" across all of the San Francisco area Craigslists. I got thousands of results and started to page through them. After a few, I started to get a little weirded out..

Lucky woman – you've found me!
Looking for lucky gamers for downtown study
Lucky, Inc. is hiring DBAs, VBScript developers, sales…
Wanna get lucky? Go to http://www.russianlovers.com
Lucky trapeze artist looking for roleplay

Seeking lucky leather daddy for sensual squeeze
Lucky ones are coming

I felt like showering, but I had found something. I clicked on the last ad, and the full text came up completely blank. There was a title, and an anonymized craigslist e-mail address, and that was it. I clicked on the address, brought up an e-mail window, looked at it for a minute, then closed the window. No point in e-mailing them, whoever or whatever they were. What would I ask: *Hi, you had something to do with the mysterious death of my housemate, who I really didn't know, who left behind a cryptic note with the same phrase that you did in an anonymous ad in the San Francisco 'items for barter' section. Who are you?*

I didn't think that was a winner. The Boston stuff got me every time. Why was he so loyal to that town and that baseball team? It was like everyone who was born north of Connecticut drank that love-the-Sox Kool-Aid, and for God's sake unless I did something soon they were going to take his body and burn it to ashes.

"Shit!" I said. "Shit! Shit! Shit!" I slammed the computer closed and started to pace back and forth, kicking aside the papers and actual-dirty clothes that littered my floor. Why didn't I keep a list of things I needed to do? What was I doing?

"What *are* you doing?" It was Jenn, home.

"What do you want to know?"

She arched an eyebrow at me. "Well, you're walking back and forth kicking your clothes around, mumbling, and swearing. I know you're not hormonal and weird because you're a guy, and I'm pretty sure you didn't just get fired, because you're too lazy to get a job, which leads me to believe that you may have gone crazy and are going to kill all of us with an axe, which I think I have a right to know about, seeing as how I live across the hall."

I stopped pacing and looked at her. She was dressed in work clothes – slacks, a white blouse, and a thin gauzy scarf/wrap thing. The sleeves of the blouse were rolled up, and her wrists were bare, which was weird. Jenn usually wore a small gold-colored watch; I had borrowed it once to take to work to see if I could freak anybody out by wearing a woman's watch. Nobody had, but I'd kind of liked the watch. It looked better on her, though.

"Why are you home?"

She sighed, turned around and walked into her room. I followed. She collapsed onto her futon bed, and I sat down on the floor. She found a remote control buried under her covers and clicked on her boom box; jazz from one of our local NPR stations played softly.

"I just couldn't take it any more," she said. "When it's not pregnancy, it's drama of the boy kind. My cubemate just broke up with her boyfriend last week, and has spent the better part of each day on the phone trashing him to all of her friends. When she's not on the phone, she's talking to the woman who's on the other side of me – it's like being in the middle booth between two sides of a food fight at Denny's. I can't take it. I have to get out of there."

"What would you do?" I asked.

"Don't know. Don't care. Anything to get me out of there and not have to deal with those idiots ever again. I'll go work at Starbucks for the medical insurance. I'm down to one person to talk with during the day, and she's all the way across the office."

"What happened to Sara?" Sara had been one of Jenn's work friends, a pixie-looking blonde girl with a penchant for old-school Chuck Taylors and much better musical taste than Jenn. Sara used to come over for beers but hadn't for a while.

"She moved. Didn't I tell you?"

"Not that I remember."

"So I probably told you," she said. "She fell for a guy who lives in Philadelphia, so naturally she decided to go there for a year and then apply to law school at Penn or Villanova. Don't ask me how that makes sense, because it doesn't."

"So now you're all alone?"

Jenn sat up, then started to unwrap the scarf from around her neck. "Yes, Alex, I'm all alone all day at a job I hate. And you're an unemployed slacker who doesn't even log in to IM any more, so I don't have that to entertain me. Thanks a lot."

She stood up and walked over to her dresser, unbuttoning her blouse along the way. I looked down.

"Look down," she said.

"Already there."

"Anyway, I'm not sure what to do," she said. Her voice was

calmer now; the rant had removed some of the bile from her system. I looked at her floor. It had been a while since she'd swept; the cracks between the hardwood planks were filled with little dust balls and crumbs from the crackers she liked to snack on. I looked up, just catching the curve of the side of her stomach as she slipped on an old t-shirt.

"I don't think I can help you much," I said. "I'll be in my room. I think I need to check Brent's eBay account."

"You still haven't done that?"

"I keep forgetting," I said. "But I just remembered."

"Get to it," she said with a grin. "Go do your thing. I'll be downstairs plotting revenge and looking around for a new job."

"I'll be up here if you feel like ranting again," I said.

"Thanks," she said. I turned around and went back to my room, hearing her say "eBay" thoughtfully as I left.

I don't know a whole lot about eBay. I've bought stuff (vintage Clash records, old posters) and sold stuff (duplicate copies of vintage Clash albums, some books), but I don't sit there at work tracking the progress of all of my auctions or grab things off of Amazon and then eBay them for a profit. Sometimes the eBay people tell me about auctions I should be looking at based on what I've purchased in the past. Nobody can have enough Buzzcocks buttons, apparently.

But I wasn't looking for an auction; I was trying to scope through Brent's account to find things out. The username and password logged me right in. I kicked myself for not checking it earlier, then got to work. A check of his profile revealed that he had been using the Brent name. At least I was in the right place. But my eBay knowledge failed me at that point. Luckily, Thomas was available on IM.

Alexbkr: You there?

Thomasrox: No, this is someone else. What's up?

Alexbkr: I'm looking through Brent's eBay account. I don't know what I'm looking for. Can you help?

Thomasrox: Irate. Livid. Can't you figure it out for yourself?

Alexbkr: I don't know anything about eBay. You do.

Thomasrox: Fine…well, keep in mind that the screens you're looking for probably won't show anything.

Alexbkr: They don't.

Thomasrox: Check and see if there's an associated PayPal account. That might lead somewhere.

Alexbkr: Hang on.

I clicked back to the Web, then went to Brent's My eBay, then to his account. Sure enough, on the left hand side of the page was a link to PayPal. A click there took me directly to a PayPal account page with an e-mail address I didn't recognize filled in.

Alexbkr: I'm over at PayPal now, with an e-mail address in the box. Should I try the login and password?

Thomasrox: N. Try using the password you already have with the e-mail addy. Most people use the same password for everything.

Alexbkr: Do you?

Thomasrox: Hell no. People with only one are stupid. I've got six or seven.

I had one password. I made a mental note to figure out a different one for my bank.

First try. The password went right through. The page was mostly blank. No dice.

Alexbkr: Nothing there, dude.

Thomasrox: probably because he's been inactive for a few weeks. eBay doesn't go by transaction, it goes by date. Check a couple of months ago.

Alexbkr: Oh, right.

Thomasrox: Do you know how to do anything?

I ignored him and went back to the site. June was my first paydirt – a $600 transaction with someone who went by the handle of *Vampyreboy*. Freaky. May and April were similar; a smattering of payments in the high hundreds, and then immediate withdrawals to an account labeled "Bank of America." Nothing earth-shaking, and nothing that really showed anything other than a guy with an eBay side business.

March, however, was a completely different matter. The sales came nearly daily instead of once per week, and they edged into the thousands. My instant messenger light blinked at me.

Thomasrox: How's it going?

Alexbkr: He's got a ton of transactions in March. All incoming – he never used this account to pay for anything.

Thomasrox: What were they for?

Alexbkr: I'm not sure.

Thomasrox: Wait, you can use Track a Sale to look up things that have already happened – even if Brent erased his records, they still keep them so people can price-compare. Then go into "other auctions by user" and you'll get the list of what he sold.

Alexbkr: I didn't know that.

Thomasrox: Most people don't. It's an eBay geek thing.

Alexbkr: An eBay geek, you are.

Thomasrox: Proudly. It pays for my beer.

I clicked back into the Track a Sale feature on the eBay side. I knew that the card Brent had sold for the record was a Yaz, so I ran a search for Yazstremski and found

23 sales of autographed jerseys.

13 retro bobblehead dolls.

3 pairs of cleats ("Worn at Fenway! Certificate of Authenticity!").

One pair of batting gloves, dirty.

One pair of long underwear (what?).

3,242 baseball cards.

Alexbkr: Dude, this is impossible. 3,000 baseball card auctions to look through.

Thomasrox: Do they have a price filter?

Alexbkr: What's that?

Thomasrox: Something that sorts out the sales by price. You could sort it down that way.

Alexbkr: Hang on…oh, it says, "Look for auction sale by" then a box and "date," "price," "user," "auction id."

Alexbkr: Only prices of $500 or more…

Thomasrox: That might make it manageable.

Alexbkr: Yep, 128. Thanks!

Thomasrox: Someday you're going to have to learn how to use a computer.

Alexbkr: Bite me.

128 is much less than 3,242. It is, in fact, 94% less. That's a good thing. But, it's still quite a few web pages to crawl through. At about forty-five seconds per page, assuming that nothing crashed, I'd still be sitting in front of a computer for close to two hours. This wouldn't have been a big deal if I'd been at my former job, where I sat in front of a computer all day, reading up on Z-list celebrity gossip (if the guy who played the skinhead friend of Eric Stolz in *Some Kind of Wonderful* had a shotgun wedding, I would be the first guy to know) and obsessively tracking the movements of Mick Jones. But since I was at home, all I could think about was the beer I wasn't drinking from the bar where I wasn't sitting, and the women who might be sitting there, or the coffee I wasn't drinking, the magazine I wasn't reading…but I soldiered on.

And I found the auction, only twenty minutes in. Two years ago, a user with Brent's username had sold a Carl Yazstremski card for over five thousand dollars. Five. Thousand. Dollars. Clicking on the user link from the historical auction pulled an "all auctions by user" list. Funny how I couldn't get that from Brent's account after he'd erased it, but I could see it here; corporate stupidity knows no bounds, I guess. The auctions list ratcheted up the screen; there were at least fifty pages of records.

Thomasrox: Anything?

Alexbkr: eyes getting blurry, I'm gonna print and look at it somewhere else.

Thomasrox: OK l8r.

I hit Print and went downstairs to the house printer. Thomas had set it up when he'd moved in. He'd gotten a deal from his company where they provided him with a printer and free toner as a way for him to more efficiently work from home. I'd never seen him actually work from home – he tended to screw around online or instant message his friends all day – but the upshot for us was free printing for us in the house. The printout ran to fifteen pages. I gathered it up, clipped it together, and went back upstairs to get my laptop and assorted stuff. Jenn was still rummaging around in her room, but she'd changed into jeans and a hoodie.

"Hey, I'm going to go down to Coffee to the People to read. Want to come along?" I said.

She nibbled on the end of her finger. "Sure. Just a sec." Jenn walked over to the other side of her room, grabbed a book and a bag, then came to her door. "Let's go."

"That's it?"

"What do you mean?" she asked.

"Well, most girls, when they say, 'Just a sec,' it means about fifteen minutes of doing weird little things that make no sense, like rearranging the carpet or making sure that all of the pens are in the right places or whatever."

She scowled. "I'm not one of those chicks, Alex. Am I ever late?"

"Not really."

"No," she said. "I'm not. Being punctual is one of my things."

As we walked out the door and down the street, I thought back, trying to remember a time when Jenn had kept me waiting. Shawna was a disaster – one time I had asked her if she wanted to hop out and get some tea and had still been waiting forty-five minutes later. I'd left and gone down the street, waited an hour and finished two cups by the time she'd shown up. Jenn, as far as I could remember, had never done that.

It was a warm walk. I was in my sandals and shorts, and Jenn took off her hoodie when we got down to Haight Street. She was wearing an old green tank top, and her arms were pale. The tank top fit tightly, and the homeless kids let their eyes follow her as we walked by.

"Spare any change, darlin'?" asked a punk with purple hair and a chain connecting his nose and right ear, "or just ten minutes with you?"

"Keep dreaming," said Jenn.

"That's what we do all day," said the kid, grinning and taking a puff off of his joint.

"Go back to Marin," said Jenn.

The kid said nothing, and we didn't look back.

The coffeehouse was half full. We ordered iced drinks and took one of the outside tables under the awning. The sun was warming the back of my neck, and I could feel my forehead dampen at the hairline, but I didn't care. Three months of fog will do that to you. Jenn took a ball of blue/white yarn, two long needles, and what looked like a scarf for a midget out of her bag, then started to knit.

"Stitch and bitch?" I asked.

"I'm knitting," she said. "I'm relaxing. 'Stitch and bitch' is a catchphrase invented by men because they don't understand knitting, and they assume that whenever a group of women get together they're complaining about their husbands or boyfriends. It's insulting, really. Don't you have something to read?"

"Yes," I said. I felt my face turning hot.

"What are you reading?" she asked over the *click-click* of her needles. Her hands dove back and forth, and her eyes followed her hand movements, flicking up every couple of seconds to look at me.

"A history of Brent's eBay transactions," I said. "I'm trying to figure out how much money he made off of them. And maybe find something out about him, too."

"Why don't you just look at the addresses the cards were sent to, and call them?" she asked. "I don't remember him being much of an eBay maniac when he was here, so most of those are probably from his old place back in Boston. If you have the address, you can get a phone number, and maybe those people will know something."

I stopped running my hand down the paper in front of me and looked at her.

"Close your mouth," she said. "Something will..."

"Fly in, right," I said. "Did you read a bunch of Sherlock Holmes when you were a kid?"

"No," she said, stopping her needles. "I just thought that it makes sense. Maybe he had old roommates where he was living before, and they can tell you about him. Or maybe he was living at home, and one of those addresses is his parents, and we can just get rid of the whole mess."

"You're a genius," I said. I clicked open my laptop and started to go through the list of sales. "I can't call them, but I can find them through their eBay user names. The odds are that they're the user name plus yahoo.com or gmail.com or hotmail.com – that should cover most of them. Hm... how do you write an e-mail that says 'Hi, the guy who sold this baseball card to you is dead, do you happen to still know the address that it shipped from so I can track him down and find his parents so they don't cremate him?"

"That probably works," she said. She smiled at me, then started the needles on their *click-clack* cycle again.

I got to it. Sending several hundred messages through eBay takes quite a while, it turns out. Still, I was pleased – the e-mail thing was the best idea I'd had in weeks.

After finishing the e-mail, we headed home. I stopped off at a drugstore on the way and bought a standing cardboard-like vertical file. When I got back home, I picked up the shockingly large pile of Brent-related paper that was strewn around the corners of my room and started to file it. I could have used Brent's vacant room for storing all of that stuff, but…well, it creeped me out. I'd spent most of my working career trying my hardest to not be the guy who files things for other people, and I'd never once put any important paper in the file cabinet with the neat hanging folders that had been next to my office desk. And now, here I was, sitting on my little couch, going through a pile of papers and filing them.

- Pages and pages of eBay printouts.
- Brent's original getting-into-the-house e-mail from our Craigslist ad.
- Copies of the documentation from the morgue, complete with my signature and a blank spot where the *next of kin* was supposed to be.
- Scribbled notes to myself of where I'd seen graffiti that had referenced the Lucky Ones.
- An envelope from Friends of the Republic of China, West Coast Brotherhood Empowerment Division., addressed to *Partner, PO Box 103, Spotend Alley, San Francisco CA USA.* No ZIP code.

Whoops. I remembered now – after the haircut I'd stuffed the envelope in my bag, not wanting anyone who was possibly related to Brent to find out what I was looking for. I'd come back into my room and tossed it on the pile of Brent-related stuff, thinking to myself *I'll get to that after having a beer...* Nice one, Alex. I hit myself in the forehead with the heel of my palm. Ow.

The envelope was glued tightly shut all the way across; it felt like it had been sealed by a perfect envelope-licking robot. No air could get through, and my fingernails weren't long enough to pick it open. I ended up slicing through the top with the small blade from my pocketknife.

Inside was a letter:

Dear Sir,

It was with great interest that we read of your request to open a dialogue with the Friends of the Republic of China, West Coast Brotherhood Empowerment Division. In particular, your business propositions re: privies was of much conversation here. We would most definitely be interested in speaking at greater length to your organization and its representatives.

As a next step, please sending us more detail about standard brands and practices in industry so as we can begin to understand the fabrication process. Pictures and specifications in metric measurements are much appreciated. Our contact information is as below, and you have the name of our representative in the United States. We hope to hear from you soon.

Best,
Liang Xi
Friends of the Republic of China

What? I read the letter three more times, hoping to make some kind of sense out of it. As it was, it could have been referring to anything from washers to crack cocaine, and none of it was specific enough to mean anything, except...well, it had to mean *something*.

I also filed what little mail that had come in for Brent since he'd died. Most of them were magazine offers or credit-card applications, and one survey from the San Francisco Department of Public Works, addressed to our landlord but somehow in Brent's mail pile. No credit card *bills,* though. No bills of any kind. Nothing financial, not even a bank statement. Brent did have that bank account, though – he would have paid rent to Thomas, who was the longest-resident guy. I knew that his PayPal linked account was at Bank of America – did Thomas have any cancelled checks from the same account? I popped open a window and sent a quick question to him, then went into his room and scanned everything I had as a backup. I was scanning everything at this point, and had stopped asking Thomas for permission to use his printer/scanner.

My phone buzzed. A little envelope appeared with a pen next to it – a text message from the same mysterious number as before. My pint-sized friend.

Can you meet me at Harrington's in an hour?

I felt my blood rising up as I texted back.

You going to do something weird again?

The return message was instant.

Harrington's in an hour. It's important.

I stewed. I don't stew much; usually my anger is more of a simmer, or maybe a poach. Why the hell was I doing this? I'd spent most of the day going through paper, and I was reading meaning into things that were probably the result of fevered Budweiser dreams. I decided to go to Harrington's and tell whoever this was to shove it, and I decided to walk; that would probably get me there in time. I checked my computer one last time.

Thomasrox: No cancelled checks, dude. Those would go to him, not to me, and I didn't make copies of checks from you guys.

Well, it was a long shot. After stuffing some notes into my shoulder bag, I left.

The sun was starting to go down, and the shoppers on Haight Street were giving way to the night-time amateur drunks. The professionals had been at the bars since noon. It's a weird transition time; the people getting off the busses are all dressed in business casual, and they all walk-run off the main street to their flats down the hill in the Panhandle or up the slope to Ashbury Heights. At Trax, the mostly-gay bar a few blocks west of us, the shaved-headed pretty boys had already started to congregate outside for the monthly Twink Night. Two cigarette-smoking dudes eyed me as I walked past, and I smiled at them. Flattery makes me feel good regardless of whom it comes from.

Most of my walk to Harrington's was downhill through the Lower Haight, where the happy hours run until eight o'clock and the tricked-out bicycles hung off the parking meters like penis pasta on a bachelorette. I reached the bottom part of my walk at Market Street and turned left past a giant white apartment building and a Starbucks that closes at six. The only people walking around are the ghostly homeless and their squeaky shopping carts. Three blocks of that, and I took a left on Larkin.

Larkin passes the public library, a big gray box of a building that takes up one square block. The local street people set up camp over the steam grates on the west and north sides to stay out of the wind and stay warm. Even this early, every grate was covered by a shadowy pile, and cardboard shanties leaned up against the walls and stretched out over the stairs. I breathed out hard as I walked past.

Larkin becomes what the city is trying to get people to call *Little Saigon*. It's a pretty sad effort – the naming effort consists of the Public Works folks hanging banners reading, "Welcome to Little Saigon" on the overhanging arms of broken streetlights. Little Saigon is really the area of the Tenderloin that serves as the very last stop on San Francisco's crack and heroin train, fifteen square blocks of dealers, addicts, and the services that keep them alive. A guy had spread out a library's worth of books on a rug on the sidewalk, nearly blocking it. As I walked by, he whispered, "Any book you want, man, horse if you need, rock, rock, rock…"

I didn't reply.

Harrington's is four blocks up from the library, smack in the middle of a bunch of Vietnamese restaurants that never open but feature groups of men playing cards with enormous stacks of money behind the window bars. The door to Harrington's was closed; the single window was so smudged and greasy that I couldn't see inside from the sidewalk. I took a breath, opened the door, and walked in.

Harrington's had all the charm of a '70s-era high school cafeteria. An old bearded guy in a baseball hat was sitting on a plastic chair next to one of the tables, nursing a not-steaming cup of coffee. Two women sat at the near end of the bar, smoking and not talking. I took a seat at the center of the bar. The bartender, who looked like

Christopher Walken after an all-nighter, looked in my direction and raised his eyebrows.

"Beer?" I said. "What've you got?"

He reached a bottle of Coors Light from under the counter and plunked it down in front of me.

"Got anything darker?" I asked.

"Nope," he said. "You asked for beer, and that's what we've got. If you want something darker, we have whiskey or some coffee left over from this morning."

I shrugged and sipped the beer. It was colder than a brushoff from a sorority girl and tasted a little better than carbonated Bay water. I was ten minutes early and had forgotten to bring a book. An ancient rotary-channel-dialer television in the corner was playing a re-run of *The Maury Povich Show* from the mid-'90s, judging by the T-shirts that the guests were wearing. The sound was down, so I wasn't able to figure out what the subject was. I think it had something to do with Satanism and youth culture, but who's to say? The early '90s were really odd. I got more and more irritated as I sipped my awful beer, and I started to mentally count the number of places in the world better than Harrington's.

1) *The Swiss Alps. Mountain huts, fried ham for dinner, Swiss beer.*

2) *Zeitgeist. Decent pool table, good beer on tap.*

3) *Tokyo. Beer from vending machines.*

4) *The beach at Zihuatenejo. The beer isn't that good, but the margaritas probably rule.*

5) *My living room. Comfortable couch, Anchor Liberty.*

"You're early."

I hadn't noticed him come in; it was my tiny Chinese friend. He looked something the worse for wear; his head had been unevenly shaved recently, and what hair he had was sticking out and up in angry one-inch bristles. A large gash was healing on his left hand, which was shaking a bit as he sat down on the stool next to me.

"Beer?" asked the bartender.

"How's the coffee?" asked the little guy.

"Six hours old," said the bartender. "It's a little strong."

"Perfect," said the little guy. "I haven't slept much lately."

The bartender rooted around for a minute or two, eventually coming up with an off-white mug.

"Cream or sugar?" he asked.

"No," said the little guy.

"That's good," said the bartender, "we don't have any."

The little guy took a sip, then screwed up his lips and frowned. "Strong," he said. "Crappy, but good."

"What do you want?" I said. The old guy at the table moved over to the juke box, where he was pressing buttons with his face plastered to the song-list window. I didn't want to be in Harrington's any more; I didn't want to walk back through the Tenderloin after dark and be accosted by the maniacs, and I could figure this out on my own without the cryptic crap. More than anything else, I was tired and didn't want to listen to him rate his coffee. I stood up.

"Sit down," he said. "You need to hear this."

"I don't need to hear anything," I said. "I need to stop spending time in crappy bars inhaling other people's smoke and trying to figure out why my dead roommate was making so much money selling baseball cards on eBay and what he was doing with the money, which has nothing to do with finding out who he really was and getting him out of the morgue so the city doesn't ashify him without his family ever knowing. And what the hell is *your* name, anyway? Wait, scratch that. I don't care any more, and I only came here to tell you that and go home."

"You can't do that," he said.

"Why not?"

"Because lots of people know that you've been asking around about your dead roommate and the wrong people might have heard about it."

He was trying to sound tough, I think. But that line, coming from a guy who made Napoleon look like Wilt Chaimberlain, ended up being funny enough to make me snort.

"Don't laugh," he said. "This is serious. Do you know what he was up to?"

"Why should I tell you?" I said.

"Because if you tell me how he was getting all of his money and actually take me seriously, I'll tell you something about what he was planning to do with it, and maybe you'll get out of this without getting into trouble."

I took another sip of my beer and thought for a few seconds. Maybe he was serious. Maybe I was in trouble. Maybe that wasn't a cold drop of sweat making its way down my rib cage. Trouble? I just wanted to find out who Brent's parents were.

"He was hawking baseball cards on eBay," I said.

"So what?" he said. "I wanted to know how he got his money."

"He sold them for a total of…" I stopped and dug through the crunched papers in my backpack, digging up the eBay records. "Three hundred and forty-two thousand dollars."

The little guy blinked twice. "Hm…." He said. "That's quite a bit."

"Yeah," I said. "Why?"

"What I know," he said. "It's not much…"

"Thanks," I said. "Now you've wasted my time and told me that someone I don't know knows that I'm looking to find something out about a dead guy. And I've come clean to you with something that nobody else really knows. You're way up on me, and for all I know you're with the guys who are trying to find me. Why am I even here?"

"No, stop interrupting me," he said. He reached down into his pocket and pulled out a many-folded piece of paper. "I really shouldn't be giving this to you, but…well, here."

I took the paper from his hand and unfolded it. It appeared to be a blueprint, or some other kind of design specification. Not a diagram or a blueprint, but a list of dimensions, diameters, angles, and what looked like several algebraic equations.

"Where did you get this?" I asked.

"I have a friend," he said. "He's from Laos, he does janitorial work for a few places, and people don't pay attention to him because he doesn't speak any Cantonese. He's a lot smarter than the people think he is. He got this for me."

"From where?" I asked.

"Your friend had sent this thing out to several places in China," he said. "Somehow it worked its way back to people here who employ my friend. He had it. My friend found it."

"Where does your friend work?" I asked.

He shook his head. "I can't tell you that. I can't be risking him."

"Oh," I said, not sure what to say to that. "Thanks."

He shrugged. "You helped me out when I was strapped. I owe you one."

"Thanks again," I said.

"Some words of advice," he said. "At the moment, nobody who knew your friend knows exactly who you are or what you're doing, but they know that somebody's nosing around. You need to be careful."

"Who are they?" I asked. "How do they know this?"

He grabbed my arm and squeezed hard. "You were stupid enough to go namedropping in Chinatown, and you asked the barber some very dumb questions. Luckily for you he's half blind and only remembers that you were a white guy with light brown hair. Since you were sitting in the chair, they don't even have a height, and they don't know what other names your friend..."

I opened my mouth to say "Brent" but he shushed me.

"I don't want to know," he said. "But if they do find out, and they find out that there's a body in the morgue that bears a suspicious resemblance to their dead former business partner and that they haven't cremated it yet...how long has it been?"

"A while," I said. "A few weeks."

"Suspicious," he said. "If they find that out, they might have ways of getting your name. You don't want them to know your name. I'd get rid of the body. If they find out, they'll link it back to you."

"What should I call you?" I said. "I kind of like to know people's names."

"Don't," he said. "If you feel an urge to get in touch with me, resist it. We're even now, and I'm leaving this town. There are too many people here who know who I am."

"One more question," I asked.

"OK," he said.

"What's with the lucky one thing? I mean, I've run across it a few times, and the word 'lucky' shows up in the name of that place you probably don't want me to talk about..."

He didn't pale, exactly, but he kind of *rippled*, a body-shake born out of a cold day on the tundra.

194

"I've heard a few things," he said. "That could be very interesting," he said.

"What?" I said. "Who are these guys? What's going on?"

His smile widened until it seemed to split his tiny chin. "That word," he said. "'Lucky.' You might want to pay attention to that. Just be careful. I'm going to leave now, and you should wait a few minutes before I go."

Yeah, whatever. He was right back in the Tom Clancy playbook with that one. Why couldn't people come up with more original sneak-around things to say, like "we're leaving together and walking to an SRO hand-in-hand so that the people who are watching us think you're a male prostitute?" It would be more effective. If *I* was putting someone under surveillance, I'd just wait and follow the guy who left the bar right *after* the guy who leaves, and whack him.

I took out my phone and looked at the number he'd messaged me from, and saved it as "littleannoyingdude." I'd call him if I wanted to. I finished my beer, and left. Navigating through the outskirts of the Tenderloin after dark was much more fun than twilight – the dealers were flitting back and forth in the gloom, meeting up with other indistinct figures, slapping hands, changing things, then flitting away. I didn't come within ten feet of anyone until I got back to Market Street and hopped a bus home.

Chapter 13

"So this is a set of instructions on how to build a *toilet?*"

Thomas nodded. "It's pretty easy to figure it out if you have a bootleg copy of AutoCAD. All I had to do was feed these figures into the program and let it autodraw for a few hours. I did that, and this came out."

"What's so special about it?"

"I don't know. I mean, maybe it's some special kind of Masters of the Universe Toilet."

"The Grayskull Flush-o-Tron? I guess I'll have to find out," I said. "Want to help me?"

"I'd love to," said Thomas. "I really would. But I have to go to work tomorrow morning, and although I've got them convinced that I'm using instant messenger to communicate with my wide variety of fictional stockbroker friends to figure out market trends, I think I'd be hard-pressed to explain why I was looking at multiple instances of toilets during work hours. I don't want to get a reputation at work as an obsessive toilet fetishist. Even if I didn't get fired, nobody would ever go to lunch with me again."

"Can you print out these pictures?" I asked.

"Sure," he said, clicking his mouse a few times. "It's coming out downstairs."

The next time I'm out on a blind date with a girl, if we play the running-out-of-questions game and she asks me when the last time I pulled an all-nighter was, I'm going to lie. I'm going to make up some story about missing a night bus and having to walk home and deciding to stay up for the sunrise, or talk about how the inspiration to put together a website dedicated to pictures of George "the Animal" Steele struck me, and I lost track of time putting it together and coming up with an advertising strategy. There is absolutely no way that I'm going to tell anyone that I stayed up all night comparing online pictures of toilets to a printout picture of a computer-aided drawing of a toilet generated from specs given to me by a shrimp who may or may not have connections to the Chinese mafia. The mafia part is cool, sure, but anyone who stays up all night looking at toilets definitely gives off a *run the hell away* kind of vibe.

But that's what I did that night. I went through a pot of green tea and surfed my way through the entire American Standard website. When I got tired of looking at pictures of toilets, I ended up looking up information about them. I learned quite a bit:

- *Webster's* defines a toilet as "a fixture that consists usually of a water-flushed bowl and seat and is used for defecation and urination," while the more blue-collar Wikipedia definition is "a toilet is a plumbing fixture and disposal system primarily intended for the disposal of the bodily wastes: urine, fecal matter and vomit." That last one seems to me to be a fortunate by-product of what a toilet is primarily for. I can't think that the inventor was thinking to himself, "Wow! I bet people will barf in this, too!"
- The flush toilet was invented by a John Harrington, who was too embarrassed to mass-produce the thing. So some guy named Alexander Cummings now gets all the credit.
- Some people who use public toilets for anonymous sex refer to toilets as "Roman Tea Rooms." English people call the practice "cottaging."
- The 2000 Nobel Prize in Public Health was awarded to three guys (Wyatt, McNaughton, and Tullett) who reported on wounds to the buttocks caused by collapsing toilets.
- Elvis, Lenny Bruce, Catherine the Great, and Kings George II and Edward the Second all died while sitting on the can. George died of an aortic dissection, which sounds like what we used to do to earthworms in fifth-grade biology class.

It was four in the morning by the time I had worked my way through the American Standard site and Kohler.com. I had wanted to start with TOTO, but they kept throwing out errors. So many hours and no dice; American Standard was turning into a blur of gravity flushes, comfort jets, air spas, elongated one-piece toilets, no-plunge models, and something called Flowise®.

Enough. I was holding my head and blinking, thanking the gods I didn't wear contact lenses – my eyes hurt enough as it was. After a quick break to refill my tea, I checked back with TOTO. Their site was finally functioning and forced me to wait through a minute long Flash introduction that featured words like "timeless," "smooth," "pure," and "striking," while showing me pictures of brushed aluminum sink fixtures and the ivory white of surgically clean bathroom floors. When I clicked through to the toilet section, the site informed me that TOTO offered "legendary flushing performance."

In days of yore, when the Geats would come back from the hunting of boars and the pillaging of the villages, yon warriors came to the privy, and there they were rid of the blockage in their loins. And yea, when the blockage was pushed down the pipes by the wondrous power of TOTO, the men would gather around the campfires in the darkest of nights and regale their sons with tales of the mighty TOTO flusher myth...

I shook my head; that kind of thought wasn't going to get me anywhere. Despite the glossy sheen, their catalog wasn't that much different than American Standard's – they let you choose between round and elongated, ADA compliant or not, one piece or two. They offered something called the "Cyclone Flushing System." I'd pay to see that; would it make a mobile home explode somewhere every time you flushed?

And then, there it was. The object of my desire. The Neorest Toilet with SoftClose seat. It looked like any other toilet, except with no tank. It had the Cyclone Flushing System, automatic operation, and a twelve-inch rough-in, which sounded dirty. It was a dead ringer for the line diagram that Thomas had printed out for me at the beginning of the night. I scrolled through the page, looking at the features and wondering what was so special about the thing, and then I saw the list price.

$9,899.

I closed my laptop and started to massage my eyes. Ten grand? For a toilet? Something was wrong with the world. But why did Brent have the design specs for this toilet sent to an underground organization in China? If he was looking to make money, that would make no sense, because the average person in China wasn't going to drop four digits on a toilet, surely.

Unless...maybe they weren't selling them in China. Maybe they were selling them *here*. Gerald had gone off to Thailand a few years back and had come back with a sheaf full of bootleg software and movie DVDs, manufactured and burned in sketchy back-alley Bangkok duplication houses. He'd sold them on eBay and made a killing. Why not do the same thing, just more high-end, and with toilets? It was exactly like the bootleg Kate Spade bag sellers on Canal Street in New York, just on a bigger scale. It made sense, especially if they were able to use low-quality electronics. Anyone who bought these things would be sorely disappointed. I fell asleep in my clothes, dreaming of animated toilets with giant teeth.

"You're insane," said Jenn the next morning. She was staying home from work for the day and was baking a batch of banana-nut muffins to celebrate. She was wearing her glasses, which she almost never wore outside of her room. I didn't mind them; they were pointed at the sides, kind of like the horn-rims that librarians all were supposed to wear back in the 1950s.

"Where was he getting the money to do this?" she asked.

"Baseball cards," I said. "He was selling baseball cards on eBay and then taking the profits from that and plugging them into this venture to sell bootleg toilets here in the States."

"Are you listening to yourself?" she said. "A woman came into the office yesterday to try to sell some pamphlets. She's a Jehovah's witness and a no-oil vegan and she made much more sense than you are making right now."

"It makes perfect sense," I said. "You're just being stubborn."

Jenn opened one of our drawers, yanked it harder to release it from where it always got stuck six inches from being closed, and pulled out a wooden spoon. She jammed the spoon into a bowl, cradled the bowl under her left arm like a football and started stirring muffin batter with her right arm. I could see the tendons in her forearm rippling as she mixed. She leaned back against the counter as she worked and stared at me with a steady gaze.

"So what are you going to do about it, assuming that your insane theories actually hold water?"

"Well, I..." my phone rang. I looked at it – the caller ID was the morgue. I hesitated, then flipped the phone open.

"This is Alex."

"Hello, Mr. Baker. This is the San Francisco City Medical

Examiner's office calling."

"I know. What's up?"

"Well, there's been an unfortunate accident."

"What?"

"Well, we were training new interns on how to do the body reduction…cremation, I think you'd call it. And the body that you're listed as the contact information on was unfortunately put in a crematorium that was supposed to be inactive for the training session. Except the failsafes were not confirmed to be on as per protocol. So when the instruction group flipped the "on" lever, instead of nothing happening, the fire jets went up, and when that happens the incinerator is impossible to re-open until the cycle is finished."

I sat down. "What's that all mean?"

The voice hesitated. "Your…um...partner?"

"Housemate."

"Your housemate has unfortunately been cremated. We don't store reduced remains here, so you'll need to come down as soon as you can to pick up the ashes."

"Wait….you *accidentally* cremated him?"

"Yes, sir. I'd like to stress that it was an accident, and the City's insurance policy will be happy to reimburse the next of kin for the costs of…"

I closed my phone. I'd waited too long. I felt empty and cold, angry and sad. I guess Jenn could see that something bad had happened, because she walked over and put her arms around me from behind and squeezed, her warm cheek touching my ear, her hands on my chest.

"I'm sorry," she said. "What now?

"I go down to the morgue," I said. "And get his ashes."

Shit.

Jenn came down with me. I didn't ask her to– actually, I told her that she really *shouldn't* come along, but she wasn't having it.

"My roommate, too," she said. "He was a decent guy, and there's no way I'm letting you go down there by yourself and carry an incinerated corpse back on the bus."

"Because two people carrying an incinerated corpse is much less weird," I said.

"Oh, save it," she said. "I'm doing you a favor because I think you could use the company. Quit this I-don't-need-anybody-lone-Dark-Knight-Detective crap and let's get on the bus. And stop being macho – it's OK to be sad. You can't be expected to do this alone, and stop pretending that you want to."

That shut me up. It helped a little bit that it was a beautiful Indian Summer day with no trace of fog, the air dry and on the verge of being warm. I put a light jacket in my bag as a just-in-case; Jenn stayed in her tank top and pointed to her upper arms as we walked.

"I get to show off the guns maybe twice per year," she said. "I don't care if I get a little cold." She was obviously trying to cheer me up, but it was pretty transparent. Her voice cracked a little on the last word.

The morgue was the same as before but the stairs outside were empty. I walked to the side of the entrance and looked to see if there was anything left of the little homeless encampment. A cigarette but had been crushed on the concrete, but that was it. Nothing remained of the homeless man who'd been living there before. We entered.

"Can I help you?" asked the woman at the desk. She twirled her graying hair around a finger, then pulled the hair free with the other hand.

"Yeah," I said. "We're here to pick up some remains."

"What's your name?" she asked.

"Alex Baker," I said.

"Oh, yes, Mr. Baker...." She turned around in her chair and opened up a file, flipping through papers with a practiced air. "They told me that you'd be coming in...they wanted you to sign this."

She whipped around and smacked a legal-size sheet of paper on the counter in front of me. The thing was filled with small letters and big words. When I read legal documents my eyes glaze over and my brain immediately goes on a journey replaying Hulk Hogan matches that I watched in the mid-1980s.

"What is this?" I asked.

"Just a release form for the remains," she said.

"Can anyone else see it? I mean, if anyone comes here and asks..."

"Not without your permission – we keep everything confidential."

"OK," I said, and scrawled my name on the blank line.

"Right," she said. "Just take this form downstairs." She stamped the paper with the word RELEASE and handed it to me. It was a three-sheet carbon. "Through that door to the elevator and down. Have a nice day."

We rode the elevator down to the bottom floor, and stepped out into the chrome-steel hallway, then through the pressure door to the room where the bodies lay. The same white-haired mad-scientist guy from before was there when we entered; he was bent over one of the gurney drawers, softly singing a song. Jenn reached over and took my arm; I could feel her shivering in the chill.

"Oh, hello," he said. "Can I help you?"

"We're here to pick up some cremated remains," I said, handing over the RELEASE form. Soft violin music was playing in the background. It was discordant – swipes with the bow followed by atonal plucking, the kind of music they'd play in a dentist's chair in hell.

"Cremains," he said.

"What?"

"Post-burn people are called cremains," he said. "Ah, yes, case 432A-I. That was such a bummer. It wasn't really Leon's fault, you know; he was new and one of the diodes had burned out, so he certainly couldn't be expected to know that was going to happen when he flipped the switch on a practice session. We all stood there and watched helplessly as the fires consumed your friend. It was..."

Creepy. I could hear Jenn breathing hard and shallow.

"Sad beautiful," he said. He shook his head slowly back and forth. A wisp of white hair dislodged itself from behind his right ear and swayed in front of his face. He took his glasses off, breathed on one of the lenses, and rubbed the lens with the tail of his lab coat. "So sad," he said.

Jenn's grip on my arm tightened a little bit. I squeezed back. I could feel her breath on my ear as she started to whisper something to me, but she was interrupted by the mad scientist.

"Right," he said. "Follow me."

He led us to a steel door flush with the wall at the far end of the room. The door opened inwards to a room starkly lit with two compact fluorescent lights, lined with file cabinets.

"Temporary storage," he said. "Usually we don't have to use it. We keep spare bulbs, cleaning supplies and fuel in here. We ran out of cardboard boxes for this sort of thing, but your friend fit nicely into one of these..." he yanked open a drawer and took out a brown plastic bag, one of the kitchen-sized ones you use to line your garbage can. Block letters on the side spelled out *San Francisco Medical Examiner.*

"It's a double-bag," he said. "It will hold the weight nicely. Here you go." He held the bag out with both hands, and I extricated my right arm from Jenn's vise grip and took it. I nearly dropped it; it weighed at least fifteen pounds.

"Weighs a bit, doesn't it?" he said, smiling and showing his teeth. "We can get rid of all of the skin and fat, but the ash from the bone is still pretty dense, even though it doesn't look it. You're all set."

"Let's go," I said to Jenn.

"Oh, you'll need this," said the guy. He scribbled a few words on the RELEASE form, tore off the pink copy, and handed me the rest. "Give the yellow one to Susan upstairs, and the white is for your records. You can show yourselves out; I have some reorganization to do in here. Have a nice day."

I slung the garbage bag over my shoulder and held it with two hands. Jenn and I walked out, her shoulders touching mine with nearly every step. I could hear her breathing quickly, and if we'd stopped I'm sure I would have heard her hammering heartbeat. Her face was flushed and shining with wetness.

Susan took the yellow copy of the RELEASE form and smiled at me when we left it with her. She tapped a few words on the keyboard, printed out another sheet of paper, and handed it to me.

"For your records," she said. "Have a nice evening."

"Right," I said. Jenn pulled me out the front door, keeping her hand on my shoulder until we made it to the street.

"What *was* that?" she asked. "Where are Mulder and Scully? Does anybody know what goes on down there?"

"It is pretty weird," I said.

"Weird? Weird doesn't cover it. We just got our roommate's

remains in a hippie grocery bag, and we're standing on Tenth Street, and you have a dead guy slung over your shoulder, and we're going to carry it on the bus."

"You know what's weirder?" I said. "I bet that isn't the first time this has happened on the 19."

She shook her head. "That's not funny."

The bus was nearly empty when it pulled up. Nobody was waiting at the stop with us, and the driver didn't look up as we boarded. Jenn put in three dollars for the both of us. We couldn't fit in one of the two-seat combinations that faced forward, so we went to the back of the bus and sat in one of the rows that face inwards, with Brent's ashes taking up the seat between us. Jenn put her hand on the bag and ran her fingers back and forth over it. I looked at her, then looked at the bag, then looked at her, then looked at the bag. The bus made its way north through the warehouses and flophouses on the other side of the courthouse. Nobody else boarded the bus, and we hopped off at Market Street.

"Quiet ride," I said. Jenn nodded. We waited on the bus platform with a few other people. A 71 bus showed up after about five quiet minutes; this one wasn't empty, but we were able to get two seats in the center-facing section near the back. We sat side by side with Brent's ashes at our feet. Jenn sat with her head down and her hair covering her face. I took my jacket out of my bag and draped it around her shoulders. It was dark green and far to big for her; it looked like she was wearing a sack. She looked like I felt: wan, her eyes red and hollow. I had run my hands through my hair so many times that it stuck straight up and out, looking like it hadn't been washed in weeks.

A bear couple sat across from us, the two of them taking up the three seats with no trouble at all. They looked alike in that way that couples who have been together for a long time look – both men wore t-shirts, jeans, suspenders, and had gray and white spattered amongst their trimmed beards. If they hadn't been holding hands, they could have passed for slightly overweight skinheads. One of them cupped his hand over the other's ear and whispered, then took out his wallet and extracted a five.

"Here," he said. "You guys should get yourselves something to eat."

Huh?

"What?" I said.

"Food," he said. "I know what it's like out there after someone steals your stuff."

I stared at the bill for a few seconds, until finally it clicked.

"Oh, no," I said. "We're not homeless. We just…"

"We've had a bad day," said Jenn. "And there's a dead guy in the bag."

"Oh…" said the bear, folding up his money and putting it back in his wallet. "I'm sorry, I just assumed."

"It's cool," I said. "Garbage bag. We look like hell. It's a natural conclusion to draw."

"I ordinarily don't give out to homeless kids," said the bear. "You're both so cute and you look so sad…" He reached up and nuzzled at his eye. "Did you say there's…"

"A dead guy," said Jenn. "Ashes."

"In a bag?"

"They ran out of boxes at the morgue."

"Hm," said the bear. "Twenty years ago *everyone* had urns lying around."

"Not anymore," said the other guy.

"Thank God," said the first. "This is our stop. You guys take care." They got up and walked out the door, then down the hill. Jenn looked over at me, then down again. Our stop came a few minutes later and we got off, with me lugging the bag full of Brent. We were a block from the house when Jenn stopped walking. I didn't notice for a few seconds – Brent was getting heavy and my arm was aching, and I just wanted to get home. I turned around and she was standing under a streetlight, leaning against it, one hand on her face, her shoulders hitching up and down.

I walked back to where she was.

"You OK?"

She looked up at me, her face smudged with tears and dirt that had probably come off of the side of the lamp post.

"No," she said. "We just went down to the *morgue* and picked up a shopping bag full of a person, and the guy there was a freak right out of late-night cable, and then the guys on the bus thought we were homeless because we were carrying a bag full of a person and we look like shit, and nobody's ever thought I was homeless before. What the hell is going on? Why are we doing this? We don't even know who this guy was, he was *lying* to us about his fucking name, and you're walking across town like a hobo too poor or stupid to steal someone else's backpack to put your stuff in. I don't know what to say, I don't know what to do, and now..." she dissolved in sobs.

I set Brent down and put my arms around her. She hugged me back, her hands cold through my shirt, and her tears wet on my shoulder. I held her for what seemed like a very long time.

Chapter 14

I didn't know where to put Brent. His ashes had stayed in the corner of my room for the whole weekend; the total bill for his storage that Susan had handed me was for $150 per day, which would *definitely* be hard to pay back. I spent as much time as I could away from my room to avoid dealing with it. The bag with his ashes was similar to our environmentally-friendly shopping bags, and I didn't want anyone to accidentally take Brent to Safeway. My choices were

1)   Hide it in a closet downstairs.
2)   Put it in my room somewhere.
3)   Put it in Brent's room.

None of those was a particularly attractive choice. Brent's room was out because I knew we would forget to take the bag out of there when potential roommates came to look at the room; explaining that you'd be moving into a room most recently occupied by a bag full of cremains was not something I wanted to do. Even worse – what if someone found that to be a plus? No way. We had two communal closets downstairs. One stored our cleaning supplies, the other empty computer and stereo boxes. Nobody ever really went into the second one except Thomas, who added a new box every few weeks as he added to his ever-expanding gadget collection. However, he'd probably throw the bag away, which meant that it would have to live in my room for now.

The bag made me nervous; I first put it in the corner behind my love seat, until I realized that it was right next to my heater, which did not actually heat my room when I turned it on, but would blaze up at random times, usually when it was warm outside. Like now. I ended up putting the bag behind my closet door, which didn't close properly and was usually open. I would have put Brent in *my* closet, but that felt disrespectful. So he stayed behind the door, a little bit of black plastic peeking out behind the knob. It was like he was craning what was left of his neck around the blue-painted wood and staring at me.

After a scary night full of dreams that Brent was reforming himself out of his ashes and trying to choke me to death in my sleep, I crawled out of bed at six-thirty in the morning – earlier than I'd ever been up when I'd had a job. I went downstairs, where Thomas was sitting at the kitchen table with his laptop, drinking coffee and clicking keys every few seconds.

"Hey," he said.

"Hey," I said.

"Coffee?"

"Please," I said. "I didn't sleep well."

Thomas filled a mug and handed it over to me. I ordinarily use cream and sugar, but I was feeling tough and took it black. My first sip tasted like the air at a convention of the recently divorced. I gagged a bit, grimaced, and swallowed.

"Sugar?" asked Thomas, grinning.

"Please," I croaked. "How do you drink that?"

"I drink redeyes when I get coffee out," he said. "Grinding to 'turkish' and then letting it sit for a bit is the only way I can get close to that at home."

I added three tablespoons of sugar, then went to the fridge to get some milk. The coffee now tasted palatable, but I could still feel my heart rate accelerating to NASCAR speeds.

"I'm trying to remember the last time I saw you up this early," said Thomas. "I think there was that one time you had a morning meeting, but…"

"Yeah, that time the company CEO came by the office," I said. "We all had to wear ties. You made fun of me for looking like you that morning."

Thomas looked down at his tie and wrinkled his nose. "I hate this thing," he said. "And the annoying part is that I don't officially have to wear it."

"Really?"

"Yeah, officially we're business casual during the week. But if you don't show up in a suit and tie, your boss calls you in and gives you this obtuse lecture about how it's important that we all get on the same page and remember that the company has an image for our customers. Except for the part where we do all of our customer contact online and on the phone, and it's not like we're videoconferencing or anything. Our customers never see us, but I have to wear a tie. Four more years."

"What happens in four more years?"

Thomas took another sip of coffee, sighed, then looked down. "I'll have my private student loans paid off," he said.

"Oh."

I looked at Thomas while he looked down and sipped his coffee. The usual dark circles under his eyes were even darker; he looked like a raccoon on his way to a wedding. He drained his coffee and stood up.

"Time to go," he said.

"You should get some sleep," I said.

"Hello?" he said. "This is the pot. Kettle, you're black. You look like hell, Alex. I always look like this in the morning. You're just never up to see it."

"Yeah, but at least I have a disintegrated dead guy in my corner," I said. "You do this every night."

He shrugged. "You get used to it. I have to have my life, and I have to be at work, so sleep has to go. It's not like I have to be particularly coherent at work anyway. Writing Excel macros isn't exactly...wait, Brent's ashes are in your room?"

"Yep," I said.

"That's severely fucked up," he said. "You should put them somewhere."

"Where?" I said. "I don't want them to get lost."

"That's your insomnia, then." he said.

"Hey," I said. "Serious question."

"Shoot," he said.

"Do you like your job?" I asked. "I mean, do you *like* like it?"

"It's a moot question," he said. "I have no choice. Asking whether I like it is pointless. They own me until I can pay off my loans." He sighed again. "I gotta go. Have a good day."

I sat and sipped my coffee, looking out the window at the blank green wall of the house next door, until steps thudded on the stairs and Jenn came down, her head down, not saying a word. She'd never been a morning person; I'd not seen her before ten a.m. on a weekend outside of the morning after the Bed Pass-Out Incident. Her eyes were half closed, and she gave off the vibe of a woman on her way to an execution chamber. She poured a cup of coffee into a brushed-aluminum travel mug, added two spoonfuls of sugar, screwed on the top, and left the kitchen.

"Hi Alex. Bye, Alex," she said on the way out.

Shawna came down last. Her black hair was tied back with a green bandanna, and she was wearing a hippie-looking skirt-over-jeans combo that looked pretty good; her legs somehow came off as longer than they really were. She looked even more tired than Jenn, and her walk was less bouncy than usual, as if someone had taken the springs out of her legs.

"Tough night?" I said.

She turned on the stove below the teapot and nodded, grunting a syllable that may have been "yes" and may have been "shit," but probably actually meant something somewhere between the two.

"Good day coming?" I asked.

"Mmmph," she said, sitting down with a thud. "No sleep. Work."

"Gotcha," I said.

"Gotta go," she said, heaving herself up from the table and thudding her way out the door. I listened to her footsteps go down the stairs and then heard the door slam as she left. I was alone in the house with a bag full of ashes and an uncertain day ahead. The teapot started to whistle. Shawna had been so tired she'd forgotten that part of the morning. I got up to turn it off, and since I was up anyway I went back upstairs, where I opened up my laptop to check my eBay messages for the first time since I'd sent out that blast to Brent's customers. I'd written to over three hundred people, and nearly fifty had messaged back. The notes were a litany of "sorry" and "don't have it" and "why would you want to know?"

Except for one – a guy who went by the handle of *Samhornmessiah*. He had actually corresponded with Brent aside from eBay on a Red Sox message board, and wanted to get some information from me directly to prove who I was before giving me any information. So I e-mailed him what I knew about Brent, what he looked like, when he'd moved into our house, and a few other minor details, using the name "Brent." Samhornmessiah must have been online, because he e-mailed back in about five minutes.

Alex,

OK, that's cool. His address before moving in to your place, or at least the address where this stuff came from, was 15 Minuteman way, Billerica Massachusetts 02037. I have it because I kept it in my address book when I bought the card from him in case I wanted to send it back. You're lucky; I've got a new computer on the way and was going to wipe this one – that information probably would have gotten lost. Hope that helps.

It did. I was able to get the phone number for that address with a single white-pages lookup. It was still only nine o'clock California time. Why not? I dialed the number, my heart suddenly pounding. I'd never made a death call before.

"Hello?" The voice was female and raw, like Jessica Rabbit after gargling lye.

"Hi, um. You don't know me, but…"

"Well, that didn't stop you from calling me, did it? Who are you?"

"My name is Alex Baker. I was roommates with Brent Scalia…"

"Oh, yes, him. What is this about?"

Him?

"Um…are you related to him?"

"No," said the voice. "He lived with us for a while."

"Oh," I said. "You were a roommate."

"Kind of," she said. "I had an in-law apartment downstairs and he lived in it for a few years after he graduated from BU. He didn't seem to mind that it had no kitchen – just a hot plate and a small fridge. He was a good tenant – paid the rent on time and never really made any noise…"

She kept talking, in the way that people do who never get the chance to talk with anyone but the people who randomly call. Their happiest times are during political campaigns and Christmas donation time. August is hell.

"Are you still there?" said the voice. "What's this about?"

I was having trouble speaking. Finally, the words came out. "Brent died," I said.

"Oh," said the voice. After a few seconds she spoke again. "Well, if you're looking for any of his things, I can't help you with that. He left me a forwarding address just in case, but he stopped getting mail here a few months ago. The mail was going to San Francisco, but I don't have the address any more."

"No, that's OK," I said. "Did he have an emergency contact or something like that on his lease? Relatives, maybe?"

She tutted. "Oh no. I remember clearly asking him about that when he moved in, and he said that his parents had both died when he was young, and he was an only child. His emergency contact was his office number – I remember because I called it once when I hadn't seen him for a few days, and it turned out he was just on vacation. He was very nice about it, and his boss certainly didn't mind talking with me for a few minutes. What a nice young man he was…"

I took the phone away from my ear, then slowly closed it. Rude, yes, but I didn't want to listen, and I couldn't handle saying goodbye. The part of the Brent's ash-bag that I could see looked like a deflated balloon. That was one mystery solved – at least Brent had given us his real name when he had moved in. The different name at work was still a sticker – maybe he was afraid to have his eBay and work worlds collide? Either way, the only person he had left was me. Us. Me. And his unborn kid. And Brent was in a bag.

"Don't worry," I said. "I'll find somewhere for you to go. Or at least a nicer place for you to wait while I figure out what to do with you. Christ, I'm talking to a bag."

My room was making me insane. I needed to get rid of the bag. The house was still empty. I got the bag out and hopped on a bus downtown. It was after the morning rush hour so I was able to get a seat next to a guy in business casual who kept looking at his watch and biting his lower lip. He got off at City Hall, carrying a leather briefcase and running to beat the yellow light across Market Street. I stayed on the bus until it terminated for no particular reason at Third Street, right in the center of the financial district. Not too many people were around; we were after the morning coffee break street rush but still before everyone took off for lunch. I walked south and saw my salvation: Hold Everything.

HE is a vertical store with a parking lot, huge shopping carts, and the demonic parking-space-seeking drivers that characterize the modern retail experience. I walked in. The greeter was a slightly overweight kid with glasses and hair gelled up into something resembling a Japanese anime 'do, minus the blue hair and power gloves.

"Hi," he said as I walked in. "Welcome to Hold Everything; what can we help you hold?"

I stopped and gave him a once-over. He was in his late teens, was probably going to school part-time, and hated his job because it required him to be nice to everyone all day. If he had a hamster at home, I pitied it.

"I'm looking for an urn," I said.

"Hm…I'm not really sure what that is…" he said. "Hang on."

"No, it's…" I said, but he'd turned around and started to punch buttons on the black PA phone behind him.

"Manager needed up front," he said. I could hear his regular voice a millisecond before the scratchy PA one. "Manager needed up front to help with a customer request."

He hung up the phone and turned back to me. "Don't worry," he said. "A manager will be right up here to help you out."

"It's OK," I said. "I can probably find it…"

"Yourself?" he said, almost laughing. "We have nearly 40,000 containers of various shapes and sizes and functions in this store, plus even more on our website, which you can access here from one of our friendly kiosks."

"Isn't that what you do?" I asked. "I mean."

His smile cracked, and I saw a little hint of sadness in his eyes. "Well, yes," he said. "But they pay me. They don't pay you."

"Good point."

His smile returned. "Don't you worry," he said. "The manager will be here in a minute."

He was absolutely literal; the manager showed up right after the greeter had said the word "minute." He was a small man with a wispy mustache and a budding combover who wore a nametag that said *Hi, my name is Don. How can I help you Hold?*

"What are you looking for?" he asked.

"An urn," I said.

"An urn…like a vase?" he said. "Well, I think the more appropriate question is – what are you looking to hold?"

This was *exactly* the question that I was hoping to avoid answering.

I'm not a fan of awkward situations leading to awkward silences, and I had tried to think of a plausible lie as to what one would put in an urn that *wasn't* the cremated remains of a former housemate, but my mind was still happily thinking about ways that Andre the Giant *could* have beaten Hulk Hogan at Wrestlemania III, and not coming up with anything useful.

"Um…it's for ashes," I said.

"How many ashes?" asked the manager.

"I can't count that high," I said. "But around fifteen pounds."

His eyes widened, and that act made his mustache flutter just a tad.

"Why in heaven's name would you want to store that many ashes? How big is your fireplace?"

"Um…" I said. Oh, fuck it. "They're the ashes of my dead housemate. He was cremated yesterday, and I can't get rid of them because he had no parents, and I'd rather store them in something other than a shopping bag until I figure out what to do with them."

You know that silence that happens in the middle of a party when someone who's really drunk starts talking and is really funny for about three or four minutes, and everyone's laughing, but then the drunk person says something like, *and then I slept with her husband and she didn't know it,* or *thank God I kicked that coke addiction without anyone noticing?* The silence at Hold Everything was just like that, without the partying and the drunks. It felt about the same. I'd kind of talked loudly because I was nervous, and when nobody responded I just kept talking louder, until you could probably hear *figure out what to do with them* all through the store.

"Hm…" said the manager. It wasn't the best way to break a silence. "I don't think we carry mortuary urns here."

As he talked, a few people came over to see what the dead-body fuss was about.

"He's looking to get rid of a body?"

"No," said the greeter. "He's looking to store the ashes of his dead roommate."

"He burned his roommate to death?"

"No," I said. "He was cremated after he was already dead."

"Oh," said the woman. "That's OK, then. You should put the ashes in an urn."

"I know," I said. "That's kind of what I was looking for, something to..."

"They don't carry urns here?"

"No, we don't," said the manager.

"That's impossible," said the woman, who was loaded down with clothes hangers and a shoe rack and clearly did not have better things to do on a pretty fall morning. "You're called Hold Everything," she said. "You advertise that you can hold everything. Well, that's false advertising. Young man, you should sue."

"I don't want to sue," I said. "I'm just looking..."

"See, if you sue and win," she said, "You can go to Pier One or Cost Plus and buy one of those really nice *ornate* urns, the kind that I put my husband in after he died."

"Now," said the manager, brushing the tiny hairs of his mustache with a nervous hand, "there's no need to talk about suing here. I'm sure we can come up with some sort of compromise."

"That's corporate-talk for giving up!" she said. "Don't you do it, young man."

"I don't want to..." I said.

"Really, suing is a bad idea," said the manager. "It'll take up lots of your time, and you probably have better things to do. Will you accept a $50 gift certificate good at any of our *other* corporate properties as a sign of our apologies, and we'll call it even?"

"Don't do it!" said the woman. "This is almost an *admission* of guilt right there."

I was pretty sure that the woman had watched way too much *Judge Judy* and *Boston Legal*, so I wasn't inclined to take her legal advice.

"Sure," I said.

Don the manager breathed a sigh of relief, took a red gift card out of his pocket, and swiped it in a reader that hung next to the phone.

"Thank you," he said. "And thanks for visiting Hold Everything! Please feel free to come back some other time." He took my arm and walked me to the door. "We hope to see you soon!"

I was on the sidewalk, my head spinning, a $50 gift card good at Williams-Sonoma, Pottery Barn, and some store called West Elm in my hand, it was eleven in the morning, and I still didn't have an urn. Great.

For the next two hours I wandered around downtown. Small groups of office people still gathered at least ten feet from the front door for their morning smokes, and delivery trucks still sat half-on the sidewalk, tilting at odd angles while the drivers ran through their schedules. Most of the men already had their sleeves rolled up in the warmth of the morning, and the UPS guys were all wearing their slightly-too-short shorts.

While I walked, I thought, mostly about Brent and how I was being a bad dead-guy's-roommate because I *still* hadn't figured out what his real name was, and if his family even existed, and if he'd had any money at all that we might be able to use to make up the extra month's rent that we now owed because we hadn't yet been able to fill his room. I knew what he'd been doing, but I didn't really know why, and the thought was starting to enter my mind that perhaps the car that had careened into him, shattering his body inside but leaving the outside weirdly intact…I shivered, and I realized that somewhere along the way I'd stopped thinking of Brent as "dead" and started thinking of him as "murdered." I was imagining something right out of a direct-to-cable Lorenzo Lamas thriller, and it was giving me the heebie-jeebies. And, that murder had cost the four of us over a month's rent at this point – none of us were rich enough to absorb that with a little pain, and I knew that the extra money was hurting Shawna. A crisp-suited guy with a Bluetooth earpiece nearly ran me over as I slowed, jabbering away.

"No, no," he said. "We really can't do much with that until we prove the market. It's just too nascent, new…."

I stopped in the middle of the street, neatly blocking the way of a homeless guy who was pushing a stroller full of recyclables. He started swearing incoherently at me, stopping after I hopped a few steps away. Whatever. It didn't matter. I'd figured it out!

Well, kind of. One of the marketing idiots at my old job had constantly talked about the need to prove the market. Whenever someone would come up with an idea for a new product or new way of doing anything, this guy would go on and on about how you had to prove the market, meaning that you had to make sure that people would buy what you were selling before you put the resources together to sell lots of it. I couldn't remember the guy's name, just that his palms were sweaty and he had brown eyes, which I only remember because he was one of those guys who always gives you a firm handshake whilst looking directly into your eyes when he sees you, even if he last saw you five minutes ago. I started talking through my Great Idea softly, to myself.

My Great Idea

1) Brent was obviously running some sort of business endeavor with this toilet thing. He worked in finance, and the card money was an investment. You only invest money in things that are going to make more money, so he obviously thought his toilet scheme was going to be more profitable than the baseball cards.

2) If he was going to sell the bootleg toilets here in the US, he and his partners would need to prove the market first, and would have built a model.

3) Which meant that they'd probably *sold* one or two of those bootleg toilets already, and if it had worked, they would have taken the next step.

4) Which meant that they'd probably registered a website in order to appear legitimate, as well as applied for a business license.

5) He'd obviously been planning the baseball card/toilet thing for a while, before he moved in with us. Once he'd figured out that his business was possibly dangerous, it would make sense to work and live under pseudonyms to make himself harder to find. His business partners would know his business name and be able to check him out that way, but if they wanted to physically find him, it would be impossible.

6) All I had to do was find the company name they were using and I could track down who they were.

Diabolical genius, this was. All I had to do was figure out the name of the business that Brent was using, track down his name, perhaps access his bank account to see if he had enough left in there to cover our missing months' rent and have some left over for

Morgan and the kid, without his business partners ever finding out who I was. I was still a little worried about what the little guy had told me. This was an easy solution: find and close the bank account, the trail disappears, and they would never find us. Three birds with one stone – all of my problems solved in one shot.

"I'm fucking brilliant," I said.

"You might be," said a voice. It was a cop – the same cop, in fact, who'd come to the door on the day that Brent died. "You OK?" he said. "I saw you from across the street and thought that you might be having a seizure."

I didn't answer right away, because my brain was still processing the part where this was the guy who'd changed my life so dramatically by showing up at my door not so long ago. Some coincidences freak me out, and this was one of them. It was like one of those moments in a Dickens novel, when the guy who you think seems to be a reprobate turns out to be the long-lost brother of the banker who's cheating the family out of the home.

The cop must have thought I *was* having a seizure, because my mouth was open and I didn't seem to be capable of speaking. "Hey, buddy," he said. "Can you talk? Do you need a referral?"

"Toilets," I sputtered.

"What?" he said. "Do you need a bathroom?" He put his hand on the butt end of his nightstick.

"No, no," I said. "I'm OK. I'm not seizing or freaking out or anything."

"You're sure about that?" he said.

"Yeah," I said.

"Well, if you're looking for a public bathroom, your best bet is to go down to the Sony building," he said. "But don't shower in there."

"No, I don't need a shower," I said. "I just need to know more about toilets."

He took his hand off of his nightstick. "You should get a drink of water," he said. "It's warm today, maybe you're dehydrated."

I shook my head, trying to think of the best way to explain what was going on to the cop.

"Bootleg toilets," I said. "Is that a crime that you would know anything about?"

He laughed. "We tend to go for the murders first," he said. "If someone's selling fake toilets, this is the first time I've ever heard about it. There's more money in drugs these days. I have some real crimes to go look for; you have a nice day."

He walked off, speaking to the walkie-talkie extension clipped onto his shoulder. I didn't care. For the first time in I-couldn't-remember-how-long, I had an idea, and it was probably a good one.

"Can I help you?"

The voice belonged to an older black man, with thick brown-framed glasses and a pointed gray beard that would have made him look like that villain from *Flash Gordon* if his voice hadn't been so soft and he hadn't been smiling.

"Um...maybe," I said. "I'm kind of looking for an urn." I didn't know why I was talking to him – ordinarily, talking to strangers in San Francisco will get you screamed at. My incredible idea must have temporarily numbed my brain.

"An urn?" he said. "Why don't you come into my shop? I've got lots of big vases – they might be similar to what you're looking for."

I looked up and over his head. It wasn't too hard to see over him; he was about five foot six with his shoes on. His store was a little flower shop, the kind that has plastic buckets full of single roses on either side of the entrance with a hand-lettered sign that says *Don't forget your sweetie today! Roses $3.00*. I followed him inside, where it was, like so many other things, larger than it appeared. He had a corner filled with potted ferns, and a shelf of cacti. Several dozen tiny green saplings were locked in a glass case under the cash register, and the counter was covered with seed envelopes. The place smelled fresh, like the kind of cleaning product they sell at hippie food stores.

"I know I've got a few things back here," he said, taking a key ring out of his pocket and opening a door behind the counter. "Most people who come down here aren't looking for real garden supplies, but I do keep these around for the customer who knows exactly what he needs, like you."

"I don't really know what I need..." I said. Clanks and bangs came from the back room as the old man rummaged around.

"Sure you do," he said. "You need this." He came out front with a black vase, about two feet high. It was a dark black, so dark that when you looked at it the rest of the world seemed to dim. The vase had a thin, curved handle on either side, making it look like one of the amphorae that populate the Greek section of art museums.

"How much is it?" I asked.

"Not so fast," he said. "You need to hold it and decide if it's right for what you need."

He handed the vase over to me. I had prepped myself for quite a bit of weight, but it wasn't much at all, really; I held it with one hand with no trouble.

"What's it made of?" I asked.

"I don't rightly know," he said. "Not fired clay, definitely, but it's strong. I put thirty pounds of dirt in it a few weeks ago to test it, and the handles held up just fine."

"It's..."I didn't have the words. Not *perfect*, because that felt weird; surely there wasn't a *perfect* container for a dead person. "Appropriate," I said. "It's appropriate."

"Twenty dollars," said the gray-bearded man. "I think that's fair."

I handed over a twenty. "Do you need a bag?" He asked.

"It couldn't hurt," I said. For some reason, I didn't want to be walking around the city with a vase this black; it would have felt a little strange. "Do you have one with handles?"

"Surely," he said.

I left with my large black vase in a Big Brown Bag, and took the bus up Market Street towards the public library. The ride itself isn't particularly far, but the eight blocks go through several worlds. At the cable car turnaround a young guy was drumming out scattergun rhythms on buckets, his bare shoulders shining with sweat as he whipped his sticks around. One block from Union Square the shiny storefronts became graffiti-tagged plywood, the litter on the sidewalk changed from the occasional drink cup to shredded cardboard, old clothes, and lumps of possessions that may or may not have contained people. Sixth Street was the epicenter; as crowded as the shopping districts but devoid of smiles, an intersection of cheap restaurants where the owners stood in their doors and hoped that the screaming junkies outside didn't scare away enough potential customers to make the day a loss.

From there the bus hit Civic Center, and I hopped off. Today was a market day; two rows of tents lined the plaza. A few tourists browsed here and there, and the usual mob of homeless were scattered about, keeping out of the way of the pairs of cops walking circular beats among the tents. I walked past sellers of pashmina scarves from India, Bolivian wood engravings, local glass art, two bead-makers, and a guy selling obscure Asian tobaccos. Nothing useful, and I continued until I reached the granite stairs of the library.

I wasn't there for a book. One time Thomas and I had been drunk and arguing about whether or not you could find a company that sold Indonesian leather products in Indiana. We hadn't reached any conclusion, but the next day he'd shown me a printout that proved that, in fact, a small store in Noblesville, Indiana did in fact stock purses, belts, and jackets made exclusively in Jakarta. He'd found the place by going to a database that businesses paid thousands of dollars a month to access, but you could get for free with a library card. Capitalism doesn't make sense sometimes.

Most of the computers at the library were public Internet terminals used by homeless guys coming in for some warmth. The screens all had the little anti-glare covers that prevented you from spying over other people's shoulders. This was a good thing; there'd been a feature in the paper a few months back where they'd exposed that 40% of all Internet traffic at the library was porn. I kept my eyes front and center as I passed a row of computers; what other people were looking at, I really didn't want to know.

The database terminals were nearly empty. Two high school kids with all-over hair and huge jeans sitting together were staring intently at a screen. They looked up as I pulled out a chair, flicked their eyes to the bag I carried, then proceeded to ignore me and click keys with the speed of a court reporter. I opened up a search window and started working. I needed to find the name of a business that had been incorporated within the past ten years, and dealt in discounted high-end bathroom fixtures. Simple, right?

Not so simple. It turned out that the search criteria in the main database that Thomas had mentioned was based around SIC codes, which are numbers that refer to types of businesses. The system was created during the Eisenhower administration, and it showed. "Ironworks and sundries," "oil exploration" and "retail." No code for "toilets." I tried to go old-school and run a search for "privy seller" but got nothing. I sighed and readjusted my legs; this was probably going to take a while.

As it turned out, it took three minutes. Finding the toilet seller category wasn't really a problem – what made it hard was that the bathroom fixture industry had its own meta-category, and there was no differentiation by product. Most of the folks in the selling-toilets business didn't go out of their way to advertise what they were peddling, or even put the word in their name. I eventually found my way in to the world of expensive porcelain by running a search for kitchen equipment, then double-checking the secondary SIC codes of the manufacturers and searching on those codes to see if there was anything interesting. I discovered codes for water filters, tea suppliers, cabinet makers, and even a local company that trafficked exclusively in hypoallergenic porcelain sex toys.

Searching was as boring as it sounds until I got to the sex toy company. I made a note of the company name on one of the little pads that the library put next to all of their computers; Thomas would be interested. Right after that, I got a hit. A Detroit firm manufactured hinges for refrigerators, several dozen varieties of doorknobs, and...brushed aluminum roll hangers for toilet paper. Bingo. I did a back-check on the toilet paper product and got three different SIC codes. 416843 was a no-go (it led me to, among other things, a dowel store) but 883419 was a good one. I managed to follow that trail to long descriptions of nearly two hundred different companies that purported to sell bathroom equipment direct to the consumer. A few geographic and time filters limiting the list to US companies founded after 2002 knocked the list down to sixty.

I hit control-P, and brought my empty vase and brown bag out to the bank of printers at the end of the row of computers. The printout took about three minutes, and cost me just under five dollars; the library charges seven cents per sheet.

I walked into the front door with the bag under my arm, carrying the vase by its handles. My wrists were tired; the trolley bus had come off the wires six blocks from home. I didn't have the energy to walk up the second flight of stairs to my room, so I sat down in the living room. I considered turning on the television, but reruns of Maury didn't seem right. Instead, I sat on a cushion next to the window overlooking the street, and looked at what I could see.

The afternoon sun was lancing through the seams in the buildings on our side of the street, giving the sidewalk a bright/dark shadow pattern. Foot traffic was fairly light; one drab-jacket-clad homeless guy was pushing his squeaky shopping cart up the street, and a few early office refugees were making their way down from the rail stop up the way.

Jenn was one of the refugees. I could tell it was her from three blocks away; she walked a certain way on the way home, swinging her right arm and holding on tight to her oversized purse/gym bag with the other. She'd probably had a bad day at work; she was walking slowly and keeping her eyes on the ground.

She made it to the door after a few minutes, a walk that ordinarily would have taken her less than one. When she got to the door, she left my view. She slammed the door behind her and clomped her way up the stairs, entering the living room, dumping her bag on the floor, and slumping into the loveseat across from me. Instead of the usual soap and skin, she smelled like man-sweat and exhaustion.

She looked at me, unscrewed the top from her water bottle, and took a long drink.

"What's with the vase?" she asked.

"For Brent," I said. "It feels right."

She nodded and took another drink. "Neat," she said. "It looks good."

I took the vase up to my room, but didn't feel up to doing the full transfer yet; I was afraid that without an oversized funnel I'd spill ashes all over my room. So I just took the whole bag and stuffed it into the vase; from the outside you couldn't see the plastic. I took out my printouts and started Googling the companies involved. My plan was to eliminate the companies that looked real and find the super-sketchy ones. That plan devolved in about twenty seconds; there was so much chaff out there, and the word "toilet" was heavily weighted towards porn sites. I hadn't had any idea that toilet fetishism was a big subset of society; to each his own, I guess.

After ten unsuccessful minutes, there was a knock on my door. It was Thomas.

"Alex, we need you downstairs." He had changed out of his office wear and was sporting a Dead shirt from the 1984 tour, Birks, and ratty shorts that had been long pants at some point in their lifetime. We almost never got to see Thomas's legs; they were right at that point of emaciation.

"Why?"

"Roommate interview coming up, dude. I e-mailed you about it this morning."

"I haven't checked my e-mail all day. What if I'd been busy? Why didn't you call me?"

He looked at me and raised an eyebrow. "Are you headed out on a hot date or something?"

"No, but…I don't have any *beer*."

"Really?"

"Yeah," I said. "I finished my last one the other night, and I didn't go to the store today."

"So do it without," he said. "The guy will be here in ten minutes."

"I'm headed to the store," I said. I may be a flaky, unemployed wannabe amateur detective with the ashes of a dead guy in a Greek-themed urn in the corner of his room, but I had my standards. No way was I going to confront the cavalcade of Craigslist freaks without beer. Before I left, I checked my e-mail – sure enough, Thomas had forwarded a response to us. He'd included the ad as a reminder.

Housemate wanted for Cole Valley Apartment. There are four of us and we're seeking a fifth for a nice, quiet bedroom with space for all of your stuff unless you do something weird with your space (see below) Yes, we're more of a home than a house. Yes, we hang out together. Yes, we expect you to pay the bills on time without turning our common space into a dungeon, 420 plantation, side Internet business, or cult recruitment center. No, we don't care if you're a boy or a girl, gay, straight, used to be a boy or a girl but are now something else. We only ask that you hold some kind of job that pays the rent. All of us work during the day, except for one slacker who just got laid off. He likes to think he's doing productive things even though he wakes up every day at ten. So it would be good if you weren't also a slacker; we don't need an enabler around here.

I made a mental note to not let Jenn post the roommate ads before I'd had a chance to see them.

The corner store was out of Anchor Steam, which was the only beer they stocked which wasn't a criminal overcharge, so I was left with a dilemma:

1) Go downscale and get a twelve-pack of Pabst Blue Ribbon for eight bucks. I hate doing this because it's what all the hipster kids do, and I didn't want to look like someone who was trying to look like he was a construction worker.

2) Spend nine dollars on any one of the higher-end six packs they had. They were all pretty much the same; constructing the beer names with the standard formula: (BREWERY NAME) + (RANDOM VAGUELY ENVIRONMENTAL-SOUNDING ADJECTIVE) + (COLOR)/(SHADE) (BEER TYPE), where BEER TYPE is "ale," "porter" or "stout."

I stared at the cooler for a few minutes, my naturally frugal self in a drag-out battle with my need to not appear to be trying to be cooler than I actually was. I finally shrugged my shoulders and picked out a sixer of Otter Creek Willow Run Pale Ale. With tax and bottle return fee, it cost me ten dollars. When I was in high school, the guys with fake licenses would charge us seven bucks for six-packs of similar stuff, and *they'd* be taking two off the top for their time. There are some things I hate about getting older.

When I got back to my house, I was damp; the evening was as sultry as it ever gets in San Francisco, as if the fog had turned invisible and heated up in the process. I wiped my hand across my forehead and it came down shiny. Voices came down from the living room, including one I didn't recognize. I was late.

"Hi" I said as I entered the living room. "Sorry I'm late."

The guy was definitely young. He was about my height – average, that is – with dusky skin and a neat black beard, trimmed to more than just a line, but much less than the lumberjack look. His khakis were neatly pressed, and his beige button-down shirt was untucked.

"Ahmed," he said. "Ahmed Bin-Alaweed."

"Nice to meet you," I said. His handshake was firm, and he looked me directly in the eyes as he shook. His eyes were dark brown, almost black, and he flitted them down to the brown bag under my arm.

"Is that beer?"

"Yep," I said. "Want one?"

"I was hoping you'd ask," he said. "It's been a long day." He had a slight accent, that lilting, musical quality that comes from a British language education. I always find that kind of voice to be reassuring; it's the kind of talk that fits college librarians and people who run museums; quiet, confident, intelligent.

"What do you do?" I asked.

He grinned. "I'm a cabbie. For the moment, anyway."

Something about the way he said it was weird, as if there was more of a story.

"There's more to it," he said. "I actually have a doctorate in physics from the University of Karachi in Pakistan, and I emigrated here a few years ago to work for a gaming company. They went belly-up, and with them my sponsored work visa. I liked being here, I didn't want to get deported, so I managed to hook up with a taxi company that needs drivers and does year-by-year visa renewals. I don't really know how it they pull it off, but nobody's come after me yet."

"Wow," I said. "Are you getting back into programming?"

"Not any time soon," he said. "Cabbing is OK; it keeps me in beer money, and there's not much politics. I can listen to podcasts of physics talks while I drive, and a friend and I schedule our own hours."

Huh. I excused myself to go to the bathroom. When I got back, Ahmed and Thomas were arguing about baseball.

"Come on," Ahmed said. "*Everybody* was using steroids. It's not like he was different in any way."

"That's such crap," said Thomas. "His *head* grew. Nobody else's heads grew."

"Sure they did," said Ahmed. "But everyone else had hair, so they just cut it shorter so you couldn't see the difference."

And so on. I was enjoying the conversation, and it wasn't solely because of the two-quick-beer mild buzz. I looked around the room. Shawna was rapt, following Ahmed's every word. Thomas was doing the same, and Jenn was leaning forward.

"So, um…" I said. "What do you do on the side?"

Ahmed turned towards me. "What do you mean?"

"You know," I said. "It's San Francisco. Most people are running a side business, so I was just curious if you had one."

"Not really," he said. "Sometimes people ask me to do some freelance programming or design, but I really don't want to do that – I'd rather do academic physics, but my visa isn't for academic work, so…at least my time off is mine. I read books and drink beer. Being cabbie with a doctorate is quirky enough. I don't need any more San Francisco cred."

"Hm," I said. "I don't wanna sound like I'm prying here, but you're not the kind of guy who's going to invite all of his bondage friends over and throw a giant torture/scat party in the living room?"

The room was silent for a second.

"Alex," said Jenn. "Can you shut up?"

"No, it's all right," said Ahmed. "I've been on the other side of the San Francisco freak show. This place I went a couple of weeks ago, they were great. Totally normal-looking guys, two of them, really clean place, they were both doing streaming-video stuff for work. Turns out the streaming video was porn, which is no big deal, but then there was the part where the kitchen and bathroom walls were completely lined with screen captures from their work. Staring at orgy photos isn't the best atmosphere for cooking, and I try not to think about sex when I'm sitting on the can. I haven't returned their calls."

We all laughed.

Ahmed looked at his watch. "I should go," he said. "Forty-five minutes is probably more time than you guys have to spare." He looked at Thomas. "You've got my number, right?"

"Yeah, it's in my e-mail." said Thomas. "I'll give you a call in a day or so, if you're interested. You interested?"

"Definitely," said Ahmed. "You guys seem all right to me."

"Great," said Thomas. "We'll be in touch."

All of us were silent as we listened to Ahmed go down the stairs. His footsteps were light, what I imagined a ballet dancer's sounded like, if that ballet dancer were wearing hiking boots. He closed the door with a soft click, and then the floodgates opened.

"Perfect," said Thomas. "He's in."

"He's cute," said Shawna.

"Knowing a cabbie would be *huge*," said Thomas.

"Not bad at all," said Jenn.

"I'm skeptical," I said.

Four heads swiveled around and looked at me. If I'd been standing, I would have rocked back on my heels. As it was, I sank even farther into the couch cushions.

"Care to explain?" asked Thomas. "If we have to interview another person, I'm gonna be livid."

"Nothing really to explain," I said. "Remember the other guy who was perfect? Remember how he looked super-normal and wanted to set up a bondage dungeon in our living room? Remember that nice little boy who ended up wanting to have his mother come by and check us out? Remember the Scientologist? We could get burned - maybe we shouldn't be blowing all of our wads over Ahmed until we find out a little bit more about him."

"I'm tired of all of this," said Thomas. "Can't we just go with him and hope for the best?"

Jenn cut in before I could respond. "I think Alex is right," she said. "We can wait a day or two. If nothing comes up, he's in. If he's got any skeletons, they'll come out of the closet."

"You think he's closeted?" asked Thomas.

"No, but I have my suspicions about you," she said. "A year and a half here and you haven't been on a single date. What's with that?"

"Thomas is totally comfortable with himself," said Shawna. "Straight men are allowed to dress nicely."

"Only if they're getting some," said Jenn, grinning.

"Guys?" said Thomas. "Um…"

"What about Ahmed?" I said. "Why don't we just go out with him? When?"

"Trivia?" asked Thomas. "Next week? Shawna, you'll have to come."

Her face fell.

"Come on," he said, smiling. "It'll be fun, I promise. If we get this guy, we won't have to pay extra rent for the next month. And I'll buy your drinks."

"OK," she said. "I'll go. But I'm going to miss my new yoga class for that. You owe me."

Thomas played dirty; Shawna was easily the poorest member of the house, cobbling her income together from three different part-time jobs and the occasional substitute-teaching gig. She'd never missed the rent, although one time she'd come very close, and would have been in trouble without a last-minute call from one of the restaurants where she occasionally picked up a night shift. She had put on a ridiculously low-cut dress and headed out there, coming back with over $200 in tips and a big smile. Since then, she'd been more careful, but the extra hundred and fifty dollars we had all forked over the previous month to cover Brent had bitten her hard. It was kind of unfair; she worked all the time to scratch out her basics and sometimes had to live on nothing but spaghetti, while I hadn't really worked when I'd *had* a job, and after my severance ran out I'd *still* make more than she did from unemployment insurance. She worked fifty times harder than any of the investment guys I'd met, men who had two-beer lunches and looks-like-work spreadsheets that detailed fantasy football teams down to a science.

But that's neither here nor there. My phone had buzzed while we were talking, and I flipped it open.

I need to see you.

It was from Morgan.

I don't want to give the impression that I'd stopped thinking about her; I hadn't. She had said she would call and hadn't. She was probably home with morning sickness, and I hadn't found out anything that I could tell her, other than that I'd let the father of her kid be burned up in the city crematorium. At this point, if she couldn't help me figure out which toilet company had been Brent's, she wasn't going to be helpful to me, and I sure didn't have anything that would help her. And I had my suspicions. Brent had been murdered; how did I know that *she* didn't have something to do with it? If nothing else, our housemate search had taught me not to believe a first impression. Even if it was stockinged and hot. But I still couldn't abandon her entirely.

Thought you hated texting.

A pause, then a message

I changed.

I hesitated, then tapped a few keys.
Where and when?
Three minutes passed, then.
Where we met the first time. It's important.
I sighed.
I can be there in an hour.
One minute this time.
OK. See you there. Be careful.
Be careful? Of what? I shivered. Morgan had now moved from an object of lust to an object of nervousness.

I changed out of my sandals into shoes and added a jacket; warm days still meant cool nights. Jenn was in the living room, wrapped in a blanket. She looked like an attractive adult girl version of a swaddling-clad baby.

"Going out?" she asked.

"Yeah."

"Where?"

"The Dovre."

She made a gargoyle face. "Meeting that girl again? Why are you still interested in her?"

"What would make you think that?"

"The part where she stood you up after you asked me for advice on wine, you haven't seen her for two weeks, and I haven't heard the name 'Morgan' in this house in that time span. Usually you can't shut up about someone you meet."

"That's not true."

She arched an eyebrow, and moved her shoulders under the blankets. "Oh really? Is this the Alex who last year spent nine straight days at Café Velo Rouge because some girl who sat next to you asked to borrow your cell phone to make a call? Who then had to be dissuaded from calling the number that was on that phone to try to track her down? Who ate eight consecutive dinners at that café on the off chance that she would come back? Who finally gave up after eight straight days of bean salad nearly caused a bathroom-based house revolution? And didn't you at one point openly consider one of those sketchy fifty-dollar Internet background checks? Am I missing something here?"

All true. Every single word she said was absolutely true. She'd left out the part where I'd taken two sick days from work, considered buying a second-hand bike so that I could fit in better at the Velo Rouge, and actually *had* paid a few bucks for an Internet search of the name "Rita" for addresses within six blocks of the Rouge, and come up blank. I hadn't told anybody about that last one; I think it crossed the line from adorably-infatuated to scary-stalker. I didn't do anything with that information, though; the search company turned out to be a Cayman Islands front for a company that then deluged me with buy-one-get-one-free credits for online gambling sites. I'm not a gambler, so I just forwarded them to Thomas, who used them to play online poker. He made a couple hundred bucks and we split the winnings. More disturbing, though, was that Jenn was right. What was I doing being even remotely interested in the pregnant woman who was carrying my dead housemate's child?

"I'm not interested," I said.

"Right," she said, laughing.

"Seriously."

She laughed harder. "Alex, you're hopeless. Most guys are easy to read, but you're...you're so transparent I can't even think of an analogy."

She was right, but she was irritating, so I didn't say what I should have said— "you're right." Instead, I said "Well, at least I might have the *possibility* of getting some," and walked out the door before I could see whether my words had done what they were supposed to do. I don't know if they did that to her, but it worked on me; I felt about as tall as a Smurf as I walked out the door. Did it get any lower than implying that you were going out to possibly have sex with a pregnant-by-a-dead-housemate woman?

I walked all the way to the Dovre, meandering over the hills to Dolores Park, where the evening junkies and young parents kept up an uneasy co-existence. The view behind me was of downtown; skyscraper lights slicing up in the evening darkness and the soft arcs of the Bay Bridge winding their way across the water to Oakland. Hiking up the hill to the top warmed me up, and I sloughed off my jacket. I hit Mission Street at 24th, where a small rally was taking up most of the courtyard of the BART station; a guy with a top hat and a waxed mustache was chanting in Spanish through a microphone and an old Fender bass amplifier; twenty or thirty people were murmuring along with him, and the families with strollers walked on by, ignoring the spectacle as if it happened every day. I couldn't read the signs, so I couldn't say what the hoopla was all about, but even if they'd been in English I probably wouldn't have known. It's not that I don't care, it's that the every-day-is-a-protest-day mentality of this town wears on you after a while. Live here three years and you'll ignore screaming mobs with the same aplomb you do a dejected panhandler, and I'm not at all sure that this is a good thing.

The smoke from the inside of the Dovre swirled out the door and up past the neon sign, giving the air itself a red glow. Inside, it smelled like stale jeans and sweaty mesh baseball hats; not the kind that Ashton Kutcher wears to be cool, but the kind that guys wear to keep the sun off during a long day hauling beams. Morgan was waiting at the bar, a tapered cigarette in her hand, sipping on a highball glass filled with iceless dark liquid, and bouncing one of her crossed legs over the other. She was wearing tight-patterned fishnet stockings under a mid-length skirt, and her dark eyes glittered when I sat down next to her. A dark green handbag sat on the bar next to her.

"Alex," she said. "It's been a while."

"What are you drinking?" I asked.

"Bourbon," she said. "It was on the rocks when I got here."

"Am I late?" I said. "Sorry."

"No," she said. "It's only one, and I've been here a while."

She let her cigarette rest between her finger, tapping it slowly, letting the ash slough off onto the bar.

"What do you know?" she said.

"Huh?"

She stubbed out her cigarette on the side of her bar stool, swiveled towards me and put a hand on my knee. "About David," she said. "Brent."

"Well…" I said. "A little bit. I mean, it's been hard to find things out, and they went ahead and cremated him."

"What?" she said. Her hand tightened on my thigh, squeezed hard enough to hurt. She leaned forward, her eyes hardening from glass to diamond. "They burned him up?"

I nodded, and she looked away. Neither of us said anything for a while; I had my questions – what did she know about Brent/David and his other life-doings? What was her having-a-kid plan? – but I didn't say anything. I busied myself watching the bartender, a man with gorge-deep wrinkles in his face and yellow skin that looked jaundiced in the dim lights of the Dovre. He was cleaning glasses with a hole-filled rag and watching the television, which was tuned to ESPN Classic and replaying the 1994 National Spelling Bee without subtitles.

She looked at me, then looked away again.

"So," I said. "Um...what?"

"What what?" she asked. "We're exactly where we were earlier. I'm going broke, I'm pregnant, I'll be showing soon and then nobody will hire me, and there's nothing new to change any of those things. Next month I'll stop paying my credit card bills. This is the worst."

Her voice cracked a bit on the last sentence. I felt a hard lump in my stomach; I felt like her credit card bills and unborn kid were my problems as well as hers.

"I'm getting closer," I said. "I mean, I managed to get into his PayPal account..."

She grabbed my arm. "Really?"

"Yeah," I said. "But there wasn't any money in it. He had transferred all of it to a bank account, and I don't have access to it." Oh, and his parents are dead. He really had nobody."

She looked down. "He never mentioned any parents or anything like that at work."

"Sad," I said. We sat without talking for a few minutes; the soft words from the sportscast that was on in the corner were just audible. The Cincinnati Reds had won that afternoon.

"I hope I win the lottery," she said. "That's the only way that this is going to work."

I sighed. "Don't worry," I said. "I'll break through somehow. Maybe I can bridge you something until I can get to Brent's money..."

She took my hand. "Oh no," she said. "I won't let you do that. Besides, you're not working right now. I couldn't do that...I'll hang on until you get Brent's money and can get it to me and the kid."

"You sure?"

"Absolutely." She took the last sip of her drink, leaned over to kiss me on the cheek, and stood up. "You're the best, Alex. I have faith in you. You can do this, I know. But…" she stopped. "I *will* let you buy me that drink." She winked at me, I felt my heart beat faster, and then she sashayed out of the bar, lithe legs peeking out below her black skirt. I wanted to hit myself. Why was I such a stupid, stereotypical guy? All dick and no brain, and now I couldn't help the one person I knew who badly needed the opposite.

"She your girlfriend?" asked the bartender. "I wouldn't let one like that sit in this place all by herself."

"No," I said. "Just a friend in need."

"Both the best and worst kinds to have," he said. "Want a refill? I nodded. Sitting and drinking with just myself, my thoughts, and my hard-beating heart seemed like an appropriate thing to do. When my drink had melted to a watery slush and I felt even worse. I left and hailed a cab home. That was it. I was going to find Brent's money and get it to Morgan, even if I had to…well, not die trying. But I'd try really hard.

"What?" Jenn's voice was in full assault mode.

"You heard me," I said. "Morgan is pregnant with Brent's kid."

Jenn gave me a look of scorn unequalled at any point in our housemateship. It was a hard look to describe – the wide brown eyes of blank astonishment combined with a slight lowering of her head and a pullback of her shoulders to effectively make me feel like a bigger idiot than if I'd been a nineteenth-century French general and said, "Hey, it's a really good idea to invade Russia this winter." She was wearing a grease-and-flour-spattered apron with her hair pulled back into a tight bun. Basically, she was a kitchen fetishist's wet dream. She huffed.

"Um…" I said. "I don't get it."

"God," she said. "Men are stupid, but you're *stupid*. Did you ever get around to putting Brent's ashes in that vase?"

"Kind of."

"Kind of?"

"They're in the vase that I bought, yeah," I said. "I just left them in the bag."

Jenn raised an eyebrow, then turned back to the stove, where she put the following ingredients into a giant cast-iron skillet that she'd prepped with half a stick of butter:

Nine eggs, separated with the whites beaten until stiff, yolks beaten

11/2 cups milk

2 1/2 cups flour

1 cup butter, melted.

She'd called in sick to work and was making Dutch Babies for Shawna and me. Shawna was upstairs taking a shower, leaving me alone to face Jenn's wrath. And wrath it was – what she'd done to the egg whites can only be described as a ruthlessly planned tactical assault. She didn't talk again until she'd hefted the entire mess into the 425 degree oven, and then she turned to me again.

"I suppose I should say I'm sorry for calling you an idiot," she said. "And I guess I'm sorry for saying it like that. But you *are* an idiot. Or she's a maniac. But it's probably both."

"Why would you say that?"

"She's pregnant and hanging out in a smoky bar drinking whiskey? Alex, I hang out with pregnant women *all day long*. They talk about fetal-alcohol syndrome and the dangers of secondhand smoke for hours on end; it's like there's this massive public health God in the sky that tracks pregnancy tests and sends out scary informational brochures the instant your pee turns something blue. Most of the women I work with won't even put their nose over a glass of wine and smell the fumes, let alone hang out in a bar where the air by itself can up your BAC. And don't even get me started on the smoke factor. That's just not happening. There's no way she's pregnant. She's taking you, Alex. How long have you known?"

I would have answered her, but I was flustered. I knew that. Of course I knew that. I had just forgotten, like I'd forgotten the letter to Brent. What else had I forgotten? I was about to apologize but Shawna flounced into the kitchen.

"Someone's pregnant? Are they going with a hospital/doctor/epidural thing, or a midwife? Maybe a water birth? One of the women in my studio was originally going to do one of the hospital things, but we've pretty much talked her into doing it the natural way, which Thomas says is ignoring fifty years of technological advancement in favor of they way they used to do things in the Middle Ages before they had modern dentistry, which I guess means that the baby might have bad teeth? Who invented the toothbrush, anyway?"

"Done," said Jenn, bending down to the oven and pulling out the skillet. I'd never eaten a Dutch Baby before, and the number of arterial hardeners that Jenn had thrown in the pan had made me hungry. The swollen, golden cake that had somehow risen and expanded to bubble outward over the rim of the skillet turned my stomach into a beast. Jenn smiled for the first time that morning, cut the thing in thirds, and served. I sprinkled my slice with powdered sugar and took a bite. Delicious – a pancake with an injection of Awesome. I polished mine off in under five minutes.

"Thanks, Jenn," I said. "That was great. And…thanks. I hadn't remembered any of that pregnancy stuff."

"You're welcome," she said, almost cracking a smile. "You up to anything today?"

"I'm going to look at some stuff online," I said.

"More Brent information?" she said.

"Yeah."

"Still?"

"Yep," I said. "I want to finish this off. If I can get to the end of this trail, we might get some rent out of it. And if I can find out who he was working with, we can try to stay out of their way."

"Want to do it at Coffee to the People?" she said. "Company is always a good thing, and I'd like to take advantage of the day off."

"Sure," I said. "I'll get my laptop."

"No," she said. "First you're going to pay for breakfast by doing the dishes. Then we'll go."

Outfoxed again. Dammit.

Coffee to the People was mobbed with high school kids. The skinny white counter guy with the chin-length dreadlocks looked like he'd just sat through a late-night marathon of *The Exorcist, the Shining*, and *the Blair Witch Project;* The last time I saw that much fear behind someone's eyes, I'd been at work and my straight-and-married cubemate had been caught downloading gigabytes of gay porn movies to the advertising area of the central server.

"Please tell me you're just ordering coffee," he said. "If I have to make one more double-decaf whatever-the-fuck with whipped cream I'm going to go to the hardware store, buy an axe, and start going Lizzie Borden on anyone sporting an Abercrombie and Fitch logo."

"What's going on?" I said. "Isn't there school?"

"Not yet," he said. "Apparently all of these kids are from the 'burbs and are on a cultural-history field trip to Chinatown for some summer camp. They decided to ditch the dim sum and come to the Haight to bother me and score skunk weed. Three of them tried to buy from me. I mean, do I *look* like a dealer?"

He had dreadlocks, wore a vintage Floyd shirt, sported two earrings and was thin in a hippie-not-hipster way, tan, and four days unshaven.

"Yeah," I said. "You kinda do."

He shook his head. "You're behind the times. If you're dealing now, you wanna look like you guys. Especially if you're hanging out in the Haight; cops will hassle the hippies, but leave the square folks alone. That's just a little tip. Don't use it for evil plans, OK?"

"I won't," I said. "Coffee, medium."

"Make mine a large," said Jenn.

"On it," he said. "Three fifty for both."

I put four down on the counter and moved Jenn's hand away from her purse. "I'll get this one," I said.

"Thanks," she said.

"Don't mention it." The hippie guy gave us our coffees; I added cream and sugar to mine while Jenn found us a table.

"When did you stop using cream?" I asked.

"A while ago," she said. "When did you start noticing what I do to my drinks?"

"A while ago," I said.

The high school crew had monopolized four of the twelve tables in the shop. They were a kaleidoscope of unkempt multi-colored hair, sparkly tongue jewels, and henna tattoos. I was fascinated by one kid who managed to keep his cell phone glued to one ear with his shoulder while one of his hands made its way down the back of the jeans of the girl to his left, and the other mechanically brought a drink to his lips.

Our table wobbled, so I had to fold a rave flier into quarters and wedge it under a leg. Jenn started to knit, clicking her needles against each other every few seconds. I took out my laptop and started to sip my coffee. It was good – dark and medium-strong, without any of the burnt over-roasted flavor that's such a problem in the post-Starbucks era.

My stack of papers was over two inches thick; I hopped online and started Googling. It was pretty mindless work; type in a company name, then check out the site. Most of the sites revealed that the fixture companies were subsidiaries of even larger fabrication businesses, organizations that put together the metal struts that hold the tires on jet airliners, axles for cars, the corrugated tin roofs for rain to rattle on in the South, and maybe a few of the bolts that they use to hold a toilet to the floor. Those guys were easy to cross off my list.

The specialty manufacturers were harder; high-quality porcelain companies that also put together custom tiling solutions, a small metal shop in west Texas that was the only American manufacturer of the linkage chain that pulls up the stopper in the toilet water tank, and several places that did metal, porcelain, and plastic work. I put most of them aside as I worked through the pile; they probably deserved a closer look.

One of the problems was that I really had no idea what a front-company website would look like, and even if I could recognize an obvious fake, there was absolutely no way that a well-put-together front company would throw up a site that would be easily recognizable as a front company. So how to tell? After an hour of digging, my *take a closer look* pile was an inch high and I'd only managed to weed out about fifteen of the sixty possibles.

I sighed and looked out the window. A woman approached the doorway, opened it, and looked in. She had blonde, scraggly hair and carried an overstuffed green military-issue bag on her shoulder and a blue-colored drink in a clear plastic cup. Her eyes were sunk so far back in her head that I couldn't see any color; they were like two little black holes in the middle of her face. With her tight, over-the-bones skin, it was like looking into the center of an unsmiling mummified skull.

I recoiled a bit when her gaze fell on me.

"What's wrong?" asked Jenn.

"Nothing," I said. The woman turned her eyes to the café again, reached for the door knob, then pulled her hand away. She staggered back, then started to trudge up the hill. Her scarred legs seemed like they were having trouble supporting her; she leaned forward under her load.

"Oh," said Jenn. "Another heroin addict."

"Her eyes," I said. "They weren't really there."

I walked up to the counter for a coffee refill, where a guy with a corduroy scally cap and colorful bandana was showing the hippie counter guy a wooden katana.

"For practice," he said. "Best of all, you can walk around with this sucker in a scabbard and nobody will mess with you, and if the cops hassle you you can just tell them it's made of wood, so you're not carrying a deadly weapon around."

"Good to know," said the counter guy.

"If you wanna buy it, I'll be outside spare-changing for a while," said the sword man. He took his paper cup of coffee and walked by me; his smell was that familiar combination of sweat and too-long-without-a-shower grime. I stepped aside.

"He comes in here every week trying to sell me that goddamned sword," said the counter guy. "I can't figure out if he forgets who I am or if he's just really persistent."

"If he was a really good salesman, he wouldn't be trying to sell you a wooden sword," I said. "He'd be selling you entire wooden sword kits, or selling you a system for making wooden sword kits so that others will sell them and tithe some of the income to you."

"I should be so lucky," he said. "I make nine bucks an hour to pay five hundred bucks a month so I can live in a closet while I go to school and pile up debt. If anyone would buy into a scheme to sell wooden swords, I'd have signed on for it long ago."

"You and me both," I said. "Wooden swords would beat working." I took my coffee, gave the counter guy two bucks, didn't wait for change, and walked back to my seat as fast as I could, spilling a bit of coffee on one of the teenagers as I shouldered by. He didn't notice; he was too busy putting his hand down the back of his next door neighbor's pants, getting the hand slapped away, and trying again.

I flipped through the list of companies again, until I realized that it really didn't matter what the websites looked like; if I wanted to, I could probably use a few simple software tools to put together a website that looked like I was running a Ferrari dealership from my home address. If you didn't know San Francisco geography, you'd be none the wiser. I switched from looking at the corporate sites to using a WHOIS directory – the kind of search that can tell you who actually who bought the server's space that hosts a given site. It went quickly, and I became absorbed enough that the incessant prattling of the high school kids seemed to fade and became more of a background din.

Bingo. There were three websites owned by holding companies with "Lucky" in the name.

Lucky Home and Work Products

Number One Lucky Products

Producta Lucky Uno

I wasn't sure about the Spanish, so I left it in. I could *feel* it, though; behind one of those three names was the group behind Brent's scheme.

When I was in ninth grade, I had felt that Cara McDonogh had really, *really* liked me, until I'd asked her to go with me to get sandwiches on a leave-early day, and she'd yelled, "*You* want to get sandwiches with *me*?" loud enough for all of the cool kids to hear, and I'd slinked away with a tomato-red face and an ego that didn't recover for months. You have to be careful with those gut feelings; they'll burn you as often as not. This one, though…this felt real.

Jenn and I went home soon after that; she had finished off as many rows as she could in one sitting, and I'd devolved from research into reading an endlessly crosslinked series of bored-in-the-office cartoons. Shawna and Thomas were home when we got there, sitting on the couch watching television. Shawna was resting her head on his shoulder, eyes closed.

Sh, mouthed Thomas. *Asleep.*

I nodded, and we walked back into the kitchen. I poured myself a glass of water and scrounged some cheese and crackers. Jenn walked over to the cabinet, pulled out metal cup-looking thing, filled it with flour, and started sifting it into a bowl.

"Sugar cookies today," she said. "I bet I can get 'em done before Shawna wakes up."

She continued to sift, dipping the cup into a plastic bag full of flour (she bought the stuff in bulk from the natural foods market down the street) and clicking the sifter trigger.

"How does that work?" I asked.

She looked at me as if I was an eight-year-old who had just pooped his pants.

"It sifts," she said.

"I know that," I said. "I mean, um…would it work for something besides flour?"

Jenn put the sifter down on the counter and put her hands on her hips. "Talk," she said. "What do you want to know?"

"Well," I said. "Brent's ashes…I mean, I didn't want to spill any of them out of the bag that they're in before I put them in the vase thing, so I just put the bag in the vase, but that seems kind of disrespectful to him. He's dead, you know? So I though that since you're always dealing with flour, you might know a good way to move the ashes without, you know, *touching* them. I don't think I could handle that."

She made a face. "There's no way you're going to use my sifter and cooking gloves to transfer his ashes. Don't ask, don't think about it, don't even have the *precursor* of that thought."

"I wasn't thinking that," I said. Of course I'd been thinking that. What I was really hoping was that Jenn would have some kind of baking-related vacuum-tube flour-transfer device that we could easily apply to the ash situation, and we could just press a button and *whoosh* Brent would be down in the vase and we could throw away the garbage bag.

"Right, and don't think about using any of my other stuff, either. I don't have anything that we could use for that, anyway, but I wouldn't put it past you guys to try."

"Us guys?" said Thomas. He had wandered into the kitchen and was spooning coffee into the pot. "What's the problem?"

"Brent's ashes," I said. "They're in a plastic bag, and I want to put them in the vase I got the other day."

"Proper respect for the dead," he said. "Gotcha. How fine are the ashes?"

"I don't know," I said. "They're ashes. I haven't looked at them. That's gross."

"Not as gross as using something that touches food to transfer the ashes," said Jenn.

"I wasn't thinking that," I said. "I would never think that."

"Yeah, you would," said Thomas. "Let's take a look at 'em and see if we can come up with anything."

The three of us trooped up the stairs to my room, Thomas's thudding footsteps drowning out Jenn and me. We walked into my room and I quickly moved my comforter to cover my tangled sheets. The vase was behind the door, blending in behind the shadows; some of the plastic was sticking out of the vase's mouth, as if the vase itself was trying to vomit out Brent's bag. We stood in a line, Thomas-me-Jenn, looking at the vase.

"Well, it could look weirder," said Jenn.

"Yeah, you could have painted Brent's face on the vase," said Thomas.

"Can we call it an urn?" I said. "Once there's a dead guy in there, I think you can call it an urn."

"Cremains," said Thomas.

"That's what the weird guy at the morgue said, too." said Jenn.

"So we should remove Brent's cremains from the bag?"

"Yes," said Jenn. "Brent's cremains shouldn't stay in the bag."
She snorted.

"That wasn't funny," said Thomas.

I couldn't help myself. I started to giggle. "Yeah," I said. "But it kinda was."

"So what do we do?" I said.

"Well, we could just take it downstairs to the porch and pour it," said Jenn. "We'll lose some of it to the air, but that's the most efficient way, and we won't end up with Brent on the floor or in the carpet."

"We can't lose any of it," I said.

"Why not?"

"Because, well, then we wouldn't have all of it, and what will we tell his...um...people?"

"What people?" said Thomas. "Nobody's really going to care if we lose a little bit. Ash floats; it's the thought that counts."

"OK, Let's give it a try," I said. "I still don't want to lose very much, though."

I was being optimistic. Pouring ashes isn't like pouring, say, sand (sand has large grains, which makes it easy to manage) or flour (flour clumps). I remember reading stories about how hard it was to get rid of all of the ashes after the eruption of Mt. St. Helens; the stuff got *everywhere*, and no matter how much people swept and wiped and dusted, it was just impossible. As I carried the bag of Brent's ashes downstairs, I noticed that the top of the untied bag was trailing a little smoke plume, kind of like an old-school locomotive. Those were Brent's ashes, floating away into the stairwell.

Transferring the ashes on the porch would have been a snap except for three things:

1) The light breeze blowing up Cole Street.
2) The tiny, tiny hole in the bag that opened up when Thomas accidentally snagged it on a nail that protruded out from the porch railing.
3) Thomas's inherent spazziness.

Jenn and I both ended up with parts of Brent on us, me on my forearm, her on her neck. Thomas was quivering when we finally finished, and I had blood welling up from under one fingernail after slipping on some of Brent and driving my finger into the railing. But, most of Brent was out of the bag and in the urn, which we capped and took back inside. I started to carry it up the stairs, but Jenn stopped me.

"I don't think you should have it in your room," she said. "It's kind of spooky."

"Should we put it in his room?" I asked.

She shook her head. "Not while we're interviewing. I think we can put it in a closet now that it's fully in the urn. Nobody will mess with it."

"You sure?"

"Even Shawna's not spacey enough to chuck something that looks like somebody else spent money on it. And it's kind of heavy. We're all too lazy to take something heavy downstairs to the trash."

So we heaved Brent's ashes into the back of the closet behind the kitchen, blocked from view by our ancient upright vacuum cleaner and headless mop.

Chapter 15

Two of the three companies that had come up during my search were headquartered in San Francisco. One down in the Mission District, one South of Market. Thomas spent an hour or so on Wednesday morning checking with some of his real-estate sources about on the building addresses, and he popped up on my instant messenger around lunchtime with the results.

Thomasrox: Record sez both addys are old dot-com houses.

Alexbkr: From the early '90s?

Thomasrox: Yeah, the one on Shotwell was the place where the guys from Webvan started up in '97. They had a ton of space and vacated quickly; there's probably still a bunch of logoed delivery bags there.

Alexbkr: What about the other one?

Thomasrox: Nobody worth anything. Something called carts.com, and I-divorce.

Alexbkr: I-divorce?

Thomasrox: Yeah,. They had this idea of making money of a community off of divorced people. I think they shut down because nobody could get along.

Alexbkr: Who'd a thunk it?.

Thomasrox: You'd be surprised.

Thomasrox: Half these guys worked themselves out of their first marriages, then go for someone our age. The trophy wives that show up for office parties are younger than me, with better clothes/legs/teeth. Effing stupid.

Alexbkr: Bitter?

Thomasrox: When one of them wanks out on his child support and the sheriff comes by during meetings to serve papers, yeah. They bitch and bitch about how their ex-wives are ruining them, then they give each other 100k bonuses every quarter and skip out every other day to play nine holes. It's great.

Alexbkr: How long 'til you get to do that?

Thomasrox: Will never happen. Will move to Paris first.

Alexbkr: Anything on what's in those places now?

Thomasrox: Looks like a bunch of companies that could be anything at all. Consolidated Products Corp, General Supplies and Services Inc...

Thomasrox: Those are the corporate equivalent of "John Smith."

Alexbkr: No Lucky Home and Work Products, Number One Lucky Products, or Producta Lucky Uno?

Thomasrox: No, but that doesn't matter.

Thomasrox: My list doesn't cover everything, and it sounds like these guys probably want to be on the down-low. Or they could have registered recently enough for the city business directories not to show 'em. Those city databases can be slow-reacting. But I know where the people behind them are.

Alexbkr: What do you mean?

Thomasrox: Neither of them blind-registered their domains. I e-mailed you the address of the domain registering party...the first two are both in China.

Alexbkr: Right.

Thomasrox: You gotta go down there and scope them out.

Alexbkr: Um, how do I do that? I can't just go "hey, I'm Alex, are you a sketchy Chinese bootleg toilet company?" They'll pull out my fingernails or something.

Thomasrox: You just need an excuse. That's easy. How many random people come by companies every day? Salespeople, venture capitalists. Be one of them.

Thomas was right – in SOMA, both types would be common and forgettable. I had the clothing to pull off either a salesperson or venture look, and I knew how both species talked. I got down on my knees and started to root through my closet. After my layoff, I had folded up my three pairs of khakis and five button-down shirts and piled them behind my shoe rack. The bulb at the top had been burned out for quite a while, making the whole experience like rooting around in a cotton-filled mole's den with a blindfold on. I picked out what felt like two shirts and a pair of pants and took them out.

They obviously hadn't been worn in a while – the pants were so wrinkled that the legs didn't quite cover my ankles, and the shirt collar went both up and down. Therein lay the problem; I didn't own an iron. Jenn had her nice clothes cleaned and pressed. Shawna didn't care. Thomas? He was probably my best bet; his work suits and Euro dancewear always looked like he had his own butler. I flipped open my laptop again.

Alexbkr: Hey dude, can I use your iron?

Thomasrox: You could, but I don't have one, so that would be kind of a problem.

Alexbkr: How do you keep your biz-cas stuff pressed?

Thomasrox: I fake-iron. My showers are long, so I just take my clothes into the bathroom when I shower. It gets 'em mostly there, then I wear the wrinkles out on the bus.

Alexbkr: Oh…OK. Thanks.

Thomasrox: n/p. You get the addresses?

Alexbkr: Yep. Thx.

I took the dark tan khakis and blue button-up shirt with me into the shower. I was already clean and didn't need a shower, but just turning on the water and leaving my clothes hanging there in the steam didn't seem like a particularly good use of resources, so I closed the little window in the wall, stripped down again and washed up. Then I scrubbed again just to waste time. Sure enough, when I groped my way out of the shower through the steam my shirt and pants had lost most of their wrinkles. Score one for Thomas. As I dressed, I breathed as deeply as I could, trying to calm down. After dressing, I looked at myself in the mirror. I felt a little dirty; I was voluntarily dressing like a wanker. Brent's ghost owed me one.

I headed down to the Mission first, hopping a bus down the hill to the big Safeway on Market Street, then walked down the hill past Mission Dolores. The old church loomed beige in the bright sun; a couple was taking wedding photos at the door when I walked by. She was in her normal dress, he was wearing a policeman's uniform. Oddly, I think he really *was* a cop; I've seen several cop-themed wedding ceremonies since moving here. Wouldn't it be kind of odd to be saying "I do" to a guy with a loaded 9mm automatic hanging on his waist? It seems stressful; not to mention the obvious nightstick-and-handcuffs kink theme. Sure, that stuff is fine, but on a wedding night I'd think you'd want to be a bit more romantic. The guy caught me looking at them as I walked past, and he smiled at me; no faketitude there. I grinned and waved back, mouthed *congratulations* and walked on.

Things became dicey as I walked down 16th Street and hit Mission. Ancient homeless men with desiccated legs wheeled themselves from bench to corner and back again, scoring two-collar rocks from the men in dark hoodies who lurked in the corners. Crones in vinyl miniskirts worked the plaza, smoking tired cigarettes, the makeup to cover their open sores flaking off in the warmth of the afternoon. I could feel them looking at me; a good chunk of the guys who dressed like me at this intersection were there to score. They made me more nervous than I already was.

East of Mission Street, the crowd got tougher; the locals here had guns. The sidewalk was shaded by a multi-story warehouse with boarded windows that the neighborhood had been fighting to develop for years. I stepped over a set of scab-ridden legs sticking out from under a pile of clothes. Liquid was dripping from the cuffs of the rolled-up pants, creating a fetid puddle below the knees.

After I passed Capp Street, most of the winos and hookers dissipated, and the street became a hodgepodge of dilapidated old houses, auto parts stores, closed theaters, and dark corners. I took a right at Shotwell and walked three blocks. The building I was looking for was at 438, kitty-corner from a gloomy-looking bar called the Rest Stop. I at the office building for a minute or two and headed over to the bar. If Brent had worked in the area, he might have stopped in once or twice. It didn't look like a yuppie-friendly place, so I took off my button-down and stowed it, rolled, in my bag. I'd have to brave the potential wrinkles, as an untucked t-shirt turned me from yuppie into nondescript neighborhood guy.

The front area of the Rest Stop was big enough for a fistfight. The red chrome-legged stools were capped with middle-aged white guys dressed anywhere from downscaling yuppie to construction-worker *chic*. Nobody was behind the bar, so I sat down and cracked open a peanut from a bowl that lay on the bar. I hesitated with the shell until I saw the sign:

All peanut shells go on the floor behind *you. If you throw them behind the bar, we will not be held responsible for what we do to you.*

I chucked my shell to the floor and popped open another nut.

The bar was quiet; I could hear the muffled crackling of the shelling and chucking over the soft Sinatra coming from the speakers in the ceiling. A crunching sound came over towards me, and I looked up into a weathered face framed by shoulder-length gray hair. The bartender was smiling just a bit, as if he'd just heard a joke that wasn't quite funny enough for a real laugh.

"What can I do for you?" he said.

"Anchor Steam," I said. "And maybe a little information."

"The first I can do," he said. "The second might be a little harder, Spade."

The beer was cold and came with a perfect quarter-inch head. Steam is brewed locally in Potrero Hill, and it's one of those things that you can't really get anywhere else. Taste-wise, it's like any number of ales, but it's just slightly off. But in a good way. I put down a twenty. The bartender gave me back seventeen. I made no motion to take the change.

"What do you want to know?" he asked.

I sipped my beer, thinking. I couldn't really ask if any Chinese gangsters from the place across the way ever came into the bar. I couldn't ask him if they got a special discount on their bar toilets (what kind of commode was in the back, anyway?) from the guys across the way in the office building. There wasn't much I could ask him that didn't sound dangerous or insane, so I went with an old standard.

"Ever see this guy in here?" I said, pulling out my scanned/printed photo of Brent's drivers' license from my wallet and folding it out on the bar. He picked it up and held it at an angle to capture the light.

"You know what's funny?" he said. "I've been pouring drinks here for twenty-three years, and you're the first dick who's ever come in with that question."

"No need to be harsh," I said.

"Dick," he said. "You know, private eye."

"Oh," I said. "I'm not…"

"Gotcha," he said. "I know how it is. I haven't seen one of your kind in a while. This neighborhood isn't tough any more. Back when I started, this was the kind of place where if you looked at a fella wrong, he'd pop you one with a fist full of rolled quarters. Now the junkies and used-up hookers are the only thing saving us from having to serve biodynamic cabernet."

"That's the way it goes," I said.

"Yep," he said. He looked down at the bills on the bar, then looked up at me. I nodded, just a bit, and he folded them into his left hand. "Your friend here in this picture, though...I can't say that I've seen him, but I can't say that I haven't. It could be...hm. I've been tending long enough to be good at faces, and I've definitely seen his face, but not here."

"Where?" I said.

"I moonlight every now and then at one of the swank places over South of Market. Bigger tabs, bigger tips, helps keep me in used books. I think I saw your friend there. Did he wear a baseball hat sometimes?"

"Red Sox," I said. "The one with the two socks, but he wore it high, not low on his face."

The bartender nodded. "That coulda been him," he said. "I have a mental picture of him drinking soju cocktails with some other guys. Three of 'em, all kind of short."

"Any of them Chinese?" I said.

The bartender nodded. "Could be. Since I'm not regular there, I don't think my face memory is as good as it is here. Your best bet is to go over to the Lux Lounge at Bryant near Ninth and talk with Gary, the regular bartender there. He's as good with faces and customers as any one. If your pal was in there more than a few times, he'll know." He paused and gave me a hard look. "Why do you wanna know?"

"Long story," I said, then hesitated. He'd given me information freely; would he talk about me to other people? He'd called me *Spade* and now I was thinking like Bogie. I'd play to his prejudices. "I'm actually a low-on-the-pole guy for the city," I said. "The company across the way might be a front for a development consortium that's going to try to turn this whole area condo. This guy is their American front guy and we're trying to find out more about his background, so I'm..."

"Scoping it out, seeing if they're going about it on the up-and-up," said the bartender. "Probably be bad if they knew the city was onto them, huh?"

"It's not good if people know that you're looking at them," I said.

He nodded. "That's OK in my book. I never saw you."

"What should I tell Gary?" I said.

"Tell him Jon sent you," said the bartender. "That's 'Jon' with no 'h,' OK?"

"You got it," I said, putting another five down on the bar. "Thanks, Jon."

He nodded, pulled the bill, and walked down to where one of the other men was drumming his fingers against an empty pint glass. I drained the rest of my beer and walked out the door into the sunshine, my heart pounding with excitement. That had been easy; it had felt like people walked into The Rest Stop with pics for the pourer every day. I wished that I had something to record the whole conversation, to see if it was really as cool as it sounded from my side.

Getting from where I was to SOMA was a tough proposition; several busses ran up the main streets, but outside of rush hours their schedule ranged from unreliable to a ghostly figment of the city's collective imagination. I hedged my bets, walking over to Bryant Street, then north along the bus route. No busses came, so I walked the whole way.

The sky had descended to new levels of gloom when I reached the intersection of Ninth and Bryant, a neighborhood that was doing the new-millennium switchover from an area of low-slung warehouses that held things that people would eventually buy, to a neighborhood of low-slung warehouses holding oversized loft apartments and Internet companies that sold things that nobody understood. The Lux bar didn't open until four. The nearest food options were a sushi place where the cheapest roll was nine dollars and a bodega with a fridge full of those white-bread-with-American-cheese contraptions. I went to the bodega and bought a sandwich that tasted like feet but only cost a dollar fifty. There really wasn't anywhere to sit, so I stood and munched on the corner, waiting and watching the traffic roar by until four.

The darkness inside the Lux was calculated; leaning back from your date would help cover up the crow's feet around her eyes or the gray in his hair. It reeked of twentysomething economic yearning and thirtysomething what-do-I-do-now desperation. Two-page cocktail menus featured house drinks with four-word names and seven dollar well shots. It was completely deserted; I was pretty sure their working clientele wasn't the afternoon drunks. Their people would be in right at five-fifteen, knocking back pink cosmos and scoping for people with similar-sized stock option packages.

I walked over to the bar, where the bartender was pulling glasses from the dishwasher and stacking them on a rubber drying mat.

"What can I do for you?" he asked.

"I'm looking for a little help," I said. "Are you Gary?"

"That's me," he said.

"Jon with no 'h' from the Rest Stop said you might be able to help me out."

The bartender smiled. "Sure. Jon's helped me out of a few tight spots on big nights. You looking for a job? We can always use a barback, but you don't look like the type who can handle slinging kegs and fifty-pound ice bags around. No offense."

"None taken," I said. "I'm kind of looking to see if you ever saw this guy around here, up until about a month ago. I think he might have worked around here and might have come in with some of the guys he worked with. Jon said you had a good memory for faces, so…" I pulled out my oft-folded picture and spread it out on the bar.

Gary squinted in the gloom, sighed, and reached behind him. The lights over the bar flared up, and I could now see the pockmarks on his cheeks. He'd either had late chicken pox or bad acne as a kid.

"Yeah, I know this guy," he said. "He doesn't come in here any more; it's been at least a month."

"Who would he come in with?"

"A couple of Chinese guys. They weren't part of the happy hour crowd; they'd usually make it in around eight or nine, on a weekday, which is weird for here. We get a good amount of folks who are looking to take the edge off after work, but the crowd bleeds off until the late-night clubbers come in at around eleven. He was a good tipper; he paid for the other guys' drinks."

Jackpot! Wait…what was I supposed to ask as a follow-up question to this sort of thing? If I really were a private investigator, I suppose I'd ask something like *what were they drinking?* Or *any broads with them?* Or, if I were Magnum, I'd be able to charm him with a smile and a mustache. But I'm not, I'm me, so I sat there and stared at the *faux*-wood bar while trying to think of something to say, feeling like even more of an idiot than I usually do. Wait...they could have come from anywhere; maybe this was just their favorite bar.

"They from around here?" I asked.

"I got the feeling they worked nearby," said Gary. "But they didn't live close. They came in on foot in the early evenings but would catch cabs when they left later. Plus, the Chinese guys were older, gray hair and such, and he was so young... Your friend paid for drinks, but he wasn't bleeding money. Regular credit cards, no platinums. If you're going to buy a loft around here, you gotta be worth a few million at least."

"Even with all the junkies and broken glass?"

He grinned. "That shit ups the property values these days. Realtors call the area 'up and coming.'"

"Hmm," I said. I now knew that Brent's fake company was most likely the one half a block away, the artfully named Number One Lucky Products.

"You want a drink or something?" he said.

"Sure," I said. "What's on tap?"

He shook his head. "We don't have taps here, my friend. All we've got is Bud, Bud Light, Coors Light, Corona, Heineken, and Amstel Light."

"Bottled beer for the frat-boy set?" I asked.

"It's amazing," he said. "So many people come in here who are worth more than the Bay Bridge was when it was built. If one more guy with a eighty dollar t-shirt, Armani jacket and slicked-back hair asks me for a 'heinie,' I swear I'm going to do something that'll get me fired."

"That'd be fun," I said.

"No," he said, shaking his head. "Some of those guys throw down ridiculous tips to show off. Those idiots are going to be my down payment."

"Thanks," I said, extending my hand. "My name's Alex."

"Gary," he said. "Glad to help out a friend of Jon's."

"You know, you look kind of familiar," I said.

"I get that," he said. "I once won three straight days of *Jeopardy*. People remember that sometimes. The memory helps in my line of work."

I got up to leave, and he stopped me.

"One more thing," he said. "They stopped coming in a little while ago, but your pal's two friends have come in since. A few weeks ago. They ordered vodkas and sat in the corner, talking in Chinese. I went over to ask them if they wanted refills and…well, ordinarily people like that kind of service. They weren't pleased. You remember when people are mad at you. Haven't seen 'em since. But…"

"But?"

"I got a really weird feeling from them. Like a mixture of danger and stupidity. Like Wile E. Coyote."

I left the bar and headed out into the street, turning left and walking the half-block down to where my database had said Number One Lucky Products, Incorporated had their offices. As I'd expected, it was a low-slung warehouse-type building, with a single glass-filed door stuck in the middle of an industrial wall. A single metal panel was next to the door, with a little speaker, telephone keypad, and digital display. A little printed sign was on top.

To access company directory, use # and * keys to go up or down the alphabet. When you have reached the company you would like to visit, press the "talk" button.

I scrolled through the alphabet, starting with Aaron, Daniel, and Saul LLC. After seeing twelve companies with ridiculous technology names, I hit my quarry. I stood there, staring at the name for what seemed like a long time, not sure if it was a good idea to try to call them or not. It was after five. If Number One Lucky Products was a normal company people would be starting on their way out right now. I stood a good chance of coming face-to-face with a group of shady characters while I stood diddling outside their door. That would be bad – the last thing I wanted was for them to remember me. I took a deep breath. Go in or go home?

My decision was made for me when the door opened. Two khaki/polo shirt guys with too much gunk in their hair came out to the street. The taller one looked at me oddly so I just said "thanks" and walked into the lobby, which was more of a wide hallway with a single elevator and a building directory on the wall. The glass on it was dusty, and some of the white letters had fallen off of the black rubber backing, so most of the company names looked like they needed Vanna White to turn over a few more blocks. I scanned down the list until I found N ber O e ck ucts, Inc. The floor number had fallen off, so they were either on floor four or five. A door to the stairs was next to the elevator. I walked.

I started on the fifth floor, which was yet another hallway with square ceiling tiles laid on a metal frame and thinning blue carpet. Brown doors led off the hallway, some with suite numbers, some with company names, and a few with neither. Walking the hallway took me less than a minute, and I didn't see what I was looking for. The stairs echoed on my way down.

The fourth floor was a clone of the fifth; the same ceiling tiles, the same tired carpet, the same harsh lighting. The only company that wasn't missing letters was Number One Lucky Products, Inc., Suite 405. I kept walking past the door, my mouth dry. I hadn't planned to actually go into their office, but that was what I was thinking about doing. Dammit. I couldn't go in there looking like me. I needed to change my look somehow, disappear. I opened my bag and took inventory.

- one copy of Jared Diamond's *Collapse*.
- Chapstick.
- A small notebook.
- A black scally cap.
- My sunglasses that were missing a lens.
- The sunglass lens.
- Gum.
- Two pens.
- A crumpled MUNI transfer.

I took the shades out and turned them over in my hand. They were cheap construction; thin bendable metal frames and easy-scratch lenses. I'd bought them at the drug store when my previous pair had fallen victim to an overcrowded MUNI bus and aggressive old women with shopping bags. I always keep a small Swiss Army knife on my keychain; I wedged the blade into the little crack between the remaining lens and the frame, and pried. The lens popped right out. Then I donned the hat and put on the lensless glasses. One of the glass frames next to the door at the end of the hall reflected well, so I could see myself. With the shade from the cap it was almost impossible to tell that the glasses were false. I no longer really looked like me; instead, I resembled an out-of-work nerdy sailor who'd done a clothing swap with a circa – 1992 Seattle hipster. Good enough to pass.

The front door to Number One Lucky Products Inc was unlocked; I knocked, waited a few seconds, and entered to a front office much like the front office of my old company; one large desk, a small potted tree in the corner, and nobody manning the reception desk. Two padded chairs were on the far wall, flanking a cylinder-style table piled with magazines. I checked them out; the selection was right out of a dentist's office: *Reader's Digest, Parade, Golf Digest, Modern Western Living, Highlights for Children,* all at least a year out of date, with the address labels cut out. It looked like someone had just raided a Nebraska Republican's recycling bin. I sat down and started reading a "Humor in Uniform" segment. I think the Army pays the *Digest* to keep putting those vignettes in; making the service seem like *Major Dad* is probably a better recruiting tool than pointing out how much time you'll spend with your face down in the mud and barbed wire two inches from your scalp.

As I stood in the quiet, I started to hear small noises that sounded like the way adults talked in Charlie Brown cartoons. I closed the *Digest* and tried to listen harder. Craning my neck didn't help, nor did squinting. Walking around helped; it was a bit louder towards the far wall. They were definitely voices, and I could tell that they were coming from behind the single door, but I couldn't make out the words. I looked around; a business-style water cooler with a paper cup dispenser stood on the other side of the room. I took one of the paper cups out and put the open side on the wall near the door.

The trick worked. Two people were talking. They sounded muffled, as if they were talking with napkins in their mouths. I could make out every word, and that would have been useful if I spoke Mandarin. Sadly, I didn't; my super-spy trick wasn't going to do me a lick of good. Unless...

I took my cell phone out of my pocket. If I could capture the voices on the ten minutes or so of audio that my phone would hold, maybe I could get a translation. I clicked the voice-note button and held it next to the cup, putting my ear close. I could tell that they were talking about something pretty intense, even without understanding a word. My hands started to shake, then there was silence from the other side of the wall. I kept the cup and hurried over to the big desk, and rapped loudly on the work surface. Footsteps approached the side door, and a young Chinese man came out, dressed in the kind of suit that makes you immediately suspicious. The cut was expensive, but somehow greasy, as if he'd rubbed it in pomade before doing a bad job dry-cleaning it. I could feel flop sweat pouring down my sides; I tried to breathe deeply.

"Can I help you?" he asked. His English was very good, with a slight British/colonial tinge to it. His *L* had only the slightest lilt; it reminded me of how kids who'd come straight from China to my high school had talked after two years in the states. I thought fast.

"I'm looking for the guy here who is in charge of buying office supplies," I said. "Would that be you, sir?"

"We...don't buy office supplies," he said.

"Yes, sir," I said. "But have you considered switching your office supply provider? My organization has incredible pricing; we beat Staples and Office Depot's advertised prices on anything from pens to Red Bull by at least five percent, and if you order online we'll drop prices an additional *two* percent! Over the course of a year for a fifty-person company you'll save nearly a hundred dollars, and in this day of Sarbanes-Oxley compliance, you have a responsibility to your shareholders to keep costs down in any way you can! All you have to do is..."

He had been looking at me patiently, blinking his eyes behind his wireless spectacles. After the bit on the shareholders, he slammed his hand down on the desk with a whiplike *crack*.

"Stop!" he said. "I don't think you understand... we do *not* need office supplies, so we will not buy your office supplies. Please leave, and tell your employer that we do not appreciate him intruding upon our regular business hours. Leave now, or I will be forced to call security!"

"OK, OK," I said. "But are you sure…"

"Enough!" he said. "Out! Now!"

"You got it, buddy," I said. "Sheesh."

I left through the front door, and waited, listening at the wall with my paper cup. The voices weren't as sharp as they had been before, but I could still hear them talking in the front room. I hoped that my phone could pick them up. They talked for about another minute in that front room, then the noise faded; they'd probably moved to the back. I dropped the cup on the floor and walked down the stairs, out of the building to the street.

I walked east and north; the opposite direction from my house. All of this detective crap was making me think like a secret agent, as in *in case those guys are watching me through some kind of high-tech watching device (you know, because they have no windows) this way they'll think that I'm headed this way because it's where I live, and they'll spend all of their resources trying to find me over at the ritzy condos near the ballpark, or they'll roust homeless people from the single-room-occupancy flophouses near Sixth Street. Anyone who lives in the Haight wouldn't waste time and risk mugging by walking through this semi-improved warehouse district at night. You'd only do that if you were rich enough to live in the condos or out-of-it enough to be in the flophouses. So I'll be totally safe if I walked from this warehouse area to about Seventh Street…*

So I walked, fast, trying to calm myself down and not look behind me. The walk from where I was to Seventh Street was not particularly exciting; warehouse after warehouse on the side of the road, with the occasional bearded man wheeling a shopping cart up the sidewalk and muttering to himself. I passed someone who had already bedded down for the night. He was lying on his side, piled under sleeping bags in the glow of a street lamp, sketching in a leather-bound blank book. I looked down as I passed; his page was full of skew lines, as if he was trying to put the lines together to make words, but couldn't quite figure it out. As I passed, he turned the page and started to make more lines on a blank sheet.

My stomach was grumbling as I crossed the intersection of Seventh Street and Mission, so I walked one more over and one more up to the corner of Sixth, one of the best intersections in the city for scoring cheap food and cheap crack. Two taquerias flanked a

Chinese/American place that advertised "Hofbrau, Spaghetti, Burritos, and Pad Thai," along with a fried chicken joint, a donut shop, schawarma shack, and a hole in the wall Saigon street cuisine restaurant – you-name-it deep-fried and served over rice noodles with chili sauce.

I stood on the corner for a few minutes. As I stood there, a woman walked by wearing no pants, a t-shirt that came down to just below her hipbones, and boots. She sashayed more than walked, and as she made her way down the street people's heads whipped around to follow her progress. You see a lot of stuff in San Francisco, but pantless is a bit much.

"You gotta love that," said a male voice. He was tall enough to be a pro basketball player, with a tuba for a voice and brown running shoes rotted out at the toes. I looked closer; the shoes weren't really brown, but formerly white, scarred, pitted and stained with street detritus and filth.

"I guess so," I said.

"That's about as good as it gets out here," he said. "Got any spare change?"

"Sorry, man," I said. "I can't really help you."

Burrito time. The two taquerias were about equidistant from where I stood, and their reputations were about the same. CanCun on the right was the consistent winner of "best burrito in town" polls in the local alt-weeklies. This meant very little, considering that the "best-of" polls also consistently had In-N-Out as the best hamburger in the city. I'd been to CanCun a few times and had sworn off their al pastor after an apocalyptic intestinal episode.

Al pastor: specially marinated barbecued pork, Mexican style. I've seen it done any number of ways, but the most common here in the city is done by taking a big slab o'swine and putting it on one of those spit-cookers that the guys who make kebabs and schawarma use. The whole thing is topped with a pineapple and rotates on the cooker until you order, when they chop off big chunks and finish them off on the grill. When it's done right, it's our answer to southern barbecue. If it's off, it can do things to your digestive system that are illegal in several states. In general, I go with an innocent-until-proven-guilty approach to the stuff, but once bitten is twice shy. You really want to be careful in matters of the colon.

I chose the place I hadn't been – Taqueria Chile Verde. It was next to the fried chicken place, which had two Asian guys manning the food counter. I've never figured out if it's racist to assume that certain types of ethnic foods are better if they're prepared by certain types of ethnic people – I mean, it's normal to be weirded out at a soul food restaurant run by white people, right? Anyway, I skipped the fried chicken, not because I have racially sensitive beliefs about food, but because I really wanted a burrito. Chile Verde was warm and dry; I ordered a super burrito with carne asada (supers add cheese, avocado, and sour cream to the normal beans, rice, salsa mix), took my chips and salsa to my table, and sat down. I was still shaking a little bit; I added *not really cut out for fieldwork* to my internal job performance review.

And as I ate, I thought. I had probably just talked with one of the guys who had offed my housemate. I shivered. My burrito came. It was warm and wonderful, with a nicely grilled tortilla and fresh salsa with a cilantro punch. My hands were shaking badly enough to make eating a challenge; I kept getting avocado on my face. When I finished, I had gone through ten napkins.

"You like it?" said the counter guy. I could barely see his mouth moving behind his mustache.

"Very much," I said.

"*Gracias,*" he said.

As I left, I had to turn sideways to squeeze through the door, because a crack dealer had taken up most of the left side of the doorway with one of those little shopping carts that retired people use at the grocery store. His was full of a monster boom box, a fishing tackle chest, and two canvas sacks full of plastic bags. He looked at me as I squeezed past, dismissed me as probably not a potential customer, and continued to swivel his eyes up and down the street, looking for the next emaciated, death-seeking client.

I walked out to Market Street, where I headed to the nearest underground rail stop one block up. A MUNI inspector was stationed at the fare gates, handing everyone fliers that looked like they'd been printed on a home computer.

MUNI Apologizes, said the fliers, *But the Underground Subway will not be Available tonight due to track, wire, and/or Train maintenance issues. Please catch the shuttle bus upstairs to Van Ness Station, where train service will recommence.*

I didn't really understand the flier. The inspector was one of those guys with glasses who looks at you as if he's pleading, begging you not to actually ask him any questions, so I headed upstairs, ignoring a guy with patchy facial scruff with a sign begging for change so that he could "feed my wife so she stops complaining" and two guys who appeared to be attempting to bed down in the same rusted-out shopping cart. By some small miracle, a number 6 bus was pulling up to the island stop right when I crossed over, so I paid my dollar fifty, cursed myself for not buying an August bus pass, and made it to my front door in just over fifteen minutes.

Chapter 16

"So what do you do now?" asked Jenn. It was Saturday morning. I'd spent the past two days lying extremely low, brooding and trying to figure out what my next step would be. I'd barely left my room and hadn't really talked to anyone, so I was incredibly prepared to answer her question.

"Hope that Shawna can translate these voicenotes," I said. She'd been out of town for some thing or another, and she'd finally responded to my calls when I rang her up for the twelfth time. She'd promised to give it a shot when she got home this Saturday morning.

Right on cue, Shawna flounced into the kitchen. Her face was sooty and her arms streaked with ash, as if she'd been off on a learn-to-be-a-chimney-sweep workshop. "Hi guys,' she said. "What needs translating?"

"Where have you been?" asked Jenn.

"Smoke-hole therapy," she said. "We went out to the high desert and built a little underground lodge, then we lit a fire with green sticks and sat down in the lodge until we had spiritual experiences. I finally had mine last night, then went to sleep, then we drove back."

"Oh," said Jenn. "I don't know why I asked."

"It's really neat," said Shawna. "We might do it again next month."

"Grab a listen," I said. My phone was hooked up to a low-tech wired headphone. Shawna put it in her ear, waited a few seconds, and nodded. "It's pretty clear," she said. "Got a pen?" She listened and wrote, pausing and rewinding every few words:

"...seriously impacts our chances of making a profit."

"Any idea where it might be?"

"Of course. There is a bank, there is money."

"Our interests on the mainland need to have this cleared up. We have made a substantial manufacturing investment, but we need funding for the raw materials. Porcelain does not grow on trees, and we need to pay painters to make them look like brushed aluminum, and falsify all of the technical features."

"Yes, I understand, but the law here is such that we cannot just go in to the box and open it. We need the key."

"And the key is..."

"The key is not a key, the key is a phrase, and those words only will allow entry, as long as we can prove a connection to him."

"He is dead, yes?"

"Yes. That was a mistake. He was supposed to pick him up and take him out to a certain site. All that came through was 'take him out,' so now we are where we are.. If we can find a person with a connection to him..."

"What kind of connection?"

"Family. Or someone who can pass."

"Where did he live?"

"We do not know. I think he lived under a different name."

"What about the family?"

"We do not know — the family names provided by our employment contact were not real."

"I see. So there is nobody?"

"No. We know that he did not live alone. He mentioned this several months ago; he moved in with several other young people. If we can find one of them, we can use those people to get to the box."

"Will they help us?"

Laughter, high-pitched. Man, they really don't laugh like dangerous guys. *"Yes. I have ways."*

"And we have the passphrase?"

Laughter. *"A sticking point, but one that can be solved. We think the phrase is in the box."*

"How..."

"Yes....lucky."

"How close are you to the people he knew?"

"Not close. We do not have pictures yet. But one of our people is working on it."

"I am glad you are so far along on this. The people back home were not pleased at the delay."

"Will you report satisfactorily?"

"When all is finished, yes. Until then, I will work with you to finalize."

"Excellent. A drink? There are bars close by.

"Wow," I said, reading as Shawna wrote.

"Wait, there's more," she said.

"What was that?"

"A salesman.. America is full of them; I need to talk with the building

management about the entrance. That was the fourth one this month; they should not be able to enter through the front door."

"Why can't they just get rid of them?"

"He was no matter. What matters is that we're very close."

The voices stopped for a second, and then I heard what was either a slow removal of all of the hair from Robin Williams's arms, or the cackle of a crazed evil genius.

"Yes, when we get that box, we'll corner the luxury toilet market! We'll be selling these to these Americans at margins so high we'll be able to retire nearly instantly! We'll be the masters of our universe!"

"Wow," I said.

"They sound like the guys in *Die Hard*," said Jenn.

"Quiet," said Shawna. "Translating isn't that easy." We shut up, and she continued writing.

"Yes, and if they ever find out that their commodes are not what they seem, we'll be sitting on a beach, earning 20 percent."

Wow. *Die Hard*, but a direct quote. There are some movies you don't quote from unless you're quoting from them as part of a quoting-from-movies game. You certainly don't quote *Die Hard* if you're trying to actually *make* a megalomaniacal speech.

"What's our plan B?"

"What does that mean?"

"When your first plan fails, you should have a backup plan. In America, they always call it 'Plan B.'"

"We will not fail, therefore we do not need a Plan B."

Jenn and Shawna looked at me as if I was supposed to say something. As per usual, I had no idea what I was supposed to say. A big chunk of me wanted to laugh – the evil masterminds were guys who based their evil on an '80s action movie. On the other hand, a whole lot of people were killed in *Die Hard*.

"Wow," I said. "They sound like they've spent too much time memorizing Alan Rickman dialogue, but…"

"They *sound* like idiots," said Jenn. "But that doesn't mean much. We should be careful, but they don't know who we are or what we look like, so we should be all right. I mean, it's not like we go hang out in dark SOMA bars where they can spirit us out into a waiting van, right? If they tried anything at the Bitter End all we'd have to do is yell and they'd be shredded by big Irish lads."

"Right," I said. "Everyone lays low. So all I have to do now is try to get what's in Brent's safety-deposit box and use it to help us with the rent and help out Morgan with her little Brent's-kid problem, without those guys finding out who we are. Great. That's easy."

"There's no kid," said Jenn. "She's full of it."

"Are you really sure?" I said. "People only lie about that kind of stuff on *Jerry Springer*. Why would she fake it?"

"Are you really that dense?" she said. " Alex, sometimes I want to hit you with a rubber spatula until you bruise."

"A rubber spatula wouldn't bruise much," I said.

She looked at me as if I'd just told her that my love interest was of a different species. "Yes, that's exactly the point. I want to hit you enough times that using a rubber spatula will leave you with a shiner. Has anyone ever told you that jokes aren't funny if you have to explain them?"

"Yeah," I said.

"Well, it's the same way with hyperbolic violence," she said. "You just made me manage to bore myself. Congratulations. So what do you do now?"

"What I said," I said. "I'm going to go down to the bank, show them my drivers' license and the death documents I got from the morgue, and get into Brent's safety deposit box so I can empty it and put it somewhere else. That way, those guys won't know where it is and they won't be able to find it."

"Not the best idea," she said. "They'll find out who you are."

"How?"

This earned me yet another scornful look. If I'd been marking those like Crusoe marked his days, I'd need a second tree.

"There will be a record of who signed for the safety-deposit box," she said. "One of the women I work with, her husband left her when she was six months pregnant, and he emptied their box before he left. She was able to track him down because he was stupid enough to leave a real cell phone number when he signed out of the box."

"Yeah, but there's no reason for them to release the bank records to Chinese gangsters," I said. "I'll be safe."

"Alex, you adorable idiot, all they would have to do is come up with a decent fake-cop ID. Brent's dead. The bank doesn't care. You've got to get that box in a way that doesn't reveal who you are, because, despite their moronic way of speaking, I sure as hell don't want those guys coming by and knocking on our door. Not just that whenever someone comes by it's bad news – either the cops telling us someone's dead or yet another weirdo potential roommate – but because it's dangerous for both you and us. We've got to think of some way to get it without leaving that information."

"Well, the only way to do that would be to somehow convince the bank that a totally fake person is the right person to give access to that box – a relative or something like that."

Jenn looked at me oddly. "You know, I had a thought."

I arched my eyebrow, waiting.

"Thomas," she said. "He does more sketchy business stuff than anyone I know. I bet he can help us."

"Help you do what?" said Thomas. He was barefoot, and had padded down the stairs from his room without us noticing. His boxers and t-shirt hung loose on his slender frame, and he tried to put a hand in a pocket as he stood in the doorway, but couldn't because boxers have no pockets, so he reached overhead and rested his fingers on the top side of the door frame.

"How dumb are banks?" asked Jenn.

Thomas snorted. "You know those guys who rob banks with their fingers inside sweatshirts? Those guys are dumb. You know what's dumber than them? Banks. The big ones are about the dumbest organizations on earth. They make politicians look practical and football look like an intelligent sport."

"What's wrong with football?" I asked. "I'm not a fan, but that made no sense."

"I was trying to point out that football is as ridiculous a game as banks are dumb," said Thomas. "It totally made sense."

"It's OK," said Shawna, edging past Thomas by putting her hands on his hips, shoving him to the side, and scooting through the door. "That's just the way he talks sometimes."

"*I've* never heard him talk using analogies," said Jenn.

Shawna shrugged. "Maybe you aren't listening at the right time."

Jenn shook her head and let her lips come up into the tiniest little smile. "Thomas, back to the matter at hand. Can you help Alex get Brent's stuff out of a safety deposit box?"

"I can," he said. "But I won't."

Jenn's smile disappeared. "Why not?"

"I won't help *Alex,*" Thomas said. "Because Alex is the wrong guy to do it." He took his arms down from the door sill and crossed the room, ending up sitting down on the counter next to the stove. The room was silent, quiet enough to hear the hissing of the gas oven.

"Look at us," he said, pointing towards himself and Shawna. "We get fake licenses and then the two of us will go in. We'll be Brent's hippie cousin housemates; nobody would believe that two stoners could be devious enough to do a con ID job. "We'll look as innocent as can be, especially if I break out my real college-stoner clothes. Dead tour shirts and stuff. If anyone ever looks at the records, the people who accessed the deposit box won't exist. "

"Oh, man," I said. I couldn't stand the Dead. Anyone under the age of fifty who still bothered to listen to their tinny, out-of-tune live performances ten years after Garcia died probably deserved to *have* to listen to it. Thomas was my exception to that rule because I liked him, and he was considerate enough to only listen to the Dead over headphones. But there was no denying his college wardrobe's authenticity. Corduroy bell-bottoms, bootleg Calvin and Hobbes logoed shirts about being one with the stars, overalls, Birkenstocks with the heels shredded out from use, the whole business. If we put him in those clothes along with Shawna…"

"We get a multicultural hippie couple," I said. "That's not bad."

"Um…" said Shawna. "I'm Chinese. Won't that make us more memorable?"

"That's a risk we can take," I said. "If anyone comments, get indignant. Big banks are going to be much more afraid of inciting a discrimination lawsuit than giving away priceless consumer information. We just don't want a record of us signing for something at the bank."

"Why not?"

"Because what we're doing is illegal," said Thomas. It's definitely moral, but just as definitely against the law."

"But we have to do it," I said. "If those guys figure out a way to get to the deposit box before us, they could get Brent's money and find us. That scares me."

"I'm in," said Shawna.

"Why don't we just go in as us?" I asked. "I mean, the fact that we live at the address where Brent lived before is enough, right?"

Thomas shook his head. "No, not really. I'll have to be related to him, and Shawna can be my wife. That, along with that death certificate, should do it. We'll have to get fakes. Let's go down to the Mission."

"What are we doing there?" I asked.

He looked at me scornfully. "Were you born yesterday? We're getting some fake IDs."

"Oh," I said. "I thought you could do it."

"My printer isn't *that* good. I can do some supporting docs, but we'll have to go to the pros for these. Go get dressed, guys. We'll leave in half an hour."

Since I didn't have to change, I went through my mail for the first time in several days; it tended to pile up when I got busy. Twelve pieces of standard junk mail, a credit card bill, and an envelope from the Office of the City Medical Examiner. I ripped it open. It was a bill.

Dear Mr. Baker,

Enclosed please find an invoice for the services the city provided to you on the 16th of September. Note that said services were triggered by a regulation covering morgue overload during a time of high system stress, and you were properly notified that this was a possibility. The total for the services is $2,254, which includes cremation and overhead fees, as explained in the release form you signed upon taking responsibility for the remains. Please feel free to stop by our offices if you wish to pay in person, or enclose the following form along with your check. Please write the bill number (top of page) on any checks. For further questions, please call our office.

Great. I stared at the bill and grumbled to myself until the rest of the house got down there. I could pay the bill, but it would make my severance go less far, and if I combined it with the money I already owed the city for Brent's storage…well, I would start becoming the poster boy for one of those "Why The Younger Generation Can't Put Down Their Credit Cards" articles that pop up in the newspapers whenever some crusty old Woodstock veteran decides to start feeling superior.

"Wow," said Thomas when I showed him the bill. "You got two grand?"

"Yes," I said. "But not that I want to pay the city. And not on top of what they're going to bill me for the storage. And they screwed up – the guy said it was an accident."

"Can we sue them? It seems like their screwup is their fault."

"We *could*," I said. "But I signed the form. I was kind of a mess when it happened. This is all my fault."

"We can probably wait it out," he said. "That's a first notice - the city's not going to come after us for that for a couple of months, at least. Maybe Brent's money is in that safe deposit box. It only seems fair to have him pay for his own funeral. If we're wrong and there's no money to be had, we can deal with it."

"We?" I said.

He shrugged. "We're in this together at this point. I mean, we're going down to get fake IDs so that we can illegally access a safety deposit box. It's like they said – 'we must all hang together, otherwise we will certainly hang separately.'"

"They *hang* you for trying to get into a bank with a fake ID?"

Thomas laughed. "No. Five to ten, probably. Don't worry about it, though. Nobody there will really care. That's the key to life in the 21st century. If you know that nobody really cares, you can get away with anything."

"*We* care," I said.

He paused. "I guess that's true," he said. "Otherwise we wouldn't be having this conversation."

We made quite the procession on the way down. Thomas had thrown on a pair of ancient tracksuit pants that barely came down to his ankles and a fake Calvin and Hobbes T-shirt where the boy and the tiger were dancing in hippie heaven. Shawna was wearing her yoga clothes under the hippie disguise, as she was planning on hitting a class afterwards, Jenn in a knee-length skirt and blouse combo that I hadn't seen before. Me? I looked like I always did – long-sleeved T-shirt under a retro-styled (but not vintage) Clash *Combat Rock* shirt, jeans and sandals. We were a college recruitment poster walking down the hill into the Lower Haight, so much that the smokers outside of Molotov's took a break from looking at each others' Casualties patches and gave us a lookover. One of them, a small guy with a bull-ring in his nose and cactus-like blonde hair, let his eyes linger on my Clash shirt for a few seconds. He met my gaze and gave me an approving nod.

"Why the Mission?" I asked Thomas.

"Alex, you're smarter than that," he said. "Why are you asking me this?"

"Pretend I'm still working and my brain is clanking along like a cubicle slave's on a Friday afternoon in September."

He sighed. "Look. When I was going to college in Los Angeles, everyone knew where you went to get a driver's license; you went to where the people who really *needed* fake IDs went."

"So where did the college kids go?" I asked.

"Not the college kids. The guys who needed an identification so they could work. You go where the migrant laborers and recent arrivals hang out. In LA you went down to the Valley; you'd drive down this big street and people would come up to you at red lights and ask you if you wanted an ID."

"How would they know?"

Thomas laughed. "It was a barrio, Alex. There was no other reason for a bunch of preppie kids to be down there."

"Oh," I said. "OK."

It made sense. Despite the ongoing encroachment of lofts and lounges, the Mission was still ground zero for people who'd arrived in the city from anywhere south of the border, the same way that Chinatown was for anyone who'd come from across the Pacific. I wasn't sure where Canadians went. We could definitely find a fake license guy if we could parse him out from the hookers, pimps, dealers, junkies, stolen-goods hawkers, black-market car-repair guys, street locksmiths, and thugs-for-hire that added to the atmosphere at Sixteenth and Mission.

But we didn't stop there; we walked south on Mission. As we walked south, the atmosphere changed from junkie street theater to Mexico City. The open-front stores blasted salsa music and display windows were piled with brightly-colored school bags, quadruple-tiered white wedding cakes, empanadas, and advertisements for wire-transfer services. I caught glimpses of Spanish-language soap operas through the open doors. When we hit 21st Street, Thomas started muttering under his breath..

"ID," he said. "License, ID, License, ID."

Nobody reacted. Families with kids in strollers, solo walkers ambling down the street, guys hanging on the corner for no discernible purpose...all of them ignored Thomas. We made it down to the BART plaza on the corner of 24th Street, where a fully in-black-with-a-collar minister sat and preached to a Latino crowd that mostly ignored him. He was yelling from on top of a box with a Spanish phrase stenciled in black.

"What's that say?" I asked Shawna, who read Spanish well.

"Repent," she said. "For the coming of the Son of Man is at hand."

"Original," I said.

"End-of-the-world people are the same in any language," she said. "But this guy's at least funny. He's comparing the fires of hell to the feeling you get after eating a habanero pepper."

"What happens now?" I said.

"We wait," said Thomas. "I mumble. And we try not to look too much like cops."

"We look like cops if Tom Cruise looks like a serious actor," I said.

"Hey," said Thomas. "I really liked what he did in *Magnolia*."

"Whatever," said Jenn, "that was so obviously one of those 'I'm a popular actor and now I want the Critics to take me Seriously, so I'll find a little part in a film that nobody understands and grow my hair out while raving like the maniac that I actually am and now everyone will think that I am a serious Shakespearian type, instead of a mostly-insane teen heartthrob turned action-hero cultist.'"

"Wow," I said. "Did he shoot you down the last time he was in town or something?"

"No," she said. "I just really don't like his movies. Did you see that car-racing one? It made me want to puke. And don't get me started on the 'Show me the money!' movie. That one made me want to slit my throat, then jump off the Golden Gate Bridge, then hang myself."

"So you're not a fan," I said.

She walked a couple of steps closer to me and grabbed me with both hands by my upper arms.

"No," she said. "I am most certainly not a fan."

"You guys looking for something?' The voice was soft, accented just a touch, like the speech pattern of a successful comedian who still makes jokes based on his own ethnicity. The voice belonged to a tall, cadaverously thin Latino man, dressed in a black hoodie and jeans despite the day's warmth. He was wearing sunglasses with black plastic frames; if he'd been twenty years younger and the glasses had been prescription, he could have been the singer in a successful local rock band. Instead, he looked kind of scary.

"Yes," said Thomas, stepping forward. He was tall enough to be able to look the guy in the eye, if he had been able to see the eyes behind the sunglasses. "We're looking for..."

"You a cop?" said the guy.

"No," said Thomas. "I am not a police officer or a member of any law enforcement organization, and neither are any of my friends."

The guy relaxed; his shoulders slumped down and he shoved his hands in his pockets.

"I can help you out," he said. "How many?"

"Just for us two," he said, gesturing to Shawna, who was standing closer to the preacher, pretending to watch him but quite-obviously hanging on every word of Thomas's conversation.

"Forty bucks," said the guy.

"Twenty," said Thomas.

"Thirty," said the guy.

"Deal," said Thomas, handing over a ten and a twenty.

The guy took a small digital camera out of the pocket of his hoodie, grabbed Shawna with one arm, and pulled her away from the rest of us. She gasped, then followed. He snapped three quick closeups, then repeated the process with Thomas.

"Address?" he asked. Thomas gave him a piece of paper with ours written down.

"Wait here," the guy said, walking off down 24th Street. I tried to watch him and see where he went; it should have been an easy thing to do, as he was four inches taller than anyone else on the sidewalk, but I blinked and he was gone.

"What happens now?" I said.

"We wait," said Thomas. "Except that this time it doesn't really matter if anyone thinks that we're cops."

We waited for a little while, maybe forty minutes, during which the following things happened:

1) Jenn got bored and got a taco from a little stand around the corner, which looked so good that I went and got a taco, which wasn't as good as Jenn's.

2) Thomas bought a digital voice recorder for $40 under retail from a teenager who was selling consumer electronics out of a briefcase.

3) Another guy tried to sell us mislabeled bootleg DVDs. None of us bought any.

4) I kept having eerie flashback to being sixteen years old, at the wheel of a beat-up Volkswagen Golf with the engine running, praying that my friends inside the Liquor Locker weren't being detained by the cops.

The ID guy came back as Thomas was getting rid of the bootleg DVD guy. Our licensing friend didn't say a word, just handed little cards to Shawna and Thomas, nodded at me, and disappeared back into the street. We crowded around to get a look.

They were perfect. I mean, *perfect,* down to the holograms and the little state of California barcode on the back. He had even put on organ donor stickers. Thomas and Shawna's organs would go to science if they happened to die while impersonating nonexistent hippies.

"Not bad," said Thomas.

"My picture sucks," said Shawna.

Thomas looked at his watch. "Still only one-thirty," he said. "We might have time to hit the bank, as long as that branch has weekend hours."

"I think it does," I said. "It's in the main Bank of America building downtown. I used to walk by it sometimes when I would go to North Beach for long lunches, and they'd have big signs that talked about their extra long hours."

"'To serve you?'" asked Thomas.

"Exactly," I said.

"It won't last," he said. "In three years they'll have bought up every bank in the city that's not a credit union, then they'll merge with Citibank, buy Washington Mutual, and there will be only them and Wells Fargo in town, and after that they'll make it more convenient for everybody by closing down on Saturdays and making teller services only available between nine-thirty and eleven thirty in the morning, when everyone else has to go to work. And they'll still somehow lose money and their stock will go down, but their president will walk off with a hundred million dollars as a thank-you for making what used to be a nice little California bank a nationwide disgrace."

"You OK, there?" I asked.

"Yeah," he said. "I just get kind of mad when I see that kind of thing. Running a fucking bank is really easy. People give you money, you give them some interest. Other people borrow money from you, you charge them more interest. A flea could do it, and I work for a company that has an entire division of newly-minted MBAs who cover banks, and write hundred-page reports comprised of total bullshit on bank 'strategy' and acquisition 'synergy.' The guys who run the companies want to see their names in the news. That's it. It's stupid."

"Should we hop on BART and go downtown?"

"Into the belly of the beast," said Thomas.

BART is everything that San Francisco's public transportation should be. The trains are relatively clean, run underground and over-ground and actually show up on time. I don't ride it much – the trains are mostly for people coming into the city from the other side of the bay or down the peninsula – but after so much time lately on busses and clanky light rail trains, the seven-minute trip downtown was a bit of a revelation.

Downtown on the weekends looks like the set of a *Batman* movie without the extras. We exited the BART station at Montgomery, and were immediately approached by a guy wearing shorts, an "Alcatraz Psycho Ward" T-shirt, and a bright red backpack.

"Excuse me," he said. "Which one of these trains do I take to get to the seals?"

"Seals?" I said.

"Yes," he said. He had a foreign accent that was difficult to place; he sounded like one of those Europeans who had honed his English as an exchange student.

"I know," said Jenn. "You're looking for the seals at the wharf, right?"

"Yes," he said. "I am looking for the wharf of the fishermen."

"OK," said Jenn. "Don't take any of these; you need to go upstairs and wait on the platform above for the really old-looking streetcars, and take the one that is going towards the water. That'll get you there."

"I have done that already," he said. "And I have asked a man up there, and he has told me to walk down here to catch one of these trains."

I groaned. "Someone was screwing with you," I said. "Trust me, what she said is right."

"Why would someone give me the wrong thing to go to?" he asked. His eyes were wide, bewildered, and a little sad.

"Don't ask me," I said. "Some people are just dicks."

"Dicks, yes," he said. "Thanking you very much."

We rode the escalators up to the surface, where the skyscrapers at Market and Montgomery cast shadows that blended into each other and blocked out the sun. Jenn directed the tourist to the correct platform and the four of us walked up Montgomery past the E-trade rotunda where they have one of those rotating LED displays that shows a stock ticker. Who reads that, anyway? Do people really look at those things, whip out their phones, make a trade, and walk on down the street, more financially viable because the rotunda people were nice enough to post ticker prices?

Thomas led us to the stairs in front of the Bank of America building, the second-tallest building in the city. The Transamerica Pyramid is the tallest by over a hundred feet and the one everyone visits. Nobody cares about the Bank, which is fine by me; the building is yet another boring vertical rectangle, standing out amidst the other Gothamistic structures because it's a dark brown rather than office-building gray. We huddled around Thomas.

"OK, here's what's going to happen," he said. "Alex and Jenn are going to go in first to scope the place and find the teller who looks like he's been there the longest – someone new will get confused by our request and want to find a manager, which is something we don't want. We want someone who hates hassle and is counting the days until retirement, someone who resents that his manager is twenty years younger, knows nothing, and gets bigger bonuses than workers who've been there forever. So, we're each going to go in and try to get information about opening an account for someone our age that has no minimum bank balance. They won't have one, because all of these fascists always charge you for the privilege of keeping your money, but then tell them that you've got a couple of grand in a savings account with Wells Fargo, and get them to lecture you on how easy it is to change the account over. If it sounds like they're reading off of a paper, they're not our person. Oh, and don't go up to anyone who's really old, either; they're probably retired and took a job as a teller because Social Security doesn't cover the bills. Jenn, you go first. Try for early to mid-fifties. It's a weekend, so be nice – everyone in there wants to go home."

Jenn mouthed a few words to herself, shook her head twice, and walked through the tinted glass revolving doors into the bank. Thomas pulled out a pack of Gauloises and started to smoke.

"I thought you quit," I said.

"I did," he said. "But I started again because taking smoke breaks lets me work an hour less per day, and nobody gives me any shit about it because everyone else takes smoke breaks. If they let me take snack breaks or beer breaks, I'd do it, but smoke breaks are the only kind you can take without someone trying to make you feel like you're costing the company money."

"You don't care about making the company money," I said.

"Right," he said. "But if it gets out that I don't care about making the company money, I won't get promoted, which means that I won't get a raise, which means that I'll have to stay even longer."

"I recommend getting laid off," I said. "It rules."

"I wish," he said. "Unemployment would cover my student loan payment or my rent, but not both."

"Speaking of that," I said. "Have you heard from Ahmed?"

"Yeah," said Thomas. "He's in if we're in."

"Oh," I said. "Cool. Nothing weird about him from my end. I guess that means we should take Brent's stuff out of his room."

"Where should we put it?"

"Maybe by then I'll have found his parents – if he has any – and we can give his stuff to them," I said.

"Given your success so far, I think we should have another plan," said Thomas. "Like giving it to Goodwill."

"Would people want a dead guy's clothes?" I said.

Thomas shrugged. "*I* wouldn't care. But I'm not weird about that kind of thing. People die, but their clothes had very little to do with their deaths, most likely."

The revolving door whirled, spitting out Jenn. She strode over, shaking her head. "Don't go for the middle-aged guy in the third window from the right," she said. "He hit on me, so I egged him on a little bit…"

"Something you *never* do," I said.

"Shut it. He talked to me for a few minutes and then he tried to impress me by telling me that he was in the management training program. I made like I was really thrilled by that, then he asked me for my phone number. I was kind of tempted to tell him that I was a management sting put in place to suss out whether or not the bank's management trainees were the kind of idiots who hit on their customers, but I chickened out, so I gave him Alex's number instead."

"*What?* Why?"

She grinned and pinched my cheek. "I'm just trying to keep you entertained. Now, if you get a phone call from a number you don't recognize it, you can say you're me and that you got a sex change. It'll be fun."

I rolled my eyes. "My turn," I said. I turned around and pushed at the revolving door. It had one of those automatic electric adjusters that moved the door along when you pushed it, so that you really didn't have to do much more than leave a finger against the door and walk forward. That takes some of the romance out of revolving doors; opening them should be a bit more effort.

Inside, the bank looked like a movie set of a large bank. The line of tellers was fifteen wide, and off to the left was a large area where young men sat behind brown wooden desks. Each man wore a shirt and tie and had draped his jacket over the back of his chair. Each desk had a flat-panel computer monitor, desk calendar, and black phone with a little headrest on the back of the handset. About ten people were sitting on couches near the desks; people wanting to set up accounts, buy houses, refinance their student loans, you name it. Everyone spoke in low voices, making the whole place almost as quiet as the dead room in the morgue.

I scanned the teller windows. The guy in the third window from the right looked a little bit older than me in an odd way, like he was trying to look only as old as I was. His hair was a shade of black that only comes with Grecian Formula, and he had a satisfied look on his face, the *I might get some* look that guys get. I don't wear that look because I never get anyone's phone number, Morgan excepted, but I know the look when I see it. The guy next to him looked like he'd just become legally able to drive, and the woman next to *him* looked like she lived on a diet of bran, castor oil, and human babies. No way.

Fourth from the left was my guy. His dark hair was receding from his forehead and his blue dress shirt had a crease visible from fifty feet away. He was talking to an older woman in a walker, and he never met her eyes as he tapped away on his terminal. Perfect.

Luckily, Bank of America was too inept to implement the one-line-for-many-windows system that every intelligent business in the world uses these days. It would be great if they could do that in grocery stores so that you didn't inevitably get caught in the super-short line that happens to contain the Alzheimer's-suffering World War I veteran who has sixty-three coupons and wants to pay by check, wouldn't it? This time, though, I was happy to have it work to my advantage.

Six minutes later I was standing in front of the teller. He stared right at his computer screen and mumbled something that may have been "can I help you?" or might have been "my hamster eats food." It was tough to tell.

"I'm looking to open up a bank account," I said.

"What kind?" he asked. His sounded as bored as a delinquent during a Saturday morning high-school history review.

"Checking," I said.

Wordlessly, he handed over a form. I gave it a quick read.

"Oh, there's a problem," I said. "I don't really have the eight-hundred dollar minimum that they say you need to have…"

"It doesn't matter," he said. "Just fill out the form, and when you get your first bill with the charge, call and yell at them and tell them that the teller you talked to said he would waive the fee. Don't even bother to tell them the name. They'll do it."

"Thanks," I said. "Bruce." His name tag read *Bruce Walker*.

"Don't mention it," he said. "Even if they found out that I'd told you it would take them six years to fire me, and my 401(k) vests in three. It's a three hundred billion dollar company. They don't care."

"Wow," I said. "How long have you been here?"

"Seventeen years and four different banks," he said. "We kept getting bought, and they kept giving me raises, and here I am, standing behind a counter. Just like making pizzas, except I make slightly more money and have to wear shirts that button all the way up."

"Thanks," I said. "I'll fill out the form."

"Sure," he said. "Glad to help."

He was perfect. Not only did he not care, whoever he reported to was probably the guy who handled safety deposit boxes, and *that* person probably didn't care that Bruce didn't care about anything. I swished back through the revolving doors to my waiting housemates.

"He's perfect," I said, smiling. "Fourth from the left, receding hairline, a wrinkle in his shirt. His name is Bruce, and he really doesn't give a shit. I think he's one step away from either pulling an *Office Space* and sabotaging the company or passing out from sheer boredom."

"That's our guy," said Thomas. "Are you ready?"

Shawna nodded. Jenn walked over to Thomas, looked up at his face, then rubbed her hand on his head several times, mussing up his hair and making a section in the back stick up, Alfalfa-style.

"That's better," she said.

"And remember what we just practiced," said Thomas.

"This'll be fun," said Shawna.

"Oh, and if they catch us, just talk loudly about nothing and walk out quickly," said Thomas. "If it goes wrong, they'll be confused and think that you're crazy. Nobody wants to mess with crazy people."

Shawna nodded, then the two of them slipped on a pair of identical two-dollar fake wedding rings and walked in.

We waited. I kind of *wanted* to stew, but instead I looked down and walked around the border of the cut-out squares in the concrete, inscribing squared-off figure eights. Three figure-eights, then four, six, eight, then ten. It had been years since I'd worn a watch, and I hadn't bothered to check the time on my cell phone when they'd gone in. How long had it been? Ten minutes, surely. Fifteen, really. Maybe twenty. Certainly long enough for them to go in and tell their story; maybe they were at the safety-deposit box right now. Jenn had walked over to a raised granite planter-box and had hoisted herself up to sit down on the ledge. I gave up my pacing and walked over to join her.

"Hey," she said.

"I'm nervous," I said.

"I hope so; I mean, it would be really good if we could get all of this together."

"I feel bad," I said. "Dragging you into this. I'm the guy who decided to look into the whole Brent thing. I didn't have to do that. Why bother? We just really needed a hew housemate, which wasn't that big of a deal, really."

She looked at me, then looked down at her fingers.

"Alex, looking for Brent's family was a good thing. If you hadn't done it..."

She stopped talking and started playing with her fingers.

"What?"

"What goes around," she said after a pause. "Comes around. At some point you have to do the right thing. You did it, and we followed."

"Is this the right thing?" I asked. "Now I feel like I'm on the hook to find a place to stash his ashes before Ahmed moves in. And with the gangster thing, why didn't we just go to the cops? Now we're here committing bank fraud."

"The cops took the death report," she said. "Nobody saw the car that hit him, they put out an APB on an unidentified car, and three days later some more people were shot in the city. They've got better things to do, and without parents or relatives to really push them, they really couldn't have done much. I feel bad that you had to do most of the work."

"Oh, that's nothing," I said. "I was unemployed."

She put her hand on my wrist. "Sure," she said. "But you still did it."

We sat there for a minute or two, her small hand on my slim wrist; I wondered if she could feel my pulse through the top of my arm, if the pounding of my heart was strong enough to echo through the bone and still be...touchable? *Audible* wasn't the write word, and *feelable* sounded pornographic. *Palpable.* That was it.

Shawna and Thomas came through the revolving doors, walking fast. Shawna was carrying a tan manila envelope, the kind of thing they send your report cards home in when you're in elementary school. Jenn and I hopped off the ledge and walked over to meet them.

"Everything OK?" I said.

"I hope so," said Thomas.

"Can we get the hell out of here?" asked Shawna. "This place creeps me out."

We walked south towards Market Street, nobody saying a word. We reached the Montgomery Street subway station and looked down into the darkness below for a few seconds. Thomas broke the silence.

"Anybody up for a drink?" he said.

We all agreed without saying any words.

"I know a place," he said.

Thomas led us across Market Street to the south side, then up one block, then left. Dave's was as low-key as you'd expect a place with that name to be. The walls were covered with autographed Z-list celebrity photographs and a dry-erase board above the bar invited regulars to leave a drink for their friends. The jukebox was playing a David Lee Roth-era Van Halen song at a low volume, and two of the ten tables were taken. Bowls of pretzels dotted the bar. The bartender was a brunette woman with an Australian accent, young enough to be still young, but old enough to see the road signs that read *middle age*. Thomas bought a pitcher of Anchor Steam and we settled into a corner table.

Shawna and Thomas sat next to each other on the bench, with the three of us across from them in wooden chairs. I sipped my beer slowly, nodding my head along with Eddies sharp riff on "Panama." Thomas laid the envelope down on the table and started to open it.

"Wait," I said. "Before we do that....what happened in there?"

"Oh, OK," said Thomas. "That's a good idea. Here's how it went down."

Thomas and Shawna walked through the revolving doors; Shawna shivered a little when she entered the air conditioning, and she flexed her toes under her Birkenstocks. They walked to the line in front of the guy that Alex had recommended. Two customers waited in front of them. Neither of them talked; Thomas tapped his feet, Shawna played with her hair.

After fifteen minutes, Bruce nodded his head in their direction and said "next." The two walked up to his window, and, as they'd rehearsed outside, Thomas started talking.

"Hi," he said. "We're like, in a kind of weird situation."

"I've heard them all," said Bruce. "Nothing's weird here any more."

"No, dude," said Thomas. "*This* one is weird."

"Yes," said Shawna. "Really weird, like, the strangest thing ever, and we're not totally sure what to do about it."

"What is it?" asked Bruce.

"Well, our live-in housemate Brent died in a car accident a little while ago," said Thomas. "And we're going through his stuff, and we have the number of a box that he had here, and we were hoping that..."

"Do you have the key?" said Bruce.

"Uh...no," said Thomas.

"Not a big deal," said Bruce. "The master key that we use is really the only thing that opens the box, you know. All that two-key stuff is fiction, because everybody keeps losing their keys. We use passphrases for everything now as backup."

"Really?" said Shawna.

"Yeah," said Bruce. "Don't tell anyone, they might fire me." His voice didn't sound like he was scared of being fired. He sounded like the play-by-play announcer at the Boredom Games.

"I don't suppose you have his name, your address, proof of death, and the passphrase?" asked Bruce.

Thomas and Shawna both produced their fake drivers' licenses and the morgue documentation. Bruce glanced at it, then looked back at the two of them.

"Passphrase?" he asked.

Shawna looked down, then up at him, her eyes as big as she could make them. Her pupils glistened. "We don't have it," she said. "It's so awful…"

"Right…said Bruce. "Any idea what it might be? I'm looking at it right here, and if you can get close…"

"Something to do with the Red Sox," said Thomas. "Probably Carl Yazstremski."

"Good enough," said Bruce. "It was 'Yaz Triple Crown. OK, we do have record of your friend having a safe deposit box at this bank, and you've got proof of address and the death stuff…what was your relationship with the deceased? Were either of you married to him?"

"It was a special relationship," said Shawna. "The three of us were…close."

"Only in San Francisco," said Bruce. "I'll put you as 'engaged.' That covers it. Hang on." He clicked a few keys on his computer, then walked to the back of the teller area, where he exchanged words with a younger man in a shimmering suit.

"What now?" said Shawna. "I think we should get out of here, don't you? I think that they know what we're doing and they're tripping one of those silent alarm things that you read about in books."

"I don't think so," said Thomas. "Look."

The shimmering-suit guy pulled out a key ring from his pocket, then touched a key fob to a drawer on his desk. The drawer opened automatically and the suit guy reached in and brought out a small key ring with three keys. He talked with Bruce for a second or two, then handed the ring over. Bruce gestured for Shawna and Thomas to follow him, then walked over to a little door at the far side of the line of teller windows. When they got there, Bruce opened the door from the other side and ushered them in.

"I should probably thank you," he said. "This breaks up the monotony of being at that window all day. Can you believe that guy's entire job is to open the key drawer?"

"Glad we could help," said Thomas. "You get tired standing up there?"

"You bet," said Bruce. He looked at Thomas, running his eyes up and down, taking in the flared legs of his tracksuit pants and the Calvin and Hobbes shirt. "I get the feeling you and your wife here don't spend a whole lot of time standing in mechanical air, huh?"

"He's not..." said Shawna, stopping when Thomas squeezed her arm hard enough to leave a mark.

"Not really," said Thomas.

"I hear you," said Bruce. "Whatever you do, don't get into banking. I'm close enough to being out of here that I can taste it."

The three walked through a doorway in the back of the teller area and into a well-lit hallway. Another bank employee was leading a customer out of the hallway as they entered, so the three stood to the side and waited as the other two went past.

"See, it's really not the best idea to have that in there," said the employee. "With the volatility of the commodity markets, does it really make sense to have ingots in a box when you could be having a professional manager handle your money?"

"I don't know..." said the customer, a woman in a conservative blue skirt/blouse combo with more salt than pepper in her hair and old-school librarian glasses. "It's not that I don't think it's a good idea, but I'm just not sure about handing over everything to another person to decide on..."

The two exited. Bruce snorted. "Asshole," he said. "What he *won't* tell her is that the bank gets commission on every transaction she asks him to make, and his advice will be to constantly buy and sell; the bank will make more and he'll get more and more out of his referral fees. She'll end up doing worse than she would have if she sold the gold and chucked it in a no-load fund, and he'll use those commissions to put a down payment on a vacation home in Costa

Rica."

"Wow," said Thomas. He started feeling like he was talking to an older version of himself.

"That's the way the banking business works," said Bruce. "Most of what we do you can do for yourself, but we don't want you to know that."

"But now *we* know," said Shawna.

Bruce laughed. "No offense, miss, but you don't really look like the type to bring down the international banking system by publicizing how much we suck. I owe you one more for making my day more interesting, though. Here we are."

"Here" was an unmarked door in the middle of the hall.

"We don't mark it so that people who would rob the place have to take longer to find it," said Bruce. "But if they're smart enough to know that we keep the keys to safe deposit boxes, they're smart enough to do some research. Our own stupidity astounds me, sometimes."

The room was row upon row of shiny boxes, flanked by little cubes that looked like voting booths, complete with purple velvet curtains and flakes of paper littering the floor. Bruce walked over to the middle of the room and took out his key ring. He used one key to turn the top lock, and a second key to turn the bottom, which ordinarily the customer key would open. He shook his head, muttering to himself. Thomas and Shawna both leaned forward to listen, but they couldn't hear anything other than a few slightly-louder curses.

Bruce pulled out the box and brought it over to them.

"Here you go," he said. "I don't know what's in here, but the thing is unlocked, so all you have to do is flip up the top, which you'll notice I've been nice enough not to flip up and look at, in case you have something illegal in there, which of course you don't, right?"

Shawna and Thomas both shook their heads.

"Good. Even if you did, we're not really legally allowed to know. So it wouldn't matter. How long do you think you're going to be?"

"Don't really know," said Thomas. "Probably not more than a couple of minutes."

"Damn," said Bruce. "I was hoping to sneak out and grab a

smoke. Oh well. I'll be out in the hall; just get me when you want to put the box back in its slot."

Thomas started to laugh, and Shawna elbowed him in the ribs.

"*Not* funny," she said.

"It kinda was…"

"No."

"OK."

They went inside the voting booth, where a single ten-inch fluorescent tube provided a harsh light. Thomas reached for the box, touched the cold metal, then drew his hand away.

"I think you should open it," he said.

"Why?"

"Just because," he said. "You knew him better than I did."

"How's that?" she said. "You went to a baseball game together; doesn't that make you like BFF?"

"Not really," said Thomas. "We're guys."

Shawna shook her head. "I don't know what's wrong with you that you can't realize that a shared experience like that can be a wonderful thing and can be the springboard for the kind of friendship that can go on for ever and ever, even a lifetime, but all you boys do is drink beer and stick your hands down your pants and then maybe you'll think about telling each other that you might like to hang out some time, but by that time you're all married and don't have any friends and rely on your wives for your social life. That's fucked up."

Thomas blinked, and would have taken a step backward if he hadn't been in a tiny booth barely big enough for a Clark Kent-to-Superman switch.

"Um…I don't really know what to say, but can you…?" he gestured to the safe deposit box.

She sighed. "Fine," she said, and flipped open the top.

"So that was it?" I asked. "No interrogation, no acting, no hemming and hawing, they just let you into the room, you opened it, and that was all that was in the box?"

Thomas nodded. "Yeah," he said. "It was kind of weird. You'd think that he would have had some old baseball cards in there or something. Just the envelope."

"We checked," said Shawna. "Thomas even licked his finger and ran it around the inside to see if there were any little secret compartments."

Thomas cringed. "I saw someone do that on an episode of *CSI* when they were looking for a little secret compartment in a metal box, and when the guy licked his finger and ran his hand around it, this little thing caught and pricked his finger, poisoned him and he died."

"Why would you do that?" I asked. "I mean, what if Brent poisoned the safe deposit box?"

"Why would Brent do that?"

"The guy's part of an international toilet conspiracy," I said. "I think at this point we can say that he was capable of pretty much anything."

"Good point. But my finger remained unpricked, and I'm still alive."

"So what's in the envelope?" I asked.

That one killed the conversation again. The envelope lay in the middle of the table, a simple brown manila envelope, clasped with a metal clasp, not full, but far from empty. I reached over and undid the clasp, then turned the envelope upside down. About ten sheets of paper fell out. We all took one sheet and looked at it.

"What?" I said.

"Huh?" said Jenn

"Um…" said Shawna.

"Oh," said Thomas. "I get it."

We all looked at it.

"These are statements – account numbers to a few different money-market based savings accounts." He shuffled through the papers. "Looks like five – that's smart, less than a hundred thousand in each so that they are insured."

"Why the paper?" I asked.

He shrugged. "For accounts like this you can usually access it with an account number and a passphrase – just like this safety deposit box. He probably used the printouts for one reason or another…

"To prove that he had the money," I said. "His business partners didn't seem to be the types who would take him at his word."

Thomas nodded. "That would do it."

"How would he get at the money?"

"He probably had an online thing set up with each bank and would have transferred it to his normal bank account, or just wired it to the people he was working with," said Thomas. "That's what I would do."

"So another password," I said. "Great."

Thomas shook his head. "Probably the one we already have. Nobody ever uses more than one, even though they're supposed to."

"Oh," I said. We sat their in silence. "What happens next?"

What *did* happen next? I had originally planned to get in touch with Brent's parents and get them to deal with our dead roommate, get him off of our hands so that we could find a new person to take care of the rent, and then we'd all go our merry ways.

But that wasn't really an option anymore, was it? What if his parents were dead? If I did have the right password, I'd now have control of over a half a million dollars, and after paying back the city of San Francisco for the cremation fee, we'd still have more money to play with than any of us had ever had in our lives. Well, with the exception of Thomas. He'd played with the stock market quite a bit in the late '90s when he was in college and made enough money to retire on, but then he'd gone on a month-long vacation right when everything went into the toilet, and before he knew it he'd been back to student loans. The whole thing made me guilty, elated, and scared as hell.

"Well, we can pay for a place to put the ashes," I said. "And we can…"

"*Don't* talk about the baby," said Jenn. "There isn't one."

We sat in silence again for a few seconds. Thomas put the paper back in the envelope, and we all finished our drinks without talking about the account or the money or Brent dying, and I didn't bring up the toilet consortium or any of the other insane stuff that had come up after Brent had been killed. Instead, we talked about Ahmed, and when he'd move in, and whether we'd be lucky enough to have him own a burr-style coffee grinder to replace our sulky can't-set-the grind blade job, whether he'd be OK with splitting the cable bill straight up, or if he'd be one of those weird anti-TV guys who would insist on parsing out the television from the Internet and paying each separately. It felt normal. It felt like things were closing.

We left the bar an hour later and two drinks happier. We hopped off the MUNI at Carl and reached our front door all in a group. Shawna led the way upstairs and went right to bed; she had to open the yoga studio the next morning at six. Jenn and I mixed two big gin and tonics and sat down in the living room to watch a bit of the E! network and snark ourselves into a decent next-morning hangover. Thomas headed up to his room to check on some of his eBay auctions and offer Ahmed the house. Luckily enough for us, the *E! True Hollywood* story was the episode about Vanilla Ice, an oldie-but-goodie repeat that made us giddier than the drinks by themselves could have. Thomas came down when we were done and told us that Ahmed was in. We toasted him in abstentia, and went to bed.

Three of us slept in on Sunday. I puttered around the house, reorganized some of my old CDs, took a long coffee break down the street with two crossword puzzles, spent some time updating my notes and re-hanging several posters, and it was early evening before I finally got around to seeing if I could log into Brent's bank accounts using the PayPal password. The first one gave me no luck, so I started to play around a little bit with the syntax, replacing "a" with an at sign and "s" with $, things like that.

I logged in on the third try with the password "Y@zm@n." The bank account login screen disappeared and an splash screen came up.

Welcome, Brent! We have noticed that your account is in excess of the FDIC insured amount. It may be in your best interest to explore other financial options. If you would like to talk with one of our high-end banking specialists, please click here and one of them will contact you as soon as possible.

I clicked the "Next" button and the account screen came up. It was a simple layout, with revealing no activity over the past month, and a column on the far right showing the account balance at $432,321.76.

Dear...God? I sat back in my chair. I had never in my life had more than two thousand dollars in any account of any kind. My hands started shaking – I couldn't possibly deal with this much money. It wasn't responsible to give someone like me control over that kind of money. I'd be able to pay the bills, and if the money just disappeared, the gangster guys would have no connection to us or to Brent any more. His fake name would put them and the banks off the trail. The gangsters could take their toilets and go back to China. I put my computer away and crawled into bed early, warm and happy.

Chapter 17

The next day dawned warm; I had sloughed off most of my covers during the night and had slept under only my sheet. I woke up early because my room felt stuffy, which always made my nose fill with phlegm, so I started making tubercular sounds the instant I got out of bed. A sheen of sweat lined my forehead, and I threw open my windows to get some circulation. The air that wafted in was sultry, as if someone had super-heated the fog in a microwave before blowing it into the city.

While I showered, I tried to figure out what I was going to do with my day. I needed to

1) look up places to put Brent's ashes
2) find Gerald and see if he had any of his usual good suggestions about what to do
3) pray that Jenn had a bad day at work so that some new baked goods would make their appearance in the kitchen.
4) do some math to figure out Brent's portion of the rent
5) eat. Definitely breakfast. That seemed like a good place to start.

The coffee pot was still half full when I made it to the kitchen, but the coffee itself was lukewarm. I filled a mug and stuck it in the microwave for thirty seconds, then popped in some cream and sugar. Metallic, but drinkable. The kitchen was a mess, which was surprising because Jenn was way too OCD to ever leave behind a messy kitchen. Usually when I left a mess like this overnight, it would be clean in the morning, adorned with a sarcastic note from Jenn.

When I finished my cereal, muffin, banana, and apple breakfast, I brought my laptop out to our covered back porch. Real estate agents would call it a sunroom, which would be all right on a sandals-and-shorts day like today, but was totally inaccurate for most of the year. We rarely used the sun room, despite its three couches and exploding-arms ancient recliner. A lack of insulation and little sun exposure made it a better place for storage than anywhere else in the house. The wireless connection was a little spotty, but it was enough for me to check my e-mail and look at the weather.

High of 92, low of 65. The newspaper had a boilerplate article up about the potential record heat and reminded people to go hang out at the pool and check on their elderly neighbors. The only elderly neighbor I knew lived two doors down, spent most of his time messing with his plants, and tried to sell me weed on a weekly basis. His arms were more well-defined than mine; I wasn't particularly worried about him. Online chores beckoned:

1) Double-checked Brent's money market accounts and then changed all of the passwords to @lexr0x, just to double-blind them from anyone else who might possibly guess at the account's existence.

2) Checked my e-mail. Most of my messages were the usual penis-lengthening exhortations that eluded my spam filter and the daily dribs and drabs from the two Clash mailing lists that I read. Two e-mails from Thomas about house bills and one from Morgan, written at two in the morning.

   Alex,

   This is really important. Can u meet me at Ritual today? I'll be there all day, but get here as fast as u can. E-mail or txt.

   M

   a. I hate it when people use the letter "u" instead of the full "you" in e-mail. If you're texting, it's kind of excusable, but when you have a full keyboard at your disposal, there's really not much time-saving in ditching the other two letters;

   b. I hate, hate, *hate* Ritual. It's a coffee house down in the Mission that's chock-full of hipsters. Between all the people cruising in on their fixed-gear bikes, the trucker-hat guys showing off their newest star tattoos, and the Web company geeks who use the place as virtual offices, it's a wonder that they sell any coffee at all. The coffee is really good. The place sucks. Still, I'd meet Morgan. We'd wrapped up the mystery as much as we could, and it was time to cut her off.

3) Googling for "San Francisco cremains services" brought me

to a place called the Columbarium. It was only a mile or so from the house; a giant old Victorian building that served as a mausoleum for cremated ashes, owned by the Neptune Society. I sent them an e-mail asking for a price quote.

My chores done, I headed down to Ritual on foot. By eleven o'clock, it was already in the mid-eighties down in the Mission, and I walked past two elderly women who were walking around with ice bags on their heads. Ritual was at 22nd; as I got to 20th Street, the sidewalk started looking like my middle-school bike cage. Three bulimic-looking guys were sitting on the front bench, smoking cigarettes and arguing about Korean films, wearing black hoodies despite the heat. I was surprised that the wax on the tallest guy's mustache hadn't been destroyed by the sweat dripping off of his face.

Morgan was sitting at a side table, her black hair up in a ponytail. She was wearing a white tank top and was tapping her fingers as she sipped on a tall glass of iced coffee. A pack of cigarettes lay on the table beside her handbag – a fancy-looking leather one that I hadn't seen before. Two shredded, unsmoked butts took up most of a pastry plate. Ritual was packed and loud, and the air was stifling. By some strange twist of fate, nobody was in line, so I ordered an americano from the guy behind the counter (long, waxed mustache, a t-shirt that said, "I heart my Internet friends") and walked over to Morgan's table.

"Alex," she said, standing up and giving me a hug. Her skin was warm and damp. "I'm so glad you're here."

"What's up?" I asked. She looked scared. I steeled myself for another plea for money. *Don't be a softie, Alex...*

"They've got your roommate," she said. "You have to understand – they know about the money, and they've got Jenn."

What? I took a sip of my coffee and spilled most of it on my face and lap; why were my hands shaking so much? I was supposed to do something, right? Should I jump up and yell "well, let's *go!*"? Should I coolly light a cigarette and whisper, "So that's how they want it, eh?" Should I start crying in shame? I did none of these things; I sat and sipped my coffee instead, trying to steady my hands and feeling my heart thudding against my rib cage. Jesus. Jenn.

"What do they want?" I asked. I didn't ask who had her. I knew. They'd found us.

"David—I mean Brent's—money," she said. "They need it because..."

"If they don't get it, their entire scheme will fall through?" I said.

She nodded. Christ. I started getting angry again; I felt like I was caught in one of those late-night Cinemax naughty-detective movies, minus the titillation and non-penetrative nudity. *Why* was this happening to me?

"What are you thinking?" she asked. Her eyes were big, almost anime-big, and her hands were inching closer to mine.

"I don't know what to think," I said. My arms were aching. I looked down at them; it was probably because my fists were clenched and straining. I relaxed them, and the pain went away.

She nodded, took out another thin cigarette from the pack and started to shred it. Her shredding was practiced; she used a fingernail to slice a whole in the paper, then unrolled it bit by bit and scattered the tobacco all over her plate. I could see a sheen of sweat still on her palms. She said something else, but I couldn't hear it over the hubbub of the Ritual crowd and the overly-skinny guy next to us blabbing about how his new approach to CSS templating was going to change the Web as everyone knew it.

"What was that?" I said.

"I'm not pregnant," she said.

"Now you tell me," I said. "I'm not surprised." Jenn had been right. I'd been worrying in the back of my mind about how I was going to take care of Brent's kid's college money when I should have been paying attention to how those guys could get to us. Wait....how had they gotten to us?

"How'd they know who we are?" I asked. "How did they find Jenn?"

"Hey," said a guy at the table next to us, "can you keep it down?"

"Sorry," I said. "No, wait, I'm not sorry. I'll keep it down if you shut up and don't try to talk to me again."

The guy blinked and shook his head; shocked. I was kind of surprised, myself; I was beginning to make a habit of telling people off in coffee shops. The guy mumbled something about how everyone should respect each others' space and public places, then turned back to his computer and started furiously typing. He was probably messaging a friend – *You won't believe what this asshole just said to me at Ritual.* I didn't care; another random Internet post about another random human interaction probably wouldn't ruin my life.

"Because of me," said Morgan.

"What?" I said. I nearly dropped my coffee, and I could feel my heart pounding again.

"It wasn't supposed to be like this," she said. "I mean, it was my idea, the whole pregnancy thing…"

The guy next to us started typing in a flurry again. I glanced over at his computer, and the words in his Web browser were *it was my idea, the whole pregnancy thing…*"

"Excuse me," I said. "What the hell are you doing, exactly?"

He stopped typing and looked at me.

"I'm blogging my life," he said, "In real-time. I've got a camera on this computer, so if you go to my website, you can watch me typing what goes on around me. It's the first-ever first-person-looking realtime weblog about the day-to-day-existence of someone who's on the cutting edge. I never turn the computer off, so even when I close it, the camera is recording the blackness that it sees and uploads it through my cellular wireless card. It's at deanblack.tv. It's Dean Black TV, get it?"

He smiled as he said this, typed a few more words, then looked at me again, leaning forward until his face was only a foot or two from mine. "Hey, can I get your names?" he said. "This is the kind of real human drama that could really help build my site traffic."

"If you type one more word," I said. "I'm going to dump my coffee on your keyboard."

He drew back from me with a look of mixed horror and fear. "You wouldn't do that! That would fry my drive completely."

"Try me," I said.

He slammed his computer closed, grabbed his backpack and hopped out of his seat, mumbling to himself the entire time, something about understanding and how impossible it was to start a venture if people wouldn't give you a chance and how social networking in the real world was so much harder. Whatever. I was kind of happy that I'd been able to say the words "try me" in such an offhand-yet-badass way.

Morgan had started to shred another cigarette.

"They told me that they'd give me a cut of it. If I got it or how to get it from you they'd give me a cut and I'd have enough to be on my feet until I could find another job," she said. "I've got my own place and my bills are really high…I thought it wouldn't be a big deal; getting guys to give you money is the simplest thing in the world. They thought you actually had it, though. But I never told them anything about you, I swear. But when I didn't have the money a week after I'd told them I could get it from you, they didn't believe me when I told them that you didn't have it, and then I kind of let slip your name and Jenn's name and that other guy – Thomas – who helped you out. They think you've got it, and now they've got her and they told me to tell you that they want access to the money, and you have to bring those passwords to Fort Funston tonight at seven, and they'll do an exchange there. I just wanted to be able to survive for a few more weeks without a job. I'm sorry, Alex. I knew you were into me, and I…"

"You used me," I said. "Because I'm such an obvious patsy."

She nodded. "It's not that you're a patsy, it's that you're…"

"What? A loser? Naïve? I'm not that naïve. You didn't tell them anything? Except for, oh, who we fucking *are*? And then they probably figured out where we live? And then they kidnapped my roommate? Why?" The shaking in my hands had spread to the rest of my body. She looked down, sideways, anywhere but at me. Wait…" I said. "They're actually doing a kidnapping with a ransom and everything?"

She nodded. "And they said not to go to the cops…"

"Because if I go to the cops I'll never see her again," I said. "Great. These guys are taking their playbook right out of *Ruthless People*, aren't they?"

"What are you going to do?" she said.

"Go home," I said.

"Can I help you?" she said.

I looked at her; she was still dark-haired and alabaster-skinned, a Smiths fan's dream come to life.

"Tell them I'll be there," I said. "I assume they want me to come alone?"

She nodded.

"That's all," I said.

"Do you have the money?" she said.

I shook my head. "No," I said.

"What are you going to do?"

I smiled at her. "Nothing I'm going to tell you."

"Will you call me?" she asked.

I'd never had a girl as flat-out hot as Morgan ask me to call her before all of this started. I'd always dreamed of what it would be like to be one of those guys who doesn't have to put himself out there, to be at the receiving end of those words.

"No," I said. "Have fun paying the bills for that bag. It might get kind of rough with those credit card companies."

"But…" she said.

"No buts," I said. "Get a credit counselor. They probably won't kidnap you. See you around."

I left.

I had absolutely no clue what I was going to do. I walked home in a daze, wondering, thinking, taking out my cell phone six different times and dialing 91, then closing it before hitting the final 1. What were they doing to Jenn? She didn't know anything – just that we had the account information somewhere in the house. In the movies, if you didn't know anything they killed you. Jesus. I had to calm down. I started listing my assets.

1) Me. I had one more month of severance, then unemployment insurance. Security, but not enough to hire a squad of ninjas to take care of my problem. Also, I wasn't sure where one would go to hire a squad of ninjas. I made a mental note to see if ninjasquad.com actually took me to anything useful.

2) Gerald. My pal still knew everything there was to know about San Francisco that I didn't know and could probably tell me a bit about Fort Funston, where I'd never been.

3) My roommates. They didn't exactly fit the mold of the ace Impossible Mission Force support team, but we'd successfully bamboozled a bank. That had to count for something.

4) The kidnappers. They weren't the brightest bunch. If they were taking all of their cues from bad crime movies, maybe the best way to get the best of them would be to see what worked in bad crime movies and Bond flicks, and then do something else.

I flipped open my cell phone and called up Gerald.

"Hey, Alex," he said.

"Hey," I said. "You at home?"

"Yep," he said. "I'm working on a project."

"Can I watch a few of your action movies?" I said. "I mean, just the endings."

"Sure," he said. "Why?"

"I wanna get some ideas," I said. "I'll tell you when I get there."

"This is so cool," said Gerald when I'd finished telling him what was going on. "It's like you're becoming this Sean Connery Bond guy, and I get to be your Q."

"Without the shoe-sole rocket launchers," I said. "And the part where we have to do something fast before they do something awful to Jenn."

"Right," he said. "But they won't. Bad-guy villains always kidnap the girl, but they never do more than threaten. It's basically in the rules. They save the bad stuff for the hero."

"That would be…"

"You," he said. "So if they catch you, you're screwed. Rope knots to the nuts, that kind of thing."

"Great."

We were watching the end of the Bond film that takes place on an island that has been turned into some kind of huge-radar doomsday device. I was hammering away on my laptop, making a list of stupid-villain tricks.

"Since they've done everything basically according to script from here on out – insane plan to dominate something, evil cackles, kidnapping the hero's nearest and dearest…"

"Jenn's not my nearest and dearest," I said.

"Really?" he said.

"We're just roommates," I said.

"Sure," he said. "Anyway, they want to meet you at Funston because it's hard to get to and nearly deserted at night. But it's a stupid place to meet because there are a million places to hide around there, so we can plan out something to foil them."

"Why don't I just show up with a fake PayPal account login and say the money's in there?" I asked.

He shook his head. "Too risky. If I'm them, I get the login from you and immediately do a transfer to another account. Hell, they could do it with a BlackBerry. So it's better to actually give them the real login, but figure out a way to keep the money. Hey, why not just give them the money?"

"It's not theirs," I said. "And doing all this has kind of tubed my job search, and I'd like to be able to pay the rent when my severance runs out. It's kind of important."

Gerald sighed. "You *could* just get a job."

"Pot calling the kettle black," I said. "And, we have to get them off of our cases. If we just give them the money, they might think there's more. They have to be gone."

"OK," he said. "We're going to need Thomas and Shawna on this. I think we can take care of everything right there."

"So what are we doing?"

"Exactly what they won't expect," he said. "We're going to go after them."

"You realize that you sound exactly like a movie when you say that?"

He shrugged. "I can't help it. Sometimes you gotta tell it like it is."

Gerald and I parted – he agreed to meet up at our house right at five o'clock. I sent text messages to the other two housemates asking them to get back early and that it was important. Thomas and Shawna got back to me in that order. I mulled things over as I headed home. When the first steps bounced up the stairs, I was sitting in the living room. I was ready.

Dan Johnson

Chapter 18

I curled up behind an old gun emplacement and checked the time on my cell phone for the fourth time that minute. It was still only 6:45. I started thinking about watches – since everyone has a cell phone now, will anyone wear a watch in ten years? Or will people wear their phones on their wrists? Or will everything just be plugged into our heads and we'll blink twice to get a readout in front of our eyes? I shook my head; now wasn't the time for sci-fi fantasies. I wrapped my arms around myself and shivered a bit. I checked the time again. 6:47.

Fort Funston is way the hell out on the south end of the beach, deep in the fog belt. And the fog was more than in; it was a solid wall of mist and damp, the kind of thing you'd expect to hide ancient monsters and armies of the dead. The fortifications were crumbling, revealing rusted-out reinforcing steel dowels that poked out of the bunkers like slashed spider legs. Sea grass and driftwood covered the dunes. The dog-walkers and kite-flyers had gone home; when the sun went down, you wouldn't be able to see beyond ten feet.

In some ways, this was a good thing, as the mafia guys wouldn't be able to see that I had come not-alone unless they had night vision goggles; I wasn't too worried about that – given the way that they seemed to operate, laser-beam-helmeted sharks seemed a more likely possibility. On the other hand, I felt completely alone, and one of the bad guys could sneak up on everyone else and do something horrible to them and leave me alone for real.

6:50. The fog thickened further, adding to the gloom. I wrapped my arms harder around myself and said a silent thanks that I'd changed from my shorts into pants, shoes, and a fleece top. I was shivering but I couldn't get up and walk around to warm up. That wasn't the plan. I wondered if Jenn could get up and walk around, wherever she was. My hand hurt; it was clenched as tight as it could go, and my fingernails had made deep divots in my palm.

6:55. Fog doesn't make noise; it's an anti-sound that quiets everything else. Even my own breathing sounded less like breathing and more like the hums of a far-away air conditioner. Underneath the thrushing of the wind and the occasional hum of a passing truck on the Great Highway, there was a whooshing sound, as if I could hear the grains of sand tumble over themselves. The footsteps next to my fortification were muffled, as if the walker was wearing slippers and stepping on piles of toilet paper.

Wait. Footsteps? I stopped breathing and listened again. Someone was definitely padding around on the other side of my concrete bunker. The thing was only about twelve feet wide and four feet high, so whoever it was was close, and walking towards the near corner on the other side. I was supposed to surprise whoever it was that I was meeting, so I hit the button that dialed Thomas on the Bluetooth headpiece under my hat and crept the other way, trying to reach the kitty-corner of the square bunker. I slipped around to the short side on my hands and knees, making each movement of my hands and knees take several seconds to minimize my noise. I could still hear the footsteps; this guy was moving slowly, taking a few steps, stopping, then moving again.

Why did I automatically assume that my adversary was a he, not a she? Wasn't it possible that the gangster guys had hired some kind of *Kill Bill*-class woman killer to whack me? Moving silently on this sand-and-grass surface wasn't particularly hard, either; I couldn't hear my own footsteps. This noisemaking person was probably not a ninja assassin; they were supposed to be quiet.

When I reached the kitty-corner, I stayed on my hands and knees but I waited, trying to breathe fast but shallow to stay as quiet as possible. Not moving made me more nervous than I already was, which made me breathe faster and sweat hard despite the chill, so I started shivering in my now-wet shirt and breathed even faster because I was cold. Fantastic. I tried to concentrate; the guy around the corner knew where Jenn was. The footsteps kept moving, and I kept crawling around, following them from 180 degrees away. I felt like I was in a Bugs Bunny cartoon, sneaking before sassily outwitting Elmer Fudd, except I was pretty sure that replacing "rabbit season" with "duck season" in a conversation wouldn't be the best way out of this.

After I'd circled for 270 degrees, the footsteps receded; whoever it was was walking away from me, toward a large open area about fifty yards away. I scurried around to the other side of the corner from where I originally had started, and peered around to see if I could get a look.

The guy walking away (it *was* a guy, and I felt a little better now that my misogynistic assumptions had been proved correct) was wearing a white suit, white shoes, and a white bowler-style hat. I think he was either trying to pull off that Kingpin look from the *Spider Man* comics or channeling Tom Wolfe. Neither way worked; he was short, and the black hair coming out from under the hat looked feathered. His shoes were spattered on the back with sand. He disappeared into the fog.

I followed, skittering from cover point to cover point, feeling ridiculous, channeling everything I'd ever learned from watching re-runs of *Predator* on basic cable, wishing for a way to cover myself in mud in case the guy I was following had infrared sensors. Would that even work? Why would the Predator's technology have seen through clothes but not mud? I shook my head and banished the thought – Arnold's tricks wouldn't help, and the plan was for me to surprise this guy and put him off-balance.

I crept along on my hands and knees, then crouched and skippered through the obstacles and mini-dunes to where I thought the border of the open area was. The white-suited guy was standing in the middle of everything, facing away from me. He was barely visible through the mist; it looked like his arms and head were blurring their boundaries; I couldn't see his hands clasped in front of him.

"Ah, Mr. Baker," he said. His accent was softly Chinese; I could hear the lilting rrrs with the amplifying effect of the fog. The words were faint. "I've been expecting you."

So much for keeping him off-balance. And I was mad. There was no way in hell that I was going to be threatened by someone who talked like this. I felt my fear going away. I gritted my teeth. Was that anger? Yep, I was mad – this jerk had my roommate as prisoner and had killed another because of his incompetence. I clenched my fists again.

"Of course you have," I said. He turned around. "You invited me here, remember?" I said. "Or did you forget already and assume that I just happened to randomly come out here? Are you dense?"

He blinked and lifted his foot up, as if he was going to take a step back, then put the foot back down and re-clasped his arms behind his back. I didn't recognize him; he had to be the guy from Number One Lucky Products, Inc. whom I hadn't seen.

"Yes," he said. "We knew you would come here. Despite your best efforts, we still have what you want, and you have no choice but to give us what we want." He laughed, an eerie-sounding cackle that would have been much scarier if what he was saying had made any sense at all.

"What do you want?" I said.

"You know what we want, Mr. Baker," he said. "Please hand it over now."

The wind picked up a little bit, sending tentacles of fog whirling all over the area. I could hear the waves crashing on the beach in front of me and the cars whizzing by on the highway behind me, but it would have been impossible to see either even if the sand dunes hadn't been in the way. The Chinese guy was looking at me as if he was expecting something; my pockets were empty of everything but my phone, wallet, and keys, and I didn't think that he really wanted thirteen dollars or to find out which Thai take-out place I had on speed dial.

So I stared at him. He stared back. We did a mutual stare for what seemed like several hours. My phone vibrated, and I reached down towards my pocket and hit a button.

"Perhaps we can come to some kind of agreement," I said.

Thomas's voice sounded through the little Bluetooth earpiece:

We see him, he said. *Chill out for a minute. Shawna will be there in a few seconds. Stall.*

Chill out because Shawna would be there? It was supposed to be Thomas and Gerald only… I was in a face-to-face confrontation at least as fraught with peril as the final scene in *The Good, the Bad, and the Ugly,* and I was supposed to chill out because my airhead hippie roommate was on her way over? What on earth could they be thinking? Shawna was supposed to be moral support only. Why had they changed the plan?

"It's simple," said the white-suited guy.

It's been a hard day's night
And I've been workin' like a dog

The voice was Shawna's – sometimes she woke me up with her singing in the shower. She never sang the Beatles, though; it was usually "That Thing" by Lauryn Hill or something by Ozomatli.

It's been a hard day's night
I should be sleepin' like a log

I'd never really thought how pedantic the lyrics to early Beatles songs really were, and it was definitely a strange thing to think about as Shawna slowly materialized out of the fog. Her long black hair was swaying from side to side as she walked, and little white earbuds were attached to her ears. Shawna didn't have an IPod; I was sure of that. She sashayed up to us, singing loudly, half-dancing, her eyes half-closed.

I thought my eyes were going to pop out of my head. Shawna had stripped off the sweats she'd worn on the way over and was now wearing a tight t-shirt and what looked like child-sized black spandex biker shorts. Her legs looked almost freakishly long and slender and...in *that* shirt her bustline belonged on the cover of *Maxim,* not on a frigid San Francisco beach. And yes, it was cold, and yes, you could tell. I snuck a look at the other guy, and he was gawking hard, his eyes almost as big as Shawna's boobs.

She opened her eyes and met the other guy's gaze. He immediately turned his head and...had he turned *red?* What kind of hardened gangster blushed at the sight of erect-in-the-cold nipples through a shirt?

"Oh," said Shawna. "I didn't realize that I was interrupting anything here...I'm really sorry. You guys should just forget that I was doing anything, or that I was even here and continue with what you were doing. I mean, it's obvious that you wanted some privacy, being out here in Funston away from the scene in the rest of the city and all, you want to be kind of discrete, so I'll just keep power walking and singing and leaving you two guys alone to, um..."

"Wait," said the other guy, stammering. "Do you think that we're here for some kind of homosexual meeting?"

"Well," said Shawna. "I mean, it's not like it's uncommon for two closeted guys to meet out here on a day when there wouldn't be too many other people around and do what comes naturally. I mean, I work near Stern Grove sometimes, and as it gets darker, you can't move but for tripping over all the dudes giving each other blowjobs in the bushes."

I and the other guy both winced.

"Not so fun, huh?" she said. "This one time I was down dancing in the Castro and I went to the bathroom because I was thirsty and I was sitting down on the toilet (but not actually sitting down, because those dance club toilets are *disgusting*) and then all of a sudden this guy's *dick* came through a hole in the wall. I was supposed to do something to it. Gross, huh?"

"What?" I said. I couldn't help it.

"She doesn't matter," said the guy.

"What do you mean *I don't matter?*" yelled Shawna. Her face was turning purple, in a state that made high dudgeon look like a yoga trance.

"I matter," she was saying. "Just because I'm a woman, oh, and yeah, I'm an *Asian* woman, just like the little subservient baby-factories that you probably keep in sex slavery in high-rise hotels in the Tenderloin, right? But we don't matter because all we are are transportation systems for the uterus, which is really what America thinks of us, but Chinese guys are even *worse*, and you can't tell me that I'm being a racist, because I'm Chinese, too." She stormed off, shouting, "Go back to China!"

That's it, said Thomas. *Go time.*

"As I was saying…" said the white-suit guy, but he stopped and was interrupted when a frisbee bonked him on the back of the head. "Ouch," he said. Not "ow or "shit" or a miscellaneous expletive, but "Ouch." Very old-school – if he'd been in a comic strip, the talk balloon would have had a jagged edge instead of a smooth one.

"Sorry, man," said Thomas, materializing from out of the fog, damp with sweat and with a wide grin on his face. "Can you get that for me?"

"Be careful," said the white-suit guy, bending down to pick up the frisbee.

As he bent down, Gerald came up from out of the fog behind him. Gerald dropped to the ground and rolled into the guy's knees, buckling them and making him fall backwards. Thomas lunged forward, caught his head and stuck a hand into the guy's mouth; he convulsed once and went limp, his eyes still open. Thomas lowered him to the ground, and then helped Gerald to his feet. Gerald brushed off his jeans, then turned around.

"Come on out!" he said.

Shawna hopped up from behind the bunker where she'd been hiding. She had thrown a sweatshirt on over her biker jersey, but was still wearing the spandex pants. The effect was still eye-popping; she usually went to yoga in loose sweats, and her normal dress was designed to be as shapeless as humanly possible. She wasn't the ugly caterpillar normally or anything, but this was…different. She ran over and gave Thomas a fierce hug.

"Omigod!" she said, "I was so so nervous and then Alex didn't really say anything, I was so afraid that I was screwing up what we'd planned, because he looked *so* surprised, until I remembered that that was our little sub-plan and then I thought it was going to be OK, and that was an amazing throw, but…did that really work?" she gestured to the guy on the ground; his eyes were open, but unfocused, the pupils as tiny as the tip of a ballpoint pen.

Gerald knelt back down next to him. "He's probably on another planet right now," he said. "At least for the next hour."

"What was that stuff again?" I asked.

Gerald grinned. "Salvi divinorum," he said. "It's a completely legal hallucinogen," he said. "You can get it on Haight Street. It's completely legal because it's such a pain in the ass. You're supposed to put a drop of it in some tea, and if that doesn't do anything for you you put a drop on your tongue, and you get this little fifteen-minute trip that feels like you're in a tunnel with things chasing you."

"Sounds like fun," I said. "What does that have to do with him?"

Gerald grinned wider. "Thomas shot a whole eyedropper down his throat. The stuff tastes like Satan's semen, so the first thing that happened to him is that his taste buds were blasted to the point where he won't be able to taste anything for a week. The effect is nearly-instantaneous, and it gets stronger and lasts longer the more you put in there. He'll be completely out of his head for at least an hour and a half."

"How do you know?"

"Because the first time I tried it the drop-on-the-tongue method didn't work, so I put an entire teaspoon in my mouth. I couldn't eat anything but applesauce and rice for a week, and I lost about three hours, during which I apparently didn't move at all, according to the guy who was watching me and chickened out on taking any after he saw what it did to me."

"What was it like?"

"Sucked," said Gerald. "I was bored in this stupid tunnel for what seemed like ten years, and then I got scared, and then I woke up screaming."

"What do we do with him now?"

"We go back to your house," said Gerald. "And we start asking him questions."

"What about Jenn?"

He put his hand on my shoulder. "That's what the questions are for."

"No, idiot," I said. "I get that. What if she's here?"

"She won't be," he said. "Villains never bring along the girl." She's stashed somewhere, waiting for a signal to release her."

"Good point," I said. "So now we have to get him to tell us where she is."

If we had been Philip Marlowe, we would have bundled the guy into a cab and slipped the driver, who would have been a small-eyed guy named Whitey, a twenty to drive fast and keep his mouth shut. In real life, there were no cabs to be had at Ocean Beach at night, so we hopped back on the N line, getting on the less-crowded second car. Our transfers were still good, because the driver on the way out hadn't bothered to mark them as done at ninety minutes. Muni's antiquated systems were working in our favor.

We sat in three rows. Gerald up front alone, Thomas with Shawna, and me with White Suit. He was nearly catatonic, muttering to himself in Chinese – he didn't stand out from a good chunk of the people who hang out on the streetcars all day. Every now and then he raised his volume to nearly a shout. The first time he did this I looked up, scared that somehow he'd called attention to the part where we had drugged and kidnapped him. Nobody cared. The three riders who weren't plugged in to their IPods stared hard out the windows, ferociously ignoring the crazy dude in the fourth row of seats.

Then the MUNI fare inspectors showed up. Their job was to

make sure that people paid the fare to get on the streetcars and busses, but they usually made it a point to stay away from the bus lines full of pee-in-their-pants homeless people, and they really couldn't do much during rush hour when trains were so packed that nobody could move at all, let alone reach into pockets and pull out transfers and passes as proofs-of-purchase. Since everyone knew that rush-hour trains were where the MUNI inspectors wouldn't be, those buses and trains were full of fare-jumpers. The MUNI inspectors preferred to hang out on night milk runs like this, where the actual inspections took two minutes, and they could spend the rest of the scheduled run on their cell phones. We hadn't bought a ticket for White Suit. Shit. If the inspectors caught him and tried to write a ticket, they'd probably call social services on him, and we would lose our only connection to Jenn. Thomas turned towards me with a questioning look. I returned one of panic. We couldn't let him be thrown off the train.

The inspectors were a typical pair – a tall, slightly overweight white guy and a small black woman with an obvious Napoleon complex.

"Tickets, passes," said the woman in a voice that sounded like Joey Lauren Adams in the crying-in-the-rain scene from *Chasing Amy*. Goosebumps popped up on my arm as she spoke. "Thank you, thank, you, thank you..." I flashed my transfer in her direction and she nodded at me.

"Thank you, passes please, sir."

I looked at the kidnapper, then at the inspector. Did he have a MUNI pass? Unlikely. Dammit.

"Passes, please," said the Napoleon woman.

"He can't hear you," I said. "He's deaf."

"Are you responsible for him?" she asked.

"Um..." I said. "Not exactly."

She leaned closer to him and said "Passes or transfers, please," with an exaggerated, slow diction, like a 45 rpm record played at 33.

"His English isn't so hot," I said. "And he can't really talk."

"He's talking," she said. "Right now."

He was. Our hallucinating friend was mumbling in Chinese, sing-songing his way through what might have been a "take me to my embassy" polemic or could have been *the Sound of Music*, translated badly. There was just no way to tell.

"Well, he can say things," I said. "But they aren't really words."

"Autistic?" said the inspector.

I nodded.

"That's rough," she said. "But he should still have a ticket."

"I gave it to him before he had this episode," I said. "But it's in his back pocket."

Can you fish it out?" she asked.

"I don't think so," I said. "He gets a little weird about physical contact."

"Well, I have to see it," she said. "I have to see every ticket."

"I'm serious," I said. "He's a mental patient, and how would it look if you guys chucked him off a bus for non-payment of a fifty-cent fare when his social worker will go to court with him and they'll produce his transfer and it will all be a massive waste of time?" As I said this, I dug my knuckle's into White Suit's ribs.

"GUG!" agreed the guy. The MUNI inspector jumped back a half step. Her partner saw this from the other side of the train and hustled over to where we were, his hand on his walkie-talkie.

"This guy doesn't have a transfer," she said. "But he's with this guy and…well, look at him."

A thin strand of drool was coming off of the corner of the guy's mouth, looking like the melted cheese in a television pizza commercial. The other inspector wrinkled his lip in disgust.

"Forget about it," he said. "Dealing with that isn't in the job description."

"But we can't leave without seeing his transfer," said the woman. "I don't want it to get out that we might show some kind of favoritism."

"Not getting drooled on isn't favoritism," said the other inspector.

"But…"

"No," he said. "When you've been here a few months longer, you'll see how it works around here. Thank you for your time, guys." The N pulled up to the stop at 9th Avenue and the two inspectors exited. I let out a long, whistling sigh. White Suit whistled a tuneless, descending-in-tone non-tune.

"Jesus," said Thomas, turning around in front of me. "That was close."

"Yeah," I said. "It was. Why didn't you do anything?"

Thomas ran a hand through his hair. "What was I supposed to do? Light the seat on fire?"

"If you thought it would help, yes."

"They're plastic seats, Alex."

"That's not the point. You should have done anything you could to distract them."

Thomas turned around and faced me fully. "Did you really need the help?"

I thought about it for a second. "I guess not, but it would have..."

"Been nice to have?" he said. "Not even. I would have screwed it up. That was fantastic. Take the credit – you're better with people than I am."

"Those weren't people, those were MUNI inspectors. They're cyborgs at best."

"Don't sell yourself short, Alex. That was brilliant."

We got home about fifteen minutes later. The train had filled considerably when we reached Carl and Cole and I had to half-drag the guy through the crowd when it was time to get off, jostling several people and going through three or four "excuse me" and "I'm sorry"s. Gerald left at that pont – he had some kind of late-night party that he wanted to get to, and he wanted to get good and stoned beforehand, so he would be able to understand all of the people. His words, not mine. He gave me a man-hug as he left and made me promise to give him a call if anything went wrong.

"Thanks for the help," I said.

He shook his head. "Any garden-variety Haight kid knows about salvo," he said. "I just happened to be here." He walked off down Cole, disappearing into the gloom.

Getting the guy up the stairs to the living room was a bit of a hassle; his legs worked fine, but his knees didn't want to bend much, so eventually Thomas and I just carried him up. Thomas brought one of the wooden chairs from the kitchen into the living room and sat the guy down on it; his feet stuck out straight in front of him, making him look like a yogi with a drool-control problem.

"We should tie him up," said Thomas. He went back to the closet near the kitchen. I took off White Suit's jacket and went through the pockets, coming up with a wallet, three dollars and twenty-five cents, a small wire, a butterfly knife, and a MUNI transfer good through the end of the day.

"Goddammit," I said, throwing the transfer to the ground. "All that for nothing. We should have gone through his pockets first. And what kind of two-bit gangster rides the train?"

"Why didn't you think of it?" asked Thomas. He was carrying two long bungee cords and a ball of twine in his right hand and a roll of duct tape in his left hand. "You've been doing this detective thing for a while."

"Because there was no rational reason he would have had one," I said. "But look...no gun."

"Isn't that a good thing?" he asked.

"I guess so," I said. "But wouldn't you have had a gun, or a friend with a gun, or some kind of backup that was above and beyond a three inch wire and a knife that you have to whip around for ten seconds to use? Unless he's some kind of kung fu badass."

"Hey," said Shawna, "Just because he's Chinese doesn't mean that he's Bruce Lee."

"Right," I said "But the kung fu thing is something I would have said if he'd been a white guy."

"Are you sure?" she said.

"Yeah," I said. "There's no default-white martial art that I would have used, so I said kung fu. I mean, *Kung Fu* starred David Carradine."

"He's half-Chinese," said Shawna.

"No he's not," said Thomas, "He's Irish, English, Scottish, Welsh, German, Spanish, Ukrainian, Cherokee and Italian."

We all stopped for a second and looked at Thomas.

"Why do you know that?" I asked.

Thomas shrugged. "After I saw *Office Space,* I kind of got addicted to *Kung Fu,* and I watched all of the episodes and watched the *E! True Hollywood Story* a few times."

"Wait," said Shawna. "I thought you didn't watch TV."

"I don't," said Thomas, "But it was on..."

"It's never *on*," she said. "Nobody here watches it, and you only watch TV when Alex or Jenn is watching."

Thomas started to turn red. "Well…"

"Did you sneak down here in the middle of the night to watch the *E! True Hollywood Story* on David Carradine?" she asked.

Thomas looked down. "Um….yeah."

The guy twitched hard enough to bring the legs of the chair up and smash them down on the floor again.

"Oh, right," said Thomas. He stretched the bungee cords from the chair posts around the guy's chest and arms, then hooked them back on the original post. He wrapped the twine around the guy's legs, then duct-taped his hands to his legs just above the knees. I'd read the phrase "trussed like a turkey" before, and our friend now fit that bill.

I went through his wallet. He had a few different business cards with several different names, but none in the name of Number One Lucky Products, Inc. I guess they were too low-rent to bother with cards. He didn't have a California driver's license, but he did have a credit card with what looked like a name imprint in Chinese characters and a passport with stamps that mostly showed some transiting between the US and China. His name was Lei Zhiang.

"Lei," I said. He didn't react at all.

Shawna picked up the passport. "No. His name is Zhiang."

"Isn't that his last name?" I asked.

"Yes," she said. "But you say the last name first. And you pronounce 'Lei' like the Hawaiian flower thing."

"Zhiang Lei?"

"Yeah."

"So what do we do now?" asked Thomas.

"We sit," I said. "And we wait for him to come out of it and ask him what he's done with Jenn. And if he doesn't tell us, we make him."

"How do we do that?"

"Thomas, you start," I said. "Talk to him like he's one of those business guys you hate. The rest of us – well, don't say anything. Look intimidating and stay quiet. Thomas, I'll follow your lead. We're trying to get him to tip where Jenn is, then we'll figure out what happens next."

"What *will* happen next?" asked Thomas. "If this guy's some kind of master criminal, won't he come after us?"

"We'll figure that out when we get to that," I said. I hoped we would – I hadn't the first clue.

We all sat down; Shawna and Thomas on the loveseat, me on the couch. Zhiang Lei continued to mutter to himself and twitch every few minutes. I drummed my hands on my knee and willed him to wake up faster. Every minute he took was a minute that Jenn wasn't back; it had been nearly a day since she'd last been in the house.

"Hey," said Thomas. "I could use a beer. You guys?"

We all could. Thomas went down to the corner store. I milled around, checking on Zhiang every thirty seconds, wondering where he had stashed Jenn, and trying to figure out how we were going to get that information out of him. When Thomas came back ten minutes later Zhiang's eyes were fluttering open, focusing for a second or two at a time. Sweat stains spread from under his armpits, making his white dress shirt nearly transparent. I could see the faint lines of tattoos on his torso.

Thomas had bought a twelve-pack of Mendocino Eye of the Hawk Red Ale, and he opened them with his pocket knife and passed them out. Even Shawna had one, though she was usually more of a wine and vodka girl. Zhiang kept blinking his eyes, and eventually he shook his head back and forth, flinging the beads of sweat from his forehead. One of them hit me in the thigh, and it absorbed into fabric of my pants, leaving a dark spot. He wasn't a bad-looking guy, really. He had that long everywhere but-uneven hair that made me think of a machine-gun wielding villain in a John Woo movie. On a white guy that hair would have made him look like he was in Journey circa 1983, but on him it looked kind of cool. His eyes stopped wavering, and I could see him really focusing on us.

"So what the fuck have you done with Jenn?" asked Thomas. I almost whipped my head around and stared at him; we'd lived together for nearly two years, and I hadn't heard that tone in his voice before. It was clipped, hard, the kind of sound you'd expect to hear if you were called into the principal's office at Humphrey Bogart High School.

Zhiang didn't say anything. Thomas sighed. "I'm going to ask you one more time. What have you done with our roommate?"

"You can't make me talk,' said Zhiang. His voice was slow and halting, as if he'd just learned how to use his tongue. "I come from the Tongs. To initiate me they tore off my fingernails, slowly, then gave me these tattoos with ink that had been mixed with my own blood. I killed my first victim when I was fifteen years old by strangling him with his own intestines. Every day I punch walls to keep my hands tough. I fear nothing, you can do nothing to me, you shall one day be groveling on your knees…"

I lost it. Zhiang was looking at us like we were children, as if he owned the room. That look was familiar to me – it was the same gaze that the management consultants used to give us when they came in to re-engineer our processes for the fifteenth time in two years. It was the smug look of the kids at the cool table at lunch, the smirk of the record store clerk when you buy a Stevie Wonder album, the frosty over-the-glass gaze of the hot girl at the bar who knows she's dipping into a lower caste by talking to you, the satisfied stare of every person who has power through circumstance and no merit of their own. The look made me livid, and the steam and bile boiled right out of me.

"Oh, shut up," I said. "We're supposed to take you seriously?" I walked up to him and started tapping him on the side of his head with my half-full beer bottle. I wasn't hitting him hard enough to make it hurt, just enough to make it annoying. "You're masterminding a toilet conspiracy and you were stupid enough to let us take you here. I bet you were so freaked out by that acid trip we put you on that you practically peed your pants. And you're sitting here quoting *Return of the Street Fighter* to us. You think you scare us? We know everything about you. The way I see it, you're on borrowed time; tell us everything, or that trip you just went on will just be the start."

I turned around and walked to the other side of the room to control the shaking, then looked back at him. Zhiang stared at me. He started to open his mouth, then closed it, then opened it again, like a sturgeon, blinking. Not afraid yet, but getting there. I'd cracked his façade; all I needed was someone else to pick up the ball. My throat didn't seem to be working; all the words were gone and there weren't any more. I needed help.

The door downstairs opened, then slammed shut. I turned around.

Had someone left the door open? We both had the same thought at the same time and turned to look at Thomas.

"I locked it," he said. "Right after I got back. I'm sure."

Footsteps tromped their way up the stairs; if Thomas hadn't been sitting across the room from me, I would have sworn that it was him coming up; the footsteps were that loud. He shook his head and shrugged. The footsteps reached the top of the stairs, and Jenn emerged, wearing a miniskirt, tank top, jacket, and leather boots. The jacket was too large, and the tank top was ripped a bit down the front; she looked like she was about to explode right out of it. She gave us a wan smile.

"Hi guys," she said. "I see you got yourselves a gimp."

The word "speechless" isn't strong enough. The three of us followed Jenn into the kitchen, where she took a mug out of the cupboard, filled it with hot water, and added a bag of Oolong tea. She sat down at the table, looked around at us, and let out a long sigh. We waited, and she dunked her tea-bag into her mug over and over. She had wrapped the little label and string around her ring finger, the one with the slightly-ragged nail. Her mug was of an old *Far Side* cartoon, the one where one bear has a bulls-eye on his stomach, and the other one is saying, "Bummer of a birthmark, Hal." Jenn was wearing one of her hot-librarian outfits – knee-high black boots with heels high enough to let her look me directly in the eye, rimless glasses, and a black skirt that was just high enough above the top of her boots to reveal a bit of knee. She sat with her legs crossed, her heel tapping her shin in time with the dipping of her tea bag.

"You must have…" Zhiang started to say.

"Shut up," she said. "Just shut up. I endured the rantings of your moron friend for the whole day today, and if you say one more word I'm going to call my friend Darren, who is actually *in* the SFPD but is off today, so he won't get busted for the kind of violent night-stick sexual abuse I'll have him do to you. Remember what those New York cops did to that guy in the broom closet? That's G-rated compared to what's going to happen to you if you open your mouth one more time."

This was bullshit on three or four different levels – Jenn didn't have a friend named Darren, and she certainly didn't know anyone in the SFPD, and the department had had enough recent scandals to make it so off-duty cops were more hamstrung in defending themselves than private citizens were. But Zhiang didn't know that, and he shut his mouth.

"So how did…?" I said. Jenn ran her finger across her throat in a slashing motion, and *I* snapped my mouth shut.

"I'll get to that," she said. "In a second. First, I want to tell this guy about what's happening down at his warehouse in about thirty minutes if he doesn't tell me what I want to know."

Zhiang's eyes widened and his mouth opened.

"Don't say anything," said Jenn.

"I'll never talk," said Zhiang.

"You just did," I said.

"I didn't," he said.

"You did," I said. "Talk, I mean."

Zhiang looked confused.

"Has anyone ever told you that you're not very bright?" said Jenn. "I mean, really, you're trying to make a killing by selling bootleg toilets. That's not exactly the Google of ideas, is it?"

"Laugh while you can," said Zhiang. "When my partners find me, you will all pay!"

I couldn't help it. I started to giggle, then Thomas laughed his horsy bray of a laugh, and we were all convulsing. It was one thing to be threatened, it was quite another to be threatened with dialogue straight out of the movie version of *Dune*.

"Let's go upstairs," said Jenn. "Zhiang isn't going anywhere. Are you, sweetie?" She gave him an affectionate pat on the head. He tried to squirm away and ended up tipping over the chair. We left him that way and went upstairs to Thomas's room.

Thomas had the largest space of any of the rooms on the second floor, with a view from his two windows that looked out over the wooded peak of Mount Clarendon. Thomas and Shawna sat on his bed, and Jenn and I stood. The whole room had the musky smell of stale incense. Jenn took the tea bag out of her cup and set it on the arm of the futon, and I turned to her and gave her a hug. She squeezed back hard. As we hugged, Thomas and Shawna joined us. I'm sure that we looked like the final scene of mid-'80s sports movie, but it didn't matter. Sometimes raw emotion gets the better of a sharply-honed sense of irony. We separated and sat.

"So they *did* kidnap me, I guess," she said. "I was out on Sunday night with Selena – you know, the one person I work with who's under thirty and not in the process of popping one out – and we were hanging out at the Thirsty Bear downtown, fending off the endless parade of post-fraternity assholes and bonding over how much we didn't want to start the week. She went to the bathroom, and I felt this hard thing in my ribs and breath on my ears. I figured it was just another one of those pervert guys who press up next to you in bars for a cheap thrill, but the voice said, 'Do you feel that gun? If you make a noise, that will be the last thing you ever feel.'

"At first I laughed a little, because, really. Who talks like that? But then he pressed the gun in my ribs again, and he walked me outside to the sidewalk, where there was this big white cargo van waiting. He put me in the back, and then we drove off."

"Whoa," I said. "What were you thinking?"

She took a sip of tea. "Lots of things," she said. "I mean, I was scared – who wouldn't be? – but after a few minutes figured that this had something to do with Brent and the toilet guys, and how scary can a bunch of toilet conspirators really be? I think I would have been more freaked if the guy driving the van had been over five feet tall, and if he hadn't been rocking out to the first Christina Aguilera album on our whole drive. And I was kind of drunk, which made it easier to take. Also, they didn't have barriers between the drivers and me or anything, and they didn't bother with a blindfold, so I could see that they were driving in circles to try to confuse me, but we only ended up at Seventh and Howard, a few blocks from where we started."

"Weird," I said.

"No kidding," she said. "Weirder was that Zhiang out there and his friend put me in this room that was *filled* with toilets. I mean, I ended up sitting down leaning my head against a bowl. Then they locked the door and there I was, with all of these commodes sitting on the floor separated by chunks of cardboard. And I sat there for about six hours. And I'd been *drinking*."

"What'd you do?"

She looked at me as if I'd told her that I was thinking about getting a job as an investment banker with Thomas.

"I was in a room full of toilets. You figure it out."

"But they wouldn't have been hooked up to anything..." I stopped talking under her withering gaze.

"Alex, there are some things we don't talk about in polite company. Were you born in a barn?"

"A hospital, actually."

She exhaled loudly. "Sometimes, I don't know why I put up with you. Anyway, I went to sleep for a little bit on some of the cardboard boxes they had piled in a corner. They finally came back this morning and woke me up, and I decided that since they talked like they were in the movies – I could hear them through the door, and they sounded exactly like the villains in *Die Hard* but with different accents—I figured they were bad guys. Then Zhiang came into the room and told me that...what did he say?"

She tapped her fingers on the arm of the futon for a second. Her nails were dirty; I'd never seen them anything other than pristine.

"Oh yeah, he said, 'You had better hope that your friends care enough about you not to try to be heroes.' I was pretty angry at that point – they hadn't given me anything to eat – so I told him to blow it out his ear and that he didn't know who they were messing with. He laughed at me and split, leaving me with the short guy and the other guy in the room outside the warehouse. Zhiang left the door open when he left. The other two were sitting around playing video games and drinking. Every now and then, one of them would look at me and leer. That's what gave me the idea."

She grinned. "I figured that if these guys had spent as much time with action movies and TV as their words implied, they probably thought that most American girls were basically *Girls Gone Wild* crossed with a bordello. So I did a little doctoring to this tank top, pulled up the skirt a bit and told them I needed something to eat. "

"So what did they do?"

"They didn't know what to do," she said. "I went up and shoved my chest into the one guy's face, and he started speaking in Chinese, so I shoved my chest into the other guy's face, and he turned really red. It actually felt pretty good, channeling my inner Jessica Rabbit. I told them that I wanted something to eat like, right now, then they started arguing. I think they were each trying to be the one who got to stick around and stare. Finally, they played some kind of rock-paper-scissors game and the little guy won, so the big guy took off. He made a point to lock the door that went to the outside with a key – I could hear the bolt shoot. After he left, I just kind of draped myself over the table where the guy was playing video games – you know the pose, lying on your stomach, legs kicking up in back. He kept getting more and more flustered, and eventually he walked over. When he got close, I took one of those little aluminum office garbage cans and jammed it down onto his head. He couldn't move his arms and started yelling, so I banged on the can until he shut up. I picked up his jacket and put it on over the tank top, and then I stood next to the door for a few minutes. When the door opened, I pushed the garbage can guy into the food-getting guy, knocked them both down, and slipped through the door. I jammed one of our mailbox keys in the doorknob so they couldn't get out. I was right on Sixth Street, a few blocks south of Market. I looked like I fit in; half of the people there were hookers."

"Wait…"I said. "Why did you go out to the bar in the first place?"

"I dunno," she said. "Looking for something different. And I had an attack of incipient middle-age, so I was out *looking* like I was trying to pick up guys to see if I still had the magic. And we'd wrapped up the Brent thing – I figured it would be safe. Oops. *Anyway,* I'm wandering around there in SOMA, walking up Sixth, where everyone smells worse than me even though I've been hanging out in a room full of toilets for a day, and three or four different guys tell me how beautiful I am, and one offers me a bag of crack for a look at my boobs – no thanks – and I tried to hail a cab, but the guy thought I was a high-class hooker looking for some action and wouldn't take me anywhere. So I'm a little mad and scared because it's dark, but I still figured those guys had no way to get out, so I was safe from them. Anyway, I waited around on Market for something like an hour, finally got an overcrowded bus because the subway was out again, punched a guy for pinching my butt, and now here I am."

"So here we are," I said. I knew what we were all thinking – Jenn was back, Brent was dead, but the guy downstairs didn't seem like the type to give up on four hundred thousand dollars without a fight. If I had been a Marlowe or Spade or Travis McGee, I'd just announce that I'd take care of it, get a pal to cast a pair of concrete boots, and chuck Zhiang into the Bay. I'd talked tough earlier, but I didn't have it in me to waste the guy. But if we turned him into the cops, what would they do? We had no proof other than Jenn's word that they'd kidnapped her, and she was now back. Since there was no apparent immediate danger, even if the cops took us seriously, the toilet gangsters could just disappear and come back some other time to try to get the money out of us. We'd have to get rid of them somehow; I just didn't have a clue how to do it.

Jenn took a sip of her tea. "Oh yeah," she said. " I think I know how we can get out of this mess."

Twenty minutes later, three of us sat around Zhiang again. Jenn and I on the couch, Thomas in the favorite chair. Shawna was hanging around upstairs; she said that Zhiang was giving her the willies. Zhiang looked like any number of guys we'd interviewed to be a housemate, except that we'd never tied any of them up.

The door opened again and footsteps tromped up the stairs. I looked around the living room – Thomas, Shawna, Jenn, me...we were all in the house. Then, who?

Ahmed walked into the living room, a heavy duffel bag in each hand.

"Hey guys," he said. "The door was unlocked. Just moving a couple of things in – I'm headed to Napa for a couple of days, but I figured I'd drop a few things off on the way." He looked at the living room – all of us in the living room, Zhiang tied and gagged in a chair, blinked, and walked back to Brent's old room. Two thumps sounded when the duffels hit the floor, then he came back.

"Got a few more things to move up," he said. "It shouldn't be more than ten minutes."

Zhiang's eyes bugged out at that. Ahmed's cabbie life had apparently made him indifferent to almost everything. It was working to our advantage. If a visitor doesn't react at all to a guy turkey-trussed to a chair, what kind of awful things are usually happening in the house, and what would we be capable of? I winked at Jenn, and she twitched her lips in the suggestion of a smile.

We all looked at each other for a few seconds, then I walked over to Zhiang and took off the electrical tape from his mouth. I didn't rip the tape off hard; there was no real reason to hurt him, and it seemed to me that causing him pain was less likely to make him want to help us out. Taking the tape off took a good twenty seconds; I had to hold the skin taut as I peeled the tape away. Even with that kind of care, it still left spots of glue on his skin. His eyes stopped bugging, closed, and he winced.

"Ow," he said.

"That couldn't possibly have hurt," I said. "Stop being a baby."

"Baby?" he said.

"Hush," said Jenn. "Be more careful. He's probably nervous."

"Nervous?" he said. "Why would I be nervous when I'm the one who's going to kill you all?" A bit of the bluster had come back to his voice.

We didn't respond to that. I sat back down. Nobody said a word. Finally, after a few minutes Zhiang broke the silence.

"What do you want from me?" he asked.

"We *want* you to leave San Francisco and never come back," I said. "Taking your stupid bootleg toilet plan with you. We want to never see your sorry, pathetic face again. Did you really think that you'd succeed in this cockamamie scheme to scam people into buying bootleg expensive toilets? It's insane. And how could you possibly make money on it? Whatever."

"*Please,*" said Jenn. "I don't think they'd be spending that much money on it if they didn't think it would have a good chance of working. I mean...did you think of it?"

"No," I said. "But that's because I'm not an idiot. Unlike this guy."

"Do you guys do anything but fight?" asked Thomas.

"Shut up!" we both said. "Keep out of it."

"Well, this affects me, too," Thomas said. "He knows where we live. We could be in some serious trouble."

"Serious trouble?" I said. "Don't make me laugh. What on earth could a guy who comes up with a fucking *toilet scheme* do to us?"

"Fool," said Zhiang. "We've already executed the plan! That money in Marshall's bank account is the last link, and if you know what is good for you, you will hand it over. He tried to prevent us from finding it with the second name at his job, because he knew we'd figure out where he was coming from during our meetings. Subtle, but not good enough. You aren't good enough either. You can't stop us now! You won't kill me. You're weak, like all Americans. I'll be back, and you'll all pay, with either your money or your lives!"

Marshall. So he'd been using a third name with these guys. Brent had been nothing if not careful. Zhiang was spluttering when he finished talking, breathing as hard as a marathoner on the last mile. The sweatstains had spread from under his arms to cover most of his shirt, and I could see the cords in his hands bulging; he was straining against the twine. Hopefully Thomas knew his knots well. Jenn's plan now hinged on me. I hoped I could sound tougher than I really was. I knelt down next to Zhiang and put a full glass of water on the floor near one of the chair legs "Wanna bet?" I said. "Tell me something."

"Don't do that," said Jenn, picking up on my cue. "We can work something out with him. They didn't hurt me, we don't need to…"

"Yes, we do," I said. "We all agreed to it upstairs, even you. Don't go soft on me. Tell me, Zhiang, have you walked down on Haight Street since you've been here, or on Sixth Street near your warehouse, or through the Tenderloin?"

He nodded. A small bead of sweat appeared near the sharp point of his left sideburn.

"You've seen the people…the homeless with their heroin needles stuck out of their necks, the sores on their faces, ranting aimlessly to people who aren't there?"

"Yes," he said. "That kind of thing would never happen if this city were…"

"Hush," I said. I put my finger on the bead of sweat near his sideburn, and ran the drop down the side of his face to his chin. I reached into my pocket and pulled out a small packet. "Remember how you got here?" I said. "You probably don't. Do you know what happened on your way over?"

He shook his head slowly.

"He looks terrible," said Jenn. "No need to freak him out more. He doesn't need to know what our little games are. Be nice."

She walked over, knelt down and picked up the pint glass of water.

"Here," she said. "At least give him something to drink." She held the glass up to his lips. He looked at me, frowned, then looked at her. She smiled at him – a smile that had more watts than an A.M. news station. Zhiang gulped three times and the water was gone. As she took the glass from him, she dropped a flyer from her other hand onto his lap. The flyer was Shawna's, and it was for an invite-only polyamorous bondage party the next weekend. On the cover was a photo of a man and a woman. The man was on all fours, wearing diapers, his hands bound behind his head and his head tied far back via a ball gag. The woman was standing over him, wielding a cat o'nine tails and what looked to be a rotating, metal-studded dildo.

"Whoops," I said. "Cat's out of the bag."

"What?" said Zhiang. "What did you...?"

"We have photos," I said. "Of you, at this."

He started to shake.

"Here's the deal," I said. "Jenn's back, so we're even as far as I'm concerned. You have a choice. When we brought you here, what we gave you before was one-fourth of this packet. I can give you a full dose. You'll be out for a very, very long time. We'll take you to the Tenderloin, then call the cops and tell them that you're ranting, raving, and headed towards Union Square to bother the tourists. They'll find you and deport you, if you're lucky enough to make it out of the mental hospital alive."

Zhiang's eyes had become the size of espresso cups; they were positively bulging out of their sockets. He started rocking back and forth in his chair, banging the legs into the ground.

"Think about that before you kidnap someone the next time," said Jenn.

"Or," I said. "We'll let you hang out here until the trip is over, then we'll take you back to your warehouse to collect your boys, and you can go back home and never come back. That's choice two."

"Hey," said Thomas. "How do we know he won't bug us?" He gave Zhiang a hard look. "I vote we just dump him." Zhiang jolted at Thomas's words – his deep voice held more gravity than mine, I guess. Zhiang started shaking his head, stuttering.

I turned the flyer over in my hand a few times. "He won't," I said. "You see, I've got a pretty good idea how to get in touch with his bosses. They have a company, they have a domain name, and the person who registered this domain name is on this piece of paper." I read out the address. Zhiang's neck twitched. "Remember the Chinese girl? She's down at the bank right now with copies. If anything happens, if I *breathe* and I think I smell you in the air that I'm breathing, those pics go out."

Zhiang's eyes widened, and his mouth moved.

"Don't talk," I said. "Nod, and you're headed home."

Zhiang nodded. We retired to the kitchen, where I collapsed into a chair. I had no idea that acting tough could possibly be that hard. My body felt like every cell had just done ten rounds with Ali. Jenn filled up a glass of water and gave it to me.

"That was so cool," she said. "Seriously. Alex, where'd you learn to talk like that?"

"Books," I said. "Think he bought it?"

She nodded. "Yeah. Next step?"

"We go back to the warehouse," I said.

"We forgot something," said Jenn. "How are we going to get him out of here? We can't use MUNI or just let him out on the street..."

There was a thump from Brent's old room.

"Oh," I said.

"You don't think..."

I shrugged, walked over to Brent's room and knocked on the door. Ahmed opened it; his clothes were in neat piles on top of Brent's old dresser.

"Hey," he said. "You didn't mention it. Is it cool if I use this dresser? I haven't put any clothes in it yet, but I'd rather just get rid of my old one and save myself the pain of moving it up those stairs..."

"No, that's no problem," I said. "Um...I don't suppose your cab is anywhere where you can get at it?"

"I can get it," he said. "Why?"

"Let's do it," I said. Thomas and I picked up Zhiang by the hands and feet. Ahmed was waiting downstairs in an idling taxi. It wasn't his car; he had called a friend of his and paid him thirty bucks to wait around in the neighborhood and ask no questions. Ahmed himself had been mellow after the brief explanation I'd given him, claiming that my request was not really out of the ordinary. Live reptiles, he had said, were where he drew the line. Ahmed's cab was an ordinary yellow taxi, with chips in the bumper paint and an advertisement for 49ers season tickets on the top. Thomas and Zhiang sat in the back seat; I took shotgun.

"Ahmed," I said. You sure you're OK with this?"

"Are you kidding?" he said. "I became a taxi driver so I could get in on some weird shit. Your friend Gerald told me a bit about this when he called it in, and this is about the weirdest shit I've seen yet. Happy to help."

"What's in it for you?"

"I take notes," he said." Someday I want to get out of astrophysics and write an episodic online drama, kind of like *Tales of the City*, but with cabdrivers as the central characters. Cool idea, huh?"

"Sure," I said.

"Where are you headed?"

"Sixth Street," I said. "Near one of the Latin bodegas."

"Let's go," he said, and slammed on the accelerator. For all of his education, Ahmed drove like any other taxi driver I'd ever seen. He barreled through yellow lights, screeched around corners, nearly de-wheeled a slow-moving man in a wheelchair, and hurtled through the SOMA warehouse district like he was driving a supercharged Batmobile. We pulled up a few blocks south of Market on Sixth, in front of a blank-fronted warehouse with a steel door. I could see a small key protruding from the keyhole; nobody had jimmied the entrance yet. Two homeless guys were scrabbling together some home-made cigarettes on the corner. Zhiang, Thomas, and I got out of the cab.

"Hey man," said one of homeless guys, a tall man with a marked stoop and gray hair gnarled into a wild nest of short dreadlocks. "Got any change?"

"No," I said. "Not today."

Zhiang took a couple of steps towards the entrance, then looked back. I squared my hands in front of my face and mimed the clicking of a camera shutter with my first finger. He frowned, then walked towards the entrance. We sat back down in Ahmed's cab and drove off. I took my cell phone out of my pocket and dialed seven numbers.

"Dispatch, SOMA station" said a female voice from the other side.

"Hey," I said. "I was just driving down Sixth, and I saw this guy – he had dark hair and was wearing a white suit, and it looked like he was trying to break into one of the warehouses there. I don't suppose that's worth checking on…"

"OK," said the dispatcher. "We have officers right nearby; they'll check it out. Do you care to leave your phone number so it's associated with the complaint?"

"No," I said. "I'd rather be anonymous."

"What was that all about?" asked Thomas.

"Remember he had a passport?" I said. "His visa expiration date was two weeks ago. When the cops get there, they'll run checks on him and his two pals, and that visa overstay will come up. They'll be deported and on a government watch list. Call it a little incentive to never come back here again."

"Slick," said Ahmed.

"Let's go home," I said. I was tired.

Epilogue

From: vikas@neptunesociety.org
To: Alex Baker
Dear Mr. Baker,

Thank you for your recent inquiry regarding cremains internment at the Columbarium. At the Neptune Society, we pride ourselves on treating the dead with the highest respect; the kind hard to get in life. We currently do have urn openings at our San Francisco facility. Our rate schedule is as follows:

- *Basic service, urn alcove, internment, monthly cleaning. $2,000 base fee + $400/year for up to sixty years. Open-ended internment: $20,000 (save $4,000!)*
- *Premier service: decorated, large urn alcove, Columbarium representative assistance for services, weekly cleaning. $4,000 base fee + $600/year for up to sixty years. Open-ended internment: $30,000 (save $6,000!)*

If you have religious requirements or are planning a service, please let us know. Our space is limited, and we cannot accept large funeral parties of more than six. If you would like a personalized package, please let me know what options you are interested in, and we can come to an arrangement. We accept payments by credit card or bank transfer to our account at First Federal, number 0000236417.
Best Wishes,
Vikas

To: vikas@neptunesociety.org
From: Alex Baker
Vikas,

That sounds great. Can I reserve an alcove for open-ended internment? I can pay by bank transfer today, if you like.
Alex

To: Alex Baker
From: vikas@neptunesociety.org
Mr. Baker,

We have received your bank transfer. Per your request, your membership guide is attached. The guide includes all rules of the Columbarium, and your personal

electronic access code. Thank you for your business.
   Best wishes,
   Vikas

I spent the morning boxing up the rest of Brent's stuff. There really wasn't much. Clothes, a few books about sports, a cell phone charger, his dead laptop. His entire life fit in four large moving boxes from U-Haul. It had been long enough that his shirts didn't smell like him any more, and the books had acquired a fine coating of dust. I finished by taping the tops of all of the boxes, and that was it. It felt weird. Incomplete.

Ahmed and Gerald showed up at noon to help me lug Brent's boxes out. Jenn came along – she was taking a mental health day from work. Her last remaining work friend had broken the "I'm pregnant" news to Jenn on Tuesday, and Jenn had put in her notice that afternoon. She was taking the rest of her vacation days this week; turns out even she wasn't tough enough to recover from a kidnapping that quickly. Some things are more than even she could take.

It was a beautiful day with crystal-clear skies and a clean smell in the air. I wore shorts and sandals and stubbed my toe on the stairs as we manhandled the boxes down the stairs. Ahmed had borrowed a minivan taxi from one of his other PhD-holding driver friends, and he refused to charge us for the ride down the hill to the Haight Street Goodwill. The street was full of late-summer tourists, some dressed like me, some sweating in large sweatshirts and heavy wool scarves. It's not *always* cold in San Francisco; some people just can't read a weather report.

The usual motley crew of homeless, hipsters and teenagers were hanging out at the Haight Street Goodwill when we pulled up. I walked in and found the guy I'd talked to earlier on the phone. His name was, oddly enough, David Brentwood. In person, he had the earnest face of a recent graduate or Americorps volunteer. He found a dolly, and I helped him lug Brent's boxes inside, while Jenn stayed with Ahmed in the cab. As far as I could tell, he was giving her a lesson on quantum electrodynamics, stopping every now and then to give good-natured waves to anyone who honked and yelled at him to get out of the way; good times. David Brentwood took inventory in the middle of the store, drawing a small crowd of people as he entered everything into a list on a clipboard. I had the feeling that most of the clothes would be gone within an hour; anything that doesn't look costume-party goes fast in thrift stores. I turned around to leave, but he stopped me.

"You forgot to estimate the value," he said. "You should, then I'll get you a receipt and you'll get a tax deduction out of it."

"Do I have to?"

"It'd help," he said. "If you don't estimate the value, then we don't get to book it as a donation, we have to estimate, and it's a pain. Do you mind?"

I didn't mind. Ugh. I had no idea how much men's clothing, or books, or a dead laptop, or a whole life was worth. I scrawled *$200* on the line, then initialed.

"Are you sure?" He said. I nodded.

"OK," he said. "Here you go." He gave me a sheet of paper. I folded it and put it in my pocket. A two hundred dollar tax deduction. I got back into the cab, where Ahmed was still going on.

"...and, in theory, that could form the underpinnings for a practical teleportation algorithm," Ahmed said. "That was what most of my doctoral work was on."

"You're wasted in a cab," I said. "You should be out doing...um...science things."

He grinned. "Most of the funding for physics stuff comes from the NSA and other government organizations – they don't like to have guys born in Pakistan getting our hands on top-secret stuff. I've been waiting for my security clearance for two years. So I drive a cab and get to talk to people. It's more fun and more money than doing a postdoc. Where to?"

"The Columbarium," I said. "Across the park..."

"I know it," he said.

The park made it look like the entire city was playing work-hooky. Sandaled couples walked arm-in-arm on the walkway near the museum, an all-dreadlocks game of ultimate frisbee had broken out in Sharon Meadow, and the hippie drum circle was loud enough to hear from half a mile away, the booming of a bass drum punctuated with the staccato hand drums and the occasional wail of saxophone and flute. We didn't say anything as we drove; I leaned my head on my hands and my elbow on the open window, taking in the sounds and the woody smell of the redwood trees. The giant domed building took up nearly a full city block; a spired fence surrounded the whole place. It looked like the love child of a run-down mosque and a Victorian house, the kind of place where the congregation keeps dying off, and they don't have the contributions to handle all of the upkeep. It wasn't too hard to imagine that the place had resident headless ghosts patrolling the grounds. The garden surrounding the building was a little wild; branches poked above and through the fence, making it hard to see the walls.

"Want me to wait?" asked Ahmed.

"No," I said. "This might take a while – we'll call you if we need a pickup."

"Fair enough," he said. "See you."

"Thanks," I said.

I punched the entry code that Vikas had e-mailed to me into the keypad at the front gate. We entered into a small front room with a curved hallway exiting to either side, and a large main room in front. My user's guide said that the rooms were named after the ancient Greek winds. Brent's alcove was in the Solanus room, on the second floor. We went up a narrow set of wooden stairs to an identical hallway that overlooked the main room. Constellation diagrams covered the walls; we walked past Perseus, Orion, and Corona on the way. Alcoves lined the walls below the star diagrams. A few sported white index cards advertising their availability, but most were occupied. Some were full memorial shrines with pictures and notes, and the vases. The whole place was deserted and quiet. It was a different noiselessness than the sterile aluminum of the morgue; this silence was warm and woody; punctuated with the faint smell of flowers. Our footsteps echoed as we walked down the hall, the noise bouncing off the walls and the remains of thousands of people. It didn't feel spooky; it felt right.

Our alcove was small, lined with dark wood paneling and clean, with a little shelf for the urn and tiny wedges in the walls for pictures and other decorations. I put the urn in its proper place, with the handles sticking out to the sides.

"We should say something," said Jenn. "This is all the funeral he's going to get."

"What do you say at a funeral?" I said.

She shrugged. "Not sure. I've never been to one."

We waited for a minute.

"I'll give it a shot," I said. "Brent, we wish we'd known you better, and I'm really sad that you had to end up here. It's not fair and it's not right, but the guys who got you are gone and won't come back. I wish we could do more."

After a minute, Jenn spoke. "That's good. Good-bye, Brent."

"We'll visit, though," I said.

We stood there for a few minutes, arms around each other, reading the plaque, looking at the vase, breathing in the silence. We left in silence, our footsteps echoing off of the constellation-studded walls. Outside, the sun made my eyes water and I blinked the tears away.

"We'll visit?" asked Jenn. "That's kind of creepy."

"If we don't," I said. "Nobody else will."

"Good point," she said. "When did you start making sense? It's messing with my head a little."

"Somewhere along the way," I said. "Maybe I'm getting better at it."

"Don't let your head swell," she said with a smile. "Doing one thing well doesn't make you Ben Franklin."

We walked home through the park, taking our time and using the smaller trails instead of the big pedestrian roads. The drum circle sounds echoed through the air, sharp percussive beats alternating with deep booms and shrill wails. A guy with dull blue tattoos on his cheeks offered to sell us weed. I picked up an errant frisbee and threw it back to the dreadlocked-ultimate players, earning a chorus of "*Thanks, man*"s. We didn't talk as we walked; there wasn't much more to say, and the city was saying enough.

From the *San Francisco Chronicle's* weekly "Police Beat"

San Francisco – *Officers responded to a summons regarding calls for help from a warehouse on Sixth Street near Mission. Upon arrival, they found that the front door lock to an office space had been disabled with a key, trapping the* *workers inside. After breaking the door, the officers discovered two men, a video game system, and a large quantity of what appeared to be toilets. The men were unable to produce identification or a reason for being there in the first place, and were carrying passports with long-expired visas. The toilet manufacturers had no record of their products shipping to the warehouse. After being detained for two days, the men were released to airport police, where they were sent back to their country of origin. Officers are still investigating the nature of the business; any information may be reported to SOMA Station.*

I was fooling around in my room as the day turned into evening, listening to *Combat Rock* at an obscene volume. Standard time had hit, so it was already dark when everyone else started to come home. I was working on my costume for the Welcome To Ahmed Not Halloween Costume Party that we were planning – my outfit consisted of sunglasses, a red-tipped cane, and a black-and-white striped shirt, and I was going to tell anyone who talked to me that they were committing a foul. I'd gotten the idea from watching Thomas watch the World Series game – he had used the phrase "you're blind, ump" at least ten times. We were expecting a big crowd.

A chunk of Brent's money had gone to the costs of the Columbarium, paying the city bills, and redistributing his back rent. Thomas had put over half of the rest aside for taxes – since the assets were in the name that he'd died under, Uncle Sam would be entitled to a large amount. I hired Gerald's accountant to handle the details. The five of us split the rest. Thomas used his to pay off almost all of his student loans, Shawna bought a lifetime membership to her studio and started taking masters classes to help her become a yoga teacher, and Jenn planned on using hers to tide her over until she could find a new, better non-profit job. Thomas kept working. Jenn spent quite a bit of time baking.

Me? Well, I put an ad on Craigslist. Nothing came from it until that night, when Jenn stormed into my room and motioned for me to turn down the music.

"Alex, what the *hell* is this?" She was carrying her laptop, and she plopped it down in front of me.

"Aren't you supposed to be looking for a job?" I said.

"I was. I was actually looking through the personal services ads to see if I could find a career counselor who'd be able to help me find something new, and I saw *this*."

I looked at the screen.

Need help? You're missing a person, or a thing, or have a problem that you just can't solve. You're not looking for someone to follow your soon-to-be ex-wife, and you really don't want to deal with hippie self-help crap. You've got a problem. You need to find something. You need it solved. That's what I do. You only pay after your problem is solved. Call Alex through this ad.

"This is you, isn't it?"

I squirmed. "Why would you think that?"

"Because you're squirming, and this is written like you sound when you think you've got a good idea. Nobody else would use the phrase 'hippie self-help crap' when advertising this kind of service on Craigslist. 'Fess up. What are you doing?"

"It's something to do," I said. "I bet Magnum got started this way. I can be like him, but without the mustache, guns, or Hawaiian shirts. I've got some money and a computer. Why not?"

"Because you're an idiot," she said. "Because without help you'd never have even come close to figuring out what happened. Because it's dangerous."

Before she could come up with another reason, my phone rang. I had made my ringtone the old Hall and Oates song, "Private Eyes." Jenn rolled her eyes.

"Hello?" I said. "Yes, this is…Baker Investigations. What seems to be your problem? Uh huh. Uh huh. OK, we should meet. Do you know Coffee To The People in the Upper Haight at Masonic? Yep, one hour."

I snapped my phone shut, and looked at Jenn. She looked back at me. Her eyes weren't blazing, but they were definitely glowing. If she had been a cartoon, steam would have been rising from her ears.

"So," I said. "Someone thinks that it's a good idea. I have to go meet them now, but…well, I'm kind of nervous about going alone, and I don't know much about what she needs…"

She sighed. "What do you want?"

"Well," I said. "It's not like you're doing anything right now, and this is a woman who has a problem that involves having a kid, and…"

"Oh God," she said. "You want me to help you out."

"Yeah," I said. "I'll give you half of whatever I make off of it."

She looked down, then up at my Clash poster, then walked over to me and put her hands on my shoulders.

"Promise me one thing," she said.

"What's that?" I asked.

She leaned forward and looked me in the eye. I could feel her exhaling on my cheek.

"Don't be…just don't be stupid," she said.

"Um. OK," I said.

"That'll do," she said. "Come on. Let's go meet our new client."

She walked out the door and into the hallway.

"Hey…" I said. "What was that all about?"

"You're not a very good detective," she said.

"Oh," I said. I walked across the hall into Jenn's room. She pushed the door closed with one hand, and took hold of my shoulder with the other. Her grip was strong.

"Now," she said. "I think that 'Baker Investigations' is a little boring. Don't you think that Mercer/Baker has a better ring to it?"

What was I going to do? I nodded.

"OK," Jenn said after a while. "We should go meet this woman. What are we going to ask her?"

"I have no idea," I said. "I thought we'd figure it out as we went along. That seemed to work before."

She sighed, went to her desk, and pulled out a spiral notebook. "What am I getting myself into?"

"Good question," I said. "Why don't we go find out?"

Acknowledgements

This whole thing started as a short story project, then eventually became a longer piece, then a novel, and finally what you have just finished. I would like to thank my writing group – Patti, Eva, Georgia, and Maggie – they started this in a workshop at San Francisco State and then kept me going with encouragement and solid criticism for over a year afterwards.

Also, thanks to Michelle Carter at State and Nina and Raphael for copyedits and early reads.

And, of course, Julie. She knows why.

About the Author

Dan Johnson lives in San Francisco, where he works full-time in software and squeezes in writing when he can. He earned his MA in fiction writing from San Francisco State, is a co-founder of burritophile.com, and has written for numerous Web and print publications. He can be found in many of the places in San Francisco where you would find Alex, or online at oilies.com.